RAVE RE

Butterflies In Heat

"How does Darwin Porter's garden grow? Only in the
mooonlight, and only at midnight, when man-eating
vegetation in any color but green bursts into full bloom
to devour the latest offerings."
– James Leo Herlihy, author of MIDNIGHT COWBOY

"Racy and wild, a grotesque but believable world
presented with robustly original perception."
– Burt Hirschfeld, author of FIRE ISLAND

"Darwin Porter writes with an incredible understanding
of the milieu – hot enough to singe the wings
off any butterfly!"
– James Kirkwood, co-author of A CHORUS LINE

"We know from the beginning that we're getting into a
hotbed that has morbid fascination for potential readers.
The novel evolves, in fact, into one massive melee of
malevolence, vendetta, and e-v-i-l, stunningly absorbing
alone for its sheer and unrelenting exploration of the
lower depths."
– BESTSELLERS

"He's outrageous...the book is extremely well written...
the bizarre, corrupt, angry, suicidal,
tragic characteristics of the cast are clearly delineated."
– Alec Wilder

Butterflies In Heat

A Novel by
Darwin Porter

STARbooks/FLF
Sarasota, Florida

Library of Congress Card Catalogue No. 97-065249
ISBN No. 1-877978-95-7

Publication made possible in part by a grant from the
Florida Literary Foundation

Cover design by Scott Sosebee
Cover photography by Russell Maynor

FOR STANLEY MILLS HAGGART

1959

Chapter One

An occasional car whizzed past. No one stopped.

Numie Chase walked alone into the night.

Mosquitoes after his blood were raising welts on his skin. No use to slap them any more. They were an army against the one of him.

How he wished he had his denim shirt back. At least that would offer some protection. But it'd been stolen the night before in that sleazy motel on the mainland. Stolen along with his thirty dollars. The hardest thirty dollars he'd ever earned at that. From a minister, no less. A man of God who'd wanted Numie to be the Devil and punish him for all his sins.

Not Numie's scene at all. But at this stage, he'd long ago forgotten what his scene was. Even if he'd ever had one.

He existed for other people. Merely a tool to satisfy them temporarily. Yet he knew he'd never really satisfied anyone in any deep and meaningful way.

Just for the moment——that was it.

For a price, anyone could have a chance to swing on him.

But the market was fading, just like the cars along this deserted stretch of road that ran by a mangrove swamp.

Trudging the highway, he found his steps quickening.

Faster and faster. If only there were a light, a neon sign, a street lamp, the headlight from an oncoming car.

Something.

Anything.

But there was nothing except the sound of frogs croaking from their secret hideaways in the swamp. The harsh symphony from the frogs was growing louder and louder the farther he walked. They knew he was there, and they were mocking him, threatening him, daring him to plunge deeper into their unfriendly terrain.

He didn't know why people wanted to live so far from the mainland anyway. So far into such inhospitable territory. Maybe the whole desolate stretch should be left to the frogs, lizards, and snakes.

He was on an island. At least he could feel the murky presence of water on both sides of him. The land was narrowing like an isthmus.

He'd lost count of the islands he'd already crossed earlier in the evening. Walking mostly, though he'd managed to hitch a ride for the first lap of the journey.

The coral islands were like a necklace dangling from the mainland, each pearl strung together by a bridge. He was going to the end of that string. To Tortuga, the point where the United States came to an abrupt halt.

From Tortuga, he'd been told, there were no more bridges. Just the open sea and the islands beyond.

In the distance, a headlight. Getting closer and closer.

The lights were on him now. Numie stood proud and tall, hoping to pass inspection.

"Please stop," he whispered.

The car was slowing down. Maybe he'd get a ride after all.

It came to a stop. The figure of a man loomed behind the wheel, but the lights were too bright for Numie to make out his face.

The driver kept his window shut, as he peered out into the night at Numie.

Numie stood bewildered. Finally, he smiled. "What do you want?" The driver called through the raised window.

"A ride, mister. Please."

"You're not a killer, are you?"

"No, I'm harmless."

Slowly the driver lowered the window. But just a crack. He was quite old, maybe in his seventies. Not only old, but tired and beat up. Two teeth in front were missing. "What's in the bag?"

"Just a few possessions."

"Lay them on the front fender," the old man commanded. "If I'm going to give you a ride, I want to make sure you're not carrying around concealed weapons."

"Okay," Numie said. Into his tattered duffel bag, he dug for his possessions. An address book filled mainly with street numbers and telephones of long-forgotten people. A pair of swimming trunks he'd found on the beach one day. Two avocados and three oranges he'd picked up when passing through farm country on the mainland. A frayed travel magazine with some beautiful color pictures of Tortuga. Finally, a leather belt with a big silver buckle he'd been trying to make for himself.

"You don't have much," the old man yelled. "What about knives? Turn your pockets inside out."

"Just a pocketknife," Numie said, emptying his pockets for inspection. He put the knife on the fender.

"I reckon you can get in," the old man called. Stuffing his possessions back into his duffel bag, Numie made his way around to the side of the battered Buick. The door was locked.

The old man waited for a long time before opening it. Finally, he leaned over and raised the lock. "Get in."

Numie got in, staying as close to the window as he could. Even from this point, he could smell the breath of the old man. He was a wino. His clothes were as old and as tired as he was. Nervously clutching the wheel, his hands were dry and withered. The car had another peculiar odor: unfixed cats.

"Who are you boy?" The old man asked.

"Name's Numie. Thanks for giving me a ride. If someone hadn't come along soon, the mosquitoes would have me dry by now."

"I hope I don't live to regret picking you up. I'm Hadley L. Crabtree. Just last month the sheriff's boys dug up five bodies on the keys. Arrested the crazy killer. Seems this guy went around picking up boy hitchhikers. He'd drive them to a deserted spot on No Name Key where he'd tie them up. This sickie got his rocks off by cutting off the peckers of these kids."

"Thank god he didn't come along and pick me up tonight," Numie said. "I need mine."

"What are you up to heading for Tortuga this time of night?"

"I couldn't find anything on the mainland. Thought I'd try my luck."

"There's no work in Tortuga," said Crabtree. "No jobs. Nothing. Any jobs down there, the kids of the local families grab them up. Most of the people there, except for some rich queers who come down in winter, are on welfare. I grew up on the island, and I should know there's no money there. Hell, it was 1947 before anybody could afford house paint."

"That's bad. I sure was hoping to find something."

Suddenly, Crabtree slammed on the brakes. "My advice to

you is to get out of this car right now. Park your ass on the other side of the road until you can hitch a ride back to the mainland."

"I can't do that. I've got to give it a try."

Crabtree started the car again. "Mark my words, boy, you'll regret the day you ever set foot in Tortuga. Besides, people there are none too friendly."

"You gave me a ride."

"I'm different. The only liberal in town. Once ran for political office just to challenge the machine. Got almost no votes, but I wanted to shake them up a bit. I was clobbered. They raised my real-estate taxes and practically drummed me out of town. Got no local business after that."

"What do you do?"

"I'm a lawyer, the only friend you beatniks have in town."

"I'm not a beatnik."

"You look like one. Come to think of it, though, you're a little old to be a real beatnik."

"Thanks."

"Some of my cases deal with possession of reefers. You young drifters down there are always going up in a cloud of smoke. Somebody's got to defend you when they throw you in jail. Actually you don't have a chance. The town is on a big campaign right now to get rid of vagrants. And after all those boy killings up on the keys, they're also after the rich queers. That's the only people who ever come to Tortuga. Decent tourists avoid the place."

"This magazine I've got has some real nice pictures of it."

"Propaganda. Of course, there's no place in America like Tortuga. Most people there have been cut off from the mainland for years. They've become inbred, very suspicious of strangers. We were just left to ourselves until the last few years when you young people started to invade. You heard we had good weather or something. No one wants you, except me. And I make my living off you. Some of those beatniks look like they don't have any money, but then the sheriff confiscates travelers checks and credit cards when he hauls them off to jail. Credit cards——imagine that. Only rich folks have those things. I've never had a traveler's check in my whole life, but they give them out to beatniks. Shows what's happening to this country."

"You make Tortuga sound like a real hell hole."

"It is."

"Why have you stayed so long?"

"I was born there, and that's reason enough for most natives. Bad as Tortuga is, you don't seem to fit into no other place if you're born on the island. We even talk different, sort of funny sounding to you mainlanders."

"Is there a place to stay?"

"Just one hotel and it's not much. Every now and then one of those mainlanders comes down and tries to build a tourist court, but the locals make it rough on him. They don't want a lot of dumb tourists running around town. But the natives are the dumb ones. Tourists would bring in some money. But the islanders just aren't forward looking. I told you, I'm the only progressive voice, and I'm seventy-six years old. When I'm dead and gone, I don't know what you young people are going to do when you get in a mess."

"If I ever do, I'll call you. Okay?"

"Don't call me unless you've got some bucks. I'm not a charity lawyer." The rest of the ride was in silence. It was calm and strangely quiet in the early morning hours.

After crossing a rickety wooden bridge into Tortuga, Numie was all eyes. Crabtree remained silent except for his heavy breathing. Tortuga was like something out of the past, its mystical beauty exotic and unearthly.

Shrimp boats and barges lined the pier, and the masts of anchored sailboats bobbed in the water. One houseboat proclaimed its name, REEFER MADNESS, in bold red letters.

The streets were rough and bumpy, occasionally broken by the octopus-like roots of massive banyan trees from the East Indies. Art nouveau lamps dimly lit the sidewalks. Jungle shrubbery——wild and untamed——and sago palms filled the yards of the old seagull gray houses. The buildings were mostly clapboard, drizzly in need of paint and haphazardly held together behind sagging Victorian verandas.

A convent with a dormered mansard roof and a central tower of stone added a note of stability. Otherwise the effect was lushly decadent. From around the world, sea captains had brought back Spanish laurel from southern Europe, the breadfruit tree from Polynesia, and the tamarind with its podlike fruit from India. Cacti flaunting its snow-white blossoms rubbed up against some of the buildings. One gave off the intoxicating smell of the night-blooming Cereus.

No lights came from any of the houses, except one lone cottage down a dark alleyway shaded by gaunt and gnarled lenten trees.

Here Numie was...at the end of the line...America's last frontier. "Pretty dead tonight."

"We're coming in from the east," Crabtree said. "That's the respectable part. Wait till you see the west side of town. It never shuts down. I'm going to let you off here. You'll have to walk the rest of the way. I don't have much gas."

"Thanks for the ride," Numie said, getting out. "It saved my life."

"That's my profession." The Buick pulled out.

Behind Numie was the Tortuga bus station, gaudily Victorian as an outsized wedding cake. The years of decay showed, though. The once-white paint was scaling, and young boys had tossed rocks through the stained-glass windows. The ornamental gingerbread work around the top was rotting away, and steep-roofed towers looked out onto the deserted street.

Slowly Numie headed down the street. To the town's one hotel. To a new life.

. . .

The afternoon sun stole between the splinters of the bamboo shades. The air was heavy, humid.

Numie was drowning in his own sweat. The limp, musty sheets were tangled around his nude body.

Where was he? What new and god awful town this time?

He reached for a lopsided wicker chair and ran his hands along its moldy frame. Then he grabbed hold of it, clutching——using it as a support to get back on his feet.

Climbing out of bed, he sat down on the chair. He had to get it all together, to face that street.

Another street, another town. But this one would be different from all the rest.

Bougainvillea in runaway colors of fuchsia, burnt orange, and pink was creeping through the windows of the ramshackle Dry Marquesas Hotel. The wildly growing vine was like a threat by nature that it could crawl in, overpower, and conquer on a moment's notice.

The deathlike air was still, broken only by the heavy sound of Numie's booted feet on the creaky steps.

The lobby was a hodgepodge. The potted plants had long ago toppled from thirst. Like the old gingerbread hotel itself.

It wasn't always this way, he'd heard. Once the lobby was filled with rich, bearded wreckers, the laughter of women who powdered their faces chalkwhite, and the swift movement of black boys who stuffed their adolescent bodies into white pants and put on cerise-colored shirts. Like those anachronistic pirates, Numie had come to scavenge.

Into the lobby men's room for one final appraisal of his body. Arching his broad shoulders, he made his six feet, two inches all the taller. That body, lanky and well shaped——the body that had brought him so much praise. It was still intact. What was he worried about? The face——angular, masculine. A few lines were appearing under his eyes. So what? That meant too many nights in too many bars. Those lines would fade in the afternoon sun of Tortuga. Smooth and bronze once more.

Leaving the toilet, he walked in a rapid, nervous stride through the lobby. His body wasn't moving harmoniously. Something inside seemed to be at work to spoil his appearance. He needed a real smoke in the worse way. But he had nothing, and only three bucks in his pocket and ten dollars in reserve in his shoe to buy anything. He wouldn't be able to pay his hotel bill unless he earned some money real quick.

The side entrance of the hotel led to a street shaded by mimosa.

A barefoot black boy was sitting in the doorway, whittling on a stick. He wore a pair of bleached-out blue jeans with a big hole in the left leg, through which a knobby knee protruded.

"Where's the nearest bar?" Numie asked.

The boy studied Numie's face for a long time. Then he put the stick in his mouth and munched on it. "White boy, did anybody ever tell you got violet eyes? They're violet just like the flower. My mama's got a pair of pillow cases the color of those eyes. I bet panthers got violet eyes, too. You ever see a panther?"

"Not since I flushed mine down the toilet. So you won't tell me?"

The boy scooted a few feet away on the dusty step.

Narrowly missing a splinter. "I don't know about bars. The whole damn town's a bar. I'll be your guide. You're one of those drifters that keep coming down to bother the people here, ain't you?"

"I've done my share of drifting, but I don't plan to bother anybody. Unless they ask for it."

"Then why do you wear that blond hair so long?"

"That's my business."

"One thing we got to agree on before I take you around," the boy said. "If I see some of my kin, I gotta run and hide till they pass me by."

"Are you ashamed to be seen with me?"

"I don't want nobody on this here island to think that I, Castor Q. Combes, showed any white-haired boy with violet eyes anything. Those eyes are gonna cause trouble for a heap of people in their time."

"They already have."

"Pay in advance, white boy. One dollar."

"Now that's a philosophy I understand, Castor Q. I've always insisted that my clients pay in advance, too."

"What kind of business you in?"

"I sell illusions, Castor baby."

"What's this baby crap?"

"I call everybody baby."

Castor was reaching for Numie's arm, pulling him along. He led the way down the narrow street. Once Castor pocketed his dollar, he lost his ability to talk.

Deep into the town Numie was descending.

"This is the pinko section," Castor muttered, before spitting into a hibiscus bush.

"What's that supposed to mean? They Communist or something?"

"Pink gold, man, pink gold. How stupid you are! This gold is shrimp——delicious, pink jumbo shrimp."

The water along the rundown port was murky, as if only dead things washed up on its shore. Fish and shrimp floated on the surface——streaked with black from the oil of the boats.

Barechested shrimpers——sweaty and unshaven——were lying around, guzzling beer.

"See those men?" Castor asked.

A group of men, mostly black, lay against the side of a dilapidated warehouse——their backs against the brick wall.

"There's gonna be trouble when the other shrimpers come home," Castor said. "Those guys are out of work, and they're gonna fight with the guys who were hired."

"Do you predict trouble all the time?"

"Seen a lot in my day."

"How old is your day? You must be all of twelve."

Castor didn't answer, licking his mouth instead. He turned down a street that looked more like an alley.

Rows of honky-tonks, advertising a paper cup of beer at fifteen cents, lined both sides of the street. The buildings seemed pieced together with crates and cardboard. Some of the box-type dwellings resembled abandoned freight cars. Naked, half-starved children played under the houses, supported by pilings. Space was too scarce for anyone to have a yard——so some semblance of front porches were attached to the hovels. Sad-faced women sat on them, sunning themselves like dogs. They fanned their faces with palm fronds and gossiped. Their eyes were strange and hollow, their stringy hair falling where it may. Dresses hung like rags from their bodies. The women twisted their necks to get a glimpse of Numie.

The children——defiant of an outsider treading on their only playground——quit their games and stood back. A pathway was cleared for Numie. The haunting eyes of these little people posed some undefined threat.

"Castor," he called out frantically. The sun was turning each object it hit into giant diamonds, their reflecting glares blinding him.

"What's the matter, white boy?"

"All of a sudden I hate this place. Forget the tour."

"Wait a minute. I got strict rules. Guys who don't finish the tour gotta pay me an extra dollar."

"No way," Numie said. His pathway cleared, he darted up the street.

"Violet eyes," Castor screamed after him, chasing him up

the alley. "Money, money, money."

. . .

"Rise and shine," came a gruff voice.

A stick was poking Numie in the ribs.

"Get your ass out of that bed, punk," said another voice, growing nearer.

Quickly Numie opened his sleepy eyes into the blinding glare of flashlight. Someone was turning on the light in his hotel room.

Two cops in uniform were standing over him. A tall, lean man was at the door.

"No funny business," the man at the door said. "I'm Yellowwood, the sheriff."

"Get your hands up," one of the cops ordered.

"What's all this?" Numie asked.

"You do what you're told," Yellowwood said. "I'll ask the questions. Now haul your ass out of that bed."

Head throbbing, Numie demanded, "You can't arrest me. I've done nothing. I know my rights."

"If you don't get your ass out of that bed," Yellowwood said, "Dave here will clobber you with his nightstick." Dave was pulling back the sheet exposing Numie's nude body.

"Sheriff, there's only one weapon on him," Dave said, "and that's not very concealed."

The other cop laughed.

Numie cringed at the way he was being eyed. Yellowwood came over and stared long and hard at Numie before commanding, "Get your clothes on. Search the room, boys."

Into his pants, Numie confronted Yellowwood. "Now you can tell me what this is all about?"

"Our informer tells me you're in town peddling dope," Yellowwood said.

"That's a goddamn lie," Numie answered. "Could your informer be a twelve-year-old psychopath named Castor Q. Combes?"

"We never reveal the identity of our informers," Yellowwood said.

"Nothing," Dave said, after going through the duffel bag.

The other cop was tearing the sheets off the bed and looking under the mattress.

"Okay," Yellowwood said, "you've got it stashed——that's for sure. I want you out of town——and fast. Tonight."

"You've got nothing on me," Numie protested.

"I said tonight——and that's what I mean. If I find you here tomorrow, you can expect real trouble."

"What kind of place is this?" Numie asked. "Running a man out of town before he's done anything."

"We don't want your kind here," Yellowwood said. "This is a good town with good people. They like to live in peace."

"I'm not disturbing the peace," Numie said.

"I don't have time for no arguments," Yellowwood said. "Tonight or else." He left, the cops following, slamming the door as they went.

The room was now in shambles, Numie's few possessions tossed on the floor.

"Tonight or else," he mocked, plopping down on the disheveled bed.

Chapter Two

Later that night, the west side of Tortuga was ablaze with life. The little shrimping port rattled with the noise of rock and roll bands. Every third building was a bar.

Young people were everywhere. Elvis Presley-style hair flowed like a river. Dress was kept to a minimum. In tight jeans, boys wore white T-shirts. One girl had removed her top, exposing her pubescent breasts.

In front of his rambling, tin-roofed hotel, Numie sat on the wide veranda in a wicker rocking chair. The air was not polluted and unfamiliar to his nostrils. It was scented with the smell of night-blooming jasmine.

Two pudgy Cubans stood under an old iron lamppost. They stared at him strangely. But he did not look back.

Wherever he went in this town, hostile eyes followed. Getting up, he made his way down the arbored sidewalk. Then he realized what he had become——a fugitive in Tortuga.

Into the pay phone, he quickly found Hadley L. Crabtree's number. After the first ring, the attorney was on the line.

"I'm Numie Chase, the hitchhiker you picked up on the keys. Remember?"

"Yeah, I know. Didn't expect to be hearing from you so soon. You busted?"

"No, I'm clean, but the sheriff and two of his men searched my hotel room. Didn't find anything but ordered me out of town, 'tonight or else.' What should I do?"

"I told you not to come here in the first place. But Yellowwood, that's who it was, can't force you to leave. He always makes these threats against you newcomers. But providing you're clean and have some visible means of support, there's not much he can do against you——except watch you like a hawk. And Yellowwood just loves to watch."

"Then you think it's safe to stay?"

"No, he'll get you in the long run, but that don't mean you have to clear out tonight. What's wrong with tomorrow night? You've come all this way. Might as well enjoy yourself before heading back."

"Thanks."

"This is the last time I'm giving out free advice," Crabtree said. "Understand?" He slammed down the phone.

By now, Numie knew where to go. Not because anybody told him. He just knew. He felt called to Commodore Philip's bar as dogs are summoned to their masters by whistles pitched too high for human ears.

Just a block from the sagging pier, the bar was a primitive two-story structure. The doors were wide and open, the interior dimly lit by colored glass buoys hung from the ceiling.

Inside there was a nautical look. Fishnets swagged from beam to beam, interspersed with conch shells, sponges, and sea fans. Crude tables for drinks had been made out of cable spools.

Around the walls were framed and unframed photographs and newspaper clippings of fishermen and their prized catches.

An occasional voice was heard, but it was the quietest bar on the street. Easy to miss.

But Numie didn't.

At the door, he paused——to listen to the tinkle of ice. Then, he went in.

Here and there in a corner, a customer sipped a drink. The faces were cold and hard——brutally appraising every stranger who appeared.

Numie took a seat on a stool around a circular bar in the center. "Scotch," he said without looking up.

"Whatever you want, I've got!" came a voice.

Numie stared hard.

Behind the bar stood a black creature under a platinum blonde wig. She was dressed entirely in white. A Jean Harlow gown, cut low.

She openly met Numie's stare. "If some trick looks at me like you just looking——burning your eyes out and letting your mouth hang open like you catching flies——I charge admission."

"The attraction doesn't interest me."

In moments the whiskey was slammed on the counter.

"Not interested!" the blonde-black said. "I've never met a john yet who wasn't interested in Lola La Mour."

"What kind of name is that? Well, I'm glad to be the first."

Lola looked defiant, pursing her heavily painted mouth.

"Some people just can't appreciate the better things of

life——even when they is as easy to come by as sticking a red hot poker into a tub of freshly churned butter."

"Some guys don't want what's easy to come by."

"You one of those racial bigots? Think I'm not people or something?"

"No, I'm not prejudiced."

"Then why are your marbles so messed up?"

"I like girls."

"What in horsefeathers do you think this gorgeous pussy is? Yeah, me. The one right up here getting inspected like a naked jaybird."

"A drag queen."

She gave him a mean look. "Well, la-dee-dah, you got some bad hang-up about drag queens?"

"No, I've seen a few in my day."

"Shit!" Lola said, smoothing down her gown. "You gonna sit there, like some steeple on a lilywhite church, laying it on me that you've seen but not touched?"

"A few have climbed the mountain. That is, those who didn't mind paying the price."

Lola blinked her eyelashes, her stance growing more rigid. "See that Facel-Vega, all glowing white, sitting out there on that street? That little sports car is all the advertising your mother needs. I must be doing something right."

"Lola," a man yelled. "Gotta move your car. De la Mer's here."

Lola shrugged her shoulders. "Dykes," she said. "The worst thing God put on this sweet earth. Why anyone in his right mind would want to go down on a woman! It bugs the shit out of me just thinking about something so disgusting. It ain't natural."

Numie turned on the bar stool.

The Facel-Vega disappeared up the street. It was replaced by a custom-made Lincoln from the 20s.

Suddenly, the door burst open. A pair of pencil-thin, red high heels emerged from behind the door. It was followed by a mountain of flabby flesh. It was a woman, a real one. "Lola," she yelled in a Deep South voice, "we're here."

Numie could not conceal his fascination.

For one thing, that citrus-orange hair she let flow in every direction. That fire-orange lipstick coating the whole area around her mouth. And to finish it off, that dress——with its lavender and turquoise flowers——dripped on all over like soup.

Lola came out from behind the bar to kiss the cheek of the orange-haired woman. "Tangerine." But no lips ever touched the sagging flesh. The kiss was just pretend.

Numie met Tangerine's twinkling eyes openly now. She was just two feet away.

He turned aside only to investigate a commotion coming from the car.

From behind the enclosed, black-curtained compartment appeared a yellow glove. Then a woman's long, yellow-stockinged legs slid off the leopard-skin upholstery and out of the car.

"Who's that?" Numie asked Lola.

"Leonora de la Mer," was the tart reply.

Leonora——all six feet of her——stood on the sidewalk of the shabby street, casting a spell. She could have been arriving at the premiere of a film. Her chin jutted into the night air, concealing the wrinkles of her neck and enhancing her nobility. To Numie, she was like something from a time capsule. A mass of fabric, all bright yellow. The pearl necklace hanging down to her waist bounced in time with her step as she moved from the Lincoln to Commodore Philip's. But her walk was a stiltlike stride——legs connected to her shoulders and the trunk of her body motionless.

From the front seat appeared a tall young couple in jeans. The man sneered at the woman and walked ahead. She yanked at his sleeve, then yelled, "You can't talk to me that way."

He turned around, glaring at her. Then he struck her across the face and stalked away.

The young woman cried out.

Leonora moved over to comfort her. Putting her arm around the woman's slender waist, Leonora helped her inside.

"Some husband! He's nothing but a prick," the young woman said. "Some day I'm going to get even with him, I really mean it."

"You'll do nothing of the sort," Leonora said, clasping her arm, "and you know it."

"I need a beer," the young woman said. "I'll buy you one,

too."

"A beer? Darling, Leonora de la Mer doesn't drink beer. *I* have never had a public fight with a lover...or invited anyone to have a glass of beer. We've ordered champagne tonight."

Leonora bowed gracefully to Lola. She even acknowledged Numie's presence with a slight tip of her head.

Lola assumed a mask of twisted charm. Her friendly attitude to Tangerine obviously didn't extend to Leonora.

"Good evening, Miss La Mour," Leonora said.

"Good evening to you," Lola answered in her grandest manner.

"Such a lovely evening," Leonora said. "That's why I thought we'd have a drink at your quaint little bar."

"Yes," Lola said, "the evening *was* lovely.

"I beg your pardon!" Leonora said, turning and walking quickly to her table.

Numie smiled at Tangerine.

"Lola," Tangerine admonished, "now don't you go being rude to Leonora."

"Shit," Lola said, "this bar ain't big enough for two Super Stars."

"Tangerine," the young woman with Leonora called, "come and join us."

"Later," Tangerine said, brushing aside her invitation for the moment. Then she extended her hand, saying, "I'm Tangerine Blanchard." Three large Mexican rings perched on her hand like snails.

"Numie Chase."

"I'm the official greeter around here," she said, smiling. "Even though Lola ain't put me on the payroll yet."

"That's *some* car and *some* woman," he said.

As he turned to look for a moment at the yellow-draped woman, she was nodding to Tangerine.

"New in town?" Tangerine asked.

"Yeah, just got in."

"And you made it to the commodore's. Right away. Well you won't be a stranger for long."

What a voice, Numie thought. She sounded like a bullfrog with a cold.

"My full name's Fern Cornelia Blanchard," she went on, "in

case you should hear somebody calling me something other than Tangerine. Fern and Cornelia don't actually suit me. Remind too many people of a southern virgin...You can call me anything you like——except, for God's sake, *Miss Blanchard*. Don't remind me."

He was learning fast that Tangerine didn't give anyone a chance to reply.

Right in front of him, she scratched. Then, she yanked her dress to straighten it, saying, "I've got on a man-eating girdle. It bites into my flesh, so please excuse all this gyrating...Where you from? I come from Georgia. A Georgia peach, my daddy used to say. But the last time he looked at me——that was right before he died——he said, `Fern, honey, you look like a pulverized pumpkin'."

"Tangerine," the young woman in jeans called again.

Tangerine looked at Numie. "Would you like to join our table?"

"I don't think I'd better," Numie said. "There's enough going on over there tonight."

"Child," Lola said to Tangerine, "could you two pipe down just a minute? You keep jabbering like a concubine from a peanut plantation. I'm getting ready to do my big number, and us artists have to get it all together right before we let it all hang out."

On a circular platform was a miniature piano. At it sat an elderly black man.

"That's BoJo," Tangerine whispered. "He's supposed to play when Lola isn't singing."

BoJo was clearly too drunk to play.

A pink spotlight was turned on the mound. Rushing over to the jukebox, high heels clanking, Lola stuffed a quarter into it, then made a selection. She raced back, landing in a huff under the soft glow.

The number on the record began, the sounds of, `C'mon and get it, honey', drifting across the bar. Lola was only mouthing the sultry song, but was not quite coordinated with the words.

A man in front laughed loudly at her bad timing.

Breaking the entire routine, Lola turned and glared before picking up with the number again.

Under her blonde wig, she bled every word for innuendo.

Undulating her hips and shaking what appeared to be tiny breasts, she leered at the audience. She licked her heavily coated lips, rolled her eyes, raised one brow——a facade of sensuality.

Even under the most flattering of lights, Lola appeared much older to Numie than she had when he first encountered her at the bar. But so much of her face was obscured by that blonde wig, it was hard to tell exactly what she looked like.

Turning around, Lola ended her number with an ass-shimmy.

The same man she'd reprimanded before with a glare now called for an encore.

Obviously pleased, Lola squealed, "Christ, give a working girl a break. Gotta take a pee." She disappeared into a back room.

Ignoring his earlier refusal, Tangerine now took Numie's hand and escorted him over to Leonora's private table.

"Leonora, Anne," Tangerine said, "I want you to meet Numie, my new friend."

"You just met him," said Anne.

"I am her friend," Numie said defiantly.

"Young man," Leonora said, "please be seated."

"Is this a papal audience?" Numie asked. Nevertheless, he obeyed her command, sitting down next to Anne.

Tangerine squeezed her plump body in opposite him.

"Do you know who *I* am?" Leonora asked.

"I've never heard of you," Numie answered, matter-of-factly.

"She's the fashion queen of Tortuga," Anne said.

"Whatever that means," Numie replied.

"I have my fashion house here," Leonora explained. "In the 30's and 40's, I was the most famous dress designer in New York. Stage stars, anyone with money and taste, came to me. I was better than any of the French designers, including that dreadful Chanel creature. Of course, I spent a great deal of my time flying to the coast to design for films."

"What are you doing here? Numie asked. "A remote place like this?"

"Leonora wanted a change of scenery," Anne volunteered. "A more dramatic climate in which to create."

"Indeed," echoed Leonora. "Don't get the idea my clothes went out of style. I've always been the pace-setter in fashion."

"Sounds like a good business," Numie said.

"And what do you do?" Leonora asked.

"I'm a hustler," Numie said. "Anyone who can pay."

"Business must be rough," Anne said.

"It sure is," Numie answered. "I'm broke."

"You'll have a difficult time hustling in this town," Leonora said. "It's filled with young men only too eager to give it away. No one really has to pay here."

"Sorry to hear that," Numie replied.

"Frankly, I find the whole idea disgusting," Anne said.

"Dear heart," Leonora said to Numie. "You must excuse Anne. She's a dreadful loser in life. That's why she's so cruel. *I*, on the other hand, who have always been at the top, am so secure I need never be unkind to anyone." Pausing to look at Tangerine, she went on, "Tangerine, sweetheart that she is, always brings young people to meet me when I visit Commodore Philip's. I want to keep in touch with the young generation."

"I'm not exactly the young generation," Numie said. "I'll never see thirty again."

"We can't be children forever," Leonora said. "Perish the thought. I possibly could help you, give you a job at my fashion house."

"Thanks, but I don't know anything about clothes."

"You don't have to," Leonora said. "We'll find something appropriate for you. Come and have lunch at my home tomorrow. We'll discuss it."

"Where do you live?" Numie asked.

"Just ask anybody on any street corner," said Leonora. "Everybody knows where Sacre-Coeur is."

"Then I shouldn't have any trouble."

"Now, what was your name again?" Leonora asked. "Numie, isn't it? *New me*. Each of us like a flower blooming eternally."

He didn't know what to say, so he smiled.

"You have a good face," Leonora said. "I liked it at once. Like a young river trying hard to find its way to the sea. Real faces are hard to find on this island... on any island. But I had a premonition I'd find one tonight. Didn't I, Tangerine?"

Tangerine gave Numie a tired glance.

Leonora said to Numie, "Now you must go. I have to talk to Tangerine and Anne. And we're going to have champagne."

"Very well," he replied, getting up quickly. "Tangerine, I liked meeting you. I'm sure I'll see you again."

"Good night, sweetie," she said. "Sure, I'll see you. Real soon, I hope."

"Good night, Anne," he said.

"I'll see you tomorrow when you come for lunch." Her face was non-committal.

"Miss De la Mer, a pleasure," he said.

She extended her gloved hand.

He paused a moment, then realized she wanted it kissed. He complied.

At the door, he put a dollar bill in Lola's outstretched hand, glittering with zircons.

"Where's the tip?" Lola asked. "We're not opposed to a few gratuities around here."

"I don't have anything extra."

"I knew you didn't have much."

"I've got it, babe, but you've got to pay for it," Numie said.

"Lola has never paid for *it*. Lola *is* paid for it."

"Night." He walked out to the street.

The black Lincoln still stood on the curb——looking battered out of its owner's presence. Here and there, its body bore dabs of black paint over orange splotches of rust.

Salt air and humid weather were supposed to be bad for automobiles. And for other things. This wasting away, so it was said, was known as Tortuga cancer.

Chapter Three

Back at his hotel, Numie raced up the creaky steps to his room. Shutting the door quickly, he rubbed his back against it, hoping the wood had living strength to keep out what was pursuing him.

His shirt, soaked with sweat, clung to his body. After he'd left the bar, the shakes had descended.

With trembling hands, he reached for a half empty bottle of cheap wine on the dresser. He put its neck to his mouth, downing it. Some of it dripped from his chin onto his clothes.

Throat burning, he stared into the black-specked mirror. He was coming apart right before his own eyes!

He stripped and got into bed. There he lay——tossing, tumbling.

He was going to make it in this town, or he wasn't going to make it at all.

At some point, he fell asleep——but not for long. He woke up suddenly, slinging his arm and knocking over a lamp.

It was still dark.

He could sleep no more. Something told him to get out of bed, find a connection, move into life. Time was wasting.

He put on a pair of jeans, nothing else. Slipping into sandals; he walked softly out.

No place to go. It didn't matter. Getting away did.

At the end of the hall, an annex was barricaded by two crossed slabs of lumber. He stepped across and turned a corner leading down to an enclosed veranda under a high ceiling.

He stumbled along the musty passageway until he banged into an old settee. On one side were rooms where seemingly no one lived. The other side faced a clump of bushes. Double layers of rotting bamboo shades kept out the moonlight.

Going on, he came upon a pedestal. On it, a marble cupid poised his arrow. Dragging his hand along the mildewed, red-brocaded wallpaper, he finally reached a corner. Here, moonlight streamed in again. The palm trees swayed gently in the wind.

He soaked up the stillness, the remoteness. For this moment, he was safe, protected. Nothing in the world could touch him or harm him.

The illusion was shattered by footsteps approaching. He backed against the wall——hiding. Then with caution he peered around the corner.

Three men were outlined in the dim light. Two were in sailor uniforms. The third was trying a key in the door. The Navy men followed him in.

Numie sneaked off in the other direction. But right away a wall stopped him. The only other way to avoid their room was to jump over a steep railing into the bushes.

Then a loud crack announced the opening of the door. Both sailors ran out. They raced up the veranda.

From the room came the faint sound of moaning. Numie moved in its direction. The room smelled of gardenias turned to dust.

"Are you okay?" Numie asked, slightly apprehensive.

"Who's there?" the man cried out in panic. In the near darkness, his half-dressed figure was sprawled on a canopy bed.

Numie flicked on a light switch, but it didn't work. Striking a match, he moved to the bed. The shrill chirp of a cicada gave him a start. Was it a warning not to get involved?"

"What do you want?" the injured man demanded. He was holding a handkerchief to his bloody nose.

"Just to find out if those sailors damaged any vital parts."

"Leave me alone."

"Gladly." Numie backed away.

"Look, could you bring me a towel?" The man's voice changed, now trusting and pleading. "Soak it in hot water. I'll pay you for your trouble."

That god-damn cicada again. For a moment, Numie was silent. He felt duty-bound to help the man; yet at the same time he wanted to run up the hall. "Sure," he finally said, reluctantly.

"But don't let anybody know I'm here."

"I wasn't planning to run an announcement in the society column," Numie answered, showing his irritation. Out on the veranda again, he was more wary than before.

On his return, the mugged man held the towel to his face. "Dammit," he said, "my head's spinning." For the first time, the entire body of the man was visible.

Numie had lit a candle. It stood on the nightstand. The man was vaguely familiar. His shirt lay crumpled on the floor. Black stubble peppered his face; and his eyes were large bulbs reaching out to draw in the light. The face was lean and hungry. *That face*. The same face outside Commodore Philip's. He was Anne's husband!

Numie withdrew. After all, he'd seen how this man had treated his wife earlier in the evening. He could muster little sympathy for him, now that he was the victim of violence himself.

"I should explain," the man said.

"What's there to explain? You wanted to get laid, but got ripped off instead."

"That sure spells it out."

"Why conceal the obvious?" Numie asked.

"What's your game?"

At first, Numie hesitated——not because he was reluctant to reveal his profession, but because he didn't want to get confidential with this man. Then he smiled wryly to himself, the very thought that a hustler as broke as he was could pick and choose among people was ridiculous. "I hustle, too," he managed to say, "but I deliver." Unable to resist a john, he was selling. "And I don't rip anybody off." That was too much hard-sell, he decided, but the words were out. He reached into his back pocket and pulled out a crushed package of cigarettes, lit one, and handed it to the man.

"Thanks," he said, smiling, his fingers lingering caressingly over Numie's. A crooked grin distorted his face.

"What were you doing down here? I didn't think anybody came here any more, except me."

"Okay," Numie said, "I didn't ask you questions. You don't ask me questions." After his earlier come-on, Numie thought it best to play hard to get.

"I'm not used to that," the man said, dabbing at the corner of his mouth with a towel. "I'm Ralph."

"Numie." The room sent a shiver through him, and he put his hands in his pockets." Look, man, I've got to go. This place gives me the creeps." Almost as if to confirm his statement, the cicada let out another shrill chirp.

"My car's parked out back," Ralph said. "Would you meet me there?"

For Numie, the invitation was an all too familiar one.

"Yeah," he agreed, "but I'd think tonight would have made you suspicious of strangers."

"I am," Ralph said, "always . . . but I need one every now and then." His eyes met Numie's.

Numie withdrew at the sight of their intensity. "It'll cost you."

"They took my, money."

"No ice, no dice."

"Wait, my watch. They didn't take my watch. It cost a lot of money. A gift from a friend."

Numie took the watch. "I prefer cash." Bargaining over sex always repulsed him, regardless of how many times he'd forced himself to do it.

"That's all I've got right now."

"It's a deal," Numie said. "I usually charge thirty dollars."

"You'll have to lower your price in this town. But the watch is far more valuable." Ralph was buttoning up his shirt. "We could go for a ride in my boat and watch the sun come up. It's the nicest part of the day."

Numie started to say no. But there was something in Ralph's last statement that appealed to him. Unlike his first impression of him, Ralph apparently had enough of a soul to appreciate a sunrise. "It sounds okay," Numie said, not wanting to sound too enthusiastic.

"Good." Ralph reached into his pocket and pulled out a ring of keys, handing it to Numie.

This simple act of trust further elevated Ralph in Numie's eyes: Was it possible that he could be mugged and robbed only minutes before, then turn over his car keys to a perfect stranger the next moment?

"It's the red sports car out back," Ralph said. "I'll meet you there in a few minutes."

"If you don't hurry, we'll miss the sunrise," Numie said.

"The story of my life," Ralph called after him.

. . .

Ralph's boat zoomed through the waters of the green-blue strait, stirring up a backlash that rained down on Numie's head. His jeans were getting soaked, but he liked the pelting water.

An early morning invitation from a stranger——just the kind of excitement he needed.

Out on the dark sea, he saw a rare world——clean, refreshing. As the boat neared an uninhabited key, the sky was turning pink. Shadows remained, though. Did the night want to let go?

"Look!" Ralph yelled. In the distance, a small island with a sandy beach came into view. Palm trees flapped their fronds in the cool air.

The sun was breaking through.

Numie shivered in his wet clothes. "Man," he said.

"It's my favorite spot." Ralph steered the boat toward an inlet.

Orange rays cut into the water over the reef. Conchs heaved forward with their permanent smiles. Purple sea fans moved in time with the rhythm of the waves; and rainbow parrot fish glided between the sulfur yellow sponges and corals.

Numie stepped over jagged pieces of rock. Then he ran down the beach, kicking the white sand. Had he ever been this free? He wanted the whole world to stand still.

"Take off those wet jeans," Ralph commanded.

"What else is on your mind?"

"To see the jewels."

The jeans were peeled from his legs. He stood proudly, meeting Ralph's penetrating stare. "Do I pass inspection?"

"Triple A."

"Before we get down to business," Numie said, "I want to look around."

"Okay, I'll be your guide," Ralph volunteered, "but that's not why I brought you here."

Numie paused. Just once in his life, he wished somebody would invite him somewhere without his having to sing for his supper.

For the next hour, Ralph revealed the hidden spots of beauty. A nest of blue-red orchids. A place where water was the color of crystal. A field of thick banana trees, bearing fruit that only wild things ate.

Ralph charted the way back to the beach. "I have a big map

at home with all these islands drawn in," he said. "I named this one after myself. I don't really own it, but I feel like I do."

Numie remained silent. As he surveyed the island, his thoughts were different from Ralph's. He felt this oasis should belong to no one in particular, but should be used by anyone wanting to get away and escape——at least for a while——the real world.

He put his hands on his hips, spread his legs, arched his spine, and tossed his head back, enjoying the fresh air.

Ralph's body trembled. He looked down the beach, squinting his eyes to keep out the glare. Then he leaned over quickly and kissed Numie on the lips.

The gentle movement met no resistance. But the kiss was not returned. Even so, it stung. Numie instinctively reached to rub his mouth.

"Are you strictly trade?"

"If you want to call it that. I'm not a kisser, but I throw a pretty good fuck."

"You can't prove it by me." Ralph's eyes glowed with an overpowering hunger.

Numie's body moved over him.

"Make it hurt," Ralph whispered. His low moans were the only sound heard on the island.

. . .

Numie lay quietly on the beach. He had raped Ralph with a savagery he didn't know he had in him. The more he ripped and tore, the more Ralph had responded. Ralph had called forth the animal in him and had found it. Ralph didn't want love, tenderness. Rather, almost a primordial attack. Were those sailor muggers actually performing a service for Ralph? What a way to get rid of guilt! Numie found himself almost wishing it could be as easy for him as well. To use the act of sex to get rid of your rages, hidden angers, the poisons that clogged the system, made a lot of sense. If you could do it. Numie couldn't.

Instead he was ashamed of himself. Not for having had sex with Ralph, but for getting too close a look inside Ralph's head.

Numie felt some strong need to convince Ralph he wasn't the beast he'd been when he was mounting him.

Ralph was toying with a silver chain around Numie's neck. Then he picked up a tiny ebony blackbird it held captive, examining it like an appraiser with a precious stone. "Why do you wear this?"

The perfect opener, Numie thought, to let Ralph know he wasn't just a hustler. Numie looked into the fully awakened morning sky as if it were a window onto the past. Then he closed his eyes. "A reminder of a friend I once had."

"Care to tell me about him?" Ralph's voice was soft, caressing, inviting confidences.

"I don't think it would interest you," Numie said, secretly hoping Ralph would ask more. If it had been the city streets, Numie would have grabbed the blackbird and rested it back on his chest. He always rebuffed anybody who inquired about it. But the safe haven of the island inspired him in ways no other place had.

"At least you had a friend," Ralph said. "People usually say they can count their friends on their fingers. I can't even raise one little pinkie. What was your friend like?"

"I met him at boarding school when I was fourteen. He was tall and shy, but great on the basketball court."

Ralph began to massage his back.

"We were roommates," Numie continued, wondering how far to go.

"Did you ever get it on with him?" Ralph asked, growing impatient.

"Hell no!" Numie said. "We were close buddies, not that kind of friends. We hung out everywhere together——even went to a school dance where we did nothing but sit around rapping with each other."

"That must have gone over big," Ralph said.

"It did." Having said this much, Numie impulsively went on. "One night Marty came back to our room. He was edgy as hell. I was washing out our socks in the sink. He took his away. Told me he'd do his own from now on." Numie was speaking rapidly, knowing if he didn't he'd never finish the story. "He sat me down on the bed. Damn, did he have sad eyes! He told me there was a lot of ugly talk going around about us. I didn't know what he meant.

"I bet," Ralph said sarcastically.

"No, I didn't really," Numie said, sorry he felt it necessary to defend such a long-ago relationship. "He said he was moving to another dormitory. He'd had a talk with the dean."

"Your friend hadn't come out of the closet."

"He was trying to tell me, but couldn't. All he could manage was he was afraid I'd hate him if he told me about himself. I didn't think that was giving me much credit."

"You were too young."

"I remember, he got up and held out his hand. `Thanks for everything, little one,' he said. I didn't take his hand. Then he took this blackbird and put it on the bed. Never returned to school after that."

"He really did believe in punishing himself," Ralph said.

"Did you ever see him again?" Ralph stopped the massage.

"Yeah, I did——sorry to say." Numie turned over, staring into the sun. "I hitched to his hometown a few years later. It was about thirty miles from the old boarding school, and he was still living there. We had dinner. It was awkward as hell. He didn't know what to say to me. A married man with two kids. Still hadn't come to terms with himself. Worse yet, he was selling insurance. And he used to tell me he was going to be a poet."

"It's stupid to think you can ever go back... to anything," Ralph said. "Me, I never had anything like that to go back to."

"I don't understand you, man." Numie got up and reached for his jeans. "You're attractive, probably loaded. I don't know why you don't have friends."

"I'm on a total sex trip. When I'm not working, I'm out searching."

"Can't you get it on with just one person?" Numie asked. "A regular?"

"No way." Ralph sat up quickly. "After I've had a guy——even when he's great in bed——I lose interest. I feel the person's no good after he's put out."

"I know where I stand."

"I didn't mean it that way. I guess you think I'm sick."

Numie nodded. "Too bad," he said, zipping up. "I thought I turned you on, and you'd want another round like manana."

"You did turn me on, but from now on you're going to have to wave the flag at somebody else."

"I see." There was a long, hurt pause. "Shit, here I was telling you the story of my life."

"I did listen."

"Sure." Numie's anger was rising. "Well, forget it. I made it up." Ralph had robbed him of something precious.

"I don't believe you." Ralph said smugly. "You're mad at me all of a sudden."

"I'm not mad at you. It's just I'm always meeting guys like you. I'd better get back to Tortuga." A tougher, more familiar shell was encasing Numie. He smiled sardonically. "For an appointment with a queen."

"I didn't know you had anything left," Ralph said. "Wasn't I sufficient?"

"You were terrific. This date's with a different type queen."

Chapter Four

Pearl Street was the dividing line between the western and eastern halves of Tortuga. Pearl Street was also the dividing line between the two ways of life: The rich and poor. Unlike most towns, the island didn't have a middle-class section to separate the two extremes. Most of the houses Numie passed on his way to Leonora's were boarded up for the summer. Deserted by the wintering wealthy, they were a sad and neglected lot on this hot, sticky afternoon.

His pace quickened, as Sacre-Coeur rose like a jagged mountain of volcano out of the sea. It stood on the edge of a short canal. Like a gaudy, many layered birthday cake, it glistened with Easter egg colors. The house was high and square, with open grillwork. At least a dozen staircases twisted outside, their steps leading to towers and balconies.

Numie was stunned. Tropical vegetation was going to devour the house. It looked as if nothing were ever cut——not even weeds.

After crossing through the garden, he walked up a layer of tiled steps to a massive carved oak door. It was wide open. Going inside, he entered a square central hall, three stories high, rising to the roof and exposing the balconies on the second and third floors.

In the center of the hall stood a fountain of four cherubs. One spat water from its mouth. Another dripped water through a horn of plenty. The third played a leaking flute. And a fourth, like the famous statue in Brussels, passed water in nature's more conventional way.

Numie pivoted at the sound of footsteps.

Anne stood there silently. In the afternoon sun, she looked more beautiful somehow. Her soft brown hair was closely cropped, and she gave off a clean fragrance. Barefoot, she wore nothing but shorts and a blouse which effectively showed off her trim, creamy body. Under thin dark brows, her green eyes seemed to see too much At first, she didn't speak. Finally, she said, "So, you finally showed up. I bet Leonora last night you'd split."

"Goes to show what a poor judge of character you are."

"No, my statement still stands. Only my timing was off. Come on in and have a seat in the patio."

Trailing her, he was shown to a wrought-iron chair.

"Let me fix you a drink," she said.

"No thanks——not at this time of day."

"I'm going to have a beer." Opening a refrigerator behind the bar, she took out a bottle. "Sure you won't join me?"

"You've persuaded me."

Handing him the beer, she paused. Those penetrating green eyes were staring at the watch on his wrist. Awkwardly, he tried to conceal it. She backed away from his chair. "I see you've met my husband."

"You know." Silently he cursed his stupidity for wearing it. "The watch?"

"Yes, it was my anniversary gift to him."

"You asking for it back?"

"I couldn't stand to touch it," she said, turning away. "If you don't mind my being personal, why did he give you the watch? He usually pays cash."

"He was short, I guess." Acute embarrassment overcame him and he wasn't a man to embarrass easily.

"Probably got rolled earlier in the night," she said. "He loves rough trade."

The beer was cooling his body. He leaned back in his chair, feeling the danger of an explosive confrontation was over. "When it happened, I can't pretend to you I didn't know he was your husband. I did know." He paused. "I saw the two of you outside the bar last night."

"If you saw that, then, it'd be foolish for me to pretend that Ralph and I have anything approaching a marriage——so let's drop the subject."

"I didn't mean to come between you."

"You already have, but I'm not blaming you. You're what you said you were, a hustler. You didn't pretend. But I know that if there's a hustler floating around town, he's bound to meet Ralph sooner or later. I'm surprised it happened so soon——that's all."

After a long silence, he asked, "Do you work for Leonora——or are you just a friend?"

"Leonora has no friends——other than professional ones. I'm

sort of a secretary."

"Are you on duty now?"

"Yes."

"What does she want with me?" Another long pause. "Sex?"

"Don't flatter yourself. Besides, you've got the wrong equipment. She's got to be with somebody new all the time. She's starved for an audience, having exhausted everybody in town. You're different. She'll want to amuse herself with you for a while."

"Like a cat with a mouse?

"Call it what you like. You're broke, Said so yourself and hustling is rough in this town. My husband is the best-paying customer you'll find, and he wants it only once. Or did you know that?"

"He spelled it out."

"Leonora will make it worth your while——whatever she wants from you. What do you have to lose?"

"Was she serious? I mean, about offering the job?"

"Perhaps, she needs help. She fires left and right. Blood transfusions are always sought after."

"I could be her chauffeur. I noticed you didn't have one last night."

"She had this Cuban, but she called him day and night. He was a family man and couldn't take her demands. He quit last week."

"When am I going to see her?"

"She knows you're here. Her bedroom overlooks the patio, and she sees everything going on. She believes in keeping her callers waiting for a respectable time. But you must never keep her waiting. She's probably had time to reach her study by now. Come this way."

He followed her to a set of French doors. Anne rapped lightly, then turned the knob. She smiled at him before walking away.

. . .

"Show the young man in," came a voice from the far side of the room.

The study was actually a picture gallery. Its walls were covered with photographs of Leonora in the gowns of the thirties and forties. Other framed photographs——some quite large——adorned every table and the entire mantel. They were overshadowed by paintings of the designer in many of her originals.

Red-velvet draperies kept out the late morning sun. And two cutout brass globe lamps with bulbs enclosed in pink cellophane cast a soft, forgiving light.

Leonora sat in a five-foot-high, Venetian sedan chair on a tufted upholstered seat of red silk. She never crossed her long legs, but planted them solidly on the floor. Most of her face was in shadow. All Numie could see clearly was her outfit: blue, aqua, and violet Turkish pants, with a matching, loosely fitting blouse. She was smoking a pastel-colored cigarette from a carved ivory holder.

At this moment, Leonora was not thinking of Numie. She had become acutely aware of the smallness of Sacre-Coeur. Granted, it was the largest house on the island, but diminutive compared to many of the private palaces and manors of Europe to which she had been invited in her life.

She needed a large stage, and the walls of Sacre-Coeur were growing smaller, threatening to enclose her on a tiny island within an island. She was a tall and elegant woman, and she needed the space in which to be, to create her own theater of life.

Suddenly, she was struck by the presence of a guest. At first, she had forgotten she'd invited him. What possible purpose on this troubling day did she have talking to this young drifter? Still, he was here; and, if nothing else, Leonora de la Mer, that old lioness of the sea herself, was a lady.

"Sit down, dear heart," she said, motioning to a big gilt armchair ten feet away from her.

The chair smelled musty to Numie. Its gilt had cracked from the dampness of the air. He sat in it, anyway——until she extended her bare hand. He got up and walked across the floor to kiss it, remembering the night before.

Her knuckles were enormous. They protruded as if trying to break free of her green-tinged, chalky hands. The hands seemed to weigh down her cadaverous arms.

As Numie's lips touched her hand, Leonora smiled benignly. Many people on this island made fun of her for insisting on hand-kissing. After all, they asked, why should a common shrimper's daughter insist on having her hand kissed? But crowned princes, deposed kings, certainly prime ministers, had kissed her hand on occasion. When she returned to Tortuga, she did not know why she should abandon the custom. Besides, she considered her hands one of her most attractive features, and she welcomed any opportunity to call attention to them.

"Thanks for having me here," Numie said. "How are you?"

"Fine." She studied him coldly. What possible interest could he have in her health? "Are you really a friend of Tangerine's?"

"Yeah," he said. "She seemed nice."

Leonora frowned. "If you like Tangerine, then you like the typically southern woman——the hog-calling, knees-apart, big-mouthed broad!"

"Wha..."

Leonora was mildly shocked at her own words. Sometimes her tongue assumed a life of its own. But having said the words, she was in no mood to retract them. It would be better to defend her statement. "Don't apologize for your lack of taste."

"I assure you, I'm not."

"I keep Tangerine around because she is a constant reminder of the gross vulgarity of the world," Leonora said.

"Do you need to be reminded of that?"

"A good question, and very penetrating. I find hustlers usually are dumb."

"I don't pretend to be smart," he said. "If I was, I wouldn't be a hustler."

"I see." She paused for dramatic effect. "Some of the young people Tangerine introduces me to don't bother to show up." She felt the time was at hand for her to appear more vulnerable to Numie. To reveal in some small way that she didn't control everything on this island. "But I knew you'd visit Sacre-Coeur."

"It's great," he said. "Besides, you promised me a job."

She was struck by his abruptness. At least, he was honest.

Of all the excuses he could have come up with, including a suggestion he was dazzled by her beauty, he preferred this direct route. "I promised you a job?"

"You need a new chauffeur."

"As a matter of fact, I do. But I think you're far too ambitious to settle for a chauffeur's job."

"I don't mind starting at the bottom and working my way to the top," he said.

She smiled. "That's my philosophy, too," she agreed.

"But it's been so long since I've seen bottom, I can hardly remember what it was like." She knew all too well what bottom was like. Every morning at four o'clock was bottom to her. But she didn't want to admit that.

"I felt pretty low last night when I was invited to your table and wasn't asked to stick around for the champagne. You knew I was broke."

"I knew," she said. Learning to eat and drink before the impecunious was a task she'd long ago mastered. "I must have appeared cruel to you. I'm not, actually. I am probably the kindest woman on this island, but I have to protect myself. If I befriend just one person, the floodgates would open. Every drifter who comes to town would know me for an easy mark."

"I didn't know that."

"It's true." She settled back in her chair. Her voice was sounding desperate, even to herself. "When I first came back here, I was besieged by people wanting favors, usually money. You can't cast your gems before beggars on the street. I've had to pretend they don't exist. Otherwise, my philanthropic instincts would take over and destroy me."

"I hope you can help me get started."

"Why should I?" she asked. She was suddenly feeling pressure from him, and was sorry she'd ever invited him here. "No one ever helped me get anything...ever."

"Because I need help."

"What could you possibly offer me in exchange?" she asked.

"Companionship."

"That is condescending."

"I didn't mean it that way."

"I'm not embarrassed to be lonely." There, she'd said it and felt better for it. To be really strong, one had to admit certain weaknesses.

"I'm not either," he said quickly, "and I've been lonely all my life."

She eyed him as if he were a rock just fallen from the sky. The subject was dangerous, and she'd have to change it quickly. "Why don't you move closer to the light? It does interesting things to your face."

"No one ever told me that."

"Your face is a mask," she went on. "Masks always reveal more than they hide. It's as if you had taken your face, gone out and exposed it to the wind. The wind blew too hard and stung you. So, you rushed back and found the mask."

"Don't we all do that?"

"Of course," she said. "But the mask won't keep the wind from biting you again."

"No," he said, "but it'll help. I'd feel really naked without it." He shifted in the armchair, crossed his legs, then uncrossed them. "Do you mind if I have one of your cigarettes? Marijuana, isn't it?"

She moved her hand through the air like a swan lifting its wing. "Yes, it is," she said. "Take one of the blue ones. Blue is your color."

He laughed. "You don't know me well enough to know my color."

"You're wrong! I know you very well. Most of the night I spent thinking about you." An obvious lie, she knew, but she liked the sound of the words.

He inhaled the smoke. Choking, he put the cigarette down. "You were a surprise when I met you. Totally out of place in this rundown town. When you arrive on the scene, people sit up and take notice."

"That wasn't always so," she said, her interest rising.

"I mean, you're really stunning looking." He was saying this not only because he believed it; but because he knew she wanted to hear it.

"I wasn't always," she said. "When I was just a girl, braces covered my teeth, and, worse, I started to grow tall and gangly."

"You certainly turned your tallness into an asset," he said. "Tall women are just great."

"But children, especially one Ruthie Elvina, used to make fun of me. They even called me `the ugly duckling'."

"They called me a lot of things, too, but that's gone now."

"Not for me it isn't. I still haven't forgiven them."

"But you became glamorous," he said. "What does it matter now what some kids thought a long time ago?"

"Showing them, especially Ruthie Elvina, what I really was has been one of the most important goals of my life. I knew I would one day rise above them. Even then, I knew."

"So, you got back at them." He wanted to change the subject, but there was a sudden fierceness and determination in her eyes. He knew she wouldn't let go.

"I knew," she said, raising her voice. "That's why I was able to take their abuse. That doesn't mean I didn't have my heart broken time and time again. Now my poor heart has so many scars I can't feel with it sometimes. I want to. But a lifetime of betrayals has left me immune."

"Is that why you can't accept me?"

"I want to. You intrigue me. But I'm afraid of you at the same time. You're a self-admitted hustler. I know you're out to get something from me."

"Whatever I take from people, I give them something in return."

"I wish I could believe that. Are you really interested in me?"

"Yes, I am. I think you're one of the most fascinating women I've ever seen."

His words set her off, her head spinning——almost in reverie. He was right. She was fascinating! She chose a role, and became that role. She showed the women of America what they could do with themselves creatively. To do that, she had to don many costumes. Her clothes were in demand——by everybody. She was now fully caught up, remembering, barely aware of Numie. Whatever she had felt, she became. Why, once she dressed up like a man and walked down Fifth Avenue. Of course, she created a scandal. She had created scandals all her life. But she wasn't rejected. She was in her power then. Women all over America adopted her styles. Never had she followed other styles or conventions. She had set them. Leaning forward, she looked full face at Numie——blinking her wild, almond eyes. "If I am fascinating, as you say I am, it's because I went out in the world to make my wildest dreams come true. Whatever I wanted, I reached out and tried to capture. Many times I came up empty-handed, but I never stopped reaching." She crushed out her cigarette, shifted her position, and reached for a bamboo fan.

He blended his fingers together, then cracked his knuckles.

"An irritating habit you have."

"Forgive me," he said.

She emerged from the darkness just enough for the light to capture the outline of her face. Her violet lipstick glowed in the shadows. "Am I grotesque to you?"

"Not at all."

"You're lying——that's good. Never tell the truth to anyone——just to yourself. Of course, you consider me a freak, unfairly, but I know what you're thinking. You're not bright enough to distinguish me from that show at Commodore Philip's bar."

"I don't think I understand."

"That awful drag creature who calls herself Lola La Mour, a cheap imitation of my own name. You obviously have had more experience around garbage than around ladies."

Too bad you feel that way." He couldn't comprehend this sudden attack. "If I've not behaved right, I'm sorry."

"And well you should be." She didn't know why she was attacking him. An impulse. Perhaps she was afraid of him as she was afraid of all strangers. "I must warn you: I'm not rushing into any relationship with you, chauffeur or whatever. We'll meet again in a few days... perhaps. By then, your manners may have improved. Good day." Her disappearance from the study left a lingering trail of intoxicating perfume.

He paused. Then he picked up one of her blue marijuana cigarettes and put it in his pocket.

The sounds of a typewriter led him to a downstairs office, off the parlor. Behind a desk, Anne was answering a letter.

"I'm afraid I struck out with the boss lady," he said, standing at the doorway.

She looked up. "That's very predictable. She likes to test people. See how much abuse they can take. If she attacks without provocation, and sees that you don't fight back, then she knows you're material for her stable."

"Thanks for the warning, but I could have used it before facing the firing squad."

Over Anne's desk was a billboard advertising, Leonora de la Mer presents THE TASTE OF STEAK TARTARE, a three-act play by Ralph Douglas."

"Is that the Ralph we know?" Numie asked.

"One and the same."

"I didn't know he was a playwright."

"He's not. The play was never produced.

"Was there a play at all?"

"Yes, Leonora was going to produce it, or so she said, When you're fishing, you've got to used bait. We accepted her invitation to come to Sacre-Coeur so Ralph could revise it. Nothing he ever wrote seemed quite right to her. The rewrites stretched on and on. Just as Ralph was about to explode, Leonora would praise him and tantalize him with her backing. I kept urging him to leave Tortuga and go back to New York. But he wouldn't. One morning we didn't hear the typewriter any more." She sighed. "I type letters on it now."

"You could have gone back alone."

"With no money? I can just imagine what that would be like. Even though I don't have a husband, I can still be taken to the grocery store in a limousine every time I want a quart of milk."

"Why are you confiding in me? You have every right to hate me."

"I just know, I can feel you're joining the household. Tangerine, Ralph, and I are the permanent fixtures. The Numies of this world come and go. You're the new me. If you're going to be joining our happy home, you might as well know something about us."

"She gave no indication I had the job."

"Nor would she. That's not how she operates. Believe me, I know her well. Now, if you'll excuse me."

Through the office doors and into the patio, Numie was blinded by the afternoon sun. The air was so hot he could hardly breathe.

From the upstairs window, a velvet drapery swung into position. Was Leonora watching?

Quickly he made his way through the open door, through

the garden, through the iron gate, and out onto the street. Then, and only then, did he slow his pace.

Chapter Five

Back in the hotel lobby, the clerk was holding Numie's key.

"The key, please," Numie said.

"The bread, man. You should have paid in advance. You didn't."

"Okay," Numie said, "I'll go to the bank. Cash a check. Now give me the key."

"Man, you've got no checks to cash. We both know you're in town to hustle our ass. You'd better find a john if you want that room back tonight."

"Okay, shithead," Numie said. "Keep the room and my possessions, too. Why not?"

On the street, the day was moving in. Numie was breathing hard.

Ralph's gold watch glistened in the sun. In the corner, Numie spotted two Cubans sitting on a bench under a palm.

"Is there a pawn shop in this town?"

"No," one of the Cubans said. "No hock. What are you selling?"

"It's gold." Taking it off, he handed it to one of the Cubans.

The man fingered it softly, then held it up and listened to it tick. "Give you five dollars."

"Five dollars——for a gold watch?" Numie said, retrieving it. "Not my gold watch." He walked on down the street.

That left his remaining chance. The black drag queen, Lola La Mour.

She repulsed him. But she wouldn't be the first person he'd slept with who did.

Walking faster now, he could almost feel her lipstick-coated mouth snaking his sweat-drenched body. Maybe he could have sex with her and blot out the vision of what she was. After all, a hustler in his position could hardly select desirable bedmates.

"Damn it!" he said aloud. "Paying for it's the only way a creep like you is ever going to get near me." Imaginary conversations he'd never have with Lola. Suddenly, he was aware he was talking to himself. But there was no one on the street to notice or care.

It wasn't that Lola was black. He'd gone that route many

times before. It wasn't even that she was a black drag queen. That was familiar turf too. It was her being both black and a drag queen in a small redneck southern town. The tolerance level toward blacks must be low enough. But toward black drag queens, the worst. Or was the worst reserved for a white hustler willing to sell his body to a black drag queen?

"What the hell?" he asked finally. "A one-time shot in the dark." He laughed bitterly at his own pun.

. . .

At Commodore Philip's, the white Facel-Vega glistened in the afternoon sun.

Inside, not one customer. Only the bartender, Lola, doing her nails.

Brushing back her platinum wig, she stuffed a cigarette into her holder with such masculine force she surprised even herself. Then, with more delicate and ladylike fingers, she lit it, blowing smoke rings into the air.

Breathing deeply, she held out her breasts, making them seem larger than they were. For the life of her, she could never understand what men saw in such things. Breasts repulsed her, particularly hers today. They were sagging absurdly.

She nervously studied her reflection in the powder-smudged mirror of her compact. Her make-up wasn't staying on right, but running in the heat wave. If she didn't repair it instantly, she looked like a clown. When the Commodore returned from the mainland, she was going to have to entice him to buy air conditioning, a plea she'd registered for the last ten years.

Suddenly, Numie appeared on the street. A feeling of triumph shot through her. She knew he'd be back. Slamming the compact shut, she adjusted her dress, and prayed that her sweat glands would stop working overtime.

She stared harshly. No woman ever snared anything by being too easy to get. "The Big Spender!" she said sarcastically. "Come to toss another buck at Lola."

He eased onto the bar stool. His left leg, held rigidly stiff, started to shake furiously. He hoped Lola wouldn't see it.

"Look at her," he thought with disgust. "Licking her chops already. She just can't wait to get me," he said to himself.

"Hi," he said out loud, swallowing hard. "You look just great today. I don't know how you manage in this heat."

"Get you!" The blood raced madly through her. Thank God she had time to repair her face. She studied him carefully. Despite what he said——about her looking great and all——she could see no desire in him. Maybe it was the heat. Or maybe, and this made a lot more sense, he was playing hard to get, too. After all, he was a hustler.

"Look, babe," he said confidentially. "I've checked out the scene in this town. You're the best-looking thing walking."

"All the bees swarm around my little honeypot." Once more she thanked her guardian angel that little honeypot was freshly scented with strawberry. Unlike some people, she did not believe in natural body odors. Why smell stale when you could sprinkle yourself with the essence of all the flowers in the field?

"Here I am." He felt defenseless before her, and he hated her, as he hated all people who had ever held power over him, if only for a moment.

"Remember what I told you. Lola gets paid. Lola doesn't pay." An obvious lie, so obvious she embarrassed herself while saying it. But in a world of total pretense, why couldn't she be allowed this one indulgence?

"Okay with me," he said, matching her lie for lie." Only thing is, my bread hasn't come in yet." Another lie. But he knew the code of all respectable liars, all people who live behind masks and facades. As long as he wasn't challenging her lies, she would honor his.

"I see," she said. "No use making you wait, though. I've been known to make arrangements for credit. There's something vulgar about cash.

"Agreed." He was glad the negotiating was over. Now he could relax, for a while. "Gimme a Scotch, a triple. I'm really dry."

"Okay," she said. From behind the bar, she emerged with a drink. Unlike the time before, she gently set it down. She smiled and looked at him with an appraising eye. Despite the fact he'd been a hustler for more years than anybody cared to remember, there was something freshly appealing about Numie. Instead of being washed up as a man, he seemed more on the brink of becoming one. The scent of him came through to her. The day was hot, but he smelled of freshly laundered Levis. Her hands traveled up and down his chest, feeling his muscles. Then they settled between his legs. There, they expertly took measurements.

"I don't have a place," he said. "My hotel's kicked me out."

"Don't worry," she said. "I live right upstairs. I'll be off in an hour; and you're going to learn what it's like to make love to a real girl."

"I can't wait."

"You'd better."

Standing up with her, he took the cheeks of her ass and squeezed hard. She reached quickly to kiss. He withdrew slightly.

Stung by the rejection, she said, "Keep it on ice, lover man. I'll warm you up." He'd pay for that rejection. Not now, but later when he was more vulnerable. Into her purse she dug out two one-dollar bills. "There's a drug store on the corner. Buy some vaseline. We're going to need it!"

Taking the money, he said, "See you later."

. . .

The Main Street was alive and bristling. Vendors selling plantain and fresh vegetables rolled their carts down the shabby pavement. In Spanish, they screamed out the quality of their produce.

Two salesmen from a Navy store stood on the sidewalk, trying to lure young sailors in. A sign, *Real Estate, Theodore M. Albury*, hung across a restored Bahamian building.

An usher was sweeping out the local movie house. And what a movie house! Completely washed in lavender, it was candy-boxy with garish decorations. Even the fire hydrants out front were painted purple.

Inhaling deeply, Numie sucked in the powerful medicinal scent of a tall, chalky mauve eucalyptus tree. It fluttered in the lemon light.

Suddenly, a green-striped white car pulled up along side him. "Boy, I thought I told you to get out of town." It was the sheriff, Yellowwood. In the front seat with him was Dave, his deputy.

Numie was scared. His eyes opened wider and wider, as a certain knowledge hit him. For one brief, terrifying moment, he wanted to run. "I'm clean, sheriff," he protested, the words coming almost involuntarily from his throat.

"You were dirty the day you were born," Yellowwood answered.

Dave was getting out. "Into the back seat, punk," he commanded. The look in Dave's eyes told Numie he meant business.

A whirl of fear descended over Numie. Leonora's marijuana cigarette was concealed in his back pocket. He had to get rid of it, and quick. But how?

"I don't know what this is all about," Numie said, still in confusion and doubt. But he was ready to do as he was told.

"I was leaving town this afternoon. Somebody owed me some money I was collecting——that's all."

"Where you're going, you won't need money," Dave said. His voice was harsh, and when he spoke he leaned closely to Numie's ear, as if to intimidate him more.

"You've got nothing on me," Numie protested, his anger bubbling.

Dave didn't take his eyes off Numie. No way to get rid of that smoke. The rest of the drive to the jail was in silence.

The first out of the car, Yellowwood led the way into the station.

"Johnny, a call for you," the desk clerk said.

"Take him in back," Yellowwood barked, heading for the phone. "You know what to do, Dave."

Numie didn't like the sound of that. His initial panic returned.

"I'll be right back to see it," Yellowwood added.

Now Numie was completely bewildered. What did Yellowwood mean by it?

Dave was joined by a gruff, pot-bellied deputy. "Hi, Hank," Dave said.

Numie was surprised that Dave actually had a much higher pitched speaking voice. Hank nodded a greeting to Dave, then coldly appraised Numie. "A good-looker," he said to Dave. Then he whispered, but loud enough for Numie to hear,

"Yellowwood's gonna get his rocks off today——that's for sure."

Numie eagerly searched the faces in the station. He was alone, hated. Was Yellowwood planning to torture him?

In the dingy, dimly lit back room, Dave ordered, "Off with your clothes. I've seen you naked as a jaybird before, so don't be bashful."

Slowly Numie unbuttoned his shirt and then stepped out of his jeans. He was used to stripping in front of men, but this was different. His clothes gave him an extra sense of protection, but that was now peeled off.

He was sweating heavily. The only light was from an exposed electric bulb overhead. His clothes off, he was standing in the middle of the room as Yellowwood stalked in.

The sheriff's beady glare began at his feet and traveled upward, lingering long over his middle. The same appraising look Numie had seen back at the hotel room.

The fact that the sheriff was displaying such an interest in his nude body remained Numie's only chance.

Hank was searching his jeans. From the back pocket, he pulled out a marijuana cigarette enclosed in tissue. "Just what I thought. He was carrying illegal drugs."

"I thought you told me you were clean," Yellowwood accused, shooting Numie a surgical stare.

Numie said nothing. He could only watch like the hypnotized victim of the coiling threat of a viper.

"Blue wrapped," Dave said, examining the dope." I thought De la Mer was the only person in town who smoked blue-wrapped marijuana cigarettes."

"Tell the guys in number nine they're gonna have some company," Yellowwood said.

Hank and Dave left the room.

Now, Numie's chance. "Sheriff, I can explain. Surely we can work something out. Just the two of us." He leaned forward slightly so that his legs strayed wider apart. Suddenly, the sheriff's billy club was smashing into his wrist. Numie fell back in pain.

"You read me wrong, boy. *Way wrong.*"

Dave was back in the room. Following, Hank was putting on a greased rubber glove.

"Bend over," Yellowwood commanded.

Numie hesitated until the sheriff moved menacingly toward him with that club again.

Reluctantly Numie turned around, bending over.

"Pry those cheeks apart," Yellowwood said.

Numie complied, feeling like a slave on the auction block. Utter humiliation.

In one quick move, Hank's long finger was jabbing inside Numie, deliberately trying to hurt. "Got nothing in there," Hank said to Yellowwood. "Not even a turd."

"Take him to the cell," Yellowwood snapped.

"Can I put my pants back on?" Numie asked, humbled and stripped of any pride.

"Hell, no!" Yellowwood shouted.

"I'm entitled to at least one phone call," Numie protested. "I know my rights."

"Fuck your rights," the sheriff barked. "Take him out."

Completely nude, Numie was pushed down the corridor.

The smell of urine was everywhere. On both sides the cells were filled with men leering at him.

"Hi, honey," a young black called out in a falsetto voice.

"You giving that away for supper tonight?"

"There's enough meat there for the poor," another yelled.

At the end of the corridor, Numie faced a tiny room with a small barred window. Hank was placing handcuffs on him. Then Dave shoved Numie into the darkened cell——so hard he stumbled and fell on the concrete. Face down. His nose was bleeding.

Gradually as his eyes became accustomed to the darkness, he spotted two men sitting on the lower bunk of a bed.

One of them was staring at Numie with glee.

Chapter Six

An evil smile was spreading before Numie's eyes.

A young man in his twenties pulled at Numie's hair——forcing his face up. Scraggly black hair covered his head; and a raggedy mustache had been spit-licked from both sides of his upper lip. A nervous Adam's apple bobbed up and down his neck, heavily veined and thick with muscles.

"I do believe little blondie has a nosebleed, Mitch," the man said.

The eerie sound of his hick voice sent shivers of fear racing through Numie.

Mitch was bending over him. Older than the other man, he had more refined features reflected in his chiseled nose and high cheekbones. His brown hair, parted on the right, was slicked down with water. His hazel eyes were kinder, not as menacing, but a snide smile was on his lips. Placing Numie's nose between his fingers, he pressed as hard as he could.

"Cut the shit, man!" Numie cried out, jerking his head away. "Can't you see I'm bleeding?"

"You should never talk back to us," Mitch said. "Jeb and I might be forced to remove some of your equipment."

"You're so piss elegant, Mitch," Jeb said. "He means we'll cut off your balls if you don't shut up."

Numie froze. Where had he heard that before? Recently, just recently. Now he remembered. The lawyer who had picked him up on the keys. Mitch was the crazy thrill killer in for sexual dismemberment and murder. Why had Yellowwood placed him in this cell? Handcuffed, he could do nothing. Dare he scream? But his jailers knew he was here already. Nothing made sense.

"You're going to shit green," Jeb said, "before this little session is over."

"Jeb," Mitch said, "you should talk more refined. You don't ever learn anything from your association with someone of my breeding." He looked at Numie. "Jeb never got beyond the sixth grade. He bores me most of the time. Was arrested for breaking and entering. Can you imagine anything so dumb when there are far more adventurous things to get arrested for?"

"What's he with you for?" Numie asked.

"Since he's locked in here with me, I'm teaching him some more sophisticated pleasures. Up to now, he'd just stick it in any hole available."

"Hell!" Jeb said. "I'll never go your full trip. You like to finish them off for good. I like mine live and kicking."

"As you see," Mitch said, "he hasn't completely come around to my way of thinking. But he will!"

"Mitch believes in sparing young men the pain he knows is waiting for them," Jeb added.

"He's right," Mitch said. "Life is only good when you're young. I'm in my forties now. Pretty soon I'll be a doddering old wreck. Already my right arm hurts day and night like pins and needles are being stuck in it. The circulation's bad. Every man has to go sometime. Why not now? Go out while you're still in your prime."

"You're crazy!" Numie shouted. "Let me up."

Blood exploded from one of Numie's nostrils, as Jeb's fist smashed into his face.

Momentarily dazed, Numie came to as a sweat-soaked cloth was being stuffed into his mouth. His voice was muffled. He tried to protest, but it was no use.

Mitch gripped him under the armpits; and Jeb grabbed his ankles. The men raised him up only to dump him on his back on the concrete floor. The metallic click of the ensnaring handcuffs resounded in Numie's ears.

The impact of the concrete caused his blood-soaked head to loll to one side. He was too weak to move. Whimpers were escaping from his throat.

Minutes went by before anybody touched him. He kept opening his eyes, then blinking them shut. What were they going to do to him? Fearful sounds of anticipation bubbled up.

A rough thumb lifted one of Numie's eyelids. "You're really scared, kid," Mitch said. "With good reason, I might add."

The handcuffs were biting into Numie's skin. Jeb was tying his feet.

Suddenly, Mitch's probing hands were traversing his chest. "So young and beautiful," he said. "How sad it has to decay."

Numie was writhing at the man's touch. Mitch's thumb and forefinger came together in a nerve-shattering pinch of Numie's nipple. Numie gasped. Mitch's hands traveled lower, reaching the pubic hair. There they slowly pulled, as Numie squirmed in pain. Then the fingers reached out and enclosed his cock.

Numie tried to struggle up, to wiggle away from that hand. But a slap sent him back on the floor again. Mitch gripped the cock tighter, applying more and more pressure.

Numie's chest was heaving. Breathing through his blood-clogged nose was hard. The wheezing sound coming through the cloth lodged in his mouth was heard around the room. The cords of his neck stood out like ropes.

Jeb's fingers enclosed his testicles. "They're such nice ones," he said to Mitch. "Do we really have to cut them off?"

"Of course," Mitch said. "He might impregnate some fine lady and bring yet another life into this miserable world. Make a person endure the torture I've had to."

Sprawled on the hard concrete, Numie was sighing with pain. Hoisting himself up, he was knocked down again. Beyond humiliation at this point, he waited to die.

Jeb was yanking at Numie's sac, seemingly trying to pull it from his body. Then his fingers encircled one of his testicles, squeezing it hard.

Eyes bulging, Numie moaned loudly. Electric shock traveled his quivering body.

"I want to enjoy this up close," Mitch said. "Do what you must, Jeb."

Mitch straddled Numie's chest, holding his shoulders back against the concrete. "I always like to stare into the eyes of the victim while the cutting is being done. It isn't the cutting I like so much, it's the look on the face of the victim. At first, the slicing is very slow. It doesn't hurt. Then you begin to feel the real pain. You won't be able to stand it. But nature has her own protection. As the cutting gets deeper, you'll pass out. That's when all the fun goes for me, and I lose interest." Holding Numie's cheeks between his hands, he asked, "Do you want Jeb to masturbate you? It'll be the last time in your life you'll be able to achieve orgasm."

Numie's head snapped from side to side to show his refusal.

"Then it's time to begin," Mitch said calmly.

A cold metal object was placed on Numie's genitals. It felt dull——not sharp at all.

A sudden force of energy shot through Numie. Heaving his chest forward, he unseated his rider. His knees found Jeb's chin as their target.

Then, for the first time, Yellowwood's face at the barred window came into view. How long had he been watching?

Both assailants got up and retreated to their bunk. A steel eating knife was dropped to the floor.

Yellowwood opened the cell and entered. "I see the boys were having a little harmless fun with you," the sheriff said to Numie. He roughly pulled the gag out of Numie's mouth and moved to untie his feet.

"They were going to kill me," Numie said, sitting up.

"Hank and Dave put you in the wrong cell," Yellowwood said. "Sorry about that."

Numie shouted. "You did this to torture me."

"Watch the accusations," the sheriff said. "You could be in more trouble than you're in now. And you're in plenty of trouble."

Hank came in. He removed Numie's handcuffs. Numie rubbed his raw wrists, then held the cloth gag to his bloody nose.

Dave entered with Numie's jeans, tossing them on the floor. "Put on your pants," he ordered. "Quit showing your bird to all these perverts."

"Damn you!" Numie yelled.

"Now, now," Yellowwood cautioned. "Overlook that, Dave. The kid got roughed up a little and he's overly emotional. Mitch is just up to his old tricks. Right, Mitch?"

Mitch didn't answer.

"And so are you, Yellowwood," Numie charged.

"I'll forget you said that, boy," the sheriff replied. "To show you how generous and considerate we are around this hotel, I'm going to let you make *one* phone call."

"Who do you know in this town?" Dave asked Numie. Now fully dressed, Numie stood in the corridor in front of the phone. "Leonora de la Mer," he said. "She's hired me as her chauffeur. Get her on the phone. She'll straighten out this whole mess."

"De la Mer," Dave said. "It figures. That broad's the only one in town crazy enough to hire you. She's always hiring beatniks. Gets you cheap——that's why. At least that explains marijuana cigarettes in blue paper." Dave dialed her number. "Speak to her secretary," he said.

"Anne," Numie said tentatively into the phone. "It's me, Numie."

"Where are you?" asked the voice.

"In jail."

"I see."

"What do you see?"

"Most drifters end up there before the first forty-eight hours," she said.

"I need help. Could I speak to Leonora?"

"Of course."

A sudden silence and then another voice was on the phone. "This is Leonora de la Mer. What do you want with me?"

"It's Numie " he said, his voice desperate. "I'm in jail, and I need help."

"Numie?" she asked. "I don't think I remember you. But then I meet so many people in the course of a day."

The deputy was listening in on the extension. He decided to break in. "Miss De la Mer, this is Dave. You know, the sheriff's deputy."

"Dave?" she asked.

"Yeah, you know me."

"I know Mr. Yellowwood, you mean."

"Anyway," Dave continued, "this kid here was busted. Carrying around a blue-wrapped marijuana cigarette, the kind you smoke."

"I beg your pardon," she said. "And I don't know that young man."

"Leonora, I was just at your place," Numie protested. "I'm in real trouble. I lifted that cigarette from your study."

"Dave, as you call yourself, it sounds to me that the young man you've incarcerated is a thief," Leonora said. "However, I won't bring charges, if that's why you're calling."

"That's not why I'm calling," Numie said. "I need someone to bail me out."

"The young man is obviously insane," Leonora said. "Apparently, he steals from me——how he got into Sacre-Coeur, I'll never know——then he wants me to bail him out. You must admit the whole suggestion is outrageous."

"Leonora, *please*," Numie said. "I've been tortured."

"You know that's a lie," Dave said.

"I have pressing business to attend to," Leonora answered. "I can't involve myself in any more of these absurd conversations." She slammed down the receiver.

"But she does know me," Numie said, holding the dead phone in his hand.

"Of course, you've met her," Dave said. "I'm sure of it. But if De la Mer says she doesn't know you, man, she means what she says."

Bent and defeated, Hadley L. Crabtree was walking down the corridor of the jail. You could smell his breath, flavored with cheap wine. His clothes——the same outfit he wore the night he'd picked Numie up, were as stale as his breath.

"Thank God you're here, Numie said. They've busted me."

The lawyer looked at him strangely——as if he didn't recognize him at first. "Busted! I'm so tired of hearing that I could die."

"It's true," Numie said. "I need you to help me."

"You didn't listen to my free advice," Crabtree said. "Which was to get out of town. I think I told you not to come here in the first place."

"The sheriff's got it in for me."

"He's got it in for everybody," Crabtree said. "I lost three cases today. Got any money, boy?"

"Not a cent," Numie said. "But if you get me out, I can work it out and pay you back."

"That makes one thousand guys——and girls, too——who have used that line on me. I'm an old man. I have to get money for my work."

"Please."

Dave walked up beside Numie. "He's got to get back to his cell," he said to Crabtree. "You going to represent him?"

"No," the lawyer said flatly.

Numie sighed. "The only liberal in town. I'm entitled to some kind of defense."

"We'll take care of everything," Dave said to Numie. He motioned to his desk. "Crabtree, you old grandpa, I've got a bottle in the bottom drawer. Take the rest of it home with you.

You've got some more court cases coming up tomorrow, and the sheriff wants you to be in real good shape."

Numie stared at Crabtree——almost defying him to go to that desk, to take that bottle.

Eyes down, Crabtree made his way to the desk.

Dave's hands were on Numie's back, shoving him down the long dark corridor.

. . .

It was two o'clock in the morning. From his bunk bed in a lone cell, a stirring of life came to Numie. Someone was shining a flashlight in his eyes.

"What in hell?" he asked, adjusting to the harsh light.

From the corridor, the lights were switched on. The other prisoners started to wake up.

There, under the cruel glow of an exposed electric bulb, stood Lola La Mour. She was floating in printed silk organdy in vibrant lemon and chartreuse. Beside her was Yellowwood, aroused from sleep.

"So, there you are!" Lola screeched.

"How did you find me?" Numie asked.

"I called the sheriff," she said. "After all, you made off with my two dollars to get that tube of Vaseline. Remember?"

When you didn't show up all night, I sent out a call for help. You fitted the description."

Yellowwood was unlocking the cell. "Why didn't you tell me you were Lola La Mour's boy? This whole thing wouldn't have happened."

"How did I know?" Numie asked.

Lola rushed into the cell, pulling the sheet back and exposing his nude body. She gave him a quick professional appraisal. Approving, she reached for his jeans. "Into these, stud," she said, "and then we're getting out of this rathole. Nothing in here but perverts." She glared menacingly at the sheriff.

"Lola," Yellowwood said apologetically, "I'm really sorry about this."

"Sorry!" she shouted. "You're sorry? When the commodore gets back from the mainland and hears about this——that's the time to be sorry!"

The sheriff motioned to his deputy. "He had this," he said, taking the marijuana cigarette from the man and handing it to Lola.

She examined it carefully. "Yes," she said defiantly. "He had this because I gave it to him. It was presented to me by De la Mer, and I passed it on to Numie. Thank God we've got it back. I could use it right now." She held the cigarette to her mouth. Yellowwood reached into his pocket and pulled out a lighter. Its flame outlined the glow of Lola's face in the darkened cell. She inhaled deeply, then looked at Numie. "He needs this more than we do," she said, passing the cigarette to him.

Numie took it, staring first at Yellowwood, then at Lola. He put the tip to his mouth and sucked in the smoke.

Then Lola took it back, leading the way up the corridor, her high heels clanking against the pavement.

"Hey, baby, look what I've got for you," a bearded shrimper yelled, waving his cock at her.

She abruptly stopped in front of his cell looking at the prisoner, her face a mask of contorted charm. Then she took her cigarette and jabbed it into his nest of pubic hair. He jumped back screaming.

"The next time you see a lady, creep, act accordingly."

Outside the jail, Lola's sports car gleamed in the moonlight. She stood to the side, as Yellowwood rushed to open the door.

Numie got behind the driver's seat, accepting the slightly crushed cigarette from Lola.

"Anything I can do to make this up, Lola," Yellowwood said, "just let me know."

She ignored him.

Out of the parking lot and up the darkened street, Numie steered the Facel-Vega and sucked in more smoke from Leonora's blue marijuana cigarette.

Johnny Yellowwood faded in the rear-view mirror.

Chapter Seven

Numie braked the Facel-Vega in front of Commodore Philip's.

He rubbed the hammerlike throbbing in his forehead between his eyes. His whole body ached.

"I hope you're not too worn out to perform," Lola said.

"Yeah," he muttered. "I can still get it on. Too bad, though, I'm in such rotten shape for my premiere."

"We have the whole bar to ourselves tonight," she said, turning the key in the lock.

Commodore Philip's was completely deserted, except for a lazy calico cat on the corner of the bar. He aroused himself slightly at the sight of Lola and Numie, then settled back into sleep.

Swinging his legs over a bar stool, Numie eyed the booze. "I need a stiff one."

"So do I, handsome," Lola said, "but I think we're talking about two different things."

"Later, later," he cautioned. "First, the machine has to be lubricated. In minutes, the liquor was racing through his body. "Now for the big question. Who in hell is Commodore Philip? Jesus Christ with gold balls?"

"My lover man," she said, pouring herself a drink.

"Is he a real commodore?"

"Sort of," she answered matter-of-factly. "Owns a boat or two. Commodores and sea captains are always gay, darling. They learn it during those long voyages away from women."

"I don't know about that, but do you really have something going with him?"

"He's devoted to me," she said. "He worships my every move. I've been with him for years. Came to work as a maid. That was a long time ago when I had dyed my hair red. He took quite a fancy to me."

"And he allows you to go around whoring?"

"*Please*," she said. "Watch your language in front of a lady. My commodore and I have worked out a compromise. He has a bad heart condition——one so awful he could go at any minute. When I started working for him, he thought I was real pretty. I started peeling everything off——everything except my red panties——thinking he wanted to ball. Then he told me the sad news. All he wanted was for me to parade around in front of him——doing *lewd* things." She sighed. "It was hard for me to think of anything lewd seeing that I'm a lady. But he told me some things he wanted, and I did them just to please him. I felt sorry for a man who can only watch."

"Maybe that's what he really digs," Numie said. "Like your friend, Yellowwood."

"No friend of mine," she said. "The sheriff's a real sickie. But my commodore is very gentle. He just whispers encouragements while I get it on with a super stud."

"The commodore must have a lot of pull in this town if you can just walk in the jailhouse and get me out while blowing smoke up his nose."

"My commodore is a very rich man, and Yellowwood is on the take. He was just a cheap crook in the bolita racket until my commodore bought the office of sheriff for him."

"When will the Commodore show up? I'd like to meet him."

"I bet you would, sweetie," she said, fingering his chin. "I'm sure he'd like to meet you too. With my Commodore, one never knows. He just pops up on the doorstep. His real life's on the mainland. He never lets me go there, though. He claims he comes to Tortuga for 'slumming'. I told him, 'Don't associate me with no slum'. He didn't, of course. My pad upstairs is very elegant. Why don't you come up and look at it? Plus what other sights I might be showing."

· · ·

Lola's apartment was a mass of white. No color anywhere, except in her face.

To furnish it, she'd dipped heavily into her experience of watching Jean Harlow and Joan Crawford movies. Lack of access to the rich furnishings once available to those two movie queens hadn't stopped Lola. She resorted to what she could find at the local stores and the city dump. Coats of white paint and yards of shiny white satin had brought renewed life to the opulent taste of another time.

In the middle of the living room stood a Victorian adaptation of a Louis XV chaise longue. The central place for Lola's operations, a way station en route to the bedroom. Hanging near it, melted tallow covered the missing or substitute bits of an overscaled chandelier. Beside the chaise stood a round ornate reed table——dominated by a lamp with a shade fashioned like an artificial lily.

Opening onto the living room, the bedroom invited with a high-posted brass bed, again enameled a glistening white. A shirred satin canopy shaded it, and filmy draperies were held back by garlands of make-believe roses and lilacs. Carefully placed against the headboard were pillows, each one different in shape, but all lacy and feathered around with fringes.

Everything designed to remind one of a heady background for seduction.

Lola held up a rhinestone-covered box beside the bed. "In here are some of my beauty aids. You'll forgive me while I make myself more alluring——if that's possible." Into the bathroom she disappeared with the box.

He slipped out of his jeans, tossing them on the white carpet.

Moments later, Lola was back. "Wow!" she yelled, squealing with delight. "I wonder if I could lose weight dieting on weenies all week." She was wearing nothing but pink panties, red Joan Crawford fuck-me shoes, and that platinum wig. Though it sagged in parts, her body was actually like a girl's: tiny breasts forming contours on a slender frame that was emaciated. Her mouth was painted a turkey red. She wiggled her hips over to the bed.

"These white satin sheets are a little much," he said, patting them invitingly.

"Men perform better on satin than cotton," she confirmed.

"Let's give it a try." He grabbed her, cupping her tiny breasts and pinching the nipples until she screamed.

"You're hurting me," she protested.

"And you love it!"

Her only response was a soft moan before plunging her mouth onto him. Suddenly, she jumped up. Her back to him, she lowered her panties, revealing her buns. Then she fell on the bed, butt up. "A five-alarm's fire's raging in me," she said.

"Let's put it out," he said. He never saw her front part, and didn't have to look into her eyes as he did his work. Deeper and deeper, he took the plunge. Lola screamed once, but it was mostly moans reaching his ears. He rode in further, exploring more.

The bedsprings were rusty and creaky——providing just the kind of rhythm he needed to do his job. She'd brag later about having had him——he knew that. But the joke would be on her. She'd never really have him. He gave them sex, but he'd never give of himself. Not to Lola. Not to anyone.

The rhapsodic sound of her voice, the way her body was turned on, the way she needed what he offered——everything blended to make him a man again after that nightmare in jail. Riding to his finish, he was the one groaning now.

Immediately recognizing the signs, Lola started to protest, "Don't, don't, lover man. Make it last all night."

Yet her contracting and pulling only goaded the inevitable. Soaked with sweat, he tensed——holding back as long as he could. But his release was violent, spasm after spasm. His energy drained, he collapsed on top of her.

She turned her head around, wanting to be kissed.

Ignoring her at first, he started to pull out. His job over, he'd earned his supper. After all, he didn't kiss fags. But the compelling hunger of her eyes——unlike the desperation in Ralph's——told him he'd better satisfy her in that way. Pressing toward her, his mouth met hers. He was quick and efficient. But also thorough, competent in his job. Kissing her was no more unpleasant than many duties he'd been called upon to perform.

The nails of her right hand dug into his back. "I need you!" she cried. "No man has ever made me feel like that. *No man.* Don't ever leave me, *please.*"

"Fuck, Lola," he said, slowly pulling out of her body——even though her muscles were fighting his going. "Who's gonna leave? I'm gonna stick around a while."

. . .

In the middle of the night, she rubbed her butt up closer to his. It was good to have someone young and alive with her tonight. All those nights listening to the commodore's snoring was more than she could bear.

In some ways, Numie was like a son-lover to her. All her life she'd wanted a son, and had cursed nature for making that dream impossible for her.

He'd come into the bar when she was at loose ends. She was fearing life was passing her by. She certainly wasn't getting any younger, and the commodore's days were clearly numbered. The prospect of her own aging——faced with that empty bed——was getting too much for her.

Numie had been more than just a robot moving inside her only hours ago. She thought he was really falling for her. She could just tell. Chalk it up to her woman's intuition. Of one thing she was certain: she wasn't just a job to him, another performance in a lengthy career. After all, he'd kissed her——and he didn't have to do that.

He'd satisfied her sexually, but he'd also awakened other longings in her——longings she'd tried to forget. She needed deep down involvement with another human being, and just not for sex either.

She'd seen desire well in Numie's eyes when she had stood practically naked in front of him. It must have been exciting for him to view a body such as hers. She could just imagine some of the tricks he'd turned——probably all with pudgy middles and everything sagging. Her breasts hadn't altogether fallen yet, and she'd strictly watched her diet. Her figure had remained trim. When Numie grabbed her breasts, she knew she'd turned him on. Her only disappointment was that he had failed to take one of them in his mouth. She loved to have that done.

Reaching over in bed, she stroked his smooth thigh with her hand——not enough to wake him up, just enough to make contact with him. Then she pressed her mouth gently against his. He moved, but didn't wake up.

How exciting he was to her!

She snuggled next to him, resting in the cradle of his arm.

Through this man lying beside her tonight she could rediscover her own long-lost girlhood.

She just knew it.

. . .

At six o'clock that morning, a loud banging was heard from

downstairs.

"What the hell?" Numie asked, turning over and sinking deeper into the satin-encased pillow.

"That's my nephew," Lola said sleepily. "Be a sweetie and let him in. He's come for that cat."

"What a time to wake up," Numie said. "Why don't you give him a key?" Nude, he stumbled out of bed and made his way down the steps into the bar.

The first rays of light were breaking through the glass panes of the door. The calico cat still slept on the bar. Taking the night latch off, he pulled back the door.

There on the early morning sidewalk stood Castor Q. Combes.

"Violet eyes," the boy shouted. "You owe me money."

"Castor, you little informer bastard. Come on in."

"You owe me a dollar," Castor said. "You didn't finish the tour. And watch who you're calling bastard, white boy."

Behind the bar Numie searched under the cash register. Some crumpled bills were left from last night. He tossed Castor three dollars. "There," he said. "Now that evens the score."

Castor fingered the bills carefully. "I hope this isn't counterfeit." Then he went over and picked up his cat from the bar. "He's mine. I've been loaning him to Lola at night to catch a big rat in this bar. But I always come and get him in the morning to feed him. I don't let him stay here during the day 'cause I don't want no cat of mine associating with the white trash who come to this bar. Which reminds me. What are you doing here?"

"Just dropped in for a drink."

Castor seemed satisfied with that explanation. "I've got to warn you about my aunt, Lola La Mour. That's not her real name. You'd better put on your clothes when you're around her. She's a queer. I won't let her touch me or even get near me."

"Thanks for the tip, Castor baby," Numie said, guiding him to the door. "If she bothers me in any way, I'll call the sheriff."

"No, you can't do that," Castor said. "He's one, too."

"Then I'll have to handle the situation myself."

Castor eyed him suspiciously for a moment. "Come to think of it, *you're* one, too. Now, get on, cat," he called as he slowly sauntered down the shabby street. He kicked an empty beer can, sending it dancing across the cobblestones.

Another day in Tortuga.

Chapter Eight

That night Numie was sitting at a quiet corner table at Commodore Philip's. A glow from within was warming his blood. That and the third double Scotch Lola had placed on his table.

Under her blonde wig, Lola was at the bar, laughing and talking with the few customers.

Impulsively, Numie slammed down his drink. What was he doing shacking up with a black drag queen? Had he come this low in his search for a bread ticket?

Getting up, he walked to the men's room. There he stood——not really needing to go, but somehow wanting to get out of the bar. He was alone in the toilet. The smell was foul, yet he remained almost by compulsion. Maybe from force of habit.

So many nights spent——wasted!——in a latrine. A dangling cock——was that what Numie Chase had to offer to the world? Was it all? He feared it was. No one had ever wanted friendship. No one ever saw talent, ability. The whole world was on a sex trip. He wasn't on the sex trip. *They* were. Everyone he met.

Head spinning, he propped his elbow against the wall. All those faceless men who'd stood beside him at latrines were on the march tonight. He could hear their voices, the dialogue changing little from town to town:

"New York's a pretty quiet place tonight, huh?"

"Not much doing in Atlanta tonight, huh?"

"This Washington goes to bed at nine o'clock, huh?"

"How about a drink?"

"How about a drink?"

"The chairs in this fleabag are uncomfortable——we'd better sit on the bed."

"Sure is hot in here. Better take off your things."

"I've got a wife and three kids."

"I've never done this before with a guy."

"A drink?"

"A drink?"

A sudden rap, and Lola was throwing open the door. "Just

checking," she said, "to see that you're not being molested."

Straightening up, he zipped up his pants and headed out. "Yeah, I'm alone," he said.

From out of nowhere popped Tangerine——a red hibiscus in her orange hair and an extra coat of blood-colored lipstick on her mouth. "Lola," she called, "the last of the red-hot mamas is gonna shake it tonight."

"If you shake that thing, the hinges will come apart!" Lola said. She embraced Tangerine across the bar, then mixed her a drink. "Go join that stud in the corner. Mind you, gal, I said join——don't touch."

By then Tangerine's back was turned. She was moving fast toward Numie's table.

"How you doing?" asked Tangerine.

"Fine," he said. He neither welcomed nor resented Tangerine's presence tonight.

She plopped down in the next chair.

No question about it: Tangerine was Halloween. She was a masquerade party. The tinsel on a tree. The ribbon on a package. More than that, too.

"I just had to see you," she said.

"You heard about my getting busted?"

"Found out this afternoon," she said. "From Anne. She called Lola at the bar."

"I'm surprised. Leonora didn't know me."

"Leonora has to have her little dramas. Too bad, too, 'cause she could have got you out. Just like Lola did."

"She can have her dramas at somebody else's expense from now on," he said bitterly.

"Well, you're okay, and Yellowwood won't bother you again. Let's don't talk about Leonora no more. I'm much more fascinating."

"You certainly are." He sighed to himself, praying that Tangerine wasn't yet another woman on an ego trip.

"I've got to talk to you. I'm really sorry Anne put down your profession like that the other night. I don't think nobody should go putting down nobody else for the way they earn a living. Whatever your work is——just so long as it's honest——it's okay with me."

"Thank you, baby. That's good to hear." Was she being

condescending?

"I really liked you, and I've been trying to figure out how I can help, 'cause I know you're broke."

"Really, I'm fine."

"Don't pretend with me. You can let it all hang out. I've got twenty dollars on me, and I could sure use your services."

"Tangerine," he said, laughing, "surely you're joking." No sooner had he said that than he regretted it. After all, a man who went to bed with Lola La Mour might also go to bed with Tangerine Blanchard.

The hurt on her face was instantly apparent.

"I didn't mean it that way," he apologized.

"You think I don't need loving?"

"Of course not! Everybody needs loving."

"Let me tell you something. The last time I went to bed with a man was so long ago I can hardly remember——he said that part of me stunk. That's right, stunk! What every girl wants to hear. He wouldn't go to bed with me, got up and put on his pants."

"C'mon," he said, "I don't want to hear it."

Ignoring his request, she went on. "Know what I did? I scrubbed myself every which way. I even used Ajax one time. But it didn't help. That smell, I can't get rid of it. I do stink. Men won't touch me."

"Stop it!" he said. He gripped her wrist to make her pay attention. "You don't stink," he said slowly——certain that she heard his words now. "Don't let some bastard lay that kind of shit on you. The guy was a son of a bitch. He probably hated women. Forget it!"

She was almost crying. "You know what I've had to do? I'm not proud of it, and I'm not trying to shock you or make you sick at your belly, but I've longed for a little loving so much. I used to have a big German shepherd." Her voice broke off. She started to weep.

"Don't cry...Please."

"I'll give you twenty dollars."

"Honey, I can't accept." He felt trapped. "Lola is very jealous."

"You and Lola?" she asked, taking his hand. "I didn't know, really I didn't. If I had known, I would never have barged in like this. I'm so happy for you all. I would never break up a relationship or interfere in no way. You've got to believe that. I'll go and apologize to Lola."

"I don't think you'd better," he said, restraining her.

"Well, okay, but if making it with me is out of the question, why don't you come back to my place for a spaghetti dinner? Lola won't mind."

"Now that's an offer I can accept." A great burden lifted, he reached for his drink.

She bounded to her feet and wobbled across the bar toward Lola. "You won't mind if I take that good-looking boy friend of yours home for dinner?"

"Not if you bring him back," Lola said. "He needs some nourishment. Just make sure you feed him some protein. And don't let him drink too much."

"Drunk or sober," Numie interrupted, "you're gonna get it."

Lola squealed.

"You trust me with Tangerine?" Numie asked.

"Tangerine is the only one in town I'd trust you with," Lola said. "Tangerine hasn't had thoughts about sex since Harding was in the White House. Why, she'd even qualify to take up a collection for the Salvation Army."

He smiled at her, rubbing her chin with his thumb. "If one of your johns comes around, I told you what to do."

"I know what to do," Lola said. "Hey, lover man, here are the keys to the Facel-Vega. From now on, you're the man in the driver's seat."

He made his way out of the bar. His back to Lola, he could drop the pretense. He'd behaved exactly as she wanted him to——the aggressive and jealous lover.

Moments later, a mountain of a woman under a citrus-orange peak was being transported up a dark street in a car much too small for her.

Behind the wheel, Numie was in control——riding high.

Tangerine lived on the top floor of a dilapidated, two-story frame house. Instead of panes, some of the windows had cardboard stuck in to keep out the rain and mosquitoes. They probably didn't.

Entering her apartment, he was surprised to find a man-sized hole in the hallway. You could see through to the apartment downstairs.

"I tried to cover it with boards, she explained. Then, one night I broke a toe in the crack. Now I just let it be." With despair she looked at her reflection in the hall mirror. "My mama never repaired nothing. Why should I?" Frowning, she brushed back her orange hair.

He walked across the wooden floorboard and stared down at the hole. "You could fall in——any damn time of the day or night. How are you supposed to get across?"

"Easy," she said, laughing. "There's two ways. Slip by on the narrow side. Or else squeeze. Which, of course, I can't do since I got so damn fat. So I leap over. Like this." Picking up the skirttails of her flowered dress, she jumped. The flesh left her body, shooting out in all directions. She landed on the other side; and the house shook.

"Have to cross this hole to get to the john," she said when she caught her breath. "Wouldn't dare try that at night though. Shake my buddies downstairs out of bed. So I use a slop jar——the same one my mama used. It's all she left me."

He laughed loudly. She was wonderful!

"Go in and take a seat," she said. "I've gotta get busy with dinner."

In the living room, he sat down on a flea market sofa.

"Don't let one of those springs ruin your married life," she called in.

"Dammit, Tangerine! You sure this sofa isn't another one of your family heirlooms?"

She stuck her head in. "Help yourself to a drink. There's a smidge of bourbon left over there on the table. Don't bother with glasses. Us Georgia gals like our liquor straight."

"Thanks." At the table, he took the practically empty bottle. Holding it to his lips, he drained it.

Head spinning, he settled back on the sofa to think of Tangerine. She *was* a clown. A sad one. But she could laugh at herself. Something he couldn't do.

The way she brought everything out in the open——nothing seemed unmentionable. Or anyway, once mentioned, it lost some of its shame.

If he could get close enough, maybe some of what she had

would rub off.

Just then, she burst into the room with a plate of spaghetti for his lap. Meatless spaghetti out of a can. She poured two glasses of red wine.

He smiled his thanks.

"Tell me something," she said, "what in hell did you end up here for?"

"I wanted a new chance," he said guardedly, fearing the immediate personal tone the conversation had taken. "What more can any man ask?"

She settled back on the floor with her legs propped up in the air.

He was startled——unpleasantly so——to see she wore no underwear. Turning his head, he tried to answer her question better. "I really don't know why I hitched a ride here. It's as far as my thumb would take me, I guess."

She propped her fleshy body on her elbows. "Tell me something, what are you running from?"

At first, he resented the question. She was prying, and his business was his own. Then he decided her intentions were good. Deliberately stalling, he pulled out a package of cigarettes and lit one. He offered it to her. When she refused, he puffed away on it for a while, then asked: "What makes you think I'm running away? You can run toward something, too."

"You're running away," she insisted. "No doubt about it. I can always tell a mile off. No wonder. Seen enough young men on the lam in my day." She leaned back, using her hands as a pillow.

The cigarette burned his hand before he felt its heat. "Hell," he said, "I've always been running from something. Must have inherited that from my old man."

"Oh, my God," she yelled, heaving her fleshy body from the floor. "I forgot the dessert." She raced toward the kitchen. "It's burning."

He didn't really hear her, couldn't care about dessert. How unlike his old man who had always insisted it be served at the beginning of a meal "in case I die before I finish eating."

He still remembered the big Nordic ape. Got his blond hair from him. Also, his cock. Every time he got a beating from the old man, he'd look into those eyes——crystal blue and cold as a northern lake in winter.

Even though he'd looked like an ape, he worked in the fields like an ox. He always walked a little stooped forward from having spent his life earning a dollar for some man other than himself. If anything, he'd shown Numie how stupid it was to be somebody's slave.

The day he skipped out, he'd taken Numie on a long walk through the fields. The chill of late autumn had been in the air. "I'm gonna make it, son," he'd said. "Real big. The next time you see me, I'll be pulling up in some great big white Cadillac."

After five o'clock dinner, he set out down the road. There had been nothing unusual about that. He never told anybody where he was going or when he was coming back. Once he was gone for eight weeks. But Numie's mama must have known something. Earlier in the day he'd beaten her severely for not having his fresh clothes pressed and laid out. Numie still recalled her standing there on the rotting floor of their front porch long after the old man had disappeared down the road and the sun had set.

"It's store bought" Tangerine said, back in the room now. She handed him a white melted horror.

Tentatively, he tasted it. "I've always had cheesecake cold before."

"I like my cake hot," she said, getting into her piece. "My mama was baking all the time. Did your mama know how to cook?"

"She made what she called creamy gravy, except it had no cream in it and lots of water, and she could make a very floury biscuit——that's about it. Any meat my old man got."

"What was she like?"

"A dumb hillbilly from the Blue Ridge. After my old man left us, she went to work in South Carolina in the kitchen of a diner peeling potatoes. When that closed down, she got a job scrubbing shit off other people's toilets."

"Not much of a life."

"In the end, the only thing she had was her religion. She was a real fanatic, praying all the time. Even when she worked, she was muttering some prayer of thanks to God. Thanks for what? Those bony arms she used to lift up to God, I'll never forget them. Her sunken eyes, like a dying calf. I saw her grow old before her time; and I swore it wasn't going to happen to me."

"My mama was the same way," Tangerine said, "'cept she wasn't all that skinny. She was constantly being born again, washed in the Blood of the Lamb. She tried to drip some of that blood all over me, but I was an infidel by the time I was three years old," Tangerine said, pouring him another glass of wine. "I started going out with men——I mean men, not boys——when I was eleven years old."

"I was fifteen before I was ever picked up," he said. "Just the year before I'd been at boarding school, and I was pretty innocent even then."

"Care to tell me about it?" she asked. "I just love to hear stories about how guys lose their cherries."

"With me, it started with my standing outside movie houses, wanting to go in. One day this bald old man offered to pay my way. Naturally, once we got inside, I got the hand on the leg. I was too scared to put him off. Or to turn him down when he wanted to go back to his apartment. Know what he wanted? Me to jerk off in front of him——nothing else. Hell, I did that all the time anyway. It became a Saturday afternoon thing, and I always ended up with five dollars."

"Didn't it bother you?" she asked.

"Not with baldy. After all, he wasn't touching me. I think the first time I felt really dirty was when I went to his apartment, and he had two friends there——one a hairy ape, the other a dainty type. They got me drunk. One of them had a camera. I thought it was for a screen test of sorts. When they dumped me near my home later, they gave me a twenty-dollar bill. That was the most money I'd ever seen in my life."

"Your mama, she just let you roam about? Sounds like mine."

She found out I'd been skipping school a lot. She was too frail to beat me up, but she got the big bruiser she worked for to do the job. I needed to hide, so I headed for baldy's apartment. He told me to go away, bolted the damn door."

"True love."

"I walked for miles that night, trying to hitch a ride," he said. "The cars just whizzed by, their bright lights blinding me. Finally, I bedded down in a clump of bushes. Next morning I hit the road again——this time for New York."

"No damn food in your belly."

"Yeah, but not for long. Two college girls picked me up, and they really liked me. Other strangers just talked, saying I was pretty young to be out on my own. Still others wanted me to put out. I didn't turn anybody down. What did I have but my body to trade for meals and a free ride? When I got to New York, I knew for sure how I was going to make my way."

"When I heard about you and Lola that night, I was really thrown a bit. I mean, is black your trip?"

"Anything's my trip. Lola isn't my first black. The first person who picked me up in New York was a black——this one quite a lady. Blacks have always been attracted to me because of my hair. For a while, it was exciting——you know, the big taboo. After a few months I had to get out, though. She told me, 'You're not chicken——more Tom Turkey'. She didn't want any 'old' boys around. I was still fifteen. But in New York when you're fifteen it isn't hard to find another bed."

"You went both routes?"

"Yeah, so I had more than my share of customers. Man or woman, it didn't matter. In fact, I still don't know which I prefer. I've always gone to bed with people I didn't like. I never had sex with anyone because I wanted to——except one time, and I don't even want to think about that tonight. I didn't want to give anything away if I could get paid for it. Survival, that's where it was at. That's where it's at now."

"If New York hustling's so great, why did you split?"

"Those beds have been harder to come by in the last few years——and I'm not fooling myself. I've got to go to work one day, get a real job, but all I know how to do is sell my meat."

"I don't believe that," she said. She strode regally over to him and gave him her hand.

He took it and held it. Dazed, he lifted his head. What did she want? Finally deciding it was only an offer of bodily comfort, he squeezed it and let it drop. He sank back on the sofa, as a silence fell over the room. "I almost never talk about myself. But I've been doing a lot of rapping on this island."

"It's hard to keep a secret in Tortuga."

He downed the last of the wine.

Out on the street again, he wondered if he felt self-pity or self-contempt. A vague emptiness was welling inside him.

Somehow he'd missed out. But missed out on what? Why was he getting sentimental about himself? Maybe because of the spirit of that glorious old hag who would love anything that came in front of her path.

He couldn't get his head together. Not one single, clear idea. He was all broken inside, his eyes hazed with booze.

All around him decaying gingerbread verandas spoke of a long-faded elegance, a Southern aristocracy dimly remembered. Now laundry hung over the railings, and children slept out on uncovered mattresses on rotting boards. Once ladies in antebellum gowns and white stockings waited under white parasols for gentlemen callers on a Sunday afternoon.

Now, today, these same veranda occupants would have settled for a decent meal.

Didn't life ever get better?

Chapter Nine

The volley of water was cold, but bracing. Numie scrubbed too hard, trying to wash away the memories of a drunken night.

Stepping out, he blindly reached for a towel.

Lola was there, holding one from her perch on the toilet stool. She kneeled on the tile and began to dry his legs vigorously.

"You really dig me, don't you?" he asked. "Now get in the kitchen and fix my breakfast."

"Get him!" Lola said, tossing the wet towel in his face. "You really think it's a man's world!"

"Freedom's something you wouldn't know anything about."

"What? You want to bring back slavery?"

"No, I just know when a woman wants a man to boss her around. Now, get my breakfast."

Stepping into his jeans, he went into the living room. There he collapsed on the white satin sofa. The smell of bacon frying wafted across.

Bacon frying reminded him of Louise of long ago. She would cook his breakfast in the morning. With his mama working in the diner, he saw more of Louise than anybody.

Where was she today? Probably on welfare in some shack in Carolina. Maybe dead. She wasn't any too young when he knew her, and that was twenty years ago.

But she laughed a lot and didn't give a damn about religion——so she was fun to be with. A gelatinous mass of a woman, black as Lola, she was short, but she always wore high heels, even when cooking breakfast. "Flat shoes are for field niggers," she used to say.

She'd walk across those wooden floors with a mincing gait, her large hips keeping a rhythm all their own. Those high heels were too small for Louise. Maybe that's why she used to say, "I never stand up when I can plop this big fat ass of mine down."

Louise spent a lot of time on her back, not always alone. During the day, she'd been Numie's mama. But at night she had no need for him. Too busy mothering men far too big to need a mama.

Those men would arrive with boxes and candy in heart-shaped Valentine boxes. Louise had the largest collection of those boxes of just about anybody. Sometimes the more considerate men would bring a bar of candy for Numie, too. Often he'd be given a comic book which the men had read themselves.

Louise would receive them in faded white lace dresses turned yellow with her sweat. She was forever lying there against the flowered wallpaper of her living room which had been stained by leaking rain.

She figured Numie was too young to care what was happening. She didn't even bother to shoo him out of the room. Each evening, the same ritual. After Louise and her main man of the night got drunk, the suitor would take down his pants——rarely take off his shirt——and mount her.

Numie was allowed to watch, or else he could go into the kitchen for some cold fried chicken Louise kept in the refrigerator. After they were through, Louise and her man would laugh a lot. Often they'd sing.

One night had been different. Her lover that time had been younger than the rest, his mustache making his broad features sinister. He smelled of shaving lotion. His skin was much lighter than Louise's, almost olive in tone. He hadn't bothered to bring Valentine candy boxes or anything for Numie.

He also hadn't bothered with the preliminary drinking. He just put a shiny ten-dollar bill right down on the table, pulled off all his clothes, even his shirt, and ordered Numie into the kitchen.

That afternoon Louise had made some fudge, and Numie decided to sample that. Later he heard Louise screaming, "It hurts...it's killing me." Grabbing a paring knife, Numie had rushed to the front bedroom. In one quick move, he jabbed the knife into the shoulder blade of Louise's rider.

Numie recalled nothing after that——nothing except a kick in the face that sent him sprawling across the room.

When he came to, Louise's watermelons were swinging back and forth over him. "I do believe you've been bit green by the jealous bug." She was laughing and smiling, giving him a loud, slurpy kiss on the mouth. She showed no clue whatsoever she'd been involved in an act of violence only hours before.

"Where's your friend?" he'd asked, sitting up and rubbing his head.

"At the hospital. It was just a scratch, but you should have heard that man carry on. Like a pig with his nuts cut off. You really thought he was hurting me?"

"You were screaming."

"My sweet little baby," she said, giving him another wet kiss. "You'll soon learn when hurt becomes heaven for a woman. I was just starting to enjoy it when you came barging in with my kitchen knife."

Suddenly, he was conscious he was entirely naked. Not a stitch on. He fumbled around, reaching for a faded quilt.

"Don't you go getting modest with me," Louise said. "Always hiding that peter. I ain't never seen it till tonight when I put you to bed."

Embarrassed and ashamed, he muttered to let go and reached for the quilt again.

Her hands snaked down his body, ensnaring the curly hairs of his lower abdomen. "You're becoming a real big boy, real big, and I hadn't even noticed. Imagine that!" She talked to his cock as if it were separate from himself, making cooing sounds. "You like Louise's warm hands on him? Look, he's growing bigger! Now just you lay back and spread your skinny legs."

Numie tried to swallow, but maybe his throat was too dry. It sounded more like a gulp.

"Tonight old Louise is gonna teach you the best lesson a gal can teach a boy. Now, just you relax. 'Cause I'm a gal who likes to take her time. Lazy Louise, they call me."

She'd been in total charge that night. He hadn't really enjoyed anything, but had been completely fascinated, completely under her spell.

After they were through, she wobbled across the floor, giggling and half drunk. She reached for one of her Valentine candy boxes and untied its shiny satin ribbon. "You get first prize tonight, you little mother-fucker," she had said, tying the red ribbon around his cock. Later she slipped the ten-dollar bill under his pillow. "That's the first time Louise has ever paid for it, but you earned it. It was good having something fresh for a change."

. . .

"Stop thinking about sex," Lola said, emerging from the kitchen with a plate of food. For one brief moment, she thought Numie was thinking of some body other than her own.

Numie gulped down the scrambled eggs, then sliced the bacon and tasted Lola's freshly brewed coffee. At least, she was a better cook than Louise. "You sure make good coffee."

"My daddy taught me," she said. "Taught me a lot of things." Her voice drifted off. It wasn't easy thinking about her old man.

"Where's he now?" Numie asked matter-of-factly, not caring.

"Dead," she said blankly. She barged into the bathroom and stared at her face in the mirror. The results didn't please her at all. Not enough sleep last night. It was hard being a sex object.

Back in the living room, she was rubbing her hands over a wooden Cuban cigar box. "Numie," she said impulsively. "Would you smoke one of these cigars? They're from Havana."

"A Havana cigar," he said, surprised. "Sure. I've always heard about them." Taking one from her, he lit it and settled back on the sofa.

She studied him for a long moment. The smell was so familiar. It brought back recent memories of the Commodore, but in some vague and distant way she conjured up her father sitting there. He sure did smoke different from Numie. "Child," she said, jerking the cigar from him, "you just don't know how to smoke."

"Oh, yeah?" he said, resentful. "What do you know about cigars? I thought only dykes smoked them."

"I resent that. For one thing, I just happen to be the daughter of the most famous cigar roller who ever set foot in Tortuga. We used to make our own on this island, I have you know. My daddy came over from Jamaica to work in a factory here."

"I'm impressed."

"You should be! Cigar rollers in those days used spit. My daddy's mouth was dry all the time."

"Don't make me throw up."

She turned from him, feeling some of the disgust herself. But the disgust was directed at Numie. He'd pay for putting down her daddy. Nobody did that. Not even the Commodore.

Back in the bathroom, she stared at her face in the mirror. Would her daddy, were he alive today, find her attractive? The little girl look was still there. *Wasn't it?*

After all, he'd told her she was the exact spittin' image of her mama. Lola had never seen her mama——she'd died giving birth——but she just knew she must have been a handsome woman.

She would have to have been, because her daddy never got over her. Lola was sure of that. "You're all she left me," he used to tell Lola, taking her after supper and placing her on his knee. He'd let her sip some of his rum toddy. It was real sweet the way she liked it. To this day, she still didn't drink anything but rum toddies.

"You liked your old man a lot, huh?" Numie called from the living room.

"Liked?" Lola asked, rushing back in, hands on her hips. "I was madly in love with him, child." She plopped down beside Numie on the satin sofa. Placing her feet on the coffee table, she smoothed an imaginary wrinkle out of her white nightgown.

"You mean, like a woman with a man?"

"Of course," Lola answered, getting up impatiently again. She wanted to talk, to tell someone, but she didn't trust Numie with this secret part of her life.

In the bathroom once more, she took off her gown and inspected her red panties. My God, a stain! She'd have to get another pair, a fresh, nice, clean one. She liked to smell fresh and clean at all times, even if it meant changing her panties twenty times a day.

Out of the top drawer, she selected a pair of red ones.

That had been her daddy's favorite color. In fact, he was the one who launched her on a lifetime career of wearing red silk panties.

She still remembered the first night her daddy got her to put on a pair of her mama's panties. He'd brought her things all the way from Jamaica——couldn't bear to part with them. Daddy kept his former wife's clothing locked in the top drawer of a closet so none of his children could get at them. But one night he got a pair of panties, real silky ones, and asked Lola to try them on. They'd both had too many rum toddies that night. But she'd put on the panties, then accepted his invitation to climb up on his knee, like she always did. "You look like your mama," he had said, "'cept for the color of your skin."

"What's the matter with my skin?" Lola had asked.

"Nothing," he told her. "'Cept your mama's skin was nearly white. All her life I never knew her to go out in the sun."

Lola resented that. She wanted to be white, too. Another dirty trick from Mother Nature, the old bitch.

Astride his lap, Lola let her daddy take her for a ride. That time, though, his hands were different from before. "You're becoming quite a little woman," he said. He'd started to tickle her thighs, even pinching her little bottom. "It's the cutest in the world," he'd said.

She'd wanted to ask him if it were cuter than her mama's, but hadn't dared.

Then he'd turned her around, with her back rubbing up against him. She could feel the warmth of his breath on her. It had been *very* exciting. She'd thought he was just playing a game. Then with his finger he'd started poking through the silk panties at her rosebud. She'd felt him grow hard. He'd rubbed up against her, but didn't try to enter. He'd kissed her right after——right on the mouth, real hard. "Yes indeedy, you're getting more like your mama every day." With that, she knew she'd pleased him. It was the happiest moment of her life.

After that night, she didn't need any more encouragement to wear silk panties. It was the most natural thing she'd ever done. Approving of herself finally in the mirror, she paraded into the living room.

"You should have been a girl," Numie said.

"I *am* a girl," she protested. "Want me to prove it?"

"No, no," he said, fearing another sexual encounter with her. "Guess you are a girl after all."

She reached over, took a piece of his bacon, held it up in the air for inspection, then devoured it.

"I want to ask you something," he said. "When did you start dressing up in drag?"

"I don't dress in drag," she said adamantly. That awful word, would it haunt her forever?

"Sorry, I didn't mean to make you pissed," he said.

"My daddy used to let me wear my mama's clothes," she said.

"That's surprising."

"No, it wasn't surprising at all. He knew I was really intended as a girl."

"You told me last night you had brothers. Didn't they think it strange to see their little brother going around dressed up like a lady."

"Not at all," she said. "I think they rather liked it."

"You mean, they *used* you?"

"Darling, used isn't the word. They gang-banged me every night."

"They probably did if you went around dressed the part."

"Daddy was working late one night at the factory, and all three of my brothers came home. They'd been drinking. I pretended to be asleep, but it was no use. I knew what they were going to do. Bill, he was the oldest, hopped on first——right in front of the other two. He was brutal. It took him a long time to get off 'cause of the booze."

"Did the other two get it on with you, too?"

"They sure did. Charley was next. I didn't like him at all. He was kinda crude like, worse than Bill. When it was over, Charley thanked Bill. Thanked him, mind you, for the privilege of socking it to me."

"It was probably Bill's idea."

"I'm sure. Henry, he's the youngest, asked, 'Bill, can I get in her ass, too'? Henry was just two years younger than me, and wasn't developed at all. But Bill let him. 'Last...and least', he said, after looking Henry up and down. He couldn't manage, and my brothers laughed at him. By then, Henry was crying."

"Did the others keep socking it to you?" In a way, he felt sorry for Lola.

"Until I left home," she said, swallowing bitterly. "I hated them, but what could I do? I was a weak kid. After daddy died, there was no one to protect me. All my brothers used me, my brothers' friends, the guys at school. My voice was too high pitched to be a real boy. Even the girls made fun of me. Her fists closed in determination. "But I swore I'd make this town eat shit one day. Now I'm the Commodore's mistress. I've shown them all!"

"You can't get even with the past. No one can."

"All I know is I can go any place in this town——right in the sheriff's office——and nobody makes fun of me no more."

"How'd you meet up with the Commodore?"

"In this very bar. He used to have amateur entertainment on Saturday night. I appeared in full regalia one night, a beautiful red silk dress with a white boa. I was stunning, even without the blonde wig. I wore a red one in those days."

"Like Tangerine?"

"No," she said, indignant. "I could never be like Tangerine if I tried. She's nothing but a cheap whore."

"So you put on a show?"

"I did the bit, 'whatever Lola wants' . . . and the crowd went wild. Ever since that night, I've been known as Lola. I added the La Mour, of course. Up to then everybody in my family used old English names."

"You still didn't tell me how you met the Commodore."

"He asked if I'd come back and perform the following Saturday night. I did and, of course, I was a sensation. That very night the Commodore asked me up to his place on the keys. He had a beautiful ranch-styled house then. It was later destroyed by a hurricane, and *we* never bothered to rebuild it."

"You were his houseboy?"

"Maid! I've never been nobody's boy, *ever*. A very, high-class maid at that. He let me dress up in any uniform I wanted. Sometimes I wore nothing around the house but a bra and panties. He always liked that very much. Still does. Before I'd been there a month, I was hiring a maid myself. My brother Bill's mama-in-law." Lola's eyes glistened with revenge. "Bill got hired as a gardener and general handyman." She smiled. "Still works for my Commodore and me. Carries out my garbage, child. He's always threatening to quit, but he's got no place to go. My Commodore sees to it that no one else in town will hire him."

"Lola, my coffee's cold," he said.

"Men," she sighed, pretending to loathe the word, but betraying her love of the sound.

Four cups of coffee later, nausea swept over Numie. What was he going to do today? Always he'd had something to do.

Hustle an early morning john in the latrine, make it to the next town before dark——or just make it.

Today, nothing, not one damn thing. Lola had seen to everything, even the groceries for the weekend. She'd need all morning to get ready before going down to that bar.

But what about him? Where could he go?

Just yesterday he was worried about his next meal. Today, with everything provided, he was feeling trapped. It was just plain crazy, he guessed.

Only thing is, something *had* to happen before the day was over. Something to make him feel alive.

Chapter Ten

At the beach, the sun was burning into Numie's skin. It was one of the hottest days of the year.

He was just lying there, getting redder and redder. For some reason he couldn't leave——although he knew he'd pay later with a burn.

A group of college age men and women on the beach were strangely disturbing. Their pastimes were harmless enough: playing volleyball, occasionally running to jump into the ocean.

Then, he knew what it was. Their bodies, so young and lithe. Bodies that life was yet to mar. He was resenting their bodies, knowing full well how ridiculous that was. Yet he couldn't help it, couldn't shake the feeling of having lost something.

Running his hand down his own frame, he became aware——almost for the first time——of a slight pudge developing around his middle. Compared to those kids, his body was old.

Countless johns and an endless string of horny women had sung his body's praise. He'd gotten his kicks seeing how his body turned people on. The thrill far outweighed any pleasure he received from a final discharge. A climax with a john was a duty, something expected. Depending on the fee, he could make that discharge passionate and powerful, or else lethargic or totally faked.

The praise of his body, so lavish and constant, seemed without end. Surely like a diamond, his body would only increase in value to satisfy and delight as yet unseen faces and orifices.

Was he finished as a hustler? The sun burned the question into his brain. Was that what was keeping him up at night?

A girl turned and looked in his direction.

He closed his eyes, feigning sleep. That girl, that damn girl! Was she still looking? Before, he'd assumed that anyone looking was doing so out of admiration. Never for any other reason. Now he was filled with doubts. Was she noticing the paunch? No more of Lola's southern cooking, the goddamn fatback. And the drink. What about that? Getting drunk every night didn't assure lasting good looks.

Without looking at the girl, he got up quickly and headed

down the beach toward the shower stalls.

Inside the old cabins, the smell of urine was everywhere. A row of doorless toilets faced a string of open showers. Three of the stools were occupied.

Numie didn't have to look into the faces of the hungry perchers. Those blank staring faces he'd encountered in every town he'd been in. They were sex watchers, eternally waiting for a show. He'd never bothered with them before. After all, they rarely had money, or rarely spent it if they did. He sought out johns with more bread... and a little more style. When approached by these sex watchers, he'd turn them away, usually with a curse.

Today their very presence was stimulating. In the past, he'd deliberately concealed himself from their voracious eyes. But this would be different. He wanted them to see his body. *All of it*.

. . .

Bulky bodies, human smells, devouring mouths, sweat-soaked busy hands——it'd been too much for Numie. He'd started to feel the walls closing in.

From the grope pile inside the bathhouse, he'd rushed out into the sun again. There he took a stool at a luncheon counter and ordered a beer.

Sexual tribute from the men was what he'd been seeking. And he'd aroused the lust hunger in their eyes. But Numie's ego satisfaction was short lived. The desperate men had left him feeling empty——worse than before. More sex tension than he could handle, even after a marathon session.

Those men would never be fulfilled, not in a lifetime of looking and searching. Would he be like them one day? Always searching, never finding.

Was he like that now?

At the edge of the beach a red sports car pulled up. It was familiar. Ralph got out.

As Ralph made his way toward the bathhouse, Numie thought he looked older somehow. The other day he was twenty-eight. Now he looked more like thirty-four. But he was still young, still slim, still attractive. There was a certain effeminacy about him, though. A diffidence. His black hair was fine and wavy, with a tendency to early baldness. His full mouth was pouty, too lush somehow to be flattering to a man. Those ever-searching eyes were his best feature. Not only wide, but opening onto thick, long lashes.

"Ralph," Numie called.

At the sound of his name, Ralph nervously jerked his neck in Numie's direction. His face was guilt ridden. "Numie, good to see you."

"You don't look glad to see me at all," Numie replied. 'C'mon, join me for a beer."

"Work keeps me pretty busy, but I needed some sun."

"There you go trying to explain things again. I told you once before, you don't have to."

"What do you mean?"

"I know why guys go to that bathroom. I was just in there myself. It's one great big suction pump."

"Oh, I was just going to change into my suit."

"You know, I don't understand the secrecy. Everybody in this town knows everything that's happening anyway."

"I'm married," Ralph said flatly.

"Get off it, man, Anne knows about you."

"*Anne*. You know my wife?"

"Yes, that queen I had to meet the other day. That was Leonora. I met Leonora and Anne the night before at the bar, the same night I met you."

"So you were the guy at Sacre-Coeur? I knew somebody was there. But *you*. Dammit, I told you this town is too small. You didn't say anything."

"The gold watch gave me away to Anne," Numie answered. "It was stupid of me to wear it."

"Of course, Anne knows. That's not why I'm always hiding. That was just an easy answer to a difficult question. I don't want to talk here. Let's walk down the beach."

The young people were still playing volleyball. Ralph gave each of the men a quick appraisal, then walked on.

"Nothing misses you," Numie said.

"Okay, you and I will drop any pretenses. I check out every basket."

"But what are you afraid of? Seems to me you've got it made

in this town. The sheriff isn't going to cause any trouble. That's for damn sure."

"You're right. He takes his orders from Leonora. From Commodore Philip even more."

The sun was high in the sky now, as Numie neared a deserted part of the beach.

Still drinking from his beer can, Ralph came up beside him. "I don't know why I'm always sneaking about. Everybody does know about me. Who am I kidding?"

"Maybe you're hiding from yourself."

"In one way you're right. Sex is still a dirty business to me. I've always wanted to be straight. Better yet, to have other people think I am. I'll go to extremes to convince them."

"Even marriage."

"Yes, that. Though my marriage to Anne was more complicated than that."

"Just why did you marry her?"

"It was an arrangement that suited everybody's purpose——my own, Anne's, and most especially Leonora's."

"How did Leonora get in on the act?"

"She'd known my father at one time. In fact, my father once got it on with Leonora. She went both ways in those days. When I came to New York, I looked her up. I'd written a play, and I was hoping to get her to back it."

"Anne told me the story."

"My version and Anne's version are quite different." Ralph's voice had a slight whine to it.

"In what way?"

"Mine's the truth."

"I see." For some reason, he resented Ralph suggesting Anne was a liar. He felt defensive of her in some way. "I could see why I'd meet up with Leonora, but I don't understand you. You've got brains, good looks, and you've got that upper middle-class look to you. I can't believe you were some under-privileged writer that Leonora had to take in."

"I wasn't. I'd come from model parents from a model suburb. The trees were vinyl, the grass artificial. You never saw garbage on the street. I knew little about life when I first met Leonora. Sure, I'd dabbled at a lot of things, but I'd never really been into anything. That's why my play was so shallow."

"A virgin?" Numie's eyes were teasing.

Ralph hesitated, not sure of Numie's reason for asking. "No, I'd had a few encounters——usually with hustlers like you in strange cities."

"Thanks."

"I didn't mean it that way." He leaned back on a slat wood bench, looking out at the sea. "There I was, considered the most desirable bachelor in my hometown, out paying rough trade for the dubious privilege of going down on their smelly crotches. Bums I wouldn't even allow in my home. His mouth restricted into bitterness. "After one of those sessions, I'd come back home, go to my room, and sulk for days."

"Your parents must have wondered."

"They just let me be. They were too busy leading their own lives to care about me. None of us ever had anything to say to each other."

Numie couldn't help but resent Ralph. How he used to want the advantages of middle-class security for himself. But to hear Ralph tell it, that wouldn't bring you happiness. Still, it sure beat hustling for a buck in the winter's cold.

Ralph lit a cigarette, crushed it out, then quickly lit another one. He wasn't exactly confiding in Numie as much as he was reliving an experience and working something out. More than that, he was taking the age-old opportunity of telling a relative stranger something he would not reveal to a friend.

Numie liked hearing these intimacies from Ralph. It made him feel less guilty about opening up and talking about Marty and the ebony blackbird that day on the island. A fair exchange, in other words. "What was your daddy into?" Numie asked, hoping Ralph would continue to talk freely.

"He was president of a company, making $85,000 a year. But one day our world caved in. He was fired just like a common ditch-digger. Not only fired, but charged with embezzlement. He hadn't saved a penny either and was very much in debt."

"How did your mama take to that?"

"A real loyal wife. She filed charges for divorce. That left father with me. I, too, was loyal. I split for New York the next day."

"What happened to him?"

"He was convicted and sent to jail. By then, I'd found a new mother in Leonora."

"Leonora doesn't strike me as anybody's mother."

"She was the most exciting woman I'd ever met."

"Still is, as far as I'm concerned," Numie said.

"I agree," Ralph said. "The more outrageous she is, the more I love it. Being gay has something to do with it. If I were straight, I'd probably have nothing to do with her. She's grotesque, really. But I love to be with her. We spend most of our evenings together. When I get up to leave, she says, 'Going cruising, darling?' She completely accepts me. Always did——right from the first."

"I wish she had me."

"She will," Ralph answered impatiently. Suddenly, he got up and started walking down the beach.

Numie wasn't sure whether he was supposed to follow or not. Pretty soon he fell into step with Ralph.

Leaving the beach, Ralph turned down a narrow street of unpainted houses. Exiles from Havana lounged in the narrow doorways, as children played on the porches. In one, a used tire had been crudely converted into a veranda swing.

"Real machismo, this place." Numie said. "Not like what I'm used to at all."

"I feel the same way," Ralph said, as if aware of him again. "I miss the sophistication of New York. Leonora embodied New York sophistication for me. I never thought that being with her I'd end up here."

A cool breeze was blowing. Numie looked up at a widow's walk, a platform where the wives of fishermen sixty years ago maintained a lonely vigil for husbands who would never return from the sea.

Ralph stopped at a roadside Cuban shack and ordered two strong black coffees for the both of them. "You may not believe this," he said, still remembering New York, "but Leonora used to pimp for me."

"Come on."

"No, it's true. The first night I met her she invited me out to dinner. It turned out to be a gay place on the upper east side. When we went in, Leonora whispered something to the manager. We got the handsomest waiter in the house. We met the kid later——by arrangement, of course——in the bar of the

Plaza. She'd bought him for me as a present."

"The only thing I find hard to believe is that Leonora would be so generous. I thought she was tight."

"It depends entirely on what she's trying to prove. I thought I'd really found a friend in Leonora although how she figured out I was gay I'll never know." Frowning at the bitterness of the coffee, he downed it. "I soon learned that being Leonora's friend left no time for anybody else. She's all consuming."

"Then how did you manage to marry Anne?" Numie was alarmed at the curiosity in his voice. It was as if he were enduring the conversation about Leonora just waiting to find out what he really wanted to know.

As if detecting that, Ralph looked at him, said nothing, then walked on down the street. At the corner he stopped. "I'm sure Anne forgot to mention it," he said sarcastically, "but she was Leonora's girl in those days."

Numie couldn't believe it! That statement was like a slap in the face. Ralph was telling a lie. Anne wasn't that way.

A new enthusiasm came over Ralph now. "The first time I went to Leonora's apartment, she was living with a broken-down actress named Joan. Leonora was even then getting on in years. She'd long ago tired of Joan. But Joan wasn't about to let go of a good thing."

"But how did Anne fit in?"

"Leonora had developed a passion for girls much younger than herself. I knew she was having an affair with someone and managing to keep it a secret from Joan. But that old dyke's suspicions were hard to contain. One day Leonora took me to meet Anne."

Numie swallowed hard. Ralph was telling the truth. He knew it.

"Anne ran a boutique called `bedtime fun'. She sold mechanical devices to lull a person into sleep. Lace-ruffled pillows that played Mozart concertos, muzzles to fit under the chins of snorers. She even peddled violet-sprinkled chamberpots. We talked and laughed a lot that day, making fun of the gadgets. Anne and I struck it off, right from the beginning."

"Leonora wasn't jealous?"

"To the contrary, she encouraged it. She wanted to have

Anne around the house more. So she told Joan that Anne and I were lovers. Joan bought the story, too."

"That sounds like a cozy arrangement." A slight bitter edge came into Numie's voice.

"Not really. Somewhere along the way, Anne began to believe it."

"You mean, she really wanted to make it with you."

Again, Ralph cast Numie a strange look. He didn't say anything at first, as if he were trying to figure something out. Then, deliberately and provocatively stalling, he asked "Want a *bollo*?"

"What's that?"

"Ground black-eyed peas seasoned with Cuban spices. Deep fried."

"No thanks."

Ralph walked over to a street corner vendor and bought one for himself. Only then, did he answer Numie's question. "Yes, she did. She'd been married once before, and she got the crazy idea that one night with her would cure my liking boys forever. Christ, women are conceited, aren't they? Anne, you see, wasn't really a dyke. But she was ambitious. As it turned out, Leonora was financing that sleepy time boutique."

"Leonora just buys people, doesn't she?"

"She's always bought her friends. She was buying me, really conning me into thinking she was going to back my lousy play. But I would have liked her anyway. I had absolutely no money in those days. I was living at Leonora's apartment. Even had to ask her for cigarette money. I'd moved out of my hotel after the first week in New York."

The summer sun was hot on Numie's head. He closed his eyes. "Did you and Anne ever...?"

Ralph interrupted. "With Anne I enjoyed the first female companionship in my life. She used to be fun to be with. Bright and in those days supportive. But I never felt the faintest desire to get it on with her. Although we tried once."

"Let's have a drink," Numie said. He had stopped in front of a former private home with a sign reading, "An inexpensive place for people with money."

Out on its deck with a view of the ocean, Numie hurriedly downed a Scotch while sitting in the shade of a giant seagrape.

At the far end of the deck, an elderly woman in a flowery dress was laughing loudly at a joke told by a man in a flowery shirt.

Ralph looked disgusted, "That's Ted Albury."

"Yeah, Numie said. "I've seen his name around town. Who's the granny?"

"Ruthie Elvina, as she calls herself," Ralph said. "Leonora's old girlhood enemy."

Signaling for another drink, Numie said, "You were telling me about your marriage."

"It was Leonora who kept insisting we get married," Ralph said. "Believe it or not; Leonora's very conventional. We did, finally. But the marriage has been a sham." Ralph drifted off a bit, his eyes on one of the waiters. "Leonora wanted us married, and she got her wish. Things went downhill after that. Once she got that ring on her finger, Anne started behaving like a real wife. I felt trapped. What made things even worse was that Anne was getting a little old for Leonora."

"She sure likes them young, doesn't she?"

"Yes sir! Leonora took up with a little Puerto Rican girl. But she liked Anne and agreed to keep her on as a secretary. I became, `My caddy, darling', as she puts it."

"And Joan?" Numie asked.

"She found out about Anne and Leonora," Ralph said. "Joan and Leonora broke up. Joan ended up on the street. But now . . . " His voice drifted off. The waiter was at his table.

"Another drink, Mr. Douglas?" the boy asked.

Ralph eyed him provocatively. "Yes, I need servicing."

"Look," the boy said angrily, "I told you the last time you were in here, I'll serve you drinks——nothing else." He turned and walked away.

"That son of a bitch is not going to have a job tomorrow," Ralph said defiantly. "Albury probably offered him more money."

The second round of drinks was brought by a different waiter.

At the end of the drink, Numie had enough courage to ask a troubling question. "Is Leonora all there?"

"Very much so," Ralph answered without hesitation. "She's very practical, especially about business. Though you'd never know it the way she carries on. Of course, she's got a ripe fantasy when it comes to her own charms and talent. But when a dollar's involved, she's got the mentality of Internal Revenue."

"How does Tangerine fit in?" Numie asked.

"Another caddy. Her duties are whatever Leonora wants them to be. Leonora's been known to change her mind in mid-sentence. Why do you want to know all these things?"

"I'm trying to get on as Leonora's chauffeur," Numie said. "Right now I'm shacked up with Lola La Mour. That's not where I'm at."

"You and Lola?" Ralph asked, puzzled. "That's disgusting!"

"It is for me," Numie said. "But I'm hanging around trying to meet the Commodore. Hope to work up something with him. In the meantime, can you swing something with me and Leonora?"

"It depends..." He paused. The sun outlined the harshness of his face. "You did give me a helping hand the other night, and you delivered as promised on the island. Sure, I can get you a job with Leonora. No sweat, I do the hiring and firing anyway. But you have to clear it with her."

"She practically kicked me out the other day," Numie said.

"Leonora always pulls these stunts," Ralph said. "They're perfectly harmless. She's probably forgotten all about it now. That is, if she still remembers you."

"I was busted," Numie said. "Yellowwood picked me up. Leonora had given me one of her favorite cigarettes and like a fool I carried it off with me. Some workout I got at that goddamn jail."

"I know," Ralph said. "Yellowwood's a sickie. But a real nice guy when you get to know him."

"No thanks!" Numie said. "I called Leonora from the jail and asked her to help me. She didn't know me."

"Why should she?" Ralph asked. "That didn't mean she doesn't like you."

"I don't understand," Numie said.

"Leonora doesn't want to be understood," Ralph said. "If she thought anybody understood her, she'd slit her wrist. Better yet, she'd slit theirs. I'll set up an appointment for you this afternoon. I'd like you to be her chauffeur."

"Great!"

"Only thing is..." Ralph paused.

Numie frowned. Now, the catch.

"You take your orders from me," Ralph commanded. "You report to me. You check everything with me——regardless of what she tells you to do. I feel I can trust you. Also, if you drive her around the island, I want to know where you take her, who she talks to. The whole thing. Okay?"

"I can play that game," Numie said. "You really handle Leonora's affairs, I see."

"Yes," Ralph said, "Anne and I have to look after her."

There was a long pause.

Ralph smiled, as if he knew all along what Numie was thinking. "Okay, as far as Anne is concerned, you're free to sock it to her."

Numie couldn't conceal his startled look. Was this another trap? He smiled. "I always like to get the husband's permission."

Ralph seemed perfectly serious. "She's horny as hell most of the time," Ralph said. "And she doesn't get anything in town——only when she goes back to the mainland. Which isn't often."

"I think she's very attractive," Numie said. "If you don't mind."

"Mind?" Ralph asked. "You'd be doing me a favor. If she's getting laid, she won't be picking so many fights with me."

"You're doing me a favor, too, in more ways than one." Numie said. "I don't like being in anybody's debt. The problem is, the only thing I've got to pay you back with right now is the old bod. And you made it clear you don't like seconds."

Ralph looked at him, his eyes traveling from head to toe. Then he glanced at the waiter who had spurned his offer. "This one time," he said, "I'm going to make an exception to my rule. Let's go back to the hotel, the place where you found me."

"I'm not welcome around there," Numie said. "They have my possessions locked up, and I can't pay the bill."

"You'll get them all back," Ralph promised. "The guy at the desk has been on my payroll for the past six years."

"Fine," Numie said.

Back at the beach, Numie looked at the volleyball players as he was getting into Ralph's sports car. So young and so healthy. Everybody...having fun. Shoulders sagging, he sat down on the hot leather seat.

Ralph pulled out of the parking lot.

The deep blue sky was shining brightly, and puffy cottonball clouds were bouncing around overhead. But Numie wasn't noticing. His eyes were glued on the street in front of him.

The first thing he focused on was the weather-worn sign of the Dry Marquesas Hotel.

Regretful, unfulfilled, and somehow betrayed, Numie was in a dark mood. Something was welling within, but the message was unclear. It was like a shipwrecked sailor stuffing a call for help into a bottle and tossing it into the sea.

Could he really expect an answer?

Chapter Eleven

In the main hallway at Sacre Coeur, Anne was extending her hand. "You are persistent."

"That's how I got so far in the world," Numie said. "At least I'm in better shape than the last time I called."

An awful moment passed, then she said, "I understand jails are rough. Particularly the Tortuga jail." Somehow she had managed to throw off his attempt to give her guilt.

He decided to persevere. "I needed your help. I was desperate."

"I hardly know you," she answered, turning away. "Besides, Leonora calls the shots around here."

She opened the glass doors to the parlor. A gray smell of death was in the room. All the perfumed scents of Leonora were lingering in the corners.

"Think I'll have any luck with Leonora today?" he asked.

"I certainly do," Anne said, inspecting the dying leaf of a rubber plant. "She's in a much better mood——or was five minutes ago. With Leonora, one never knows." She twisted her fingers at her waist. "At least my husband was impressed with you."

He couldn't understand this sudden possessiveness in her voice when she spoke of Ralph.

"First, the watch," Anne continued. "Now calling Leonora from the factory to make an appointment for you." She paused, a wry smile on her face. "It's nice to know you're good at your work."

He knew better than to get angry now, so he just returned her smile. "That's the kindest thing you've ever said to me."

After the briefest possible glance, she led the way back to the patio. "Care to have a beer with me? It'll be a long wait. Leonora wants to punish you a bit."

"Sure," he said.

In the afternoon sun, Anne gleamed. Her hair was wet as if she'd just emerged from the pool before putting on her shorts and halter. The blouse, almost transparent, revealed her breasts, the brown nipples jutting through the material.

"About my work," he said, taking the beer from her. The

other night at the bar you made it clear what you think of my profession. Disgusting!"

Her cool hand reached out, but had no place to go——so it fell awkwardly by her side. "I shouldn't have said that. I can never keep my opinions to myself."

The very noise of her breathing suddenly drove him to attack. "I think it was a rotten thing to say, considering you've done a little whoring, too." He stood back, waiting for this accusation to hit her.

"*Whoring?*" Her voice was incredulous.

"That's what I said. Ralph told me you were Leonora's girl."

Miles of open country lay between them at this point. She seemed to draw some sort of reassurance from deep within before she spoke. "Oh, that," she said softly.

"Yes, *that.*" He was surprised at the sharpness in his own voice. Why was nailing Anne so important?

She slammed down her beer on the patio bar. Now, she was angry. "I owe you no confessions or explanations."

"You ripped into me, and I know why. You didn't want to be reminded of how you got your start."

"Damn you!" she said. Now her facade was melting. On the verge of tears, her face was contorted. Suddenly, she regained control. "Leonora wasn't my start." She wiped her brow. "This afternoon sun gets me down. In many ways," and now she was talking in just a faint whisper, "she was my end."

"I'm sorry," he blurted out. He'd touched some response within her with which he couldn't deal. "I shouldn't have brought it up." He focused on her mouth so he wouldn't have to look into her eyes. "I was hurt the other night——that's all. Just trying to strike back."

Anne's expression became thoughtful at that moment. "That son of a bitch I'm married to told you the truth for a change. I was her girl...sort of." Sipping her beer slowly, she said, "Now that you know that, I really have to explain."

Turning from her, Numie didn't want to hear it, even though he'd baited her. "You and Ralph always want to explain things."

His revelation had unleashed a damn of fury. "I don't intend to leave the impression I'm a lesbian. That's far from the truth." Sitting cross-legged in front of him, she added, "Quite the contrary as a matter of fact."

"I didn't think you were." He was growing impatient. "Christ, I know you can be somebody's girl without being a dyke. Let's say you had to survive and forget I even brought it up. After all, you're a married woman. I can see the ring on your finger." The statement was made in awkwardness. He regretted it instantly.

"Don't be sarcastic," she shot back. "That ring was put there by a far better man than Ralph Douglas will ever be." She settled back in her chair. "That was my first husband's ring. Nick." His name was said like a breath of fresh air. Then a frown crossed her face. Her voice was far away. "After he was killed in a car crash, I never took it off——and I don't intend to. *For any man.*"

The prospect of hearing her story alarmed him. "I didn't know you were married before."

"Not only married, but very much in love. If Nick had lived, I would never have gotten mixed up with all the sickies of the world."

"You must have been very young."

"Sixteen at the time."

"I assume this was up north."

"And how. Polish parents from the Bronx. 'Polacks', Nick's parents called us. Nick was an Italian from Brooklyn. 'Wop', my parents called him. We met, fell in love, got married——even though I was still in high school and our parents were totally against it. A real Romeo and Juliet."

"Your parents let you? You must have had to get married."

"I did." She said that proudly. "But I lost our baby. A miscarriage. We never had another one, and I really regret that." A radio beside her was playing music softly. Abruptly she flipped it off. "After Nick's death, I've regretted it more than ever."

"What kind of man was he?" Now he was genuinely interested.

She looked at him, as if she weren't certain if he should know. "The wildest, most exciting man I've ever known," she said impulsively. "A real striking guy." She sat up. "A black crewcut and large deep brown eyes." She smiled to herself. "Under his left eye was a little scar. A perfect V. He never told me how he got it." Her voice drifted.

All of a sudden, Numie was jealous. Jealous! He couldn't believe it. He'd never been jealous of anybody in his whole life.

Anne's vision seemed to falter for a moment, but then it came back in full force. "He was a big man——big boned and very handsome. He had large hands and one of the most beautiful mouths I've ever seen on a man. A deep, resonant voice. And he loved to drink beer. A pleasure we shared." She sipped from her own can. With her other hand she fanned her face. "When I lost him, I lost everything."

In the afternoon sun, Anne was getting drunk. The more she drank, the more she talked.

Eager now for whatever information he could pick up, Numie stopped drinking after the first beer. He lay silently, letting the sun burn his face. But somehow it felt good, cleansing. "How did you meet Leonora?"

"A girl friend of mine worked for her," Anne said, settling back. "Leonora always hired inexperienced models in those days. Said photographers gave them bad habits."

"Was this right after Nick died?"

"Not right away. When Nick died, I didn't do anything for the first few months. By then, I had no money and got a job as a clerk at Klein's." She sighed. "But that was nowhere. Then this girl got me an interview with Leonora. She had convinced me I could be a model."

Numie smiled to himself, remembering all the people who had promised to help him become a model. "For a little girl from the Bronx, meeting Leonora must have been some show."

"It was. I can't forget the first time I saw her. I was scared to death. If she told me to jump out the window, I would have. I was ushered into this big office. French furniture, everything in chintz. Lilacs all over the place. Such a sweet odor I knew I was going to be sick. In the corner was a big head of Nefertiti."

"Who's that?"

"A queen of Egypt, can you believe it? I didn't know who Nefertiti was either at the time, but I soon found out. Even though she doesn't have the nose for it, Leonora thinks she's a reincarnation." Anne was squirming in her chair, restless as a young deer. Her eyes were bright and mischievous now. They almost hid the fact she was drunk.

Numie was finding some vicarious thrill in hearing about the job interview. It was a foreshadowing of what he was about to face. "Did you get the job?" he asked when she didn't say anything for a while.

"Yes, but I never did any real modeling. I know now Leonora just used the job as an excuse to make me."

"With your figure, I think you'd make a terrific model."

"Thanks, but it didn't work that way. My figure was much too round for a high-fashion model."

"You at least tried, didn't you?"

"Briefly. Leonora always worked with the photographer. She was like a choreographer——wanted me to feel free and relaxed, the natural look. I was a wooden Indian. Completely under her control. She was hypnotic, really."

He was like a voyeur today, but he really wanted to know. That led him to ask hesitantly, "Going from Nick to Leonora must have been quite a jump."

At first Anne didn't say anything. Then she replied, "It was. I couldn't have gone with another man then. With Leonora, it wasn't anything like with Nick. Boring, actually. I didn't like it, but then again I didn't know how to say no. I was so naive."

"Sounds like you were lost more than anything else."

Her hand ran down her thigh. It was wet and hot. "It was soon clear I wasn't going to make it as a model. So Leonora opened up this bedtime shop for me. The offers I got running that place you wouldn't believe."

"I, of all people, would believe them."

Suddenly, Anne got up, stretching in the sun. "Looks like Leonora is going to make you wait all afternoon. Not me. I'm going to sleep——I feel dizzy. She'll send for you when she wants you." Anne headed across the patio toward the parlor.

"Anne," he called, jumping up.

She turned to look back. Squinting her eyes in the glare, she said, "Whatever it is, it'll keep till tomorrow." Then she was gone.

What did he want to ask her? He didn't really know. Yet he'd called her name. Too much sun. Maybe he'd better wait in the shadows for Leonora to summon him.

Alone in the patio, Numie was growing languid in the late of the hot day. Another beer from the refrigerator, and he was sinking into his chair, sipping slowly. A stirring of the wind woke up a giant elephant-eared philodendron.

It was good to be alive. In spite of his trouble, he hadn't felt as hopeful in months.

If he were back home now, he would just hear his mama say, "Son, your sap is rising. A bad time. You could get into a heap of trouble. I'll pray to Jesus."

But he was in Tortuga, a long way from home. Nobody spoke of sap rising any more.

Another sip and his eyes were closing, dreaming.

So Anne had her Nick. Well, he'd had someone, too. At least for a little while. That day on the deserted island with Ralph, he'd mentioned but didn't tell about his second love, his real one. The thing with Marty never came off. With Lisa, it did.

Lisa, the little beatnik girl who was a beatnik before anyone knew what that was.

She had picked him up in her van one night when he was hitching. He remembered it so well. She'd just sensed what he was feeling without telling her anything. She also seemed to care, and he was a complete stranger.

When she found out he had no place to live, she invited him home with her. Home was two hundred miles away in a rickety farmhouse in upper New York state where she stayed with four other people, including an old woman known only as Grandma.

In her early seventies, Grandma physically was nothing but creases and furrows. But her spirit was much alive. She lived for just two things: bowls of Campbell's soup which she devoured and her "weed" which she smoked until she faded into a coma every evening.

Grandma welcomed Numie right away. "The more the merrier," she said. Then she confided, "You kids think you discovered marijuana. Shit, my old man turned me on to it back in 1914. Been going up in smoke ever since."

After putting her to bed, Lisa told Numie: "Grandma owns all this land. Lets us live here. We raise chickens, pigs, and goats. Two of us are vegetarians, but most of us are meat eaters."

Then she took him to a tiny room where twin girls were sleeping. "They're mine," she said proudly. "Phyllis and

Dell."

"Pretty as can be," Numie said. "Who's the daddy?"

"I don't know," Lisa said matter-of-factly. "It really doesn't matter. We don't have daddies and mamas here. Anybody who loves can be a daddy or mama. Kids should learn to accept love from everybody."

"Accept, but not always expect," Numie said.

"That's too cynical. Love must start somewhere, and on this farm we believe in spreading it around."

The other members of the farm crew included Bob and Spence, two young dudes from New York City. They shared a room upstairs——and they were very much in love. Both had run away from home. Spence's parents were very wealthy, and they objected to his having a black lover. Not a male lover——but a black one.

Maria also lived there. She was from the city, too, but she had no one. Her face was badly cut in a knife fight in the South Bronx. She stayed in her room most of the time.

In her embroidery-covered blue jeans and Indian moccasins, Lisa was a charmer. Not pretty, but appealing in her simple outlook and openness to life.

"You're in deep trouble," she said to Numie. "Very unhappy. Stay with us. We want to help you. To give you love."

By the hand, she led him to a room with straw mats on the floor. A Chinese lantern cast a dim light.

"Numie," she said softly before reaching out.

Not thinking, not guarded, he just responded to her warmth. Never before had he held anyone like Lisa. Her tiny figure, her long red hair, the smell of her flesh, her gentleness——all of her inspired him. His fingers traced a line down the contour of her bony back. In return, she kissed his eyelids.

He pulled her close, burying his mouth in her neck. Her lips soft and sweet loved him back, tasting his ear as he tasted her.

Then the calmness was over. Plunging his tongue in her mouth, he demanded more. She was eager to give. Inside her, he was in command, riding and taking. His hands found her breasts, large for her body and tipped by big brown nipples. Skin meeting skin, fondling and smothering——never such femininity and smoothness. A crescendo of sensation, and it was over.

Too soon.

He'd made love to a woman-child. No one had ever given of herself so freely to him. Nor had he ever returned love in such a way. Nothing held back, everything delivered. He lay on top of her, moaning softly, completely drained.

Completely in love.

The next day Numie joined the other commune dwellers. Spence liked to plow in the fields, but Bob preferred house work. Numie joined Spence. Distrustful of strangers, Maria finally had dinner with them on Numie's second night.

In three days Lisa's twin girls were calling him daddy. He liked the sound of the word.

Returning from the garden, Numie found Lisa in the kitchen making bread from carob flour. The smell of coffee filled the air.

"A few days in the country air, and you've gotten rid of that pasty New York City look. You look like a man should. A little color in your face."

"Thanks," he said, moving to kiss her.

She gave herself to him right in front of the twins.

"You'll burn the bacon," he said, breaking away.

"I read the other day that bacon's probably the worst thing you can eat," she replied. "It's just as well."

May stretched into June, one day going by much like another.

Numie was never bored, though. Or never too tired to make love to Lisa.

Summer quietly appeared, the yellow of forsythia giving way to the bright red of roses. The leaves on the chestnut tree in front of the farmhouse turned from lime to dark green.

As hot weather came, the tree no longer shaded Grandma. She spent more time in her bed and less in her favorite rocker.

August was a little windy, but the trips with the twins into the hills were still long and leisurely. Lisa always packed a picnic lunch. Goat bells and sundowns——the month came and went so quickly.

September brought a chillness to the air. It began around four o'clock in the afternoon. By eight the nights were growing cold. Lisa, though, was still warm.

She was by now deep into vegetables. No more animals were

to be slain, not even a chicken.

One day in early autumn, Numie was overcome with a passionate desire for a hamburger. He headed for a roadhouse run by a heavyset man from Cleveland. Devouring the juicy hamburger, Numie ordered another, this time with a lot of onion to disguise the taste of meat on his breath.

Back at the farm, something was different. A new van was parked in front, with an Oregon license plate. The twins were playing.

Picking Dell up, he asked, "Whose van is that?"

"It belongs to daddy," she said. "He's back."

A chill came over Numie. "What do you mean? I'm your daddy."

"No, our *real* daddy," Phyllis said defiantly.

Putting Dell down, Numie headed for the living room. Empty. Then the sounds, those unmistakable sounds, coming from the bedroom upstairs.

On the bed, *their* bed, Lisa's long swan neck was bobbing up and down on the cock of a handsome giant of a man, with long blond hair and blue eyes. He was like a bigger version of Numie, his body radiating power and masculinity.

Sensing Numie's presence, Lisa looked up. "*Numie.*" The sound of his name was like an accusation. "Paul and I are busy now," she finally managed to say.

"Who in the fuck is Paul?" Numie asked.

"He's my loving man," she said, her eyes filling with fear.

"Can't you hear?" Paul asked, rising up on his elbows. "The lady said we're busy. By the way, thanks for looking after my chick this summer while I was up in Oregon finding us a farm."

Dumbfounded, Numie stood and stared.

"Now if you'll pardon us, we've got some business to finish," Paul said. "Or do you get turned on watching a big dick get sucked? Bob told me when I asked about you that you're a queer hustler. If you want me, you'll have to wait till Lisa's had her fill."

Fists clenched, Numie turned and walked rapidly down the stairs, through the living room, and out onto the front porch where the twins were playing. He paused silently. Phyllis and Dell looked up at him, but he ignored their stares. In a nervous stride, he crossed the yard, heading down the path.

"Numie," Lisa called, chasing after him. She was wearing panties but no cover for her breasts. "I can't help it." Catching up with him, she clutched his arm. "Please try to understand. I love Paul. He's not like the rest of us here. Not loving and kind. More selfish. But I just love him. Always have. I thought he was gone for good, so I never mentioned him. It hurt too much to talk about it. But he's come back. Plans to take me and the girls to Oregon with him. I've always wanted to see Oregon. It's supposed to be so nice there. And they are his girls, too."

Numie looked at her long and hard, then touched her hand, removing it gently from his arm. "Good-bye, Lisa," he said softly. "Summer's over."

"Numie," she called out again to his neck.

But he didn't look back——not at Lisa, not at the twins, not at anyone. His eyes were fixed on the open road ahead.

"NUMIE," the falsetto voice of Leonora called out across the patio. "You're late, as usual!"

Chapter Twelve

His hand on the doorknob, Numie hesitated, then entered an upstairs room.

"Watch the stairs," Leonora called. It wasn't just the stairs that made her issue the warning. It was a way she had of calling attention to her presence.

Going down three steps, he was in a semi-darkened sunken chamber. The shutters were closed at the windows, and the room was badly ventilated, like attics on a summer day. On the table in the center lay Leonora. A short, fat woman was leaning over her. Against the wall a steam cabinet stood——with other machines. Rows and rows of bottles lined the shelves of this beauty parlor.

"So, you decided to apologize for your outrageous behavior?" Leonora said imperiously. She was not really trying to add to his discomfort, but wanted to remove all guilt from her shoulders.

Numie was so taken back he didn't know what to reply at first. His body tightened, then he said, "Is that what Ralph told you?" He sighed, not expecting her to answer. "Yes, I'm sorry," he managed to mutter softly. Then in a slightly louder voice, he asked, "Let's forget it, okay?"

"Come closer, young man," Leonora said. Youth filled her with gnawing despair, and she was constantly calling attention to it.

"Tangerine," Numie said, surprised, making out the outlines of her features for the first time. "I didn't recognize you."

"Please, darling," Leonora interrupted, slightly peevish that he was looking at Tangerine and not at her. "Don't interfere with Tangerine's work."

"I was just speaking to her——that's all," Numie said, this time not bothering to disguise his anger. "Why is it so dark in here?"

"I keep the room dark," said Leonora. "*I must.*" This excuse didn't seem quite plausible, so she covered her eyes with one hand. "Light destroys my eyes."

Moving toward her on the pile carpet, he saw Leonora more clearly now. She lay stark naked on her back, skin gleaming.

Tangerine was rubbing an oily solution into her legs.

Leaning over the body, Tangerine presented her cheek to Numie to kiss. "Sorry I conked out last night."

Leonora resented this display of intimacy over her body. "Numie," she said sharply, "Tangerine shouldn't drink that cheap wine. See that she doesn't. It's wretched for her skin." She smiled. "When I take her out, I give her champagne."

"*I know*." He shifted his weight from one foot to the other. That was really rubbing it in!

Sensing his discomfort, and fearing she had gone too far, Leonora said, "Now, don't be bitter. I know you're finding it hard to forgive me for not bailing you out of jail. But I don't reward thievery."

"You did offer me one of those cigarettes," Numie protested.

The torrid heat was beginning to bother Leonora——that and the conversation. "It really doesn't concern me now. You must expect to pay the penalties in life." With that, she planned to dismiss the subject for all time.

Protected by the near darkness, he could stare freely at her nudity. Her breasts were surprisingly firm. Amazing for a woman of her age. And she had no pubic hair. It was all shaved off!

Leonora was clearly aware of what he was doing. In fact, she was enjoying it. To add to that enjoyment, she decided to signal his attention. "So," she said, indicating surprise, "you're a voyeur!"

"I'm sorry," he stammered, stepping back. "Why don't I come back——when you're dressed?"

"Don't be foolish, *mon cheri*." Taking hold of his hand in a convulsive grasp, she held it to her breast. It had been a long time since she let a man put a hand on her breast. It was not erotic or stimulating in any way. What was, was the pride in knowing that her breasts were still quite firm. "We're all voyeurs. In one way or another." Slowly she released his hand.

Although he'd been used to seeing people nude all his life, he'd never felt like such an intruder before as he did in front of Leonora. It was like interviewing the president of the United States when he was on the toilet. "About the job..." he said.

"Oh, yes," she answered, miffed that he didn't comment

upon the texture of her breasts. "You're desperately in need of work." Her neck had started to ache. "Actually, I don't have a job for you."

"But you need a chauffeur," he pointed out. "And I'm an excellent driver."

"As I said, I don't have a job for you." She assumed a casual tone of voice. "But Ralph claimed you were starving. Frankly, I feel sorry for you, knowing how difficult it must be to find work in *your* line." She never hired a man without making him feel it was an act of supreme charity on her part.

"Will you give me a job?" he asked, more eager than ever for a commitment from her.

"All right, all right, darling," she said impatiently. She was the one who should be applying the pressure. Numie would have to be taught manners. "Don't bore me with details. That's what I pay Ralph for."

"But he said you had to okay it."

Numie was right. But she couldn't let him get away with it. Reaching for a large shimmering handkerchief, she gingerly dabbed at her perspiration-laden brow. "*Everybody* depends on me for *everything*."

A kind of fury rose inside Numie. Leonora had the power to humiliate totally. He hated her at this moment——hated his coming to her.

She searched for his face in the darkness, but couldn't see. The Numies of the world could never understand her——never understand that she must live her life like that of a great actress, filled with glamour and impulse. She couldn't confine herself to hours or time schedules. At any time of the day or night, he'd have to be at her beck and call if he agreed to be her driver. Best she inform him, "My heart never knows from moment to moment where I'll need to take it. Sometimes, late at night, I just like to ride around the island——deep in meditation."

"That's okay with me," he said, though he didn't mean it. Her presence seemed gargantuan. It wasn't that she was tall. More than that. In the shadows, she loomed like a giant, majestic bird descended from another planet. Compared to her, he just disappeared. Never so unimportant and insignificant.

"*I run my world*," she said, rising slightly from the table on the power of her own voice. She wasn't thinking of him now, but of the vicious attacks made upon her in this town. Numie would soon hear the lies spread about her, if he hadn't already. She was certain Ralph had fed him plenty of information. But she had to let Numie know she didn't care what people said about her, as long as she remained true to herself. "I have tremendous self-discipline," she said, "and I demand the same of my employees. I'm driven by an unrelenting passion for quality, and that, too, I demand of all those who work for me."

Numie felt he was floating in slime-green still water on this torpid afternoon. Always in pursuit of the point, he asked, "What will this all-consuming job pay?"

Aghast at his impertinence, she decided to penalize him severely by lowering his salary from what she had considered. "Sixty-five dollars a week," she said emphatically.

The statement was a blow to him. "I've made that in one hour before," he protested.

"Not lately, I presume." She never liked to attack anyone on the subject of age, because she felt too vulnerable. But it was always her final recourse.

Properly insulted, he bit his lip and decided to take another approach. "I can't live on that."

"Tangerine makes only fifty dollars a week," Leonora volunteered. Was Numie too stupid to see that she wasn't the state dispensing welfare? "Of course, there are fringe benefits," she added, fearing he'd turn her down. Then she realized she could not promise too much. She'd present the fringe benefits in negative terms. "I'm sure you'll sponge all your booze off me——not to mention marijuana! You'll probably take all your meals here. There are plenty of bedrooms."

"I need some clothes every now and then...something," he said, feeling his appeal for higher wages hopeless at this point.

"There's nothing to buy on this island. Certainly no clothes——other than my gowns." She sat up briefly, staring hard into the near darkness. "And I assume that's not your scene." Actually, she couldn't be sure. Everybody was dressing up in drag these days. "Further, if you're ambitious, you'll rise within the ranks. Tangerine was just a maid when I came here. Now she's my personal masseuse." She said that as if Tangerine held the highest position in court.

Slowly he walked the room. The air was growing heavier. It smelled of strange solutions——like a chemical factory.

With Tangerine massaging her breasts, Leonora went on, "You'll have to be my bodyguard as well. The town is filled with Peeping Toms looking for life. They roam the island at night. Having no life of their own, they must depend for their thrills on seeing somebody who does."

Was she serious? He decided to assume for the moment she was. "Well, Leonora, you set yourself up for that. Everywhere you go, you make it your own stage. You open the curtain, and you perform. Naturally, the natives show an interest."

Was he insulting her? "But I want to keep my audience at a distance," she protested. "That's why I had to put a huge gate and a high fence around Sacre-Coeur."

Tangerine was applying pressure on those aching neck muscles. "They know *I'm* here, and the hungry bastards want to get close to *me*. Just to touch me——that would delight them to no end."

Realizing that he had touched her and hadn't responded properly, he said, "You're an amazing woman, and people sense that. I did the first night I met you."

"Thank you," Leonora said. "Better yet, I should compliment your judgment."

Hoping for an advantage, he said, "If I'm to be your bodyguard, too, it'll cost you seventy-five dollars a week."

"Very well," she replied, amazed at how cheaply he could be bought. "But with that kind of salary, you'll be limited to three drinks and two beers a day at the patio bar."

"It's a deal." In some way, his acceptance seemed like a sentence instead of a victory. "When do I begin?"

"Consider yourself employed as of this moment." Her voice seemed to reverberate through the beauty chamber.

"You've already had your quota of two beers for the day. I peeked through the window at you and Anne." That must have surprised him, she thought. It'll show him who's in charge. "However, before midnight you're entitled to three drinks. The drinks can consist of not more than two shots a glass, and you have to use the ordinary brand of Scotch."

"Thanks a lot." Leonora certainly knew how to put a servant in his place.

Leonora hesitated. She was on the verge of a command——a tasteless, vulgar command. But so secure was she as a lady she knew she could give the order and not sacrifice dignity. "Now, Tangerine, *the ultimate massage.*"

Tangerine paused awkwardly, her hand at her throat. She looked at Numie.

He was horrified and filled with loathing for Leonora. "Isn't it about time I left?" he asked pointedly.

"My darling," Leonora said mockingly, "you're bashful. A professional, bashful? How quaint!" A very cross look consumed Leonora's face. "No, you're going to stay here and watch. I loathe insincere embarrassment." She slammed her fists down on the board.

Numie didn't know what to do. He was desperately unhappy.

"Leonora, honey," Tangerine said, "this awful headache's bothering me. I just can't get rid of it."

"Excuses bore me," said Leonora. She knew she was coming on as a monster, but some demonic energy was in control, forcing her on and on. She couldn't give in to reason. She'd have to pursue her command to its finish.

"I'm not really making excuses," Tangerine said, "but I don't feel well today."

"You're making these complaints because Numie is here," Leonora said. "I know you too well." Leonora was an autumnal beauty, that she knew. But a beauty, nevertheless. It seemed altogether appropriate to her that some homage should be paid. After all, her life began practically at the beginning of this century, and she should have faded long ago. It wasn't sex she wanted, it was worship and tribute to her endurance. Deciding to press her case stronger, she said, "I hope I don't have to remind you how hard it would be for a sixty-five-year-old alcoholic to find work in Tortuga."

At this point Numie wanted to grab Tangerine's arm and force her from the room. Let them take their chances somewhere else, regardless of the odds. But he stood motionless, paralyzed by the magnetism of Leonora.

"I'm grateful and everything for the job," Tangerine stammered. "Really I am. Just this once, though, I don't want to do it. Tomorrow I'll be fine, I just know it."

"Let her off," Numie said.

Leonora sat up. She wasn't used to being challenged. "Keep quiet!" she demanded. "You have just started to work for me. Lesson number one is to carry out my orders without question."

Numie relaxed. "Okay," he muttered. He felt different somehow. After all, this was a ritual that had been enacted between the two of them many times before. Maybe they both needed it. He'd seen worse things in life. If their scene called for an audience, he'd be the unwilling participant.

"As for you, Tangerine," Leonora said lying back down again, "you either do the work I hire you for——or go see Anne about getting your final paycheck." Her facial muscles relaxed now. After an initial flare-up of rebellion, both of her servants had succumbed.

Tangerine's face collapsed, then she braced herself. Resigned to her task, she slowly moved her fingers between Leonora's thighs.

Her breath heavy now, Leonora was holding Tangerine's wrist in a tight embrace of fingers.

Numie turned away, but could not blot the sound. It seemed to last forever. He thought of other things. Sailing out on the sea, the air, clear and fresh. How Tortuga looked at daybreak when the sun just seemed to rise right out of the sea.

Without a climax, Leonora pulled Tangerine's hand away. Tangerine straightened up and reached for a lavender satin robe. She gently placed it over Leonora's body. Then she slowly made her way to the bathroom.

"That sure is some robe," Numie said. "It's real pretty."

Leonora was acutely embarrassed. She had wanted to embarrass Numie instead, and let him know who was completely in charge at Sacre Coeur. But at this moment she was all too aware of what he must be thinking of her. She had to shift attention away from what had happened. Seize upon anything. What had he said? Her robe was really pretty. That was it! "Don't ever use the word 'pretty' with me," she said. "I like things ugly or beautiful——never 'pretty'."

"Christ," Numie said, irritated to the point of leaving. "I can't say anything right. You're a designer, and I thought your robe was pretty. Surely there's nothing wrong with that. I like the color."

"At least you appreciate color," she said, sitting up and wrapping the robe around her. "Before I entered haute couture, everything was blue, grey, brown, or black. I introduced sunflower yellow, raspberry pink, lime green, carnation red. I revolutionized the industry." Slowly she raised herself from the table, slipping her arms into the sleeves of her robe. "A good massage is imperative for a healthy body. And as you seen, my body is *very* healthy."

"It's a very beautiful body," Numie said, wincing slightly. "I could only envy Tangerine." There, he felt better for having said this obvious lie. He was back playing the role of whore again——the only part he knew.

She looked up at him. At first she was tempted to thank him, but that might indicate she was susceptible to flattery. Instead, she answered, "I know."

Leonora represented everything he hated. Yet he was strangely attracted to her. Did he secretly want her? Not for her body, not for sex certainly, but for some quality of life she had. She was somebody, and he was nobody.

Life had allowed her to be herself; and he hadn't been given the chance. She flaunted her achievements, making him more and more aware of his lack of them.

She was fucking the world, and doing it out in the open——in broad daylight, regardless of who was looking on.

Leonora walked over and stood before a full-length mirror, opening her robe to expose her nudity. "Whenever I designed for a woman, I always had her come before me, pull off her clothes——and just stand there."

Leonora was carefully programmed. Every gesture——the waving of her manicured nail, the turning of her lacquered head——was choreographed to suggest spontaneity. Yet the overall effect was rehearsed.

Hands on her body, Leonora continued, "Each creature is unique. I allowed the natural contours of the body to inspire me." She glared defiantly in the mirror, challenging it. Then her face assumed a Sphinx-like charm. "Sometimes I learned——sadly——that women didn't really know who they were."

At this point Leonora seemed suspended in her self-created

space. Numie's rays were bouncing all around her——but not penetrating, not reaching her core.

"I always had a solution for women like that," she said finally. "I told them to go home, stand nude in front of the mirror, just like I'm doing now——for days at a time if necessary and get acquainted with themselves. Then come back to my salon when they figured out who they were."

Leonora was now swimming in her own firmament. The glow from her was a greenish patina, as she slowly moved her ringed hands up and down her body.

"I could never dress anybody who didn't possess self-knowledge. I don't believe in attiring manikins——rather, real people. People with flesh and spirit. Once a woman realized what her personality was, then I could sharpen and define it. But I couldn't create it." Leonora was hypnotized by her own reflection.

Her sudden spell allowed Numie to observe the salon more. It was a real vamp's chamber——complete with white satin curtains, a white fur rug, and tasseled mirrors. Lots of satin pillows and assorted bric-a-brac. Overhead was a crystal chandelier.

"What do you think of my room?" she asked, as if suddenly aware of him.

"A little campy."

"Campy! You don't understand what's fashionable. I've always known——even when people denounced my work as historic."

"I'm sure that true quality never goes out of style."

"The most sophisticated thing I've ever heard you say. Do you know dresses I designed in the thirties are being sold in New York, Paris and London? Right today! I'm having an amazing renaissance. And people said I was through."

She was completely intoxicated by herself. Narcissism on a cosmic level. Crawling into her past, she found the true thread of her life in the re-emergence of her former self. She was no longer real——rather, impersonating herself.

"What a glorious comeback it's going to be for me" she said breathlessly. "The tangos will return. Dancing cheek-to-cheek. Can you imagine? We have nearly survived the fifties, darling. The bobby socks phase is over. There's hope for mankind yet."

An eerie feeling hung over the room. It seemed to have been preserved under glass from another time. On her dressing table stood crystal powder boxes, long cigarette holders in the colors of the rainbow, and a glittering array of perfume sprayers in mother-of-pearl. Silk lingerie, blouses, hats, handbags, shoes, negligees——enough clothes for thirty well-dressed women.

Leonora followed his eye. "Surprised you, didn't I?"

"What do you mean?"

"My heretical departure in lingerie. I've always refused to wear pink, black, beige, or white. I demanded everything close to my body to be made in burnt sienna. I'm sure Queen Nefertiti must have preferred the same. This so-called bizarre color in underwear shocked the world. But it was copied. The constant bore of being imitated, yet I know it's my destiny."

Her performance was illusory, and now it was time for relief. Leonora instinctively knew that for her whirring ascension to linger in Numie's mind, she'd have to fade. To return to earth, she'd have to go it alone. Nothing remained except a plausible dismissal.

"I'm going into my sauna now," she said on cue. "Let Anne know where I can reach you at all times. Good day." Clutching her robe around her naked body, she disappeared through a curtain.

Tangerine was back in the room.

Numie stared at her for a moment, started to say something, but thought better of it.

She looked sheepishly at him, then wiped beads of sweat from her face. Going over to a large French window, she threw open the black velvet draperies, letting daylight pour through. At the window, she said, "I've been about to suffocate all afternoon. This vamp stuff's not for me."

"Why do you do it?" he asked.

"Do what, dumpling?"

"Let her humiliate you like that?" he asked.

"She's my friend," Tangerine answered defensively.

"Is she?" he asked in a sharp voice. "Really?"

"My, what a lot of questions you got. I ain't had much sleep. Woke up in the middle of the night with a splitting headache. So, let's not be getting philosophical."

"Okay," he said.

"I guess I need her," she said, like a little girl lost. "She needs me, too. Other people don't understand her. But I do. She don't want to be mean. But she's afraid——like the rest of us. Of growing old. Of losing her looks. Of life. Just like us."

He walked over and put his hands on her flabby cheeks. Then he stared into the warm fire of her eyes. "I'm not knocking what you do to survive. I've done that and more. I still do."

Her eyes twinkled. "I just feel bad you had to watch. I'm ashamed to do that——especially in front of you."

"We'll forget it," he said. "How long have you known Leonora?"

"Twelve years," she said. "Leonora just arrived one day——after being gone from Tortuga for ages——and took back her house. I was working as a maid for Ruthie Elvina. She's the tightest bitch on this island. Ruthie Elvina was paying me twenty-five bucks a week, and Leonora advertised for a maid at fifty. So I took her up. She'd brought Anne and Ralph down with her." Tangerine paused a second, then went on. "I know I don't know a lot. There's a lot of things I can't talk with her about. Important things. But I listen. And with Leonora, listening is mighty important."

"She's damn lucky to have a friend like you," he said, smiling. "You're okay, Lady Blanchard. I like you."

"You'd better," she replied grinning. "Or else, I'll spank your butt." She walked back to the window——breaking a spell. "After one of those massage sessions with Leonora, I've got to have a shot of only one thing——corn liquor."

"You can't take Georgia out of the girl," he said.

"Hell no," she said. "I grew up on bootleg liquor, and I drink all this fancy bottled stuff, but it just never wets my whistle like a little moonshine. Let's go back to my place and drink some. My apartment's not fancy, you know, but I wouldn't trade it for all the Sacre-Coeurs in the world."

Chapter Thirteen

"What is this stuff?" Numie asked. "Rat's piss?"

In the middle of the living room, Tangerine paused as if she didn't hear correctly. Then she said, "This is just the best moonshine south of Georgia. Got it shipped down by my kin. What would you know about good moonshine anyway?"

"Had my first drink of it at the age of nine."

"Now who's gonna waste good moonshine on a kid of nine?" she asked.

"My Uncle Pete, that's who. A real bootlegger, pot belly and all." He downed another foul-tasting swig. "His two boys forced half a cup down me the first time I played with them. I vomited then, but it was better than the lumpy flour gravy Ora——that was Pete's wife——fed us kids."

"Lumpy flour gravy," Tangerine said reflectively, almost nostalgically. "We spoke of that before." She ran her hands up and down her body. "I wouldn't be so fat today if I hadn't slurped down so much of that stuff."

In the dim light of her apartment, her orange hair was like a fright wig. Her loose-fitting, tacky dress was the same strident color. Slowly she danced around, spreading the odor of cheap perfume across the room.

The naked light bulb, though dim, was cruel to the harsh canals of her face. In the corner a worn-out fan sputtered, but kept stirring up the stale hot air.

For a moment of isolated time, Tangerine was forgetting where she was. Rocking forth on her feet, she shook her fleshy body. "Yes, indeed," she said, "I remember the days when men liked a lady with a little meat on her bones."

"Many of them still do," he said. "I'm told a big ass on a woman turns on a lot of Cuban men. They're all over town."

"Yeah, but everyone I know wants a teen-age girl from the nunnery." She sighed. Taking a stiff shot of moonshine, she added, "It's not just being big. It's everything! I read in the paper the other day a checklist of no-nos for the Playboy Club. To be a bunny, you couldn't have wrinkled eyelids, sagging bosom, flabby underarms, bulging tummy, creepy neck, droopy derriere (I guess that means ass), and rippling thighs. I measured up perfectly to every no-no."

"You're not all that bad," he said, sorry for the way the conversation was going. Everybody seemed to be issuing a lament to old age. Even himself!

"Times were different once," she said. A slight smile crossed her mouth. She was obviously remembering one of those better moments.

"Tell me," he said, "I really want to know. When was Tangerine Blanchard getting it on in a big way?"

"World War II, man, when I used to ride the rails, the happiest time of my life." Her feet bare as a beggar's, her body sogged with liquor, she plopped down on her favorite sofa. "I was a bit ripe even then, but a lot of young men treated me like a real beauty." Her skin was an unnatural color, like pink angora. "I was every fighting boy's gin mama. I always had a drink in my bag for every soldier, sailor, or marine." Her breathing grew heavier. "A little loving, too, if he wanted it."

In the white clamshell dust of this unbearably hot afternoon, he was slightly nauseous at the idea of Tangerine's sex life. But he knew she wanted to share her former triumphs, and he'd have to listen. "You must have kept busy——all those horny guys away from home."

"I sure did," she said proudly. "Never met so many uncut virgins in my whole life. Christ, this country in the early forties turned out nothing but virgins, or so it seemed at the time." She brushed under her eye. Was it a tear? "But I loved them all, especially the virgins." Her voice softened. "I was real tender with them."

Tangerine was slipping back, he felt dangerously, throwing a veil over the past, making it sound better than it was. Perhaps that's why he asked pointedly, "Didn't you think you were being used?"

She sat up, one breast practically falling out. It was as if his question had never occurred to her.

He decided to press the point. "By guys who didn't care where they got their rocks off?" After he'd said that, it sounded unnecessarily cruel——and he hadn't meant it that way.

She fell back again, shaking hard like a woman in labor. "Honey, I wanted to be used." Reaching for her moonshine again, she had a voice more blurred than before. "It didn't matter what they had——a foot-long sausage or a three-inch piece of spaghetti. Just as long as they were in pants——that's all that mattered." Through sunken eyes, she looked over to him.

He smiled, knowing she wasn't telling the truth.

"Well," she said, "pants wasn't the reason. They had to want me. I never turned down a man." She paused. "Unless he was black, of course. God intended birds of a feather to flock together."

From where he was perched on the living room floor, Numie reached out and gently encircled her ankle. "Now don't you go letting your Georgia prejudice come out. After all, I'm related to black folks."

"What on earth do you mean?" Tangerine asked, not knowing whether to take him seriously.

"Remember that Uncle Pete I was telling you about? And Ora of the lumpy cream gravy? Ora told me she was Puerto Rican, but one of the farmers who lived nearby said, `Boy, your aunt's as Puerto Rican as a native of the Belgian Congo'."

Tangerine was relieved. "That don't make you colored."

He nodded. An awkward moment came. "Let me get another glass," he said, heading for the kitchen. "This peanut butter one's badly chipped."

In the kitchen mice were playing in moldy garbage. "Hell, Tangerine," he called.

She didn't respond.

At the door, he said. "Why don't you ever clean up this damn mess? You're breeding mice."

The heat of the room hung like gauze over her. "I've spent my whole life cleaning up after somebody else. I made a vow that in my own home, I'd be just as dirty as I wanted to."

"But the roaches will eat you alive."

Tangerine looked over to the window where bougainvillea was creeping in. She sighed wistfully, almost anticipating a breeze that never came. "Who's to say they don't have as much right to live as we do? They were on earth long before we came along."

He turned and went back to the kitchen. The mice darted under the sink. Picking up a dirty glass, he washed it thoroughly.

Back in the living room, Tangerine was getting drunk. The

moonshine was powerful stuff. In the hot air, she was puffing like an old bulldog. Folding the material of her dress, then adjusting it, she asked, "Do you think this dress looks good on me?"

He flung her a glance, almost a wild appeal for her not to seek compliments. Leonora had demanded enough to last the day. "It matches your hair perfect."

"Leonora hates the way I dress. I guess what I wear is the only way I have of defying her. But I'm grateful and all. If it wasn't for Leonora, I'd still be a maid."

"I think she reminded us of that just this afternoon." He poured more moonshine from a Mason canning jar. The liquor was tasting better the more he drank. Maybe moonshine was an acquired taste.

The air, so impure and unendurable, seemed to be leading Tangerine into meditation. "Yep," she said, "I'm her personal masseuse now, but until that promotion I was a maid most of my life. Ever since the depression."

"That shatters my illusion," he said jokingly. "I thought you were the madame of an elegant bordello...at least."

"I wish it was true," she said. "No, I'm just a damn scrubwoman. Daddy got me going. He couldn't feed me, so he hired me out. I worked as a maid to anybody who was rich."

"Well, you're still with a richie."

"Leonora's a real richie. When I got my start, a family making twenty-five dollars a week was 'rich'. You could imagine what my wages were."

"I couldn't, but I know what it is now. Fifty dollars a week."

"I couldn't even save up enough money for a pair of high heels. I've always loved high heels. They make me feel so thin."

A fly buzzed the room. An echo of the past drifted across. He sat up, jerking his shoulder. My God, he thought. It was the remark about high heels that did it. Tangerine was a white version of Louise, his long-ago black mama. Louise used to endorse high heels for the same reason. "You lived through the last of the Old South, didn't you?"

"Sure did. I can still see myself, trudging along some dirt road somewhere, with my old cardboard suitcase held together by a piece of rope. No money, nothing——just two or three feedsack dresses and the name of some dumb ass farmer who wanted slave labor in exchange for a roof over my head and something to eat."

"I guess you were lucky back then just to have something to eat."

"I didn't get much," she said sadly, "although you wouldn't know it to look at me now. Sometimes the families I worked for wouldn't let me eat at the same table with them. Made me eat in the kitchen or else out on the back porch with the coloreds."

"Mama and I always had collard greens. Sometimes we never had anything else, but she'd always manage to stir up collards." He was enjoying this moment of camaraderie with Tangerine, revelling in their communal bond, like part of the same family.

"Fern Cornelia, as they called me back then, never got near the pork chops, though. Sometimes I'd go over the bones after the folks had finished with them. But no one ever left much meat on the bones in those days."

"I've had to eat other people's leftovers. In New York I used to go into restaurants and sit down at tables after diners had gotten up. People were always leaving lots of food on their plates, and I'd finish a few off when I was real hungry——which was a lot of the time."

"Wasn't you chased out?" she asked.

"Plenty of times, but I kept alive."

A sound was heard against the screen door. Tangerine jumped up, waddle-assing across the floor. The wooden boards creaked. Opening the door, she grabbed up the afternoon paper. "I want to show you something," she said. "It's on the editorial page." Through bleary eyes, she thumbed through the paper. "I always know where to find him, even without my glasses on. *There*."

He glanced at a column with a caricature belonging to one Mike Morgan.

"Little Mike," she said. "He really made it big. A big-time newspaper columnist."

He could smell her stale breath. Backing away slightly, he said, "Never heard of him."

"You never heard of Mike Morgan?" Her surprise was

genuine. "I thought everybody who knows how to read has heard of Mike Morgan. You can read, can't you?"

"Sure, I can."

"He was the son of the nicest family I ever worked for. Good folks up in Tallahassee. His daddy was a college professor——mathematics, I think. Always wore a straw hat. His wife was real smart, too. Had a college degree. I'd never met a woman with a college degree in those days. She was sickly, though. Stayed in her room most of the day reading Charles Dickens."

"So one family was good to you?"

"Only one. But it's little Mike I remember the most. I guess I taught him what to do with that little pecker between his legs."

"Child molester." Though he said that for humor, he noticed that Tangerine seemed offended.

So taken back was she, she forgot what she was saying. She chose not to comment on that. "He was mighty grateful to me at the time. Wanted to feel my big jugs. Said he loved me. Yes, indeed, he became a real important man." She seemed to be crying.

"If they were so good to you, why did you leave?"

"They fell on bad days and couldn't afford to keep me," she said.

"What became of you?"

"I worked my way south. After the war, I was a maid in some of the finest hotels on Miami Beach. Real good tips, too. Of course, I drank it up or else spent it on some man."

"I never kept a penny I ever made either."

"I thought I'd always be young," she said. "I couldn't believe I'd ever turn forty. Other people, maybe. But not Tangerine Blanchard. I was no longer known as Fern Cornelia."

"Not me," he said. "By the time I was twenty-five, I knew forty was on the way. I know it now for sure. You're supposed to make it by the time you're forty. If that's so, I'd better get busy."

"How many of us make it? When we're young, we all think we're going to be rich one day. Never met a southerner yet who didn't think he was going to be filthy rich."

"Come to think of it," he said, "neither have I."

She was still standing in the middle of the floor, shifting her weight from one foot to the other. "What a silly fool I was——scrubbing shit off other people's toilets, just like your own mama, and dreaming about some rich man in a big car coming along to sweep me off my feet and take me away with him to a big southern plantation with big pillars out front." She brushed the hot air with her flabby hand. "Me, just standing around fanning myself all day long and looking pretty for him."

This was such a farfetched fantasy he felt compelled to match it with one of his own. "I've had my dream, too. Of wanting to meet some rich lady, real good looking, who'd be so turned on by me she'd want me to come and live with her. A nice lady who'd peel oranges for me and massage my feet and let me lie around all day——doing nothing but make love to her."

"You still have a chance," she said sadly. "I don't." Her eyes were glassy.

"You mean you think I'll find my rich lady?"

"You'll find her," she said. "Only it won't be just exactly like you dreamed up."

What did she mean by that?

The fan sputtered, then began a dance of death before petering out. The air was still, broken finally by the sound of mice in the kitchen.

The afternoon was slowly fading.

Chapter Fourteen

It was an hour before the sun would sink into the Gulf of Mexico. Gulls wheeled in the wind; and herons washed their naked legs and three-toed feet at the edge of the sea.

Taking off all his clothes, Numie plunged into the water. It was warm and soothing to his tired, overheated body.

Back on the cream-white shore, he surveyed the skeletons of two high-rise condominiums——the dream of some entrepreneur who hadn't reckoned with Tortuga's resistance to change. With their blank, gaping windows, the unfinished buildings overlooked a tangle of mangrove.

A sign read, Rentals by Theodore M. Albury. Immediate Occupancy.

On his return, before he crossed the dividing line of Pearl Street, he passed once more the ghostly balconied and porticoed houses of the monied class. Their Victorian towers were sentinels against the night, their wide verandas entwined with bougainvillea.

Numie imagined a green shutter closing quickly as he hurried by, but maybe it was the wind. The faint breezes of evening had started to blow in from the sea.

Suddenly, he stopped. From one of the windows of a gray, wooden-framed house, a skinny arm lolled lopsidedly. Perfectly innocent perhaps, but in this unfamiliar setting everything was mysterious. Was it a boy? Dead? Numie continued on his way.

Instead of taking the familiar route, he impulsively cut down one of the alleys. It was overgrown and forbidding, but it led to light. At the end of the jungle, he emerged into the graveyard of Tortuga.

Without walls, it was a field of tombs built above ground. Long-faded plastic flowers and wreaths adorned many of the mausoleums, some with Grecian pillars and highly ornate, though rusty, wrought-iron fences, and gates. Cracked and broken, the tombs of the poorer folk ominously were like brick ovens. Moss covered everything like fungus.

Wandering aimlessly down the paths, Numie stopped in front of the most elaborately adorned mausoleum. Signs of workmen lay on the ground——empty bags of cement and a wooden trough. Someone had just died.

Symbols of death were rampant. Cherubic angels brooded over the neoclassic monument; and two weeping Niobes in Grecian gowns flanked the entrance. Gothic, lacelike spires rose from the roof, and the fence was surmounted by gargoyles and leafy finials.

Under a lyre in the center were these words:

LEONORA DE LA MER
born, Tortuga, September 13, 1895
died, Tortuga, September 13, 19___

The last two numbers were blank.

Underneath, this brief inscription:

Celebrated international beauty and world's leading couturier.

A ringing of bells brought Numie out of his shock. A group of black boys were chasing a trio of underfed goats across the graveyard, the animals racing over the mounds.

A chill descended. Numie made his way fast from the cemetery, as daylight was fading.

A woman sitting on her front porch brought a resurgence of life. Humming and rocking in her chair, she lulled her baby to sleep as it sucked from one of her pendulous breasts.

"Those mighty fine people out there in that graveyard," she called to Numie.

Startled, he managed to say, "For sure."

"Mighty fine people," she went out. "I used to know a lot of 'em, and I reckon I'll be joining them myself one of these days. Mighty fine. Some of 'em still come around to visit me late at night."

Not knowing what to say, Numie walked on.

The row of little houses facing the cemetery were like cubicles, with shantytown front porches——many with missing or weather-beaten boards. On these porches big black men lounged on gliders or else perched on tattered automobile seats——a kind of social center at evening. Some freely passed bottles of liquor over to their next-door neighbors for a swig.

One house in between, the worst of the lot, was empty. The same sign he'd seen at the skeleton condominium was dug into the ground out front: Rentals by Theodore M. Albury. Immediate Occupancy.

Next door a white-haired black and his wife were reaching with a long stick, trying to shake avocados from the top of the branches.

At a house on the corner another much older black man sat rocking on his front porch. Almost bald, with skin like a brown prune, he wore frayed shorts and tattered tennis shoes. He'd erected a crudely lettered sign, "I will give you the best shine in the world for ten cents." A complete ornately decorated shoeshine stand——big enough for two customers——stood on his porch.

"Shine, mister man," he called to Numie.

"No thanks, old-timer," Numie said. "I'm wearing sandals."

"That's the trouble with this island today," the shine man said. "Nobody wears shoes no more."

"What kind of business do you expect down here?" Numie asked. "Why don't you work on main street?"

"I was there for forty years," he answered. "Got too old. The younger ones chased me out. I retired here, thinking I could still keep my old customers. A few of the loyal ones drifted over, but I guess they've forgotten about me by now. Who knows? They might come again one day, and I'll be sitting right here ready for them."

Numie smiled. "Good luck. Next time I wear shoes, I'll be right over."

"Sure would appreciate the business," the old man said. "Times been kinda rough since I retired." His voice drifted off, and his glassy eyes wandered to the graveyard before him.

The sun had set.

. . .

El Chico restaurant beckoned, a gathering place where Cubans and blacks met for chicken and yellow rice with black beans. Magenta, orange, and blue strips of neon cast a false glow.

Inside the place was bustling, nearly all the oilcloth-covered chrome chairs filled with hungry, beer-drinking diners. A Cuban mother and her two daughters——all cast from the same mold——were busy tending the eight formica tables. One of the daughters had a gold tooth; the mother, three. Each one wore platform shoes with ankle straps, and each was weighed down with heavily lacquered jet-black hair, piled elaborately on their heads in a high-rise coiffure.

The stocky mother motioned Numie to one of the six mismatched rickety stools at the counter——once the carport of the one-time filling station, but now enclosed by horizontal louvers. Overhead a wooden-bladed fan slowly revolved. The jukebox blasted out the latest Havana music.

"*Picadillo* and beer," Numie said, giving his order of spicy Cuban chopped meat to one of the busty daughters.

She gave him a sisterly smile before hurrying back to the kitchen. "Papa," she called, "*picadillo*."

Sipping his beer, Numie swerved to stare into the challenging face of Castor Q. Combes.

"Violet eyes," he said. "This is where *I* go to eat. You following me?"

"No, Castor, it was pure chance."

The waitress reappeared with Numie's order.

Perching on the stool next to Numie, he told the waitress: "Some Spanish bean soup and stuffed *boliche*."

"Don't you want your usual frozen banana daiquiri?" the daughter asked.

"You know I always have that." Castor was impatient. "I don't have to ask." After the girl left, he said, "Cubans sure are dumb. I should give my business to a soul food place——don't know why I come here."

"They serve you frozen daiquiris——that's why. Aren't you pretty young for that?"

"My age is none of your business," Castor said. "White people are always messing into black people's business."

The daughter returned, bringing both Castor's soup and his meat course. She went back into the kitchen and emerged with the frozen banana daiquiri. Writing out the tab, she stuck it under Castor's plate.

Arrogantly he removed it and placed it alongside Numie's *picadillo*. "The white boy's paying."

"I swear you're a little hustler," Numie said. "I should be your agent."

"You still shacking up with Lola?" Castor asked.

"For the time being——until something better comes along. I've got a job, driving for Leonora de la Mer."

"Another crazy one!" Castor said. "You sure do like the crazy ones."

"I hang out with you, don't I?" Numie asked.

"No you don't *hang out* with me," Castor said grandly.

"The only reason I'm sitting here with you is because it's a public place of business. If we was together in a social situation, I wouldn't be caught dead with you. I won't even let my cat socialize with your kind."

"You little brat," Numie said. "The only reason you're sitting here with me is because you're planning to rip me off for the price of a meal."

"Talk at mealtime bores me," Castor said. "So, if you don't mind." Scooting over one stool, he removed his *boliche* and proceeded to devour it, alternating between slurping on the daiquiri and the soup. At the end of his quickly consumed meal, he got up and headed out.

"Enjoyed dining with you, Castor baby," Numie called. "See you around."

"Not if I see you first," Castor said. "I got no business with human garbage."

Numie smiled as the boy left. Never had he enjoyed getting insulted as much. Finishing off his meal and paying both tabs, he left.

The street was dark. On the corner a man was closing his two-story food shop for the night. A few drops of rain were hitting the wrap around tin roof which extended over the sidewalk. Huffing, he was lifting a bushel basket of orange-green papayas.

Quickly Numie fell in step with him, giving a helping hand.

"Hard work," the Cuban said.

Numie handed him the final baskets of avocados and red plantain.

"Your reward," the shopkeeper said, coming from the back. He handed Numie a cone of guava ice cream. "Thanks a lot, bubba," he said.

"Thank you," Numie said. "It's real good."

The rain seemed to have changed its mind. Just a few drops now.

Numie was deliberately stalling, not wanting to face Lola. He wished he could be by himself tonight. He didn't want to have to relate to anybody. But that would be freedom——and he'd never known that.

Taking the long way home, he stopped off at the gaudy Victorian bus station. The beer seemed to have gone through his system in minutes.

A few sailors, a Cuban and his heavily made up girl friend, two elderly tourists, and an old fisherman waited in the lobby for the final bus in from the mainland for the night.

Numie hurried by——heading for the men's room.

Inside the marble floor smelled, and the long porcelain urinal had long ago yellowed.

Sighing in relief, Numie splashed noisily. Eyes closed, he allowed this moment to help ease the tension that had been slowly building since he left the Cuban restaurant.

Finished, he started to zip up, but stopped short. His attention shifted to the lone booth. Someone had chiseled a hole in the partition, and an eye was clearly observing Numie. Underneath the raised partition two booted feet rested.

Still at the urinal, Numie started to shake himself. After all, a customer was a customer. He certainly needed the extra money.

The eye was staring intently.

As his cock hardened, Numie edged closer to the hole.

The eye withdrew.

A shuffling inside sent a note of alarm through Numie. Zipping up quickly, he rushed out the door.

The station master was just coming in. "Hope you gave the sheriff a good show," he said.

Numie stopped in surprise. "The sheriff? You mean, that's Johnny Yellowwood in there?"

"Sure, I've got to summon him now. He's wanted on the phone. Emergency downtown."

"What did you mean, a good show?" Numie asked.

"Kid, you're naive," the station master said. "The sheriff likes to look at guys take a leak. Been hanging out in that very booth ever since he got back from the Korean War." The station master walked in the toilet. "Johnny," he called, "you wanted on the phone, bubba."

Down the deserted street, Numie glanced back at the steep-roofed towers of the Victorian station.

He didn't know why he was shocked, but he was. More by the station master's bland acceptance of the sheriff's perversity than by anything else, he guessed.

In minutes, the sheriff's car——siren blazing——whizzed by, heading for downtown.

Chapter Fifteen

Numie was hurrying up the steps to Lola's apartment. At the door, he paused for a moment, swallowing a lump in his throat, then went in.

An ashtray narrowly missed his head, crashing against the door.

"Where in hell have you been, mother fucker?"

"Lola! You could have hurt me," he said. He moved toward her, wanting to strike her, but resisting the impulse.

Hands on her hips, she just stood there in red panties and a bra. Glaring. "I'll teach you to cheat on Lola." The idea that he could find anyone in town more exciting than her filled her with rage.

"You don't own me," he protested, feeling right at this moment that she did. "Besides, I haven't been screwing around."

"Don't stand there with that shit-eating look on your lilywhite face. Do you think for half a second, I'm gonna take your word for that?" All of a sudden, she started looking calm and collected.

How could she possibly check up on him? The desk clerk at the Dry Marquesas?

"I'll know soon enough if somebody's had you." Smug superiority broke out all over her face. "There's one test no man can fake."

He sat down on her white satin sofa with a thud. What she had in mind was all too apparent. The heat of the afternoon still burned in his skin. He closed his eyes, not wanting to think about what was going to happen. He just couldn't give in to her so easily. "Bitch!" he shouted in disgust, opening his eyes quickly and sitting up. "I've been at Sacre-Coeur. Got me a job as De la Mer's chauffeur. After all, you told me yourself: you get paid, you don't pay."

Lola's face softened. Was he telling the truth? Men, particularly white men, told so many lies. "You really mean that? You gonna pay me for the privilege? You're not just sitting there spitting out lies...'cause if you are..." She was touched. No one, except the Commodore, had ever offered to pay before. The whole idea flattered her. "I know you ain't gonna get much money from De la Mer, that tight dyke. You don't have to give me all *that* much. After all, I already own a Facel-Vega, and my commodore pretty much takes care of my needs."

"I'm telling the truth about paying," he said, lying. My God, she was really believing him! "Starting tomorrow morning, I go to work."

"Don't sweat it, darling," Lola said, a sudden hollow feeling in her stomach. On a second look, she didn't like his taking a job as De la Mer's chauffeur. The whole idea of her main man driving around that cunt tossed and turned her stomach in a bad way. But she didn't want to appear too insecure. "Christ, you'll be safe with *that* bull-dyke. She wouldn't know how to take care of a man if one lassoed her with it." But what about Anne? Lola would have to consider the possibility of that horny bitch cutting in on the action.

"Tangerine told me that De la Mer's got no pubic hair. Any girl who'd shave that off must be sick."

"First real job I've ever had," he said.

"Well, that other work you've been doing is harder than planting taters. *I* should know. And with us ladies, it's much easier to peddle our pussies than it is for a man to get it up."

"I know, I know," he said impatiently. He struggled to sit up, the elastic band of his swimming trunks biting into his skin. He wanted to take a shower, but thought it too risky right now to pull off his clothes in front of her. "Got anything to drink?"

She looked over at him, admiring his tallness, those broad shoulders, the way the damp T-shirt clung to his chest. "Yeah, stud, you!"

Numie's heart sank. Nervous fingers ran through his hair. "Come on, I told you I wasn't fooling around today. Besides, it's too hot."

She liked watching him squirm. "Not as hot as it's gonna be for you in a few minutes. Child, this room is gonna be so hot that even the Devil hisself would run out for a breath of fresh air."

On the bed, he lay with his eyes closed. No feeling in it this time. No pretended moaning or groaning. She was doing all the work. So many times, the same experience. Meaningless. How could it satisfy anyone? But it did. It always did. Those endless mouths draining him. But he knew how to give. Now, it was about time. Suddenly pumping, he held her blonde-wigged head down and rode to an unspectacular climax. "Do you believe me now?" he asked with hostility, jerking her head up to look in her bloodshot eyes.

Those eyes were on fire. "And how!" she said, raising herself up on her elbows. She nuzzled her knees into the warm bed. "You ain't had nothing since little old Lola last climbed the mountain."

A sudden panic came over Lola when she saw the time. "Christ, we're gonna be late, and I gotta get some respectable clothes for you. Can't have you looking like you just washed in on a shrimp boat." Jumping up, Lola adjusted her bra and started rushing around the apartment, turning on all the lights. She had to see how she looked in the severest of glare before trusting her appearance on the street. Over her shoulder, she called back, "Tonight, you're gonna meet some *high class*."

The bed became quicksand for him. The idea of going out and being introduced as Lola's boy friend made him quiver. "And who is so high class?"

"My people, real people," she said, resenting his asking. With a sharp tweezer, she resumed her eyebrow plucking. "Not that De la Mer crowd of phonies." The image of Leonora de la Mer for one brief moment seemed to blot out her own reflection in the mirror. She practically spat back at it. "Miss Distinguished herself, that De la Mer. I ain't met no bull-dyke yet who's *that* distinguished."

. . .

In her exotic Indian wrap-pants, open to the thigh, Lola was a blaze of color as she marched down a side street off main. She stopped in front of a men's store, admiring her glamorous presence in the glass.

The clothing shop was so small you could miss it unless you were searching. "This is where high-class people go," she said over her shoulder, detecting to her horror what looked like dandruff. She couldn't be sure, though. Her vision was getting worse, but she was not a gal to wear glasses. "The guy who runs this place——he don't bother with trash."

Inside the store, Lola pranced down the narrow aisle, supremely confident of the impression she was making. "Good evening, David," she said, assuming the same grand manner she had with Leonora.

"Miss La Mour, a pleasure." The shopkeeper was plump and bald, a nervous type. The thick lenses of his horn-rimmed glasses exaggerated the size of his eyeballs.

"Thank you for staying open just so we could pick up a few fun things," Lola said.

"Anything you or your commodore want, I'm only too happy to oblige," David said.

Turning to Numie, Lola wondered if he were properly impressed at how David was treating her like a lady. He didn't seem to be. That prompted her to say, "*My* commodore owns this entire block."

"You mean," David corrected, "your commodore and Miss de la Mer."

Lola was piqued. When David's lease came up for renewal, she would see that it wasn't. The very mention of Leonora de la Mer's name filled her with loathing in the extreme. "Well...I guess she might own a building or two. I can't really mess up my mind with what she owns or don't own. We're here to look at some clothes for this buck. Name's Numie."

"Hello," Numie said. He dug his hand into his pocket. The hairs bristled on his neck.

"Hi," David replied in a high-pitched voice. He looked at Numie intently before his nervous eyes darted away. Turning to Lola, he asked: "What does your young man have in mind?"

This question only increased Numie's discomfort. David wasn't even giving him the dignity of making up his mind. Eying a rack of slacks, Numie started to say something, but was interrupted.

In one quick move, Lola crushed out her cigarette right on the tiled floor. "We're going out tonight with Ned and Dinah. I'm sure you remember Ned, don't you?" She cocked her head and turned her most accusatory gaze upon David.

David was flustered. "I'll never forget him," he muttered.

"As you know," she went on, "Ned always shows basket.

I want Numie to do the same." She glanced imperiously at Numie, challenging him to defy her.

The look was familiar, an obvious copy of Leonora at her most haughty. "Hey," Numie protested, "don't I have something to say about this?"

"Child, I happcn to be paying the bill," Lola said sarcastically. She feared her position was being seriously threatened in front of David. "When you get enough bread to pay the bill, then we'll welcome suggestions, I'm sure."

Numie swallowed hard. He'd had his fill.

"Don't you understand nothing?" Lola asked. "I can't have Ned putting on a better show than you. You just can't get it that I'm not only doing a favor for you, but for the whole mother-fucking white race."

"Some favor!" Numie said.

"A well-built man like you shouldn't be embarrassed," David added. Eyes narrowed, his lips set in a sheepish smile.

The man's coyness not only made Numie uncomfortable, but added to his increasing anger. "I'm not embarrassed" he said. "That's not the point. I don't like being ordered around like this."

"It's okay," Lola assured him. "With David, you can let it all hang out." This was said with such authority she hoped to end all argument.

"I understand what you're looking for, Miss La Mour," David said, moving quickly. "Something nice, slim, and snug. I have the exact item. Bet it'll fit without alterations."

"It had better," Lola said. "Got no time for alterations." She wet her lips, then, looking into a full-length mirror, decided she needed more lipstick. She'd have to coat it on heavy to compete with Dinah. Opening her purse, she noticed her watch. "We're practically due at their place right now."

"What's your waist size?" David asked.

"Thirty," Numie said, sighing.

It was a signal to Lola that he had decided to cooperate.

"Better check that," David said, his lips curling in anticipation. From a nearby counter, he took a tape measure, wrapping it around Numie's waist. "Right you are. And now the inseam." Dropping to his knees in front of Numie, he placed his hand inside the seat of his crotch.

Instinctively Numie withdrew at his wet-fingered touch, then stood firm.

"Watch and make sure you take the right kind of measurements," Lola said, hawkeying every move.

Numie tensed. The bald man clearly repulsed him——too many echoes of his past.

Getting up, David buzzed to the back, returning with a pair of white slacks. "Try these on."

Looking around for a dressing room, Numie asked, "Right here?"

"Sure," Lola said, "we ain't got no time for formalities."

"I'll draw the blinds up front," David said, hurrying to the door. But he was back in a moment.

Lola was boring her eyes into Numie.

Sucking in his breath, he started to strip. Tossing his shirt aside, he slowly unbuttoned his fly, sliding out of his jeans. He wore no underwear. Kicking his sandals aside, he stood straight. He grinned nicely, but it was one of defiance.

Lola was enjoying exhibiting him. It showed David the kind of white man she was capable of attracting.

David, though, was nervously mopping beads of perspiration from his forehead. His thin lips were twitching.

"The pants, man," Numie finally said.

"Oh, yes," David managed to say, his Adam's apple bobbing up and down.

Numie squeezed into the pants. "They're hardly my size," he said.

"Go on, try them on," Lola ordered.

The fabric clung so tightly it was all Numie could do to zip them up. "They pinch like hell," he said, grunting.

"Those pants do just what I want them to," Lola said. "I'll show that Dinah a thing or two." A snarl of dark jealousy consumed her face. She applied even more make-up, as if to cover it.

"Even the length is perfect," David said, mincing forward.

"Thanks," Numie said. "I'll take that as a compliment."

Still in a nervous sweat, David said, "I didn't mean it that way...what I meant..."

"It don't matter," Lola said with a snort. "We got no more time for explanations." Snapping her purse shut, she turned around. "That cotton-knit sweater with the short sleeves is just right, baby."

Numie slipped it on.

"And this tie," David said anxiously, "for his belt. A great outfit!"

"Charge it to my commodore," Lola said, parading to the front.

"Thanks for your business," David said, panting like a puppy. "It's always a pleasure to serve you, Miss La Mour." He turned to Numie, his eyes wandering instinctively to his crotch where they lingered. "And you're welcome here any time you need anything."

"Don't you go worrying your *bald* head about his needs," Lola said, casting him a murderous glance. "They're well taken care of." She possessively linked her arm with Numie's, strutting out into the darkened street, her wrap-pants flaring into the night.

In the Facel-Vega, Numie dreaded another night with Lola. He had to leave her and soon, yet he wanted to stick around to meet the Commodore. To turn against Lola now would ruin everything with the Commodore. And the Commodore seemed to run this town. Numie wouldn't have much of a chance at anything unless he continued to please.

After freshening her make-up, Lola grabbed hold of Numie's arm again. It was comforting to have a virile man at the wheel.

It was all he could do not to pull away from her. His stomach was churning, his blood pounding with rage. He was resenting Lola for exhibiting him back at the men's shop. Who did she think he was? Some prized stud who'd perform tricks at her command?

Look at her, he thought. What a slob! She was so glamorous, she kept telling everybody. Yet everything about her was cheap and vulgar.

She disgusted him, yet he feared her in some strange way. He stared at her, barely disguising his hatred.

Even without her contacts, Lola knew she was being eyed intently. Lust, she suspected, was burning in Numie's eyes. Smiling, she patted him affectionately. "I know you're hot for my gorgeous bod," she said. "What buck in his right mind wouldn't be? But I can't put out your fire——not now. Later,

later."

Eyes back on the road, Numie did not answer. A day with Lola was a terrible dream, but maybe it would all be over soon. Any minute he'd wake up and find his life had taken a wonderful new turn——and he'd be free.

Her fingers now snaking up his arm made his skin crawl. But still he drove on.

Just the sight of her face, those obscene lips, made him feel unclean.

This creature had him in her power.

And he'd allowed it.

But how in hell could he get out without ruining his last chance in Tortuga?

"Slow down," she called out. "We'll miss their place in the dark. All these nigger shanties look the same to me."

The hot night had forced everybody from his shanty. Lazily the people lolled on their porches or else hung out their windows, swatting mosquitoes. An ice-cream vendor's cart tinkled across the cobblestones. A child, refused money for a cone, cried out.

The screen door to Ned and Dinah's had a gaping hole in it. The boards of the little front porch were rotten.

Lola didn't bother to knock. Barging in, she said, "Girl, get your skinny ass out of that bedroom. You got company, child. *Class!*"

"Lola," Dinah called from the back bedroom. "Get a drink and park your fanny, honey. I'm getting into something real sexy."

Lola quickly looked at her wrap-pants, fearing Dinah was going to appear better dressed than she was. "I can't drink that rotgut liquor Ned steals," she said. "You know my commodore will let me drink only toddies, made with aged rum."

"I ain't got no liquor to age around here," Dinah yelled back. "Ned drinks it up too fast."

Their little three-room shanty couldn't have looked shabbier. After the day it was built, no one had ever cleaned it up. Lopsided bamboo shades covered the windows in the living room. Their ruffled, graying valances——once stiff and white——were limp from dampness. In front of the frayed sofa where Numie was sitting lay an imitation Persian rug; and cabbage rose-patterned linoleum had been placed under the dining table in the corner.

"Well, have your boy friend——if he's here——pour me a drink," Dinah called again. "Bottle's in the kitchen."

Lola grandly motioned for Numie to get a drink. Being waited upon, once so exotic and uncomfortable for her, was now perfectly natural.

Frowning, Numie was heading for the kitchen. Greasy oilcloth lined the open shelves. He opened the refrigerator for ice. Looking in, he caught sight of moldy lumps of leftover food and slammed the door. Shades of Tangerine's apartment. To get a glass, he pulled back a plastic, orchid, polka-dot curtain over the sink. Immediately, a pair of cockroaches ran out, darting down the wall and under a fire-engine red bucket. He poured some cheap whiskey into the glass.

Back in the living room, he was making for the sofa...and Lola.

"Dinah's lover man ain't here yet," she said. "He's always late." For about the ninth time, she inspected her lips in her compact mirror, then slammed her purse shut. She moved closer to Numie, whispering under her breath.

"Probably knocking off a quick piece somewhere, if I know that buck."

Numie withdrew slightly, not inviting this intimacy.

Lola noticed that he had seemed to pull back. Did she have bad breath? She decided she was mistaken. "Ned can go one round after the other. No letting up."

Numie's eyes flared. "And how would you know?"

"I saw him ball five chicks in one night," she said, deliberately on a campaign to make Numie jealous. "When he finished the second round with each of them, he begged me to get him another set."

"You exaggerate," Numie said with disgust, perfectly aware of what Lola was doing. He didn't feel jealous at all, however. He just wanted to go out on the porch and breathe some fresh air. "If super fly's so spectacular," he said with a biting edge to his voice, "what are you doing with me?"

"Now, don't you go getting your feathers riled," she replied, a smile crossing her face. She could just sense the jealous fury inside him. "In the black community, I'm always known for dating white johns."

Numie sighed. He saw the picture clearly. Tonight was part of the same exhibition that had begun at the men's shop. "What am I? Some sort of status symbol?"

Lola resented this. "Honey, don't flatter yourself. You were nothing till I got you out of jail and put some decent clothes on your back."

"Thanks!" He was just about ready to get up and walk out when he was interrupted.

At that moment, Dinah barged into the room. She was wearing hot pants two sizes too small and a blouse that showed her breasts. Her mouth was red coated, flaming. A spray of freckles covered her light-brown face, resting under a coppery Afro hairdo. She was strutting around the living room, showing off her trim, boyish figure.

Numie was contrasting her natural beauty to Lola's contrived look.

Lola fumed. "Child," she said, "you put on too much lipstick."

"*You're* one to talk," she answered. Then smugly she said, "Besides, Ned likes to work it off." Her eyes searched every nook of Numie, beginning at his feet. The tight pants were creating the desired interest. "Ain't you gonna introduce me to your good-looking stud? My, is he handsome! Blond hair and blue eyes——what a turn on."

Lola smiled triumphantly, delighted that Dinah was pleased at her latest acquisition, yet nervously jealous at the same time. "Numie, Dinah," Lola said.

Numie smiled at her. She was that breath of fresh air he needed. He wasn't particularly attracted to her, but he admired her openness and frankness after having lodged so much time putting up with the posturing of Lola and Leonora. Glad to meet you," he said, handing her the whiskey he'd poured in the kitchen.

Dinah tongued her lips, making her lipstick all the more vibrant. "I knew Lola had something special, the way she talked on the phone. But I had no idea——no idea a'tall——that it'd be this good." Her expression suggested she wanted to get plugged into the action. "Why, if Lola hadn't already staked her claim, and I wasn't holing in here with the most jealous stud south of Birmingham..."

"I think this conversation has gone far enough," Lola said, burning with irritation. The evening wasn't going at all the way she planned it. Dinah was stealing the show. Those god-damn hot pants! If only Lola had legs she could show off. But hers were bony. "Where's Ned?" she asked. He was her one hope. He'd throw a little cold water on that brazen black pussy. "I'm not used to waiting," she announced.

Ned was suddenly at the door. Dressed entirely in white, he was an attractive animal, tall and big boned. He had light brown skin, with a velvety complexion. His lips, handsomely full and sensual, gave way to a greeting smile of gleaming white teeth. He held his strongly cleft chin high in the air. His nostrils——broad, but carefully chiseled——sniffed the foul smell of the shanty. Piercing their way into Numie was a set of copper-brown eyes.

Numie stared back at Ned, but he was tense. Ned was too cocky and belligerent for his taste.

"Baby," Dinah squealed, running toward Ned. He picked her up in the air as he kissed her, his bulging muscles clearly prominent in his white T-shirt.

Lola glanced first at Numie, then at Ned. The men's eyes were like headlights tonight. All those beams were focused directly on Dinah. "Cut out this disgusting spectacle," Lola demanded, getting up from the sofa, tossing her boa on the arm. "You don't seem to realize, Ned Papy, there's a lady present." Back arched, she stood proudly, the way she had seen Leonora enter the bar the other night.

"Well, Miss La Mour," Ned said, breaking away from Dinah. With a leer, he looked Lola up and down. "Forgive me for not showing the proper respect. After all, I'm just a cheap, common field nigger——not a grand lady who lives at Commodore Philip's, goes off on yachting weekends, and is seen about town in a *white* Facel-Vega."

Lola was fuming. Ned's look——the arrogance of it——was the same look lilywhite mothers gave her. But she controlled her temper. Ned resented her because she'd made it big, and he hadn't. It was the resentment the very poor reserve for the rich. She decided she was going to behave in a most ladylike manner. "I want you to meet my escort, Numie."

"Put it there, Numie," Ned said, extending a broad hand.

"Glad to meet you," Numie said, with as much vigor as he could arose. The prospect of a long evening with these people lay heavy on his stomach.

Ned smiled. "Dinah's a pretty lucky girl, wouldn't you say?"

Numie was taken back. Was Ned asking for a compliment? He couldn't be sure. "What do you mean?"

Ned seemed piqued that Numie didn't get the point right off. "Having me for her old man," he said, like an irritated parent to an unruly and stupid child.

"For sure," Numie said, hoping to sound as noncommittal as possible.

Ned glared. He seemed itching for a fight. "I'll take that as a compliment, *white boy*." Letting go of Dinah completely, he took a menacing step toward Numie. "Or was it a proposition?"

Numie backed away, hoping to avoid a bad scene. "A compliment."

"I think there was a little proposition there, too," Ned accused.

Lola nervously ran her fingers through her blonde wig. She stepped between them. "Numie don't go that way," she practically hissed in Ned's face.

Ned grinned contemptuously at her. "Miss Rubber Tits," he said, "you don't seem to get it. Hanging out with you makes him gay."

"He's strictly the man," Lola protested.

Ned pulled up his pants to emphasize his merchandise more prominently. With a sneer, he glanced down at what Numie was showing. "Any time you want to get it on, baby, you're welcome. If you've got the bread."

Numie swallowed. He was used to being insulted, and he thought he could handle this, too. "Thanks for the offer," he countered, "but I'm fully booked."

"Besides," Dinah said petulantly, linking her arm with Ned's again, "when I get through with that hose tonight, it won't be able to put out no fire nowhere."

Ned looked down at her, then he smiled. "That's one promise you're going to keep, bitch." He grabbed her again.

"You got me all messed up," Dinah said, trying to break away. "Come on, Lola, let's freshen up before we go out with our old men."

Reluctant to leave Ned alone with Numie, Lola finally consented to follow Dinah to the back bedroom.

Into the kitchen and out with two glasses of whiskey, Ned offered a drink to Numie.

"Thanks," Numie said, accepting the glass, but feeling acutely uncomfortable in Ned's presence.

"You're welcome, *white boy*.

Numie sat the glass down on the top of an old television set. "It's going to be a long night," he said, the irritation in his voice clear. "So let's cut the 'white boy' thing. You're black and I'm white. Now we can sit around and talk about that phenomenon all evening. But it won't get us far."

Ned's face froze. At first Numie didn't know if he'd gone too far.

Then that face broke into a smile. "Right you are," Ned said. "But I just can't resist socking it to white boys, though. My people have taken so much shit from you guys, I like to toss a little of it back in your face."

Picking up his glass again, Numie said, "Don't throw any at me." Then he smiled, too, to soften the edge between them.

"Got nothing personal against you," Ned said, pulling off his shirt and using it to mop under his armpits. He also seemed to be flexing his muscles. He rolled the shirt in a ball and tossed it into the corner. "It's just that my heart's burning."

"Just?"

"Yeah," he said, turning and glaring. "On fire with rage." He banged a fist into the palm of his hand. "I hate white people, every one of 'em."

Placing the glass back on the television, Numie was heading for the door. "That tells me where I stand."

"Nothing personal," Ned said, going after him and laying a hand on Numie shoulder. "Stick around."

"I didn't think I was welcome."

"Shit, man," Ned said, breaking away in disgust. "You think you've got some patent on being white? I could pass for white if I wanted to."

To Numie's surprise, he flashed a triumphal expression only

outclassed by Lola herself.

"In fact, I once hitched to Chicago, and people took me for white." He searched Numie's face carefully. "Well, maybe Puerto Rican. But they sure didn't think I was black."

"Did that turn you on?"

Ned's temper flared again, but he held the reins on it. "For a time it did," he said.

Numie thought this was the only honest statement he'd made all night.

Ned plopped down on the sofa, resting his feet on a table strewn with cigarette ashes. "I liked getting it on with white women who would have died if they'd known it was a black man tearing into them." He frowned. "But then I made up my mind that was nowhere. I'm black and proud of it. Black is where it's at, baby."

"I think being who you are and being proud of it is out of sight."

"Not with Lola, it ain't. She's a white nigger."

"What do you mean?"

"She's still freaked out she was born black. Not just black, but blue black. There's no mistaking the color of that pussy."

"You don't sound like you're her friend at all. I thought you were."

"I'm no friend of that dumbass queen. Not Ned Papy, baby." He raised his booted feet slightly from the coffee table, then slammed them down again.

Finishing the bitter, cheap whiskey, Numie sat the glass down for the final time. He glanced toward the bedroom door, where he heard nothing but giggles. "Then why are we here?"

"She's here because she likes to take us out and show off her sports car, her fancy clothes, and her latest white boy friend."

"Does that impress you?"

"We ain't impressed, my Dinah and me. The only thing that impresses us is that she pays the bill."

A silence drifted between them. Even before the evening had gotten under way. Ned seemed to have already had a lot to drink. Numie was hoping at this point to find an excuse to leave. "Maybe Lola and I had better split back to the bar. After all, she said herself she didn't know when the Commodore was going to show up."

At the mention of that name, Ned sat up. "The fact that she's got the Commodore don't turn me on either."

"I didn't know you knew him."

"Oh, he calls me every now and then to...perform. Bores the hell out of me, but I get it up for his pleasure."

Numie immediately asked himself if the commodore would want the same from him.

"Can't stand the bastard," Ned went on. "Talk about color. Just as Lola is pure blue-black, the commodore is ghost white. Palest white I've ever seen. So delicate——like you think he's gonna go at any minute, first time somebody comes up and says boo at him."

At this point, Dinah appeared at the door.

Lola trailed. "I'm just standing here," she said, barging in front of Dinah, "looking at you two rotten excuses for men." She ran her hands up and down her body, relieved that both men were staring at her now. "You've got the two most gorgeous pussies in town——and you don't deserve us."

. . .

In the heart of blacktown, the Hollywood Palace had lived many lives. Originally it was an opera house, with twin wooden domes on its facade and simulated arches leading to its two-story interior. In those days, it was once the border between the black and white sections of town. But now the area around it had been consumed by blacks, except for a sprinkling of Cuban families.

With not enough lovers of opera to keep its doors open, it was converted to a cigar factory. Streamers of nut-brown leaves——ready for cigar rolling on the ground floor——had hung from the balcony. The old seats had been removed, replaced by long tables where black men and Cubans worked hard hours.

When tobacco was no longer imported, two entrepreneurs found the money to open a night club and cocktail lounge. On Saturday nights, such as this one, the whole black community showed up.

Leading her pack, Lola stood in the neon glare of the club. My daddy used to slave here," she said to Numie. "Those goddamn white men draining all his spit day by day to make their cigars."

Numie was vulnerable, exposed standing out here on the sidewalk under the harsh lights. The men lounging against the wall made him feel like a moving target.

At the door, Lola flashed her membership card. "This is strictly a private club," she said over her shoulder.

Ned and Dinah trailed her in.

Numie lingered behind until the smiling eyes of the fat woman guarding the gate assured him it was okay. As he entered, music from an Art Deco jukebox filled the air. Sawdust covered the floors, and the smell was of sweaty bodies and cheap whiskey.

He was the only white man there. Eyes sought him out, and at first he was afraid. Then he relaxed. Those eyes weren't menacing——rather, amused at the show. A freak show, that's what they were. Lola and her white boy friend. It was clear to Numie that because he was there as Lola's white boy, he was no threat to the other men. Besides everybody was too busy having a good time.

Lola was well known. Many men called out her name. However, no women acknowledged her at all, turning from her presence whenever she got near them.

Lola was gleeful, though she tried to act cool. Here, for the first time, Numie could see how many men wanted her. Let the women snicker and turn from the sight of her. They were half out of their minds with jealousy.

A rancid patina lay over the club. Tiny strings of theater lights were strung from a central chandelier, laced with cobwebs. Many of the bulbs had burnt out, never to be replaced.

Lola directed Numie to a high-backed booth that had been slickly covered in red and gold oilcloth. Ned and Dinah followed.

Lola grabbed Dinah, pulling her along to the former stage of the opera house. It was now a dance floor. Grandly Lola ascended the central winding staircase, fringed by ornate plaster banisters. From a rear projection booth, an ever-changing spotlight sent shafts of colored lights upon the dancers.

The spotlight picked up Lola and Dinah——and stayed there. Deftly Lola moved to the center, quickly pushing Dinah to the periphery of the glare. She could have asked Numie or Ned to dance with her, but it was important at this moment to show up Dinah in front of the huge crowd. Even though Dinah was younger, Lola knew all the men were looking at her, Lola. And why not? She was far more devastating than Dinah. As Lola danced, the other customers backed away, acknowledging her position as star performer.

A five-piece combo had replaced the jukebox sound. The men were blasting out hot rhythms to keep the palace rocking.

The drone of chatter ceased in the smoke-filled room. The crowd was reaching a moment of high intensity.

To the rhythmic thumping of a congo drum, Lola under her blonde wig was love goddess of the island, beautiful, radiant, alive——all woman. Moving her body rapidly, she could feel the devouring eyes upon her. For her, the room was filled with desire.

As the drums reverberated, her pants whirled around the floor, seemingly having a life of their own. Her dance built as the drums grew louder and louder. Faster and faster she moved. Her gyrations were incredible. She just knew every man in the room was erotically breathless.

For one moment of panic, she realized she had no finish to her number. She'd long ago pushed Dinah to the wing. The bitch was drunk anyway.

Then it came to her.

She'd have to do it.

A spectacular finish.

Reaching for the hook that held her blouse, she unfastened it in one lightning move. Her breasts popped out in the red glare.

Silence.

The music stopped.

Lola retreated from the spotlight. Everything had gone wrong. But, no. The shock was over. Her act was met with thunderous applause. The shock, she now knew, had been that she had breasts at all.

Spinning from the floor, she was back into her blouse, heading for the women's toilet in the rear. Covered by fabric, her boobs jiggled as she pranced down the urine-smelling corridor.

Men reached out, pretending to grab her breasts.

"Are those jugs for real?" one man called.

She ignored him.

"Show us what else you got," another man yelled.

Closing a red door behind her, she enjoyed this moment alone in the women's toilet. A sigh of relief came over her.

Fortunately, she'd remembered to cover her breasts with diamond-shaped pasties before leaving the apartment tonight. It would have been vulgar to show nipples.

In the booth with Ned, Numie was eying the cut-out glittery stars of cardboard dangling from the ceiling, turning fast or slowly, as big electric fans swirled the hot, humid air around.

Ned was drunk and getting drunker. "I sell my chick," he said.

This confession came out of the blue. At first, Numie didn't think he heard right, and certainly didn't know what prompted Ned's telling it. "Lay that on me again," he said. "Dinah told me you were the most jealous stud south of Birmingham. Something doesn't fit."

Ned eyed him skeptically. "I'm jealous only if she ever gets it on with another black man. I'm not jealous of those jellybelly white pigs she can't even stand." He downed another healthy swig. "They're nothing to her. She hates their weak guts."

Numie was trying to control himself. He wanted to keep Ned friendly and talking, but knew Dinah was a supremely dangerous subject. Still, he blurted out, "Why sell her at all?"

Ned pulled hard at his tree-trunk sideburns. "Survival, man——the same reason you're shacking up with that crazy drag queen." He lowered his voice almost to a whisper. When he spoke again, it sounded more like a hiss. "I hate every white man who's ever fucked Dinah. I sit in the living room at night listening to them get it on with my chick in the bedroom. My bed! Sometimes I want to cut off their pea-sized balls."

Numie squirmed uncomfortably in his seat. This talk about castration brought back the chilling nightmare of Yellowwood's jail. "But you still sell her?"

"Hell, yes," Ned said, sitting back and talking louder. He put his booted foot up on the chair. "I'm a man of leisure. Never worked a day in my life, and don't intend to." He signaled the waitress for another round. "Not when I can find some pussy to do it for me. I've spent most of my time in bed, and that's where I plan to stay."

"You got it made, sounds like to me." Numie didn't mean this. It was just something to say. Even though he was getting drunk, he didn't like this camaraderie between Ned and him. Ned was relating to him like a fellow "player," a pimp and prostitute himself. Numie was resenting the company he kept, even though he knew he deserved the label.

A new drink in front of him, Ned was talking again. "Made like hell! The people in this town look down on me. Even my own people." He slipped his feet off the chair and planted them on the stained floor again. "But the mayor calls when he wants a piece of black ass——which is pretty often. If he sees me on the street, he won't look my way. After dark, so to speak, it's another story. He brings me liquor, and we get drunk together."

Numie was trying to play it cool, let Ned do the talking. He held back with any more questions, figuring he'd asked enough.

"You got a lot of bread stashed away?" Ned asked him.

"Just enough to keep me in some eats," Numie answered.

"Something to drink, a tin roof——that's about all I got, too," Ned volunteered. "The white guys, my customers, would turn against me if I got too successful."

"I know a lot of people believe whities can't stand for blacks to get ahead," Numie said. "It's supposed to freak them out. But I found people, regardless of their color, often can't stand for their own friends to get ahead, much less anybody else."

Ned looked at him as if that were about the dumbest observation he'd ever heard. "Shit, man, if I had a fancy house and car, like those New York pimps, these redneck cats down here wouldn't give me no more business. They'd figure out some way to take it from me. So I don't come on too fancy, like that fucking Lola. Long as I can get by without work, like I told you, it's okay with me." He rubbed his broad nose.

Numie glanced apprehensively to the rear of the palace. Lola still had not come out of the women's toilet after that disgusting spectacle. Numie was just sitting there dreading the moment when she'd come and join them. In this crowd, the less attention he called to himself, the better.

"What do you want out of life?" Ned asked abruptly.

Numie had absolutely no answer for that one. "Just to get by," he said, copping out.

"I tell you what I want," Ned said, "not that you asked, but I'll tell you anyway. Fill my gut and get all the pussy I can handle, which is one hell of a lot. Man, I succeed at that. The living's easy." He rubbed his stomach. "I know how to control women, and other men are jealous as shit of me. Lock up their wives when they see me coming."

"Lucky man."

"Everybody——man, woman, cat, or chicken——wants old Ned to sail up their lazy river," he said. "Why, when I go to the vegetable market, even the honeydews start vibrating."

"Come, let's dance," Lola said, appearing suddenly. She tickled Numie's nose with her boa. Eagerly she was waiting to hear his reaction to her performance.

Numie glanced first at Ned to see if he were finished, then at Lola. He felt trapped between two clashing egos.

The combo was getting tired by the time Numie reached the floor. His head was spinning, and he wanted to lie down in some soft bed somewhere. It'd been a long day.

"What you and Ned rapping about?" Lola asked sharply, growing angry that Numie didn't comment on her show.

"He's been filling me in on the facts of life," Numie said, dreading the eyes looking at him.

"Ned Papy talks big and looks big, but he's no match for Lola La Mour." She reasoned that Ned had probably been telling unflattering lies about her. Leaning close, she whispered into Numie's ear. "Did he let you in on the big secret? He's madly in love with this here lady looking at you right now." She stepped back, seeking a light, any light, so she could shine. "Yeah, me. Always trying to get in my perfumed drawers."

Numie was startled.

"Promises he'll leave Dinah any minute, day or night, for a chance at my honeypot." She looked into Numie's eyes. Was he doubting her word? "The stud's crazy for me," she said more emphatically. "I'm driving him up the wall." Waving her boa madly, she danced across the wooden floor, the sound of her high heels echoing across the old opera house.

The night wore on. Most of it spent by Numie alone at the

booth. The liquor numbed him. He hoped the more he drank, the more anesthetized he'd become. He wanted to blot out everything. He didn't belong here. Trouble was, he didn't know where he belonged. If any place. Just hang in, pass the time.

At the peak of her energy, Lola never missed a dance. At one point, Ned pulled off his shirt, and he and Lola danced a dry hump in the center of the stage. The crowd wildly cheered, clapping their hands in rhythm.

Ned was coming on strong with Lola. Could Lola be telling the truth? Did Ned really dig her? But, no, it was just an act.

Besides, that chick was mad. Christ, now Numie was calling Lola a chick. Lola was no chick. She was a man. He must remember that. It seemed easier to think of her as a chick than a man. What could he call her? *It*? Nothing seemed to fit. Where did the real world leave off and the fake one begin? Quit thinking, for God's sake, he told himself. Stop racking your brain. Let it rest in peace.

Head swimming something fierce now, Numie made his way outside the club for some fresh air. It was nearly dawn.

In the distance, a church carillon sounded its morning chimes.

Chapter Sixteen

The Facel-Vega careened into the driveway of Sacre-Coeur. With nervous anticipation, Numie slid out from behind the seat. Leonora was in her rose garden. A white fedora and large, oval-shaped sunglasses concealed most of her face. Her silk jersey dress, soft and voluminous, was like a Greek costume, except she'd tightened it around her thin waist with a belt. In white strap sandals, she walked to her favorite rose bush, fingering its soft mauve flower, in perfect harmony with her dress color.

"You're late!" she accused, perking her head like a caged bird. She knew he wasn't, but wanted to put him on the defensive.

Her charge was like a bolt to him. He stood in the garden with uncertainty, mustering the courage to reply. "No, I'm not," he protested. "I just got the call ten minutes ago you were ready to go out."

"Never mind," she said, brushing the hot air with her hand. "I don't have time for excuses." Her lips curled slightly as she regarded the sun. She hated it. Why couldn't the world always be dark? It was so much more mysterious and romantic. "I want you to drive me out by the beach."

Still stung by this forbidding autocrat, Numie just stood there for a moment. Then, recovering, he opened the door to the rear compartment of her black Lincoln, helping her inside.

She slid onto the leopard-skin upholstery, seemingly sinking into it. She was a hopeless sentimentalist, she knew. Riding in this car, remembering all the people who'd ridden in it with her, got her through many a difficult day.

In the driver's seat, he was examining the dashboard. He could feel her piercing eyes, boring into the back of his neck.

"Hurry up," she called on the earphone. Her anxiety was mounting, as it always did when she paid these four calls out by the beach, although they were part of her weekly routine. "I don't have all morning."

"I was just checking something," he yelled back, barely disguising the anger in his voice. He was not interested in presenting valentines to the old monster in the rear compartment.

She didn't respond. The engine's groan blotted out her thoughts for the moment, as Numie carefully inched the wide car through the narrow gate.

Numie would be just one in a long line of chauffeurs who drove in and out of her life. He would be no worse, no better, than the rest. With all of them, she'd tried to establish a human relationship, but every time she reached out she sounded more like a tyrant. For some reason, she seemed to say and do all the wrong things. Every time she extended her feelers, she feared she did so badly, even menacingly. They were cut off. Surreptitiously she watched people, eavesdropped on their conversations, observed their body movements, their mannerisms——all this in an attempt to relate to them.

From afar she studied Numie. His skin was good, his chin showed some character. But yet he had the look of the unapproachable about him. He was like a lithe, white statue——all orderly and immaculate.

Inspecting the carved emerald glittering on her perfectly shaped hand, she smiled to herself. It was a smile of self-contempt. Here she was this morning riding in the little claptrap honky-tonk of Tortuga, wondering in her desperate loneliness how to relate to a chauffeur who was a former prostitute.

She, Leonora de la Mer, who had been adored by kings, even a president of the United States.

Along the northern shore road, a mile out of town, the houses ended abruptly. He stepped on the accelerator, sending the Lincoln zooming up the road. In spots, the pavement was cracked or broken by rubber tree roots shooting out in all directions in search of nourishment. In back, Leonora was sitting quietly.

The scents of August were in the air.

Numie stared intently at the road he was taking to the barren, northern corner of the island. Rows of bent-over, blight-plagued coconut trees grew along the way. Here, a deserted hamburger house, its faded letters, Sweet Daddy's Bar, still visible. There, a gigantic blanket of philodendron vines covering an abandoned Civil War fort.

He was still sleepy. Anne's call had wakened him less than

twenty minutes ago.

What was Leonora up to, asking to be driven to this remote section of the island so early in the morning? She was not saying a word. In the rear-view mirror, she loomed from her serene position——eyes steadfast.

"Slow down," came her commanding voice over the earphone.

In the clearing, almost completely obscured by clumps of banana trees, was a wooden shack, with a patched tin roof and unpainted walls.

"Pull in here," came her second order.

"Are you getting out?" he asked, after he'd opened the rear door for her.

"No, darling," she said, "not this morning." Reaching into her pearl-studded purse, she carefully handed Numie two one-dollar bills, fingering each to see that none had stuck together.

"What's this for?" he asked. The mystery was growing by the moment.

Leonora looked over to him. Should she tell? Bring Numie into her confidence? "For the voodoo queen inside," she finally said. "You can go right in——no need to knock."

"Voodoo?" He hesitated. Was Leonora crazy? "Just give her two dollars and split? Why, if you don't mind my asking?"

"Her reward," Leonora said softly.

"For what?" Numie was determined to know. After all, he could be walking into some sort of trap.

Leonora touched her breast softly. A sharp pain was shooting through her chest. "When I was very young and all the other children were making fun of me——the ugly duckling, remember?——that sweet old soul in there told my fortune." The pain subsided. "Bless the dear heart, she's still alive."

"What'd she tell you?"

"It's a long story. Do you really want to know?"

"Yes, if I'm going in there. This place gives me the creeps."

She gave him an extended look. "It was at a county bazaar to raise money for our boys in World War I. She had a little booth. Everybody was in costume. I, a gypsy girl." She paused a moment, trying to recall if she were beautiful then. "I still remember what the voodoo queen said to me: 'You will suffer great hardship. But in the end you will triumph over your enemies. You will go far in the world, dazzling friend and foe alike with your charm and talent. One day your name will be known in every corner of the earth'."

"She told you all that?" Those lines sounded more like something Leonora would say, not some voodoo queen.

"Of course, she told it to me," Leonora said, her patience tested. She had been told something like that. Not the exact words, maybe, but close enough. "Do you think I just make up things?"

"No, but why the two dollars?"

"I give her that every week," Leonora said nonchalantly.

"Two dollars a week?"

"Naturally. You may think that extravagant for a fortune told so long ago. Back then, I paid a quarter. I've always been generous, as I've told you. It's a fault, I know."

Numie had just the opposite reaction. Leonora was about the tightest woman he'd ever encountered.

"Ever since I returned to Tortuga and found out she was still alive, living in this horrible poverty, I've paid her this gratuity."

"Why doesn't she go on welfare?" Numie asked.

"I've tried to get her to avail herself of public assistance, but she's too proud——and I, of all people, understand that." Leonora sank back into the leopard skin. "The only thing she has to live on is the money I give her."

Taking the money, Numie was heading for the shack, feeling he was part of some ritual between Leonora and the voodoo queen he didn't understand.

A tall shrub beside the front door shimmered and glistened, with bits of glass, mirror, and tinfoil tied to its branches. It reminded Numie of a Christmas tree. But what was its real purpose? To scare away evil spirits?

Inside the main room was dark and rancid smelling. Unpainted walls held a bizarre collection of voodoo artifacts. Pinned up was a double-page spread of a nude white girl, surrounded by pictures of animals. Underneath it was a childlike drawing of Satan, mounted on velvet. On a shelf rested dried chicken heads in Dixie cups. Held by a purple and gold ribbon were a group of chicken feathers, a collection of snake skins, and oddly shaped cutouts of bright tin.

On a carpet in the corner lay a huge beast of a mulatto woman. Her eyes were closed. No longer brown, her skin was almost elephant gray. Huge rings of colored glass covered every finger; and bracelets of brass and wood dangled from her neck and both arms. Purple lipstick, put on badly, coated her thick mouth. In one limp hand she held a voodoo doll. Her hair was a bleached-out yellow gray. Suddenly, she opened her eyes. They were like those of a caged animal, their vision cruel. With her long red-painted nails, she started to claw at the voodoo doll.

"Hi," Numie said. In the dazzling heat, he stood fascinated. "Miss De la Mer's here. Parked right outside." His nervousness was growing. "Told me to give you this." He placed the two dollars on a low brass table holding a group of lit candles.

Her stare continued.

Not knowing what to say then, Numie looked up at the ceiling. A pumpkin-sized mirrored ball revolved back and forth, casting a psychedelic illusion, as it picked up the reflection from the candlelight below.

Propping herself up on the cushions, the woman raised her head. "Whose errand is it you running?"

"Miss De la Mer's." He felt he was really looking at a freak now. "She's right outside waiting in the car."

"Let the white bitch wait!" She shot him a look that could burn skin.

At first, he thought he didn't understand. "What did you say?"

"You heard me the first time. Let her wait." Her face twisted as she raised herself higher on the carpet. "That white bitch, coming around every week with her no-good two dollars. Giving me money——like I'm a common nigger. She don't know who she's talking to."

The wind from the ocean blew a broken shutter, sending it banging against the shack. Numie jumped as if hit. "Just who are you?"

The woman's face was filled with contempt. "That's none of your business." Then her face softened. "Except I'm proud of who I am. I'm Erzulie."

"That's a strange name."

"Not strange at all," she practically hissed. "If you wasn't so dumb, you'd know that's the name of the Haitian Venus. But I don't have time to start educating the messenger boy of that white bitch."

Numie was growing increasingly irritated. If Leonora had a feud going with this queen of the freaks, let Leonora handle it. He almost turned away in disgust. But curiosity drew him into one more attempt to learn something about Erzulie. "She claims you told her fortune when she was young."

At this, Erzulie spat. "The bitch is older than I am." She wiped something off her chin. "She's got me mixed up with a woman who died thirty years ago." Erzulie spat again. "Besides, I'm no goddamn fortune teller."

"Why don't you straighten her out?"

She broke into a spasm of desperate giggles. "I've told her fifty times, but she don't believe me." Erzulie's teeth were yellow fangs. It was as if she'd sharpened them. "Said I'm senile and don't remember." That giggle again. "Thinks I'm crazy, she does. She don't know she's the crazy one." Her voice echoed through the house.

The feeling was eerie. The rancid smell of the room was now penetrating to him. "I've got to go."

"Give her one message from me, seeing you're running a telegram service around here. Tell her one day I'm going to make a doll and get her!" Staring him right in the eye, Erzulie laughed loudly.

Even the hot sun outdoors, the blinding glare, couldn't blot out that crazed look.

Back in the Lincoln, Leonora said, "You took long enough. Was she grateful?"

Numie sighed. He'd run from one mad woman to another. "Sure was," he replied. "Couldn't live without your weekly gift."

"So many people, so many depend on me," she said, sinking back once more into her soft leopard skin.

In the distance was a playground, its meager grass slowly consumed in a dust bowl. Steel lids of garbage cans, smashed whiskey bottles, and old beer cans littered the grounds, along with popsicle wrappers.

In the back, a tangle of bushes propped up a sagging fence,

on which a rusty Nehi beverage sign rested. Someone had tried to build a shanty, but had abandoned it. Tarpaulin lay over the unused materials.

Leonora surveyed the scene. She feared she looked tired today. It had been more than a week since she'd last slept well. At the playground she always liked to appear looking her best. "Our next stop," she called to Numie.

"Here?" he questioned, thinking he hadn't heard correctly.

"Here!" she said more firmly.

Helping her out, he led her over to a broken-down picnic table. In the distance, four boys were playing ball.

"The first night I met you, you said you liked to keep in touch with the young generation," he said. "Is this how you do it?"

Her tension was visibly surfacing, and his question infuriated her. "Don't be impertinent."

"Didn't mean to be," he said, fearing her anger. "I just didn't know you liked kids, that's all. In fact, I would have guessed the opposite."

A disturbing memory nudged her brain, but she was fighting its coming into focus. "I loathe children." The statement didn't seem quite complete. She added, "Especially one called Ruthie Elvina."

Numie surveyed the boys playing. "Then why did we stop?"

In the glare of the sun, she looked up at him, but chose not to answer. How could she explain it to this simple hustler? She used to play on this very ground when she was but a young girl. A school had stood nearby, but it burned down. She hadn't wanted to join in the games, but her teacher had forced her. None of the other children ever wanted to play with her. The boys always made fun of her, always calling her a scarecrow. Slowly she ran her hands down her side, as if to assure herself of its curvaceous line.

The girls hadn't wanted to have anything to do with her, but they never jeered. The boys always did, though. She grew to hate them, considering them the cruelest and most heartless creatures on earth. Men were hardly better, but boys were the worse.

She got up and walked back to the car. Reaching the Lincoln before Numie, she opened it for herself.

At this point, a red-haired boy, fifteen or less, braked his bicycle at her side.

She raised her hands to her face to shield it from the dust. Who would dare intrude on this private moment of hers?

Tan and lean, the boy was wearing tennis shoes, a T-shirt, and jeans.

Catching up with them, Numie contrasted the boy's openness to life with Leonora's elaborate dress and haughty manner.

"That your car, lady?" he asked.

Annoyed, she tried to control her temper. "Yes," she said stiffly, hoping the boy would go away.

"This is a pretty swell car, but I know an old Rolls-Royce that's better. Also this black chick I've seen has got a white Facel-Vega."

That did it! Arching her back, Leonora glared at the boy. "My automobile is the finest on the island——a Lincoln custom made in 1926. It has everything."

"Is that a phone?" the boy asked, peeking inside.

"An earphone so I can speak to my driver up front," she said. She'd decided to let the boy have a look. He couldn't be left with the impression that Lola's Facel-Vega was better than her limousine.

"I thought I knew a lot about cars," the boy said, "but I ain't never seen a car with a phone in it."

"It's not a telephone," Leonora said.

"Is that a real leopard?"

"Yes," she said coldly. "If there's one thing in this world I can't abide, it's imitation leopard skin."

The boy stepped inside, putting his knee on the seat, running his dirty hand across the leopard skin. "Wow!"

"Do you mind getting out of my car and out of my way?" Leonora asked harshly. When the boy didn't budge, she seized his shirt and yanked.

The boy quickly got out.

That memory nudging her brain, she knew what it was. It moved to the forefront. This teenaged boy could be the grandson of the one of long ago who'd led the pack taunting her. The exact image, or so it seemed.

The boy stepped back. "I was just taking a look," he said,

puzzled.

"Look some place else," she said, climbing into the compartment. She slammed the door shut, narrowly missing catching the boy's fingers.

He jumped back. "What's the matter with her?" he asked Numie.

"She just doesn't want to be bothered, kid," Numie said. "Simple as that."

Behind the wheel, Numie pulled the Lincoln out of the playground. He called back to Leonora. "Just where did you get that leopard skin?"

"A famous novelist whose identity I don't care to divulge presented it to me," she said. "He killed the leopard on a safari in Africa. I took the skin, but turned down the proposition." She welcomed this opportunity to present a more glamorous picture of herself to Numie, after her difficulty at the playground.

Saying no more, Numie kept his eyes on the road straight ahead.

Few things shocked or surprised him any more. But it seemed that Leonora had deliberately tried to catch that boy's hand in the car door. Maybe Numie was exaggerating, but her cruelty appeared profound. Did she hate that much?

The same fear he had about Lola's madness was consuming him about Leonora. Would he be safe with her? Or would she turn violently against him the moment he displeased her?

He'd have to be more careful with her. After all, he didn't want to get his hand caught in any car door. Or, in anything else.

Sighing, he took a deep breath. For this job, he was getting seventy-five dollars a week. What a joke! Now he knew why he'd never wanted a regular job before.

On the earphone again, Leonora was urging him to stop. There was nothing in sight this time, except fields of mangrove.

Helping her out, he wanted to say something about the boy, but thought better of it.

Shading her sunglassed eyes from the sun, she pointed to the deserted fields. She was filled with pride. "This land is all mine...and Commodore Philip's."

Numie took a deep breath and squared his shoulders. "You

and the commodore seem to own everything in town."

She smiled at him, feeling confident and self-contained. "We do a great deal. We're partners in real estate."

"Sacre-Coeur, too?"

"No," she said. "That's the only thing I own in my own name. The bar is totally his. Even my fashion house is jointly owned."

He surveyed the wide expanse. "What are you going to do with all this land?"

"Develop it some day," she said, "when the price is right. Turn it into high-rise condominiums." A bird flew over her head, and she ducked almost in fear. Regaining her composure, she advised, "Hold onto land, Numie. It's going to be the most valuable thing there is."

Was she kidding? "I can hardly buy land on my salary," he said pointedly.

She looked at him harshly, realizing what she'd said and how ridiculous it sounded. If she didn't change the subject soon, he might be hitting her for another raise. "Let's not talk about money, darling. It's not only a vulgar subject, but bores me this hour of the morning."

Their next stop was the Sunset Trailer Court. The main sign to the camp was held up by a pair of round pillars made of conch shells cast in cement. Another sign out front promised free showers and laundry, but warned of no pets.

Helping her once again from the car, Numie was puzzled. "This is where my daddy and mama finally ended their days," she said. "At their paradise in the sun. When their house burned down, along with my school, I got this for them."

Inside the picket fence surrounding the camp was a trailer off to the right. It had been here the longest. Since 1947, she remembered exactly. Funny, she thought, looking at it now, but it had been considered luxurious at the time. "That's where they lived," she said, waving her hand.

"What do you want with that thing?" he asked.

"Sentimental reasons," she said, turning her back to him.

Hibiscus growing from the trailer's tiny front patio made access to the door difficult, but she refused to have it cut. Behind the foliage, the boxy trailer was made of plywood, and the humid weather had done cruel things to it. Its tires had long gone flat and were rotting. The orchid paint had peeled and cracked, revealing previous colors of slime green and yellow. A sagging flower box nailed to a small window held plastic tulips.

Leonora inserted the key and went inside, shutting the door in Numie's face.

The air was stale inside. Very little light came in, as the cracked window glass was fogged. In the center of the room was a fold-up card table and a pair of bridge chairs shaded by a pink silk fringed lamp.

She sat in her usual chair, after carefully dusting it. Her eyes drifted around the trailer. For a few minutes every week, she came here——just to sit and meditate. For as long as she lived, she wanted to remind herself of her origins. It was worth the price she paid.

That price was staring at her in a photograph her mama had tacked to the wall decades ago. Norton Huttnar, her miserable excuse for a husband, and the most hideous man she'd ever met.

She shuddered just thinking about the repulsive bastard. Except for this weekly interlude, she tried to forget how awful he was. But she remembered all too well.

Very old and very rich, with a fondness for teenage girls——that was Norton Huttnar. He'd first spotted her at a dancing class, right in Tortuga. Her body was starting to fill out some then, and she was on her way toward becoming spectacularly attractive. He owned Sacre-Coeur——which was his winter house, though he spent his summers in Southampton. At first he'd been interested in Ruthie Elvina, but then his interest had shifted to Leonora.

Why did she marry him? The answer was all too obvious. One look at where her parents ended up was all the reason she needed. In those days, she would have done anything to get out of Tortuga. Every night, the same. Her daddy would come home drunk, smelling of dead fish. He'd beat hell out of her mama, and Leonora had to watch. Once she stepped between them, trying to break it up, but he'd bashed her mouth in, knocking out her two front teeth.

When Norton had wanted to marry her, her daddy had been only too willing. Besides, her future husband had offered to set her daddy up in business.

A tear came to Leonora's eye. She was literally purchased like a slave on the auction block. She was only sixteen years old at the time.

Norton, the son-of-a-bitch, was seventy four!

She'd been so innocent on their honeymoon until Norton introduced her to the bizarre. She'd been in bed, lying there terrified, and he was spending an eternity in his dressing room. Finally, the door creaked open. When she saw him, she screamed.

Never in her young life had she ever been confronted with such a thing. There Norton stood, his mouth painted like bee-stung lips, his cheeks heavily rouged. He was wearing a white wig, the color of eggshell——three tiered at that. He'd painted his eyebrows jetblack with mascara, even though the gray still showed through.

His flamenco red harem pantaloons were held up by spaghetti straps. You could see right through to his jockstrap studded with pink pearls. He'd painted his breasts a turkey-comb red, and had pasted sequins around them. Iridescent beads dangled from his neck. Red silk stockings covered his legs under those pants. They were held up by garter belts, trimmed in lace. He was teetering on heels dangerously high for a man of his age, his shoes glittering with rhinestones.

Right in front of her, he'd parted those red lips and removed his false teeth. Remembering, she fell back against her chair.

That awful kewpie doll face. That sagging chin, those thick jowls. As he got closer to her, his disgusting perfume made her want to vomit. And he was wearing pancake makeup. She held her breasts. She could still feel those horrible gums working over her tender breasts, sliding up and down, slobbering over her. She'd clawed his back. He'd taken it for passion, but it was really punishment for violating her.

After she'd endured that night, she knew she could endure anything. No experience she'd ever had since equalled the horror of her wedding night. But she'd been determined. While Norton was assaulting her, she had tried to fill her mind with beautiful fantasies to blot out what was happening. But his bestiality had been so overpowering it had destroyed her dreams.

She'd known that if she failed him, she was doomed. What did she have waiting for her back in Tortuga? At the time it would have been possible to put up with anything. And she did. Night after night until Norton was finally dead. She still was grateful that he'd lived for only four more years. But those were the four longest years of her life.

She smiled in triumph and rose to her feet, a little wobbly on the trailer floor. She'd inherited everything after Norton died. And she'd earned it!

With Norton's money and the influential contacts she had made as his wife, she was launched into fashion.

The rest was history.

Outside the trailer again, Numie looked up at the Royal Poinciana trees blanketing the camp. Their leaves were fern-like and delicate, and many of them had scarlet and orange blossoms.

Noticing where he was looking, Leonora said, "When I was a child, we called this the flame tree. These trees always made me sad."

"Why?" he asked, wondering what she'd been up to in the trailer.

"They are so beautiful from June to September, but then long green pods filled with seeds appear on them. In winter, these pods turn black. The tree is bare of both leaves and flowers and looks strangely forlorn."

"They're mighty pretty now."

Eyes fixed on the tree, Leonora wandered over, reaching out to touch its bark. She fingered it, her nails digging in.

"I used to imagine those pods were dead bats sleeping through the winter. I kept praying for spring when they would fly away."

Chapter Seventeen

The road was winding along the water's edge. It was of rough coral, without streetlights or fencing. He braked the Lincoln as they neared a neon sign that read, simply, JOAN'S.

In the back seat, Leonora motioned for him to go ahead.

He looked up the driveway, then shifted gears. The car bounced along the rock-strewn road until a square, two-story white building emerged from behind a stumpy key lime grove.

The house was an acid green. The second story had a long balcony, each cut-out spoke painted a different pastel. An overgrown passion vine devoured the railings and posts, climbing to the roof. It provided a screen for two women, sitting in a row of rockers and peeking out. Overhead a string of colored lights continuously blinked.

Opening the door for Leonora, he helped her out. The piercing cry of birds meant the morning was far advanced.

Leonora's hand touched her hat. "This house used to belong to a Baptist preacher," she said, amused. "A real redneck." She clutched the fedora again, seemingly protecting it from the birds. "Built in 1875. Wish he could see it now."

Eyes glued to her every move, Numie wondered what new adventure she was taking him on. "Is this a restaurant?" he asked.

Leonora shook her head then looked in the direction of the house. She laughed. "Yes, dear heart, the garden of delights!" Then she walked quickly up the steps, ignoring the women on the porch, and passing through cranberry-etched glass doors into the central hall.

Numie trailed her, noticing how fresh and exotic she was in contrast to the shabby setting. In the hallway, he paused.

Down an open mahogany staircase came a short, stocky woman——dressed in a tailored salt-and-pepper tweed skirt, a shirt with a man's necktie, and a jacket that almost concealed her enormous bosom. Her bleached, brittle hair was cropped short, and she wore no makeup. She gasped when she saw Leonora. "You didn't tell me you were coming."

A sudden revulsion swept over Leonora, the same feeling she always had when she saw Joan. Her loose, flabby skin infuriated her. Leonora's eyes met Joan's, and they maintained locked for a moment. "Joan," she said sharply, "this is Numie."

As he shook Joan's hand, he sensed her trembling. "Glad to meet you," he said. Was he looking in on yet another vendetta?

"Hello," Joan said, hardly noticing him.

Crossing the foyer, Leonora said, "You knew I was coming." She'd always liked to nail liars on the spot. Turning again, her face was a mask of brutality. "You smell like you've just had a whole package of Clorets."

Joan looked like a little girl caught by her mother at something evil. "I was just chewing some gum."

Leonora carefully removed her fedora, enjoying the suspense she was creating. She turned almost in profile, knowing this was the best frame for her splendid jaw. "I think you've been cheating me," she accused, fascinated by the strident tone in her own voice. "I was making more money last month."

Joan's hands went up in a defensive gesture. "I turn over all the cash to you. I've never cheated you."

Knowing she was giving a performance for Numie, Leonora replied, "You cheated on me the second night we were married. Stop the pretense!" She barged through the beaded curtains into the parlor.

Numie couldn't have felt more awkward. He rocked a bit on the balls of his feet. He gave Joan a tired smile. The smile was not returned.

Joan ran after Leonora. At a cabinet in the parlor, she removed a wooden box, opening it to reveal some marijuana cigarettes wrapped in colored paper.

Leonora eyed them contemptuously. "I want a lavender one today. It fits my mood."

"I don't understand how you can smoke those filthy things," Joan said, "and complain because I take a drink now and then."

Rage shot through Leonora. How dare Joan equate her filthy habits with those of Leonora's. "A drink?" she almost screeched. "My dear child, you finish off a bottle of Scotch a day. Have ever since I've known you."

Numie was much the uninvited guest, yet at the same time

he knew he was a necessary audience to watch them play out their little drama.

Joan looked over at him. "Now you're giving this kid the wrong impression." She offered Numie the wooden box. "Here, have one."

Leonora intercepted. Those were her cigarettes, and Joan was giving them out as if she were the host. She claimed the box. "He doesn't smoke. Gave it up years ago. Doesn't drink, doesn't like girls, doesn't like boys——and he's not an addict. So you can't do anything for him. Do we understand each other?"

Joan bit her lip. "Perfectly clear."

Leonora felt needlessly immersed in details. If only there were somebody she could trust. "I want last night's earnings. Numie and I will wait." Leonora sucked in the smoke from her cigarette.

The parlor was dark except for the hall light streaming in. The red-velvet draperies were closed to the early morning sun, their cords limp and dirty. At first the furnishings were impressive, though upon closer inspection they were tacky and frayed. Leonora was sitting on a three-piece mission oak sofa covered in electric green satin. Along one wall was a curious row of mismatched straight chairs. Some well-thumbed girlie magazines lay on a console table under a stained-glass lamp.

The stale air nauseated Numie. "Unless I'm way off base here, this is a cathouse. And you're the madam."

Leonora felt her face redden and her muscles tighten. "Right about the first part," she said. "As for the second part, you're crude and insulting. I should fire you for that. I'm the landlady——nothing else. Another piece of real estate I own with the commodore."

The idea of Leonora owning a cathouse amused him. "But it is a cathouse?"

"If you want to call it that," Leonora said, bristling at his remark. "I prefer to call it JOAN'S. *That* one has found her true calling here."

Numie wondered for a moment if he should ask what was on his mind, then decided to come right out with it. "You were married to her?"

Leonora touched her finger gently against her right earring.

She feared Numie was questioning her taste——with good reason. "I lived with her, regrettably. More accurately, she lived with me. Lived *off* me I should say."

At this point Joan entered the room. "Now don't go telling him that," she said petulantly. "When I met you, I was a talented actress. I gave up a promising career for you."

Leonora sighed at hearing once more this ridiculous statement. She turned to Numie, dangling her marijuana cigarette in the air. Then she looked over at Joan. "A bit player in Hollywood with large breasts giving head to every producer who put it on his desk."

Numie was shocked at Leonora's earthy statement. Although she was usually such a lady, he was aware she could abandon that pretense in a second if the mood dictated.

At first Joan didn't say anything, looking hurt. "That's a damn lie——and you know it. I had many parts in films."

Leonora smiled, knowing she was in complete control of the situation. "Yes, the type shown at smokers."

"Legitimate films," Joan protested.

"Forgive me," Leonora said to Numie. "Joan did appear in some legitimate films. She was seen in 'We're No Ladies', as one of the drunken whores in a barroom scene. Central casting certainly knew what it was doing."

"I was a star," Joan said. "I don't care what you say. If everybody in Hollywood hadn't been a fag, I would have been even bigger. I weighed ninety-eight pounds."

"Now it's one-hundred and seventy-five," Leonora said with loathing in her voice. Obesity horrified her, yet she was surrounded by it. Both Tangerine and Joan.

"It's the work you force me to do. She likes to humiliate me, Numie, by making me hold down a job here."

Numie instinctively backed away, not wanting to get caught in this quarrel.

"Even putting my name up in lights," Joan said.

"Darling," Leonora countered, "you always wanted your name up in lights. Now your dream has come true."

"But at this disgusting place. All I ever wanted to do was settle down to a normal, healthy relationship with you."

"The only time you were ready to settle down with me was when no one else wanted you," Leonora accused.

"That's a lie!"

Abruptly, Leonora rose from the sofa. In some way this confrontation with Joan had excited her. "Is Maria ready?"

"Yes," Joan said meekly, a defeated look crossing her face.

"Have the money when I come down," Leonora said. Quickly she left the room, disappearing behind the beaded curtains.

In her sensible shoes, British tan oxfords, Joan went straight for the liquor cabinet. Hands quivering, she poured herself a stiff drink of Scotch. "Have one with me?" she asked. "I hate mornings, and this makes it easier."

"No thanks," he said. "I hate mornings, too, but I've got to get through the day. That won't help."

Nervously she was staring at him with her large, brown eyes. She was a colorless woman, blanched out by time. Her face was too full, too beefy, but there was a vague semblance there of some faded beauty. She was wiping perspiration from her high forehead, peaking under a receding hairline.

"You're in charge here?" he asked.

"You might say that——completely against my wishes, let me tell you. Leonora knows how I hate men, and night after night I have to deal with the crudest slobs. Drunken sailors and smelly shrimpers."

"Lot of hate around here," he said, hoping she wasn't directing more at him. "Leonora hates little boys. You hate men." He peered at her closely.

"I didn't always," she said. Her voice seemed drained of any tone of character.

A long silence fell over the room. It was the kind of silence you could hear.

Finally, Joan spoke. "I'm just another Tangerine, another caddy. Leonora always picks up the outcasts and makes them totally dependent on her. Are you her latest acquisition?"

Resentment flared. "You might call it that," he said sourly. "Nobody's offered to put me in the movies, take me away with them on their yacht, or install me in a castle."

"Well, that explains why you're driving Leonora around and taking her shit," she said, weaving slightly. "Does that broad know how to dish it out!"

"Now, now, you're talking about your former husband."

He was deliberately being provocative. "Leonora demands to be treated with more respect."

"I think I know a little more about Leonora's demands than you do." Arrogance surged through her body.

"She at least found a job for you." He stopped and faced her. "None of my former johns ever did that. Strictly one-night stands."

"You're a hustler?" Her face was cold and expressionless. "I should have known."

"So are you, baby." His voice was larded with resentment. "Forget the labels."

"Only difference is," she said, "I know I'm washed up." She made herself smile. "You're so sure of yourself I don't think you've got the message yet." She quickly left the room before he could reply.

Her charge left him fuming. He hardly needed a brokendown whore to tell him he was washed up. The more he tried to forget her remark, the more he thought about it. She had known where to strike. He settled back to think about it.

In some ways, he was lucky to have lasted as long as he did as a hustler. At least, that was one way of looking at it. Starting at fifteen, he was now thirty-two. A good seventeen years lodged on the job. Obviously time was running out. He had to get into some other line of work. He could just see himself now, filling out a job application. Under previous experience, he could list seventeen years of having his cock gobbled.

Here he sat in a room where God only knows how many whores had met their johns for the evening. Where did it get anybody? After seventeen years of hustling, he found himself right back where he started. Nothing to show for anything, except the wear and tear on his body. The bloom was off the flower, that was for certain. Still, he was in demand——even if it were by a black drag queen. But Ralph had found him attractive as well. How long could his appeal last? Each year counted.

Actually he had more of a chance in Tortuga than he did in New York. The competition there was rough. Why, kids played hookey from school and came to town from as far away as small cities in New Jersey "to work the queers."

At first, his hustling had been different. He'd felt he was hot shit when people paid money for his body. After a boyhood of being told he was worth nothing, it was good to see cash on the line.

With no education and an undefined ambition, he could have found some kind of work, couldn't he? Was washing dishes any more demeaning than having people too old or too repulsive to attract lovers make love to your body? A thousand mouths before he was eighteen. Maybe five hundred asses. Each and every one wanting to be stuffed.

It was a vicious circle, hard to drop out. You kept running the damn rat race until you were kicked out. But what use did society have for aging hustlers? Numie couldn't think of one. Not one.

One cold January day in a New York bar on Forty-Sixth street, he'd been drinking with two other hustlers. Usually he didn't hang out with hustlers, but he'd been lonely and depressed that day. Christ, you had to talk to someone sometime. The two men had been drinking heavily, fantasizing mightily about the big break. Both were past their prime. Both had never even gotten near that big break, and certainly were farther from it now than ever.

"Cut the shit, man," Numie finally said to one of them. "Your best days are behind you. It's going to get tougher, not better." The hustler punched him in the mouth. Numie didn't strike back. He'd deserved it, he figured.

Out on the street, he realized what he'd done. He'd attacked the one thing that hustlers had to hold on to. Dreaming about that big break kept the guy going.

Numie also realized what he was attacking. A future vision of himself. Would he end up as pathetic as that hustler, waiting for something to happen, yet knowing it never would?

Ghosts were filling up this parlor too quickly. Maybe he did need that drink. Better yet, one of those lavender-wrapped marijuana cigarettes. No, blue. Leonora said blue was his color.

Just then, Leonora herself entered.

"May I have one of your cigarettes?" he asked nervously, like a child caught with his hand in the cookie jar.

"Yes, if you *must*." Her expression was savage.

"Not if you feel that way." His face drained, he closed the lid on the wooden box.

"No, no," she said impatiently. "Take the damn thing——and give me one, too." Eyes blind with the strain of people, she added, "Let's not talk about something trivial all morning."

Blue smoke drifted up from the dark room. The light coming in through the door revealed the vague outline of Leonora's too white face.

"Well..." he sighed, inhaling deeply. A dog barked outside.

"Don't ever say 'well'." She adjusted her dress. "It's not dramatic."

"I'm too tired to be dramatic." A fly buzzed the room.

"If you have something to say, say it with all the force and power of your body. No matter how foolish it may sound. Foolish statements said with authority sound less so." The sun was high in the sky, and she was growing increasingly warm, fearing she was overdressed for the occasion.

He blended his fingers together, then cracked his knuckles.

"Please, don't do that," she ordered. "It annoys me." She knew she was being a bitch, but the scene with Maria upstairs had upset her so much she had to take it out on someone.

"I'm sorry," he said, fearing he would one day drown under the weight of his endless apologies to Leonora.

"You're always sorry about something," she said. "I'm even getting tired of your being sorry." The whole room had a musty stoginess, and it was making her ill.

"Dammit," he said. "I don't know how to please you." His voice was harsh and choking.

"You're all alike——monsters." She moved slightly into the terrific silence following the accusation. The house itself seemed to have fallen asleep.

"I am not." Why was she doing this to him?

"Yes, you are. Ralph and Anne, Joan——all monsters."

From the hallway came the sound of rushing feet, light like a young girl's.

"If we're such monsters, why do you put up with us?" He mopped his face on his sleeve.

"Darling, if we kicked the monsters out of our lives, we'd have no friends." Her hand gingerly smoothed down her dress. Was Maria running down the steps?

Joan was back in the room, money in hand.

"I can only trust this to be an honest accounting," Leonora said. The birds screeched over the house again in a way that was menacing to her.

"I told you, no one's cheating you." Joan's face turned to putty. "Here it is."

Leonora rose. "Leave it on the table for Numie. Never give me another manila envelope. I want the money in scented envelopes...envelopes scented of lavender." She turned slowly in the middle of the floor, then faced forward, and marched out.

"You must be kidding," Joan said.

"No, I am not, as you say, 'kidding'," Leonora called back. "I don't even know what the word means. I'm a woman who has the power to indulge her whims, and I intend to do just that."

"Okay," Joan said, sighing, "lavender scent it will be."

"One more thing," Leonora added, "about Maria."

"Yes."

"The child has ceased to amuse me. She's lifeless. Lies there like a limp doll, almost as if drugged." Leonora shuddered with disgust at having had sex with Maria.

"She's only thirteen," Joan protested. "What do you expect?"

"I expect her to consider it an honor when I come out to pay a visit." She turned and stared at Joan, amazed that she could not get the point.

"You're expecting too much. She told me she doesn't like to do certain things, especially with women."

"I am no ordinary woman," Leonora said, feeling put upon for having to defend herself.

"I, of all people know that, but that's not the point." Joan's fear was showing.

"I have no more time to listen to your excuses. It seems I've heard nothing else for half my life. Until you make the Garden of Delights live up to its name, I shall not come here again." She was heading for the porch, leaving an undefined threat in her wake.

"Listen," Joan whispered to Numie, "say a good word for me if you hear her putting me down." She was perspiring heavily.

"I've no influence with her," he said. "I think if I advised her to do something, she'd do just the opposite." For the first time, he mustered up some sympathy for Joan.

"But try," she pleaded. The big clock in the hallway struck the noon hour, and Joan jumped.

"Why are you asking me to do you a favor? You just attacked me for being washed up." His sympathy went as quickly as it came.

"I didn't mean it. I get mean when I drink."

"Then you must be mean all the time." Someone in the back was cooking tomatoes, and the smell was spreading everywhere.

"You bastard!" She wet her mouth and arched her back, reminding him of a bull moose readying for battle.

"Numie," Leonora called from the porch. "How dare you keep me waiting!"

"Coming," he yelled, scooping up last night's take.

The smell of the cooking faded as he reached the porch. The sea air was fresh there, aided a bit by the faint delicious perfume of flowering bushes.

He could hear Joan whispering to somebody in the hallway inside.

The clock struck the noon hour once again. Then the door was slammed shut.

A dog from under the porch barked at Numie.

The familiar black Lincoln was parked in the shabby yard. Hurriedly, Numie crossed the grounds to reach it.

Deliberately hoping to shatter the foul mood coming from Leonora in the rear, he turned on the radio. He glanced back at her, expecting a reprimand, but her face was waxed.

He cut off the radio anyway.

Speeding frantically along the beach, he had an urgency to reach their destination.

But he knew Leonora had no other place to go.

And neither did he.

Chapter Eighteen

Chino's Cafe stood on the corner of Water Lane and Shark Street, about half a block from the shrimp docks. An overgrown banyan tree with airborne roots had lifted up the right end of the building nearly a foot, including its lean-to porch. No one had painted anything...ever. The entrance door, wired back so that it was always open, was strung with a beaded curtain. Numie went in.

The cafe was jumping. Shrimpers in for a late lunch of green turtle steak and conch chowder filled the little oilcloth-covered tables.

On a lone counter rested a large urn of bitter, black coffee. Chipped cups and mugs stood upside down on paper toweling. Nearby were three large cans of evaporated milk.

All eyes turned and looked in Numie's direction. But by now he was getting used to stares. Ignoring them, he headed for a deserted table in the far corner. There, he ordered a cup of coffee and settled back.

Flies buzzed around a chrome stand, holding the remains of a key lime pie. On the wall were clusters of enlarged snapshots of shrimp boats, their owners grinning or glowering.

Everywhere he looked no frills, no fuss, no curtains, no pretense——as bareboned as his soul this day.

Forty-five minutes and three cups of black coffee later, he still didn't know what to do. The afternoons were long and heavy in Tortuga, and Numie was growing increasingly restless. Leonora had retired for the rest of the day——so he was free. Lola, thank God, was getting her beauty rest before her appearance in the bar tonight.

Then a familiar figure at the door. Anne, carrying a package.

He didn't know why, but her very presence stirred something within him. Maybe it was because he was bored. At any rate he was genuinely glad to see her. He got up quickly, heading for the front. "Let me help you."

She looked startled, almost as if she didn't recognize him. "Oh, it's you," she said. "Never expected to find you at Chino's." For a moment, she hesitated, then surrendered the package. "Thanks."

"Come join me for a cup of coffee," he said. He glanced quickly around the cafe. The presence of the other men made him nervous.

"I'd better get back." She smiled.

"Please," he said. He was afraid he was sounding desperate.

She gave him a short laugh. "Okay, if you ask that way." Winding her way through the crowd, she added over her shoulder, "I didn't know you knew how to say please."

He smiled, raising his eyes. "I know how to say a lot of things."

"I bet you have quite a line." Her lips were close to his ear.

Was she flirting? Leading her to his table, Numie ordered more coffee.

Silence fell. The utter silence of a hot afternoon.

Her brow was shiny, and her lips also shone in the bright light. Occasionally she would glance at him, but no thoughts came to mind——at least nothing that needed to be expressed.

As he sat looking at her, he sensed forlornly that his life had to change. He couldn't go on living as he was.

"I must tell you something," she whispered confidentially. "On this island you run into everybody you know at least three times a day." She sipped her coffee, eying him, then glancing at the other men in the cafe. "It's fantastic——hopeless if you're trying to avoid someone. I should also warn you that the major industry is gossip." She wiped her forehead. "If word gets back, Lola will be jealous."

His cozy feeling building with her collapsed at that remark. She was baiting him. "Don't remind me of that..." he said sharply. "I'm enjoying this afternoon." His flare-up subsided quickly, and he was at peace again. "Now that I've got some real female company."

She laughed softly at this compliment. "I've never gotten on with Lola at all," she said, "although Tangerine likes her. Leonora can't stand her either, but the commodore is Leonora's closest friend——so she tolerates Lola for Philip's sake."

"What gives with Lola and the commodore?"

"I don't understand such relationships," she said. Her voice was low, plaintive. "At times I'm so normal I seem like an oddball in this crowd."

This made him wonder how she classified him. "Your life is hardly normal."

"That doesn't mean I wouldn't like it to be," she added quickly. Surprisingly, she caught his hand and held it for a fleeting moment.

A tingling sensation rushed through him.

After dropping his hand, she seemed embarrassed, her eyes no longer looking at him. "Speaking of normalcy, how was your morning with Leonora?"

The afternoon sky was lit strangely, giving everyone a yellow glow. He paused, thinking of her reaching for his hand, not hearing her latest question. Then it sunk in. "You can imagine, I guess. You know better than anyone what a morning with Leonora is like. Voodoo queens, cathouses." He sighed. "I'm glad to have an afternoon off from her, too."

"Me, too," she chimed. "I'm out shopping right now because I can't stand being in the same house with her, even though she's retired to her private quarters. She's driving me crazy." Her lips trembled. "And Ralph is no help. He's completely on a sex trip. He's not even a companion. I never see him any more, which is just as well, I guess."

An ache of desire skidded along his spine. "I think he's very foolish to neglect a wife like you."

She was taken back. "I take that as a compliment." Nervously she stirred her coffee. "I'd like to say you're very nice yourself. Which raises a question. Can't you do better than an aging drag queen?"

He frowned at her reluctance to drop that one subject. "Do better with who?" he asked. "What do you have in mind?"

A couple of boys went by to the toilet in the rear, and she used this momentary diversion to avoid answering him. Then she said, "You're the man."

He was searching her face, but it told him little. Hands clenched, he rose quickly.

She looked up at him. "You realize I'm only teasing."

"Sure," he said, reaching down for the last of his coffee. He could feel his neck redden.

"Is it ever hot!" she said, getting up. "Let's go back to Sacre-Coeur for a dip in the pool."

· · ·

The hot bricks of the patio burned through Numie's sandals. At the opposite end of the Olympic-sized pool, Anne was removing all her clothes. Big breasted, with an hourglass figure, she had tanned skin, smooth and inviting. Laughing at his surprise, she jumped into the pool backward, her arms outstretched. She splashed him with cool water. "Bashful!" she yelled.

"Like hell!" he called back. He felt his body flood with excitement. "I'm joining you," he told the wet head emerging from beneath.

"Can you swim in big waters?" Her look was provocative, challenging.

He felt ready for the challenge. In moments, he was out of his clothes——every piece of them, and was heading for the diving board. Bouncing once, then twice, he executed a perfect dive in her direction. Surfacing, he came up by her side. He capped her head with his hand, dunking her. "That's for wetting my clothes," he said, as she emerged again.

She tried to dunk him, but he escaped, swimming to the other side of the pool. Splashing noisily, she was hot on his trail. He swam past her, going up and down the pool's length, enjoying this respite from the day's tension.

"Let's rest up," he said when she finally caught up with him.

Her body seemed ignited. "But I owe you a dunking," she protested.

"It'll wait." On impulse, he pulled her close, pressing his lips against hers. He kissed her hungrily, his tongue slipping inside her mouth.

She responded, but it was weak, passive. Then she broke away.

His innocent play with her had now become self-conscious.

Out of the water, she was reaching for a towel, wrapping it quickly around her nude body.

He, too, got out of the pool in his search for a towel. Drying himself, he sprawled on a pad in the sun. Suddenly, he felt exposed in her presence. So he wrapped the towel around his body, as she had done.

Anne was filling her mug of beer. "You've got a nice body," she said. "Or is the man supposed to say that to the woman?"

"If he is, and I haven't, I'd like to return the compliment now." The sun was drying his body, and he stretched luxuriously in its glow, marveling at the beauty of the Tortuga sky. Her compliment had gotten rid of the self-conscious feeling that had crept over him. The other day at the beach, he'd been worried about his body. Now he felt perfectly secure with it.

She seemed to be studying him. "We're about the same age, aren't we?" she asked. "I'm thirty-two."

This bolted him upright. Age, especially his own, was about the last subject he wanted to talk about. "Yes," he said hesitantly, not knowing why she was asking.

"Ralph's thirty-four," she added as an afterthought. Finding a comfortable spot on an adjoining pad, she lay back. "Why does the world belong to the young?"

"You're young," he answered quickly, hoping she would drop the subject. Even though they were the same age, she was obviously much better preserved than he was.

"No more than you are," she said. "Let's face it. You consider yourself old."

A look of alarm crossed his face. He reached for sunglasses. The savage glare of the sun was too much for him.

"I'm always thinking I'm old," she went on. "But isn't it stupid?"

"In your case, very," he said.

"I don't feel old."

"And why should you?" he asked.

"The world when it looks at me makes me feel old."

"I'm the world," he said, "and I'm looking at you. And age is the last thought on my mind." He lay back and closed his eyes. The sunglasses were providing a shield against reality for him. But then on their glass a film of his fleeting youth, speeding life started flashing before him. Opening his eyes wide, he still couldn't get rid of those pictures.

"I often wonder what it's going to be like when I'm older," she said. "I know I'm pretty good looking right now. But what will happen in a few years?"

He grabbed some of her beer and drank thirstily from the

mug.

"I see those older women up on the mainland panting after young studs," she continued, oblivious to his rising agitation. "And the way they're treated in return. Those bastards like to make the old gals not only pick up the tabs, but crawl while they're doing it."

Her haunting eyes were staring at him, but he lay back on the mat——hoping to become indistinguishable in the white glare.

"I sit by the pool day after day, feeling the world passing me by," she said.

Her entire conversation was unbearable to him. It was he who was feeling the world passing by, but he didn't want to be reminded. He hoped to find escape with her, not this torture.

"I see myself getting old at Sacre-Coeur, sharing a cold brother-sister relationship with Ralph," she said.

He swallowed hard. That prospect did not entice him either. "After thirty in life, one starts taking the leavings," he said. After he'd said it, he didn't know if he really meant it. It was something to say.

"But are the leavings all that bad?" she asked, sitting up and staring intently at him with her large eyes.

He didn't say anything at first. Had he insulted her? He wasn't sure what she was asking...and why. "I guess I've automatically given in to the world's retiring me while I'm in my prime. Never thought I'd have much chance fighting back."

"But you've got most of your life facing you," she said, still intent with her gaze. "Of course, you can't go on playing chicken to a lot of youth-starved perverts."

For some reason, this statement angered him. It was an anger directed not so much at her, but at his increasing frustration in life. "Yeah," he said, "well, just what is waiting for me?"

"You can be yourself for a change and find out what that's all about."

Before he could reply, or even think about that, Ralph was at the poolside, slowly sipping a glass of Scotch. "Hope I'm interrupting something."

Anne was angry and wasn't trying to conceal it. She was also acting guilty. "I see my philandering husband has finally returned home for his supper."

Ralph's eyes were on fire. "My neglected wife seems to be doing okay for herself." He eyed Numie, softening his glare. "Hi."

"Good to see you," Numie said, covering himself better with his towel.

In one quick plunge, Anne cast her towel aside and was back in the pool, swimming deep this time and emerging at the other end. "Come and join me, Ralph," she called. "We've both seen you nude before."

"Forget it!" Ralph called back. "She's really into this nudity thing." Then, remembering, he added, "Guess you are, too, up to a point."

"It doesn't bother me," Numie said. "I used to think we learn it from our parents. But that's not true. My mama had sex with her clothes on."

Ralph sat down on a chair near Numie. "I saw my mother naked——or partially naked——only once. She didn't know I was home, and she came barging out of her bedroom into the living room, her bathrobe swinging open. I saw her breasts before she spotted me. She actually screamed. Can you imagine?"

"Why?" Numie asked, genuinely puzzled.

"Then she said the strangest thing. She told me if my father ever found out about this, he'd beat me to within an inch of my life. What had I done? I was just sitting there."

Numie was enjoying this confidence, yet at the same time he was resenting Ralph. He felt he had been building a mood with Anne. Now it was ruined. Ralph brought out the bitch in her.

Dripping wet, Anne was beside them.

Ralph turned and gave her a hostile look. "Dammit," he said, "put some clothes on. If you could see how disgusting you look."

Numie winced.

"Disgusting to you, maybe," Anne retorted. "Numie told me I have a very lovely body." Reluctantly, she reached for her towel, wrapping it around herself again.

Ralph stared at Numie.

Numie didn't say anything, but lay back, closing his eyes, not wanting to get involved in a triangle, but moving deeper and deeper into it. When he opened his eyes again, he looked at Anne. She was drying her hair and itching for a fight.

Seeing she had Numie's attention, she said, "When Ralph and I got married, I don't think he'd ever seen a woman completely nude before."

"What I'd seen or hadn't seen was none of your damn business," Ralph said, finishing his drink.

Anne was persistent, the same way she'd been about Lola. "After a few weeks, I got Ralph to play a little game with me. He didn't want to, guess I forced the issue."

"As you're inclined to do from time to time," Ralph said sarcastically.

"I thought I could break down his disgust at looking at the female body," she said. "We started watching television, and getting our dinner, completely nude. But the experiment never worked. To this day, Ralph can't look at me without repugnance showing in his face." With this she dropped the towel, letting it cascade to the ground. Before both men, she was completely naked.

Numie was seeking some excuse to leave, but couldn't find one. Once again he felt trapped, the way he was with Leonora and Joan. Ralph and Anne actually wanted him here.

"You even forced me to touch you," Ralph accused, practically spitting out his words.

"Since when does a wife have to force her husband to touch her?"

"It wasn't to be that kind of marriage," Ralph countered.

"That's for damn sure," Anne agreed. She turned to Numie. "Ralph did try, I must say. We had a few experiments, but they were disastrous."

"I don't care to have my sexual inadequacies discussed in public," Ralph said, picking up his empty glass.

Wistfully, and very unrealistically, Numie was still hoping for a late reprieve from this conversation.

"I'm sure Numie knows more about you sexually than I ever will," Anne said.

"Cut it out," Numie said. She was really making him angry.

At first she seemed surprised that he'd reprimanded her. Somehow she'd been counting on his support. Then, looking at both men in front of her, she added, almost under her breath, "If only Nick were alive."

Impulsively, Ralph crashed his empty glass on the bricks around the pool. "Nick!" he shouted. "If I hear his name one more time...just one more time. I've warned you."

Numie got up. To hell with both of them. He was leaving for more peaceful oases.

"Just a minute," Ralph called to him, grabbing Numie by the shoulder. "Did she tell you about her precious Nick?"

Numie turned back, glaring. "I think she might have mentioned him," he said.

"I *bet* she mentioned him," Ralph charged. "The love of her life. Let me tell you about the love of her life."

Numie tried to break away, but Ralph held him firmly.

"If you tell that awful lie," Anne shouted. "I'll take something and strike you. Don't listen to him, Numie. It's a lie."

He sensed her rising panic.

She put her hands to her mouth and started running from the pool. "It's a lie! A lie!"

Again, Numie tried to leave, but Ralph practically pushed him into a chair. "Hey, cut it out, man," Numie said. "I'd better go help her."

"She doesn't need your help," Ralph said. "That great love, that Nick, was a fantasy. Sure, she was married to a Nick. A cheap hood from Brooklyn."

"Come on," Numie urged, "I'm not into life histories."

Ralph totally ignored him. "Leonora and I found out all anyone needed to know about Nick. Even Anne broke down one night and told us what he did to her, the love of her life."

"Listen, I've already told you, I don't want to hear it." Numie settled back, shutting his eyes, as if that would blot out Ralph. "I long ago learned, and you should know it by now, don't take people's illusions away."

"But I'm always being unfavorably compared to that gangster," Ralph protested.

"Let her keep the memory," Numie said. "It's probably all she has."

Ralph got up and walked around to the other side of the pool. He put his hands on a railing and looked into the deepening shadows of the garden. His voice was tired when he spoke. "*Love of her life* one night brought three guys home with him when they had an apartment in the Bronx."

Numie smiled forlornly. Somehow he knew the end of the story. He was deeply sorry for Anne, sorry she'd never really had anything.

"Then this Nick stripped nude right in front of everybody," Ralph continued. "Knocked hell out of Anne, and demanded she blow him. When she refused, he kicked her in the belly."

Numie was experiencing Anne's pain.

"She was pregnant," Ralph said, "and that led to a miscarriage. Even though she was screaming with pain, he fucked her while the other guys watched, then held her down while they took turns."

The memory of catching Lisa in bed with her lover flashed through Numie's mind. That was his emotional outrage. Anne had known worse.

Ralph's hands dropped to his side, and he looked up to the still blazing sun. "That's Nick! That's the love of her life!"

. . .

The afternoon was slowly fading, the sun sinking. The lights in the pool and around the patio were turned on. In a robe, Numie was thinking Sacre-Coeur was much like a stage setting. Unreal, somehow.

On his fifth Scotch for the day, Ralph joined Numie at poolside. "Sure you won't have another drink?" he asked.

"No, my limit for the day." Ralph's glass looked reassuring. "Leonora has put a limit on my booze."

"Fuck her!" Ralph said. "I'll get you another drink." He started to get up.

Numie motioned for him to sit down. "I don't need any more." He placed his hand on the back of his neck to massage a sudden pain. "I've got to be joining Lola at the bar."

Ralph sighed. "That's what I want to talk to you about. I think you should leave Lola."

Numie forced himself to laugh. "I think I should leave, too, but I need the bread."

The shadows were now creeping across the garden. At the

top of a set of stairs, the single bulb of a Spanish lamp was turned on. A dark figure moved along the loggia.

Unbuttoning his tie, Ralph said, "This sounds crazy coming from me, but I've been thinking about settling down."

Numie was startled.

"I've spent most of my life cruising," Ralph went on, "and it's leading nowhere. I'm beginning to want something more permanent."

His drunken, yet steady, gaze was causing Numie acute discomfort.

"Like, I find myself in bed reaching over and secretly wishing someone was there."

"We all wish that," Numie said, still embarrassed to be talking this personally with Ralph.

Getting up and pacing the patio in circles, Ralph said, "Okay, so that person doesn't love me as much as I could love him. I'm aware of that, for Christ's sake. I can live with that."

The idea of Ralph ever loving anyone was more than Numie could imagine.

"I don't expect total devotion," Ralph said, continuing his monologue. "But I do want respect. The rough trade I've patronized treats me like filth." He stopped abruptly. "And I feel like filth when I've finished with them."

Numie sniffed the air. It suggested exotic flowers, the names of which he didn't know. He looked up at Ralph. "Just what are you leading up to?"

"The day on the island when I kissed you."

At this, Numie sat up. Having sex with men was one thing. Talking about it later was yet another.

"To you," Ralph said, "that was nothing. I know hustlers don't like to be kissed. But it was a big event in my life. I'd never kissed a man before——not even my father on the cheek."

Numie brushed his still wet hair out of his face. Could Leonora be overhearing this conversation? Worse, Anne?

"Now isn't that ridiculous?" Ralph asked. "I've sucked their cocks, but never kissed them on the mouth. Somehow sucking a cock always seemed more impersonal than a kiss on the mouth. I know it should be the other way around. But kiss you I did."

The soft dazzling strokes of sunset broke through the trees, making images on the sparkling water. From an overhanging branch, leaves fell into the pool. Birds darted about. The bugs and flies of a Tortuga night were about to begin their descent.

"You had sex with me twice," Numie said emphatically, "although you told me you never went in for repeats."

"That's right," Ralph answered. "I never told you this." He reached for Numie's hand which was reluctantly offered. "But the second time with you——at the hotel——was much better than the first."

"Thanks," Numie said, slowly retrieving his hand. "I try to please."

"This afternoon I was out cruising——and I spotted some pretty good-looking numbers."

Numie withdrew. Was Ralph going to compare him unfavorably with the other men on the beach, the way Numie had done himself?

"Then I started thinking," Ralph said. "I wanted a real man, one who knows how to make love. Not some weak little boy lying on his back waiting to be done so he can collect money. Suddenly, those boys on the beach were one big turn-off. You came to mind. What would a third time be like?" He leaned closer to Numie, looking in his eyes. "I don't know what's happening to me."

Was this a dream or a nightmare? Numie wondered. Was Ralph really serious? "I think you're getting a crush on me."

Ralph smiled. He wasn't insulted. "Can you handle that?"

The night was growing darker. Numie had a sudden urge to jump back into the pool. "That's a big question. I'm very mixed up right now." He turned to look at Ralph. "I don't know what to do."

"Let me decide for you," Ralph said, moving closer. "Tell Lola——right tonight——to fuck off. Then you move in the guest cottage here."

An ominous feeling of impending doom came over Numie. "I can't do it just like that. I've been waiting to meet the commodore."

"What do you think he's going to do for you?" Ralph asked.

"I've been carrying around this hope he'll like me and give

me a real job. Maybe on one of his boats or something. He has a big yacht."

"Bullshit!"

Numie stood his ground. "Why'd you say that?"

"He'll just use you and toss you overboard."

"I know how to swim," Numie said defiantly. "Besides, I see he owns a lot of property in this town."

"So what?"

"Maybe he'd let me manage something," Numie said. Ralph was treading on one of his few hopes, and Numie was growing more defensive by the minute. "I can't get very far in this world on the seventy-five dollars Leonora is paying me."

"Move in here," Ralph said, waving his hand in a grand gesture, "and I'll double your salary."

This offer surprised Numie. "Now that's a pretty good deal."

"Only thing is, I've just canceled that invitation I made to you."

"What invitation?" Numie asked.

"That you can sock it to Anne."

Numie swallowed hard.

"Now that I'm staking my claim," Ralph said, "I don't want her filthy hands on you. Hear me?"

Resentment burned through Numie. "I hear you."

"I feel I can get very jealous, and it's a new emotion for me."

"I bet you'd be pretty good at it," Numie said with a slight touch of sarcasm in his voice. "I've got to be going."

"I want you back here tonight," Ralph commanded.

At first, Numie stood glaring at him. He didn't like to be ordered around like this. Everybody on this goddamn island seemed to be his boss. "See you later," he said in a vague, non-committal way.

Ralph grabbed Numie's arm. "You're forgetting something."

Numie started to pull away, but finally stood still.

"When you leave your *lover*," Ralph said, "you kiss him good-bye."

Numie's lips brushed Ralph's. He closed his eyes, thinking of something else.

"Not like that," Ralph said, grabbing again. Ralph not only kissed hard this time, but bit Numie's lower lip.

In pain, Numie jumped back. "Why did you do that, man?" he asked, ready to strike Ralph at this point.

Through drunken eyes, Ralph looked up at him. "I just want you to remember who you belong to. The pain on your lip will remind you."

In the night air with a sore lip, Numie decided to walk back to Commodore Philip's. For a hustler whom Joan had said was washed up——just this morning at the whorehouse——he was getting more offers than he could handle. Not quite out of the game yet.

But unlike the offers in his past for one-night stands, these were entangling. Lola or Ralph, each offer was strangely disturbing. He foresaw little good coming from either.

To begin with, he didn't like Ralph, and he positively hated Lola. Further, he'd always been a loner. He didn't know if he could take to the role of being someone's boy. Especially someone he didn't like to be with that much.

At first he was a little flattered by Ralph's offer, but then he started to resent it. His manhood up for sale to the highest bidder. Ralph just seemed to be buying him, taking him without his consent. Yet Numie had clearly placed himself in that position. So why resent the person who took the option? Rather, be grateful.

He was complaining too much. The guest cottage at Sacre-Coeur was one hell of a lot better than the filthy subterranean toilets of New York's subway system.

As he neared the bar, Lola's white Facel-Vega was gleaming under the streetlamp. But behind it was a 1938 Rolls-Royce.

He knew at once the mysterious Commodore Philip had returned from the mainland.

Chapter Nineteen

For the occasion, Lola was wearing a satin evening blazer covered with huge sequin dots the color of cherries. Behind the bar, she spotted Numie, then said, "'Bout time you showed up. *He's* back!" A tall cooler in hand, she rushed to a table in the rear.

There sat Commodore Philip.

At the first sight of him, Numie's heart sank.

Dressed entirely in white, the commodore was a strange creature. A straw hat rested jauntily on his miniature head, held on by a long neck from which loose flesh dangled. The neck gave way to a large, beer-barrel trunk, carried on spidery legs. He took off his hat, laying it on the table, and brushed back his wildly flowing silvery hair. Then he returned it to his head. His heavy face was lined and colored a sickly gray.

Lola placed the drink in front of the commodore, patting him on his stooped shoulder. Her insides were churning with disgust. He'd returned too soon, planning to horn in on her scene now that she'd bagged an attractive blond stud. She turned to Numie. "Every time my commodore comes home, it's Sunday chicken time."

The commodore's beady eyes fastened on Numie. He gently spat a drop of blood into a large, white handkerchief, then sank back into his seat. The position was just right. His head was on an exact parallel to Numie's waist. "This the stud you been raving and shouting so much about——you'd think you were at a holy-roller meeting, the way this gal's been carrying on."

Lola frowned at this revelation. She didn't want Numie to know how special he was.

The tiny white lights in back sent narrow beams to the front of the room, creating a touch of intimacy and privacy in the bar tonight.

Numie couldn't have been more disappointed. "The commodore's a slob——can't take his eyes off my crotch," he thought to himself. "Numie Chase," he said out loud, stepping up to the table.

The commodore was breathing heavily, as he always did when he returned to Tortuga. To him, the whole island tasted of forbidden fruit. His eyes traveled to Numie's face. "I know who you are, and you know who I am. So let's not take up a busy man's time with introductions that ain't necessary." He grandly waved his hand in the air. "Sit down, boy, 'cause I get dizzy looking up all the time."

"Thanks," Numie said, easing into a seat opposite this aging relic with his satanic goatee.

Blinking her false eyelashes, Lola nestled up to the commodore, possessively linking her arm in his.

Philip immediately imposed a barrier of studied indifference between them. "What you drink, boy?"

"Scotch," he replied. For some reason, Numie found he was clenching and unclenching his fingers into tight fists. There was an air of turbulent suspicion about the commodore. Just as Leonora seemed to have emerged from a 1930s time capsule, the commodore went back even beyond that. He was antebellum.

"Sunshine," the commodore yelled back to the kitchen. This shout brought on a coughing spasm that lasted a full minute. At its termination, the commodore spat some more into his handkerchief, then reached for a pill in the upper breast pocket of his white linen suite. "Scotch, huh," he managed to say.

"I'll get it," Lola said, hoping to avoid another shout and another coughing spasm. The sight of blood made her positively ill. Pretty soon the commodore would be asking her to take that dirty handkerchief upstairs and fetch him a clean one.

He pushed her back in her seat. "You're the lady of the manor tonight, you pretty little pickaninny. You ain't waiting on nobody, 'cept the boss man here." The white light coming from the back was beaming right on Lola. Christ, she was getting old! But she was the best pimp in the world, and he didn't plan to let her go. He'd settled in with her, the only person he'd ever known who gave in to any demand——no matter how outrageous. "Sunshine," he yelled again. Then, in an aside to Numie, he added, "He's my cousin." This was said as if it were the world's largest secret.

When Numie took in the full presence of Sunshine, he understood at once why the commodore wanted to keep their relationship confidential.

From the kitchen had emerged a sunken-faced, ghostly young man, about twenty years old. He'd inherited the commodore's spindly and immature legs, carrying around a trunk two sizes too big.

With prolonged and increasing loathing, the commodore studied Sunshine, then said, "Brought him from New Orleans. Works for me up on the mainland, but I decided I needed him more now in Tortuga. Get this stud hustler here a Scotch."

Numie frowned at being openly talked about as a piece of flesh. He sucked in his breath, preparing for a long evening.

"Christ, Phil, got all I can do to cook that grub you asked for," Sunshine said, in a high-pitched, petulant voice. "Got no time to run drinks."

When the commodore spoke, he sounded exhausted, as if the patience of a long life was giving way. "Do what I say, boy, or else you'll feel my boot in that skinny ass of yours." After Sunshine left, he turned to Numie. "That boy's like the rest of our family——just got no ass on us at all. Two skinny cheeks and some bones. Not enough padding to sit down on."

At this, Lola perked up. She needed some outward display of the commodore's affection which she could show off in front of Numie. "But you like my curvy little mounds, don't you?" she asked.

The commodore cocked his head to one side. Her question brought back a distant memory of some stale horror he'd rather forget. Winking at Numie, he took off his straw hat and jauntily tipped it to Lola. "Your black ass is a creamy little doorway to paradise," he said, pinching her breast.

Lola squealed with delight, except he didn't have to say black, did he?

Sunshine plopped the drink down in front of Numie, then disappeared into the kitchen in back.

Philip's eyes blazed for half a second, then faded into a motley gray. "Now Scotch indicates one thing about the personality. Shows an awful lack of imagination." At this observation, he broke into giggles. His opinions always amused him. He never knew what he was going to say next.

The glass was poised at Numie's lips. He decided to ignore the insult. Insecure johns always felt it necessary to insult him. "What's that you're drinking?" Numie asked, hoping to turn the spotlight off himself.

The commodore broke into a smile. As he fingered his chilled glass, he was remembering another day and a fine southern lady——all dressed in white and real high class——who introduced him to this drink, as well as a few other pleasures of life. "It's Roffignac, one of the best drinks of New Orleans. That's where I come from." He said New Orleans with such love and feeling it seemed as if God's anointed came from that city.

"Never heard of it," Numie said.

The commodore slammed down his drink.

Suddenly, Numie was aware of the misunderstanding. "Of course, I've heard of New Orleans. I mean I've never heard of Roffignac."

The commodore broke into giggles again. "I know, Mr. Stud Hustler, you've heard of New Orleans. You've been there, all right, I remember distinctly giving you a blow job one night at Mardi Gras."

Lola was stunned. Fury came over her. The commodore had already met her discovery. Violently she drank from her rum toddy.

Numie sat back. The commodore was lying. He knew that, and Numie knew that. He was waiting for Numie to challenge him, and Numie was determined not to give him that confrontation.

When the commodore realized he'd get no response, he went on, "I didn't expect you to hear of Roffignac. Now that's made with whiskey and Hembarig syrup. Hembarig syrup is a sweetnin' that ain't on the market no more, but I got some. And where I got it, I ain't telling." He shoved his tall cooler in front of Numie. "Taste it," he ordered.

Numie sampled it. "Not bad," he said, "sort of raspberry syrup flavor."

"Phil," Sunshine yelled from the back. "It's your goddamn sister Amelia on the phone. *Collect* from New Orleans."

For one brief moment, the commodore sank silently into himself. Breathing in, he puffed himself up like a balloon.

"Phil," Sunshine screamed again.

Slowly lighting his cigarette in its ivory holder, the commodore rose to his wobbly feet.

Lola handed him a silver-tipped cane.

Eyes clenched, he gazed toward the pay phone in the rear. He seemed on the verge of suffocation. "Would you kind people excuse me while I take care of this untimely intrusion from one's personal relations?" His ebony cane leading the way, the commodore shuffled along the beer-stained floor to the rear. His voice drifted back. He seemed to have summoned all his energy and strength to create a booming sound of robust health. "Sister Amelia, don't tell me that's you on the phone, my precious little darling. A woman of your advanced years should surely have gone to meet her heavenly reward. You ain't calling from heaven, are you?"

Amelia's tired, exasperated voice was still the same. "There you go again, making fun of me. Well, I just called your doctor, and he tells me you're not exactly in the best of health either."

The commodore burned at her words. "Since when have you acquired an interest in medicine? I always thought you were a practicing Christian Scientist?"

"You are my only brother," Amelia said, "and it seems fitting and proper that I take a sisterly interest in you. I know that all of life is predicated on us old folks moving on to make room for the new additions."

The commodore gave out with a deprecatory chuckle. "The way I see it," he said, "you figure I'm gonna be giving up my ground space before you, except what is allotted me in the cemetery." There was a long silence at the other end of the wire. He used the time to look at the badly chipped paint on the mustard-colored walls. He probably should have had this bar painted years ago, but now didn't plan to do anything about it. It was too late! He moved slightly out of the way. A ceiling fan was turned right on him. He couldn't run the risk of catching pneumonia.

"Now, that is an accusation that is simply not supported by the facts," Amelia finally said.

"Then what is the purpose of this telephone call?" the commodore asked. "If I recollect correctly, until I hit it big in real estate I never received one letter from that big old house in Vieux Carre."

"You know as well as I do that I was laboring day and day and night with sister Blanche Mae. A tubercular in the household is hard on the living. There was no money coming in, no money at all. And that awful Cajun gal——knocking on the door day and night——claiming falsely you were her legitimate husband."

"I was!" the commodore said defiantly.

"Philip, there are things in this world better left unmentioned."

"Then why did you bring her up?" he asked.

"I know that sometimes a dying...I mean a man not altogether well."

The huge expanse of his chest caved in. The air just went out of him, and he seemed too weak to breathe any back in. Slowly his lungs started to fill up again. He clasped his hand over the receiver so that Amelia couldn't hear his heavy breathing. A gold chain with little trinkets hanging from it crisscrossed his chest. When the trinkets started moving, he knew he was all right. "You might as well come out with it, Sister Amelia. To you, I'm already six feet under."

"Well, we can pray to the good Lord you'll live to be a hundred, but then we must face the realities of life."

"I think my family could smell a gold coin if it was forty miles ahead on the dirt road."

"Now that's a ghastly lie. Greed is a sin, and I've never sinned the way you have, Philip."

"Are you referring to what was commonly known as my kinky nocturnal habits?"

"Please, all these years I've turned a deaf ear to the vicious rumors spread about you. I've always tried to hold my head high in this town."

"I will ask you again. What is the purpose of this telephone conversation which is costing me my hard-earned money?"

"I want you to invite me to Tortuga to look after you."

The mountain that was the commodore suddenly blew up in volcanic flame. "That would be like putting the most hungry, red-eyed, fang-toothed, saliva-dripping wolf to guard the most succulent of spring lambs."

"I resent that!"

His heart was accelerating, and his forehead was beaded with perspiration. He whipped the white handkerchief out of his pocket to wipe the sweat. But when its blood smear appeared, he quickly concealed it from himself.

Amelia seemed to be mustering her courage. "I know that when a man is in ill health——and I have it on the best of authority you're not altogether yourself right now——he's liable to do something downright crazy. Some hussy's liable to come along and make a grab for everything you have. Things that properly belong to the Le Blanc family, not some foreign invader wanting to fill her head with gold teeth."

"Sister Amelia," the commodore said with strained courtesy, "if you had been to the dentist within the last forty years, you'd know that nobody orders gold teeth no more."

"It was just a matter of expression. I know how susceptible you are to designing females."

"You mean the Cajun gal, my former wife?"

"That matrimonial status I've never accepted. I never saw any marriage license, and I think it was all a terrible joke to humiliate me and our poor dead tubercular sister and the pure memory of our departed parents, God bless their eternal souls."

He looked at his gold watch and stuffed it back in his waistcoat pocket. "This conversation has gone far enough. I do not own stock in Southern Bell. Something tells me you've heard more than just my medical report."

"As a matter of fact, I have. The word is, you're in Tortuga keeping company with a cabaret entertainer of ill repute."

Puffing, his face reddening by the minute, the commodore said, "You've been correctly informed, my dear, correctly informed." The room was going slightly black. "I might be planning to take the next express to the pearly gates, but I'm gonna do you one last favor, Sister Amelia."

"Now for the first time this evening during this seemingly interminable conversation, you are making some sense."

A wry smile crossed the commodore's lips. "I know that if I have to pack up and ship out tomorrow, you'll be all alone in this world. We're the last of the line in the Le Blanc family. You never knew a man, Sister Amelia, and I knew too many."

"What do you mean by that?"

"A private reference——forget it. I am indeed planning to take upon myself a wedded wife." He chuckled almost to himself, the idea blossoming. "At least, with me out of the picture, you'll be left with a sister-in-law."

"Philip!" The shrill pitch of her voice came all the way from New Orleans. It was almost as if she didn't need the telephone wires.

Gently he placed the receiver back on its hook. A faded photograph of him on the wall stared back. He'd caught a big one that day, topping every man he took out on his yacht. The old commodore was quite a man, he mused to himself.

Then he said out loud, "Still is, goddamn it!"

Sunshine was back, placing an array of appetizers on the table.

Settling in once again, the commodore surveyed the offerings. "Eating's an art with me," he told Numie.

The whole idea of food didn't set well on Numie's stomach.

Nervously, Lola was casting glances at the commodore. Telephone calls from Sister Amelia always filled her with anxiety.

The commodore continued to ignore her, even though he knew she was dying to learn the particulars of his recent conversation. "In the past long years, the pleasures of the table have been denied me by my doctors." Then, chuckling almost to himself, he said, "Also, the pleasures of the bed. Tonight I've decided to change all that."

A lump rose in Numie's throat. Surely the commodore didn't have him in mind.

"Hell, I'm gonna die anyway," the commodore said. "As all men will. Why not die getting some enjoyment out of life?"

Lola pretended great concern. "You're not going to die," she said in baby-talk. "I'd kill myself if something ever happened to you, daddy." She sat back, sipping her drink. That statement was a little far-fetched, she reasoned. Better tone it down a bit next time around.

He didn't pay her any attention, his eyes riveted to the dishes placed before him. "Just look at these goodies," he said, almost to himself. "Shrimp whets with Trappey's Torrido sauce, hot oysters Diablo with Tabasco, Bayou bouchees with crawfish, and St. Louis souse." He breathed in heavily. "Ain't seen food like this in so many years I forget what it looks like, much less how it feels swimming around in my gut." He rubbed his stomach, then looked over at Numie. "Dig in, boy."

"I don't know what anything is," Numie said, not wanting any of it. "But it sure looks good." Gingerly he started helping himself.

"My grandmother's iron skillet produced some of the best vittles I've ever eaten," the commodore said, his voice increasingly boisterous. "Sunshine, he's from her side of the family, can cook almost as good." He downed the rest of his drink. "Sunshine," he yelled again. "You forgot what I told you. Got that Piper-Heidsieck chilled?" We're gonna have Piper-Heidsieck with every course. Ever had champagne, boy?"

"Yeah, once or twice," Numie said, sensing a troubled look in the commodore's eyes. "I almost got some my first night at this bar. But I was asked to leave before the bottle was served."

This amused the commodore immensely, enough so that it brought on another coughing spasm. "Must have been Leonora——she's the only one who orders champagne in this place other than myself." He handed his much-used handkerchief to Lola. "Fetch me another one," he ordered.

He made her want to throw up! She quickly left the booth, but was back in just a few minutes with a freshly laundered one.

Sunshine appeared with the glasses and bottle.

No one said anything for a long while. When the commodore ate, he was like a hungry man away from food too long. He smiled to himself, knowing he was taking poison into his system. But it was mighty good poison. "Used to put away bigger meals than this," he said to Numie.

"You will again," Lola cooed.

He turned and kissed her on the nose. "Yeah, along with the good food; this black hussy here is just what I've always wanted."

Lola beamed.

"Of course, the commodore added, "I had to have the poor thing's teeth fixed. They were just plain rotten, shaped like a dog's teeth when I first met up with her."

Lola was crestfallen. She couldn't stand calling attention to any imperfection. "Now don't you go telling family secrets," she admonished, examining a red fingernail and pretending she wasn't crushed.

Numie wasn't paying much attention. He kept noticing the

awful lighting in this bar. It made both the commodore and Lola look like dead things.

Sunshine was back with a pot of soup.

The commodore smelled it, then accepted it. Once when he was a boy, this soup had been the only thing he could swallow after a bout with diphtheria. "My mama always kept a pot simmering on back of the stove," he said, ladling out a bowl for each of them. "Always putting her stock and herbs in it, a *soupe-en-famille*."

Lola disliked the portion he gave her. "You gonna make me fat, sweet baby."

Again, he paid no attention to her, lost in his own memories. The only way he'd been able to live with Lola all this time was to blot her out until he needed her services. "When an old man's dying..."

Lola started to protest.

But just one hostile glance from the commodore was enough to silence her. "As I was saying before I was almost interrupted, when an old man's dying, he likes to go back and dig up the best of his past. A pot of soup——that's my past. Now try it, boy."

Numie tasted it, but didn't like it. He smiled instead, saying, "It's good. Never had food like this before."

"It's Creole gumbo," the commodore said, "made with God only knows how much crabmeat and some Red Devil sauce to spice it up." He stopped talking for a while. The only sound in the bar was the commodore's slurping.

Lola was fidgety. Finally, she couldn't hold back any longer. "Just what was on Sister Amelia's mind?"

The commodore stopped slurping long enough to look at her, but he didn't really take in her face. "Everybody in the world is after my money——except Lola. My Lola would be with me, even if I was the poorest man in Tortuga." He laughed under his breath at the absurdity of that statement. "Which I'm not, incidentally," he said to Numie with a twinkle in his eye.

Lola relaxed now. This was the kind of compliment she liked to hear. Of course, it was a complete lie, but she was pleased to know how she'd fooled him.

"How can you be sure you're going to die?" Numie asked.

"A man knows when he's gonna die——at least if that

man's got some horse sense." His voice sounded truly hurt. "My old ticker won't even hold up for an operation——that's what my doctors fear."

"What kind of operation do you need?" Numie asked, only in an attempt to make conversation and not out of any genuine interest.

The commodore eyed him strangely, almost debating whether he should explain. "Sons of bitches up there on the mainland think I've got cancer in my gut," he blurted out.

Numie was shocked at this candid admission.

Lola remained silent. She was long ago aware of this bit of information. In fact, she'd prayed for the growth of that cancer for so long she thought God had not heard her.

"Those bastards," the commodore went on, "They're like pig castrators. They like to stick knives in you every damn chance they get." He shuttered at the prospect of the oncoming surgery. Either that or else the Red Devil sauce was talking back too soon. "I grew up in Bayou Country, wrestling alligators. Now look at me, falling apart."

Lola started to tell him how handsome he was.

But he glared at her so savagely this time, she shut up immediately. "Pretty soon it'll be time to kick off around here. First thing I know, the town will be erecting monuments to me."

"I'm really sorry to hear you're in trouble," Numie said, almost wishing he hadn't. That seemed such a weak observation.

"My precious baby," Lola said, taking the commodore's arm again. Right in the middle of his soup, she asked, "Give your sexy mama a great big kiss. A gooey-sweet one." The very smell of that mess of blubber sitting next to her caused her to wince. The commodore's mouth on hers aroused such an awful squirming feeling she practically misfired right at the table.

Numie looked away. The commodore kissed like he slurped soup.

Again, silence, as each of them finished his soup.

"Now I know the pleasures I've got in mind for myself are causing me to risk a stroke," the commodore said. "After all, I'm not a fool. My blood pressure's so high the doctors have stopped counting." He brushed away some of the soupy crabmeat he'd dropped on his white linen suit.

Lola used her toddy to cleanse away the aftermath of his kiss. "Course it's sometimes dangerous for my commodore to be around me. I've been known to raise men's blood pressures something awful."

Numie looked toward the entrance. He kept hoping someone else would come into the bar tonight. These two colossal egos were about to consume him.

"Yep, I've really decided," the commodore said, "it's this lack of poon-tang——ain't no good for a man." He stopped for a moment. Did Numie think he was a babbler? The stud didn't seem to be paying too much attention. "I've been sitting on the sidelines too long, when I should have been out there scoring touchdowns." This observation amused him. He almost wanted to chuckle, but suppressed it, fearing another coughing spasm.

Sunshine was placing more dishes on the table.

Numie was not just full, but was feeling really sick now. This is cracklin' salad," the commodore said, holding a bowl up in front of Numie's nose.

It was all Numie could do to restrain himself. "Same thing you make cracklin' bread out of?"

"Same thing," the commodore said, genuinely pleased. "At least you've heard of something. Beginning to think you wasn't too bright." He stopped again. A vague feeling of self-mockery came over him. For some reason, he was compelled to defend himself in front of Numie. "God in his infinite wisdom gave me more sense than most men. Then in his devilish way he went and surrounded me with morons." He glared at Sunshine when he made this accusation.

"Christ, Phil," Sunshine said, "I never pretended to have a lot of book learning, but I shore can cook."

"And suck cock," the commodore interjected. He waited quietly for Numie's reaction.

Numie was having a hard time swallowing some of the crackling salad. He vaguely looked at his empty Scotch glass when the commodore said that. He was beyond the point where such a statement could shock him. Too many men had come right out and asked him if they could suck his cock. Only thing was, he never talked about it at the dinner table.

"Phil," Lola admonished, suddenly pretending to be a grand lady. "Now, mind your manners."

The commodore for a moment was bubbly happy, like a dirty little boy onto something evil. "I showed Sunshine how to do it when he was twelve years old. And he took to it like a calf with one of its mama's tits." He spit out a crackling onto his plate. "When Sunshine ain't in there stirring up raccoon pie, he's out going down on every shrimper on the waterfront." Picking up another bowl, the commodore handed it to Numie. "This here is okra salad with minced shallots."

Numie lit a cigarette right in the middle of the meal. The idea of discussing sex at the table——especially Sunshine's sex life——was just too much of a turn-off.

Sunshine was soon back with the main course: fried pickled pig's feet.

"The vegetable sidedish here is pokeweed," the commodore said. "Its berries are poison, but the green is mighty delicious. Want some?"

"No thanks," Numie answered, trying to figure out how he was going to get out of here peacefully.

"Shit, boy," the commodore said, "hope you're a better fuck than you are an eater."

Numie's face reddened. He'd just about had it!

"I was born and raised on pokeweed," the commodore continued. "The reason I know its berries are poison is that I fed some to our milkcow one day——and she up and died on me."

Lola was sitting there contemplating all the white mothers she'd had to entertain in her life. Right at this particular moment, she'd like to stuff some pokeweed berries down the commodore's gut.

"That cow started foaming at the mouth," the commodore said. "Her legs got all wobbly, just like mine are getting now. She fell down right in the pasture, moaning all the time."

Numie crushed out his cigarette. The commodore won the prize as a dinner conversationalist.

"Started to swell up," the commodore said. "That cow got twice her size. Her head just lolled to the ground, and I'll never forget those big wide eyes staring at me like I done something wrong, real wrong, 'cept I didn't know the berries were poison." His throat grew constricted. "First brush I ever had with death," he said softly, almost to himself. "Now that damn old Bessie is getting revenge on me for killing her." He looked at the pickled pig's feet Sunshine had place before him, then pushed the plate away. He didn't want to be reminded of animals dying right now. At this point he was feeling too much affinity with their plight.

Again, an interminable silence while Numie tried his best to finish the main course.

"Sunshine," the commodore yelled into the kitchen again, "keep the Piper-Heidsieck coming out here, boy." The champagne might relieve the awful constriction that kept building in his throat. Maybe that's where the cancer was spreading, taking on a new base of operations, preparing for his destruction. He gently fingered his throat, yet at the same time wanted to reach down and pull out whatever was there, preventing him from breathing properly.

Two bottles of champagne later, Sunshine was putting the dessert on the table.

"A little sweet-tater pone," the commodore said, dizzy and bleary eyed.

"Can't eat any more," Numie said. "I'm full."

"Lola said you were a man," the commodore replied, "but you don't eat like no man I've ever met." He was remembering the days he used to pick up fishermen down in Bayou country, stuffing their guts and getting them drunk on cheap whiskey before they gave in to his amusements.

Lola, meanwhile, was devouring the dessert. "I like everything real sweet."

A cynical smile crossed the commodore's lips. "Lola even thinks my gas is sweet."

"Now don't tell that," Lola said, no longer bothering to conceal her growing irritation.

"I'm perfectly serious," the commodore said, daring her to challenge him.

Lola's chest heaved, and she pressed a fist to her mouth.

Numie felt he was always coming out as part of a hate triangle on this island.

"People ask what I see in Lola gal here," the commodore

said. The champagne had warmed him, and he was once again feeling in a good mood. "I often have gas, have had all my life, and Lola is the only person who'll let me get rid of it in her bedroom. And she doesn't even strike a match——nothing insulting like that."

Numie slammed down his fork in rage. He, too, was drunk, but enough was enough!

Slurping some champagne, the commodore was on a demonical tear to display his power over people.

A bad memory of Leonora crossed Numie's mind. Despite their completely different posturings, there was an amazing similarity between her and the commodore. It was easy to see why they were friends.

"I understand..." The commodore paused, looked over at Lola, then glanced back at Numie. "I understand you've been shoving it up Lola's glory canal since I been gone."

Numie looked him straight in the eye. "You might say that."

"It's okay with me," the commodore said. "Only thing wrong with it, I wasn't there to watch. Now don't get me wrong. I'm not one of those voyeurs like my buddy, Johnny Yellowwood. I like a little action just as much as the next guy." He reached over and fingered Lola's breast. "I also like to get into a little black pussy on the side." Then he dropped his hand back at his side. "But these last years have been hard on me."

At this point, Numie was too drunk to think up a good excuse to leave.

"We gonna go upstairs," the commodore said. "Just the three of us."

The prospect of that horrified Numie. He hesitated, then said, "I think Leonora wants me to drive her around the island tonight."

The commodore's mouth fell open in surprise. A hustler wasn't supposed to act like this. "I can arrange things with Leonora," he suggested with a leer. Seeing the disgust on Numie's face, he added quickly, "And I'm a most generous man, when I want something. How's a hundred dollars sound, boy?" His hand groped under the table for Numie's crotch.

Numie hastily rose, pushing back his chair so that it made a screeching sound. It was hard for him to keep from puking right on the old bastard. He took a deep breath. All he wanted to do was get out of this bar as fast as he could. He began to back away from the table. "No thanks," he managed through clenched teeth, "I'm not into that tonight." He turned and walked quickly out of the bar, afraid to look back.

Out on the street, Numie paused in the night air. The most money he'd ever been offered for a sex act. And he'd turned it down. Why this new-found independence? What did it mean?

At this point, Castor Q. Combes, holding his calico cat in his arms, appeared in the doorway of the bar. "Violet eyes, one more night I'm gonna see if my cat can catch that rat. Got a feeling that rat is bigger than my cat."

Ignoring him, Numie headed up the dark street.

A nightmare, the same bad dream, always haunted Numie. It was spinning through his mind now, except he wasn't asleep.

In the dream he was standing outside a great mansion, somewhat like Sacre-Coeur, and he was looking through the tall, wrought-iron fence. Inside the women were elegantly dressed. The men, courtly and charming.

Along came a beggar woman. Her face was eaten with cancer, and her ash-colored clothes were rotting on her humped back. Spotting Numie, she stared at him, then started to scream. It was forbidden to look at the people in the garden.

Suddenly all eyes turned on him. He started to run, but his legs were paralyzed. The elegantly dressed women and courtly men changed before his eyes. Their faces became the faces of wolves, with fire-red eyes. They were moving toward him, and he couldn't escape.

Hands reached out, pulling him through the fence. Thrown on the rough, cold earth, he was knocked and beaten, his clothes ripped from his body. Fangs were watering. He was going to be devoured!

Looking up at the sky, he saw the moon go behind a cloud, leaving the garden in total darkness. He couldn't see anything. Then the mouths were on him. They were eating him!

At this point, he always woke up.

On the street corner, he stopped under a lamppost. The dream seemed like the nightmare in the Commodore's bar. So real he forgot for a moment where he was.

"Hustlers are a dime a dozen," he'd been told, usually by men stinking of cheap wine and holding five dollars in their hands. "You're hungry, punk, so better take it." He'd often taken it in desperation only. Always he'd feel more rotten afterward, going into the men's room, trying to wash the stench of tobacco juice off his cock.

Weren't hustlers supposed to be insensitive? Weren't they supposed to fuck anyone who could pay the price? He was up for grabs——had said so about himself many times.

Yet he was glad he'd refused the commodore. Maybe it was a final act of defiance before he surrendered completely to the forces on this island. Maybe he should right now pull off all his clothes and streak down main street, yelling, "Take me, take me," to anybody who wanted him. If anybody did.

But what if he couldn't perform any more? Were his juices drying up? Could he no longer get it up on command? He certainly hadn't wanted to with the Commodore. He'd never had this problem before. Always he'd been able to blot out the object before him, losing himself in some fantasy to sustain the act until it was over.

There was something about Tortuga, though, that was draining him, making it impossible for him to perform in his profession.

Had all those mouths of long ago robbed him of his manhood? Could it, like an oil well, be used up one day?

In the patio of Sacre-Coeur, the light from Anne's room was clearly visible. Ralph was probably in the guest cottage waiting for him. Leonora, hopefully, was asleep.

He couldn't go to Ralph. Just couldn't face his demands tonight.

He wanted warmth and comfort...and love.

Almost blindly, he was up the spiral staircase and gently tapping on Anne's door.

"Who is it?" she asked.

"It's me."

"Oh," she said sleepily. "Come on in, the door's unlocked. What's the matter?" Propped up in bed, a sheet wrapped tightly around her body, she was reading. She stared at him from behind the hair in her eyes.

"I've come to make love to you," he said softly.

She paused for a long moment, wondering if he were serious. Then she put down the book. "Of course," she said, "I wasn't going to let you if you asked, but seeing you didn't..."

Chapter Twenty

By ten o'clock in the morning, Numie knew it was going to be the hottest day of the year. He could just feel it in the air. The white sun was taking all his juice, draining him senseless from where he sat around the pool. The humidity was so stifling it gave him a dizzy head, the kind you get when you smoke too much in places without enough oxygen.

He cursed the relentless heat, his miserable headache, and the general state of confusion in his life.

Stripping out of his jeans, he raced across the bricks, their heat burning his feet, and plunged into the pool. Instead of cool refreshment, it was like a lukewarm bath. He quickly got out and dried himself off.

Lying in the shade, he still couldn't stop sweating in the oppressive heat. Nor could he think sanely this morning. There was that trapped feeling again. But trapped by whom? Leonora? Lola? Ralph? Anne? Himself?

He couldn't blame the heat entirely for the dullness in his head. First, there was that gnawing reality of last night spent with Anne. It had not been casual sex. It was more like it was with Lisa——warm, tender, loving, his giving because he wanted to give, and her receiving because she wanted to receive. She really gave, too, in the loving way a woman can.* He wasn't having to perform, as in a sex circus.

He was too experienced and had sex with too many people to get emotionally involved after a roll in the hay. Yet after he'd kissed her goodbye this morning, he sensed she felt too that there was more to it than one night's passion. A commitment somehow.

The catch was, her husband was waiting in the guest cottage to begin a new arrangement with him. He'd stood Ralph up for Anne. How was he going to explain to Ralph why he hadn't shown up? And after last night how was he going to explain to Anne his living in the cottage with Ralph?

A shadowy feeling of some vague threat moved over him. He was getting too involved with everybody. It could only lead to trouble. Then where could he go? Now he was asking that damn question. Where to go after Tortuga? Was it truly the end of the line? He could hardly imagine himself making the trip back up the road to the mainland.

There was a hope, still not clear, that he'd make it in some way on this island. He wasn't asking for much——just something. He seemed to have moved through the island in a trance, reacting to other people's outrages and requests, not controlling them himself, as he felt he should. Giving in——that's what he'd done——not stating his own wishes more clearly.

He'd had sex with Lola, Ralph, and Anne. Each one different. One, the past night spent with Anne, a moment of bliss. The other with Ralph, a time to play stud, yet he wasn't humiliated or demeaned. The third with Lola was the worst——strictly from hunger.

He had to get himself together. He couldn't——or wouldn't——go back to Lola and that commodore. That was too sick. Even for him.

Anne, he was trying to convince himself, was just one more person along the way. Loving, kind. But he had nothing to offer her. If he went back upstairs to that room where he'd spent the night, what could he say to her? She was just another hired hand at Sacre-Coeur, same as he was.

That left Ralph. Ralph was in control, Leonora's right-hand man. After Numie had angered Lola and the commodore, Ralph was the only person who could save him now from the sheriff having him run out of town. It seemed a cowardly thing to do, but he had to go to Ralph and put himself under his protection.

He desired and wanted Anne's warmth. But it was never that simple. He was in no position to stake a claim on what he himself wanted. The only thing he could do was make himself available to the person who wanted him. Of the three, Ralph had the clear edge.

Feeling numb from head to toe, he was heading for the guest cottage...and Ralph.

. . .

Ralph was asleep in a double bed.

Not wanting to wake him and not very fresh from a night spent with Anne, Numie headed straight for the shower. He stood under the water and tried to wash off the heat of the morning. Much colder than the pool, the water did the job. It ran so cold it must be well water, chilling his body to the bone. Maybe if he stayed here long enough, he could freeze his brain, make it free of doubt.

Still confused about his thoughts of Anne, he was squinting his eyes shut and turning them directly under the cold spray. As he opened them again, Ralph was there with the shower curtain back.

"Hi, lover," Ralph said, patting him on his wet ass. "I stayed up for you, but must have fallen asleep. Didn't hear you come in." With that, he was gone. No explanations needed.

Numie's stomach was still twisted in a tight knot as he came out of the shower. Don't let your wanting Anne get you in trouble, don't make any false moves, he kept telling himself.

"Here, let me dry you off," Ralph offered.

"Morning." Numie kissed him on the mouth.

"That's more like it," Ralph said. "Sorry about biting your lip. I was uptight about your going back to the ebony queen's."

Numie gave a little shudder and walked to the window. Outside on the patio there was no sound of life. "The commodore was there," Numie said, casually drying himself. "He invited me for one of the biggest dinners of my life——tons of champagne, spicy food."

"That's strange," Ralph said. "The commodore can't drink. Bad heart. He's on a rigid diet."

"Not any more." Numie's eyes narrowed, and he drew a deep breath. "He's going to have an operation for cancer."

Ralph's eyebrows raised in surprise. "It's amazing he's still around."

"I think he's trying to do himself in first," Numie said. "One last fling." His nostrils pinched, as he shook with rage. "There's just one problem."

"There's always a but," Ralph said. "Now what is it?"

Numie hesitated before speaking. "Part of the commodore's last fling was his wanting me to sock it to him. I couldn't do it."

"Of course, you couldn't," Ralph said. He picked up the towel Numie had dropped and resumed his drying. "You're mine now. Didn't you tell him?"

Numie's face grew distorted, and his shoulders slumped forward. "No, I didn't want to cause trouble. I know the commodore is Leonora's partner."

Ralph's anger flared. "Let me handle that. I saw you first."

Numie wearily crossed the bedroom, heading back to the bath. Over his shoulder, he said, "Lola saw me first."

"I can handle her or him...or it!"

Numie sighed, his eyes a little glazed. "You're a better man than me if you can."

"What can she do?" Ralph asked, walking toward him. "You're with me now. Besides, I don't think she's that interested."

Numie was breathing more easily now. He'd thrown Ralph off the track. "Perhaps not."

Before the bathroom mirror, Ralph nervously combed his hair. "We've got to get down to the fashion house. Let's take the Lincoln. When Leonora wakes up, you can drive back and get her."

"Okay." Numie finished dressing.

In the living room he heard Ralph at the door. "Oh, it's you. Morning."

Who was he talking to? Numie wondered.

"Take these letters down to the office," came a woman's voice.

My God, Numie thought. It was Anne.

"They have to be answered today," he heard her say. "Why did you spend the night out here? What's the matter with your own room? Been trick or treating again?"

"I've got a surprise for you," Ralph said. "Come on out here, lover man."

The trap Numie was fearing all morning just snapped shut. To delay any longer would only make it worse. Numie held his breath, then walked into the bedroom. "Good morning," he said.

At first the only sound heard was the dry whispering of the palm trees in the patio. Anne's hands went instinctively to her mouth. "Numie!" she gasped.

"Don't look so startled," Ralph said, with a smile. He reached for her arm.

Biting her lower lip, she jerked back.

Numie's heart jumped. He wanted to run and throw his arms around Anne. But all he could do was stand there weakly, while others decided his fate.

"You might as well get used to having Numie around," Ralph said. "I may be your husband, but Numie is my new husband."

Ralph's words were like a knife entering the back of Numie's throat.

"When did this marriage take place?" Anne asked, retreating into sarcasm.

"Last night," Ralph said, "after you left the pool."

"I see." Anne turned and walked rapidly out the door.

"I never knew her to be that jealous of me before," Ralph said.

"Look," Numie said, not concealing his anger, "that was a pretty tough line for a chick to hear from her old man. Do you have to call me your husband, for Christ's sake?"

"Yes," Ralph said, growing stern. "It's part of my coming out of the closet. Too long I've hidden around and kept things secret. I'm fed up with that. This shouldn't surprise you. It was you who convinced me. You ashamed to be my husband?"

Numie stared unblinkingly at him, his eyes narrowing, and his mouth tightening into a thin line. "Not at all. It's okay with anybody else. But in front of Anne... come on, man."

Ralph clutched Numie's arm until it hurt. "Anne will have to get used to it." He waltzed around the room. "So will Lola. So will her commodore. So will Leonora." He came to a stop in front of Numie. His face was stiff and expressionless. "So will you."

. . .

The palms fluttered in the first real wind that had stirred this morning.

Numie parked the Lincoln in an adjoining lot, then trailed Ralph up the flower-lined path to an old gingerbread house.

Except for its size, no one would know it was a house of fashion. Only a small sign outside——fashions by De la Mer——provided a clue.

Inside, the reception room was empty. A melange of flowers, monumental polka dots, and bold zebra stripes competed for attention. Everything, a monument to the ego of Leonora de la Mer.

Pictures on the wall showed her with prominent figures of her heyday: Tallulah Bankhead, Walter Winchell, even Franklin D. Roosevelt. More pictures, of Leonora in her elegant, extravagant gowns.

Mannequins displayed her latest creations. The range was vast: everything from Scarlett O'Hara dresses in white lawn to *femme fatale* stuff——skirts slit up to the crotch, long and tapering bare backs.

The room itself was like a theater setting. White bird cages from Edwardian days hung in the corners. Pink hollyhocks scaled the cerulean walls. Like a Tiepolo ceiling, clouds floated overhead. Fitting rooms were shaped like gazebos in white trellis; and the lighting was from art nouveau lamps. The wind from outside was gently rustling the lavender organdy curtains.

"What a place!" Numie said.

"She really *was* big," Ralph answered.

Numie's fingers ran along the smooth arm of a mannikin. "Who buys her stuff now?"

Ralph sighed. "About eight old dowagers, one who has retired to Palm Beach and owns a string of newspapers." He sat down at his desk, as if he were reluctant to begin the day.

"They were with her in the old days, but they never switched to Dior or any of the other post-war designers. They still like Leonora's distinctive look." His voice sounded burned out. "She's finished elsewhere."

Numie's eyes slowly took in the salon. Though immaculate and fresh appearing, the room was unreal, as if it had never known people. "But she said they were selling her dresses in Paris and London."

"Her old ones——that's true. They have a certain antique value today." He paused for a long moment, as if he found the silence profoundly comforting, then went on. "In these crazy times, anything is fashionable, including gowns Leonora designed in 1935. She's not really taken seriously, though."

"She was probably through by the time you came into her life," Numie said.

"That's right——and how it hurt her." A touch of rare sympathy entered Ralph's voice. "All her grand posturing today is to cover up that pain."

"She sure made others feel a little bit of it, too."

Ralph just looked at him, making no comment. He propped his feet up on his desk. He didn't seem to have much to do today. "We would go twice a year to Paris to see the collections. We went to every showing, then we'd dine at Maxim's or Tour d'Argent. In the old days, she'd been given the best tables in the house. But it was all different when I went with her. We were tucked away in some corner. Once on a crowded night we were turned down."

"That must have been a bitter pill," Numie said. "I can't imagine anyone saying no to Leonora."

"I think she returned to Tortuga because it gave her a chance to recapture a bit of that grandeur she'd lost in New York." He suddenly sat upright. "Let's face it. In Tortuga, Leonora is the grandest creation there is."

"For sure." The stirring of the wind lasted only for a little while, and then it, too, succumbed to the inertia hanging over the island.

. . .

In the late afternoon, two incidents were conspiring to taint Leonora's mood.

Seated in a throne chair, she was clad in turquoise ostrich feathers. In her chalky hands, she held a letter with a newspaper clipping.

It was addressed and delivered to her, even though its anonymous sender in Palm Beach used the name she was born with, not Leonora de la Mer. The old postman had remembered Leonora and had delivered it to the fashion house. Even now, she couldn't bear to repeat her real name. It was so hideous she'd never breathed it to a soul once she left Tortuga.

Norton Huttnar, her late husband, had insisted on using that name. Norton and one other person, Ruthie Elvina.

Leonora had to invent a name right for her. Why go around with an awful name if it's just as easy to be known as Leonora de la Mer? Too many people begin by accepting their names, then all the other dreary names things are called. The next step, she knew, was in accepting the world's standards of thinking and behaving. If she had ever done that, she realized she would be doomed for certain.

The second thing this vile letter-sender had done was to enclose a newspaper clipping. In it, one of her clients was described as wearing a "preposterous creation by the one-time popular dress designer, Leonora de la Mer."

Tears came to her eyes. It was amazing how approval flowed in and out of a life. The moment you allowed yourself to think you're saturated in it, that's the moment the tide goes out and leaves you stranded. She clenched her long fingers, crushing the letter even more. The tide had gone against her. She knew that. The strain of maintaining differently was weighing heavily upon her. At some point in life, each famous person——harlot or saint——becomes a public joke. There was a time in New York when just the mention of her name would invoke laughter. The laughter reserved for a has-been still trying to maintain an illusion of former glory.

She regained her composure. Suddenly, she felt flippant. Momentarily she had conquered her depression. After all, life was one great big masquerade. You have to know who you are and what you want——and not be afraid of either. That's how she climbed so far. The letter fell from her hand. "And, dear heart," she said softly to herself, "that's why I've had so far to fall." Her voice seemed to drown in the well of its own despair.

Nervously she pressed a buzzer, summoning Numie to her office. Instead of the letter, her hands held a marijuana cigarette, wrapped in red.

"Are you stoned all the time?" Numie asked, realizing belatedly how impertinent that sounded.

She didn't seem to notice. "If that's what you call it," she said, annoyed at herself for explaining any of her actions. "I've smoked marijuana since 1932. I don't plan to abandon it now that it's become a popular middle-class pastime."

"That makes sense," he said. "May I have one?"

"No, you cannot," she said harshly. "I don't like my employees smoking on the job."

He frowned. "You're the boss lady. May I at least sit down?"

"Of course," she said. "Ralph says I have to treat you more democratically——not so much like a servant——now that you're one of our little family." A wry smile crossed her lips. "How is married life?"

His face reddened. "I'm not married to anybody," he said defensively. All this talk of marriage was really getting to him. "Ralph and I are together——that's all."

"Call it what you like." Remembering her own name change, she said, "I've always believed in being inventive about names or labels people give to things." She stopped talking, and the cigarette fell from her hand.

He quickly retrieved it, returning it to an ashtray on her desk.

She didn't seem to notice his action.

He shifted uneasily in his chair.

She spun around and glared. Was she aware of his presence for the first time? He had the distinct impression she had forgotten he was in the room.

"I think you've made a major improvement in your choice of partners," she said. "Lola La Mour, after all!" Her smile was sweet yet menacing. "Of course, both Ralph and Lola are cop-outs; a sign of weakness, of not being able to stand on your own feet."

His throat was drying up by the second. "I think you're comparing me to yourself. You have the guts to make the world listen to you. But you're different from me. You have talent, something to sell to the world."

"Never admit to your own weakness," she said, virtually shouting. "You have to be convinced of what you are so powerfully that others will feel it, too." She reached into the ashtray and handed him the marijuana cigarette. She was amused when other people finished cigarettes or drinks, even food, she had started. "Or else..., you've got to run so hard that for a few years your weakness won't expose you. But eventually it will. Rest assured of that." Her voice grew threatening. "It always does."

He smiled gently, the comfort of the cigarette relieving him of the anxiety she'd aroused. For a long while, he didn't speak, enjoying the rest of her cigarette although he questioned the wisdom of smoking the red paper when blue was his color. She had touched a chord within him. Like her, he wanted to fly across the sky on the wings of a giant bird, feeling his power. But he was a loser already.

"You've lost your innocence," she said, "and found nothing to replace it with."

That statement shot the wings right off that bird he was flying across the sky.

"The world saw to that innocence soon enough," she said. "One is not meant to keep it——no more than I was."

"Were you ever innocent?" he asked.

"God knows, I was the most innocent creature who had ever lived until I met my husband, Norton Huttnar."

"You married him."

"A mistake I'll live with forever," she said. "He was such a degenerate. But he taught me something. The whole world is degenerate and depraved."

"That's some lesson," Numie said, uncomfortable with the conversation. "When was your innocence completely gone?"

"By the time I was seventeen," she said. "I was thoroughly jaded——like so many other seventeen-year-olds in the world. Degeneracy and depravity didn't matter any more."

"What did?" he asked.

"I realized then we all play the same sinful roles. The only thing that seemed important was how we chose to deceive the world."

"That's a pretty tough forecast, but I guess you're right." The cigarette was finished now, and he wanted another one, but was afraid to ask.

"I know I'm right." Her eyes opened wide. "At twenty, though, we realize who we're deceiving——ourselves." She was fighting back tears.

He got up and reached for her hand. "Are you okay?"

She jerked it back quickly. "I'm all right," she said, concealing her face from him. "I'm a Virgo, a cursed sign. If born under that sign, your brain never lets you alone, but haunts and tortures you night and day. I worry too much, care too deeply."

He felt powerless to help her in any way.

"Now you must leave me alone to meditate." She glided like some wraith into the throne chair. "I will sit here until darkness comes. Just be here to pick me up in my car, but only when darkness comes."

. . .

Later that night, Numie was sitting alone in the patio of Sacre-Coeur. Ralph and Leonora were getting ready for dinner.

The world was slipping into darkness around him, and he felt in danger of going with it. Someone switched on the lights in the patio, and the effect was like the headlights of the attorney's car that picked him up on the mosquito-infested keys.

Missing since this morning, Anne walked through the gate. She looked at him briefly, but comprehensively.

A strange shiver moved up Numie's spine. It seemed impossible that he had ever touched the flesh of this cold stranger, much less had her touch him.

"I knew I'd find you here," she said. The sound of her voice was a shock to him. It seemed totally detached from her body, lacking in any real feeling.

He studied the cool remoteness of her eyes. "About this morning . . ." He really didn't know where he was going with the explanation.

She intervened in time to save him. "Here," she said harshly, thrusting some bills at him. "Thirty dollars. Isn't that the usual stud fee?"

He smiled bitterly to himself, accepting his punishment and having no desire to retaliate. "Stop it," he said softly.

She laughed a small laugh. "You performed very well. Ralph was right. You are good in your work."

Hurt and humiliated, he handed the money back to her. "It wasn't like that at all. And you know it." He wasn't remembering their love-making that night, but their time in the pool, the liquid movements of her body.

A flash of resentment crossed her face. "Take it, damn you. A male prostitute needs to get paid for his hard labor."

"Don't rub it in," he protested.

"All these years," she said, "and I'm still naive about men." She gave him a long, level look. "I hope you and Ralph are going to be very happy together. He and I certainly weren't." She turned and walked quickly away.

"Come back..." he called, but his voice echoed in the darkness. She was gone. The stillness of the garden moved in on him. Once beautifully landscaped, it was now overgrown, like the emotions in this household. Behind her high wall, Leonora had hoped to buy solitude. Maybe, Numie wondered, all of them were tainted with Leonora's original purpose.

Leonora herself paused briefly in the garden, spying on Numie. She was surely mistaken, but she was receiving vibrations of having stumbled upon a lovers' quarrel. She had heard strange noises coming from Anne's room late at night, but had dismissed it as the wind. Was it possible for Anne to be in love with Numie? She'd have to caution the poor girl against male hustlers. She knew, but possibly Anne didn't, that male hustlers were too damaged to love...ever.

After an appropriate interlude, Leonora's voice resounded across the patio. "Dear heart," she said to Numie, "it's going to be a very special dinner tonight. Just Ralph, you, and me. Somehow it didn't seem right to invite Anne. Amy Vanderbilt never wrote anything about the etiquette of the situation." Her hand was a pearly shadow moving through the night air. She held it up, suggesting the promise of the evening. Yet it could also hold a dagger. "Furthermore," Leonora said, "you'll be delighted to know: we're having champagne."

Chapter Twenty-One

Numie stood in front of Commodore Philip's bar. The doors were wide open. In back an old black man was mopping the floor. Flies buzzed around the sticky waxpaper hanging from the ceiling, waiting to capture them.

Dreading this moment, he'd returned to reclaim his possessions. At first he considered abandoning them completely, but he wanted that duffel bag back. It'd been with him through worse situations than this; and he had to have it. It was his traveling office, and he felt lost without it.

From the upstairs boudoir, Dinah was racing down the steps, clad only in a skimpy see-through robe. She made a sleepy face, eyeballed him, and let out a soulful sound: "Lookee who's here! Lola's so pissed at you, stud, she could rip your thing off. Has that black bitch been carrying on 'bout you!"

"I've come for my things," he said.

Behind the bar, she said, "Let me scarf down some strong whiskey. Till I get some stuff swimming around in my gut, I can't think straight."

He swallowed hard. "Is Lola up?"

"Was just a minute ago——not only up, but bouncing around like some whore in heat ready to take on the whole navy."

"Where's the commodore?" The question came out like an angry curse.

"He's in the cottage out back. Went there groaning and bellyaching that we was gonna give him a stroke for sure." She jiggled the ice in her glass. "He didn't retire, though, till Ned and I earned our bread. No two cottonpickers ever worked harder for the man than we did last night." She smiled suggestively. "Heard you got all high class on 'em and swished your tail right out of here."

Numie glanced back at the street, as two effeminate-looking older men with dyed hair paraded by. "It wasn't my scene."

"Mine either, but a gal's gotta live. That magic wand of the commodore has clean run out of tricks."

"Is it okay for me to go up?" Numie's voice resounded across the bar. "To get my things?"

"Sure," Dinah said, slurping the rest of her whiskey. "Lola

ain't got no bodysnatcher up there waiting to sell you into white slavery."

Numie stood tall in his khakis an and desert boots, preparing himself for battle. Up the steps two at a time, he was pounding on the door to Lola's apartment.

Irked at the interruption, Lola yelled, "Come on in if your drawers are clean." She reckoned it was probably that annoying cousin, Castor Q. Combes, asking for another dollar.

Bracing himself, Numie walked in.

In her red silk panties, Lola was on the bed with Ned. He wore nothing. Blinking her eyes, not sure she was seeing right, she sat up. Anger flooded her system. "Lily-White, the prick-peddling bastard has returned to the scene of the crime."

Numie stood there stunned. The only thing he could think of for a moment was that the room smelled of Campbell's chicken noodle soup. "I've come for my duffel bag and my clothes," he managed to say, avoiding looking directly at the bed again.

Ned said nothing, just stared at Numie with a mocking grin.

Before Lola spoke, her mouth began to shape itself for cannibalistic devouring, like that of a hungry lioness. "The wardrobe I bought for you, you mean." She kept trying to read Numie's thoughts. He felt she was trash, that was for sure. She was torn between two conflicting emotions: That of trying to act like a lady and that of creating the impression she was the type of gal men wanted to rape.

"What wardrobe?" Numie asked, now confronting her eye to eye. "A pair of pants and sweater paid for with the commodore's money. You're welcome to keep them." Lola disgusted him. She was nothing but a bragging, jiving, exaggerating bitch!

"Just a minute," Lola said, propping her elbows on her hips and jiggling her breasts a little to enhance her sexual allure. "What makes you think you can barge in on a lady when she's entertaining a gentleman? A *real* man, I might add. Look at that thing. Isn't that the biggest salami you ever laid eyes on?" Leaning over, she said to Ned: "Numie whipped it out for my commodore last night. It was soooo tweensy-weensy we couldn't even see the thing. My commodore asked me to go get his bifocals!"

Numie burned at the fact that it was said in front of Ned.

"Aren't you talking about your own endowments?" Numie asked.

"Honey," Lola said sarcastically, "of all the things I've pretended in life, *hung* ain't one of 'em."

The very presence of Lola seemed to be clouding his brain, like darkness moving in fast on a winter's afternoon. "I'm here just to get my things, that's all!"

Whiskey glass in hand, Dinah was back in the room. She flipped on a television set, turning up the sound. "Look at all these goddam white mothers, advertising all these grand things just to tempt us. They know we can't afford them. Some of us are lucky to even have TV. That's the way they have of torturing us."

"I'll get your things when I'm good and ready," Lola said irritably. "Don't want you messing up my gowns." She settled back on the bed, determined to prolong Numie's farewell as long as possible. She wasn't going to be dictated to by any white trick in her own apartment. The commodore had dumped on her all the white man's crap she planned to take in this lifetime. It was feeling mighty good to toss a little of that shit back. "God only knows what you white trash would steal if I wasn't looking. First, I've got some unfinished business to attend to." She turned over in bed, pulled down her red silk panties, then ordered Ned: "Ride the range, cowboy." Panting, Lola hawkeyed Numie with hatred in her dry eyes.

He looked away. His eyes darted around the room, as if seeking some door of escape from this mad moment.

Chewing gum and drinking liquor at the same time, Dinah called over to the bed, "He in there dirty and deep, Lola?"

"If he was in any more, child," she yelled back, "he's be coming out like an oil derrick in China."

"He can cum a ton," Dinah said, her eyes transfixed on the kiddies' cartoons on the tube.

"Baby," Ned was huffing in Lola's ear, "I'm filling you up so much this time you gonna be water-logged."

The sound of their engines grew louder and louder in Numie's ears. Then something clicked, and he tuned them out completely, a trick he learned to do when he used to sleep in all-night movies and people were having sex all around him. Going into Lola's closet, he was rounding up his possessions.

He tossed his newly bought white slacks and sweater on the floor. Under a red sequin gown, he found his precious duffel bag. As he was leaving, Lola and Ned were in the throes of orgasm. Lola was moving hard now. She wanted Numie's memory of her to be this spectacular finish. After his temper cooled down, pure jealousy and lust would drive him back to her.

Outside the door, Numie didn't know whether to celebrate or prepare for a fast getaway.

In the bar downstairs, he paused briefly, as if he'd forgotten something. Suddenly, the cat belonging to Castor Q. Combes appeared from under a table. She was dragging a dead wharf rat, huge in size. Numie cringed at the sight of it.

Bounding down the steps two at a time, Ned landed on the wood floor, still zipping up his sailor pants. "Don't get pissed at Lola, man," he said. "Us spades are just better in the sack——every queen knows that. When I'm sailing into a chick——or in Lola's case, whatever——I'm on home turf."

"You're welcome to her," Numie said sarcastically. "The commodore, too." Turning to go, he was in no mood for Ned's gloating look.

"Now don't you go heaping no big favors on old Ned. Sweetheart, *you* can have the commodore." He opened a beer.

Suddenly, the thought of Anne flashed through Numie's brain.

Ned said, casually, sipping his beer, "Only thing I like 'bout him is his bread."

Numie smiled uncertainly. He was sure that Ned was somebody's sexual fantasy. But not his! "I've got to go."

"Shit, man, I've come all the way down here to express my sympathy for you." He anchored, feet and all, on the top of the bar. "To shower some hot attention on you. In some ways, you're a nigger like me——forced to peddle your meat in whitey's country."

Numie paused, taut with anticipation. A sense of unreality moved over him. Ned was obviously here for a purpose. And it wasn't sympathy.

"You've been outclassed, man," Ned said. "The commodore told me so last night. Black meat is in."

Now Ned's purpose was altogether clear. Ned was enjoying

his little moment of triumph.

"There was a time a honky dude like the commodore would have got it for almost free," Ned said. "Me, he'd get free. You, he'd slip about ten bucks to." He grinned. "Now there's a premium price on black meat. The finest choice sirloin is cheaper. Dinah and me are two colored children who'll continue to put out for white mothers like the commodore——but we want to hear the jangle of coins. You, on the other hand, your stock is nowhere, man." He slammed the beer down on the bar as if to emphasize his point.

Numie stood defiantly. He knew better than to meet Ned's challenge, yet he couldn't resist the bait. "We'll see about that."

"Gotta spell it out, huh, like in school?" Ned asked, swinging his feet over the bar and making for another beer. "You are retired, cat! As of last night, retired! Off the meatrack! Used up, man! There ain't no more free meal tickets coming your way."

"That right, huh? See that red sports car sitting out there?" Christ, now he was talking just like Lola, pointing to her Facel-Vega.

"Man, I don't have blinders on."

"That belongs to Ralph Douglas." Numie hiked up his pants. "For what I've got, he pays and pays plenty." He turned and walked from the bar.

Castor's cat had now dragged the rat onto the cobblestones outside. Another stray was showing interest in the dead prey. Castor's calico growled, staking her claim.

Tossing his duffel bag into the front seat, Numie felt he'd cheapened himself in front of Ned. But Ned had hurt, cut through right to the quick. How sad, Numie thought, the only rejoinder he had was to claim status as someone else's boy.

He was driving to Chino's Cafe where he'd met Anne yesterday afternoon. Only the bitter black coffee there could get rid of his disgust with himself. With that black coffee, he hoped to burn out his own self-loathing and cleanse his system. Maybe that was what Dinah was doing with that whiskey so early in the morning. Maybe that was what whores like himself had to do.

How long could he stay commercial? Even with Ralph, he

had his doubts. For Ralph, a few weeks with Numie could be no more than a tryout, an experiment. In no time, Numie could be back on the streets.

How to become the buyer instead of the seller? He never could figure that one out. But even when he retired as the seller, he knew he'd never purchase sex off anybody. If it weren't given freely, he wasn't going to have any.

He meant that.

. . .

In the late of the afternoon, while everyone at Sacre-Coeur was in siesta, Numie brought Ralph's red sports car to a stop before the gingerbread Victorian bus terminal.

Tangerine ran through the Dr. Pepper screen door. "Thank God you're here to kiss me good-bye."

"I got your call," Numie said, slamming the car door. He looked her up and down. She was in her Easter parade finery, and it was causing her to perspire heavily in this August heat wave. In a loose-fitting pink dress, she had draped a too small black patent leather belt around her large waist. Her purse and open-toed pumps were also in black patent leather. The cracks had been smoothly coated with Vaseline. Over her arm she carried a foam-backed, silk-looking purple raincoat.

"Like it?" she asked, smiling. Some of her mascara had started to run in the intense heat.

"You look great!" he said, lying. He wound his arms around her, as she snaked in tight. "Where you going so sudden like and all dressed up?"

"I'm leaving Tortuga," she said, kissing his lips. Her breath smelled of gin. "Leonora, everything. I'm walking right out after all these years." Reaching into her purse, she held up a pink handkerchief. "My life savings. Three hundred and twenty dollars and seventeen cents. All tied up real neat."

The sky was growing hazy, the way it does when thunder clouds move over before a storm. "What's the rush?" he asked.

"I'm in love," she said, squeezing his arm. Then as if she didn't expect him to believe it, she repeated. "Really in love. Thought it would never happen. But it has." She sounded like a little girl.

He didn't trust her feeling. Her voice was too giddy, too desperate, as if she were trying to convince herself. "Who you in love with?"

Just then, the screen door opened again. "Come on, Tangerine," a man yelled. He stood in the doorway, his lips tubing around the top of a gingerale bottle. The liquid wasn't gingerale, but gin. With dirty fingers, he patted away the drippings on his mouth.

"That's him," she said proudly, her eyes blazing. "Hayden." She ran toward him, snuggling into the cradle of his arm. He backed away. She covered the rejection by reaching for the gingerale bottle. Swigging down about two ounces, she handed it back. He took it and with the same dirty fingers elaborately cleaned the bottle top. That one action told Numie all he needed to know.

Hayden was like an old tough in a leather jacket and levis. His face was pockmarked, his complexion the color of beets.

"I want you to meet my best friend," Tangerine said.

Numie didn't want to shake the man's hand, but did so anyway.

Hayden would not look him straight in the eye. "Shit, gal," he said, turning away, "I ain't got no time for socializing with best friends or even enemies as far as that goes." He tossed the bottle into an open garbage pile caught by a wire fence. "Give me the money, and I'll buy the tickets."

Impulsively Numie also reached to rescue the life's savings Tangerine was so trustingly handing over.

The pink handkerchief stuffed quickly into his pocket, Hayden disappeared fast, slamming the Dr. Pepper door.

"You sure like them friendly," Numie said.

She took his hand, saying softly, "You wouldn't believe it to look at him. But last night——I met him in a bar——he was so loving and kind." She gave off a smell of rancid wetness. "That's why I asked him to go back home with me to Atlanta."

"Atlanta?"

Two boys waiting on a bench turned up their transistor radio.

"Yes, I come from there," she said. "Hayden's gonna find work up there in Georgia ...somewhere. I'll have to send for my things." She frowned. "He don't like none of my junk, so I'm leaving everything behind."

He looked deeply into the trusting eyes of this tender, loving woman. "Even your slopjar?"

Her lips quivered. "Even that."

"You must love Hayden a lot to leave that behind." He glanced nervously through the plate-glass window into the terminal. No one was at the ticket counter.

"I'm gonna introduce him as my husband," Tangerine said. Her breath was coming in swift takes. "My other two sisters——younger than I am but a hell of a lot uglier, let me tell you——they both got husbands." She was squeezing his arm again, but applying more pressure than before. "Don't you think it's about time I caught one?"

"The time is ripe," Numie said. The announcer on the transistor radio was talking about nostalgia. Then the sounds of "Pink Carnations" drifted across the oil-streaked courtyard of the terminal. "But Hayden comes on strong. Sure you're doing the right thing?"

"You bet your left nipple I am," she said. He detected a tear in her eye, but reckoned it might be a speck of dust. "Now, don't you go putting him down, sweetie. You're just jealous 'cause you can't have me." She nudged him under the chin.

"That's true," he said, smiling. "But he strikes me funny——that's all." The screeching of brakes brought four Cubans in a 1957 baby-blue convertible to a halt near the entrance. All of them scrambled out a door painted with a three-foot snake. It was almost fluorescent. Turning to look back at Tangerine, Numie asked, "What did you tell Leonora?"

Tangerine dropped her eyes, saying, "Oh, I just couldn't bring myself to tell her anything. I know I should have. But Leonora gets hysterical at the idea of someone running out on her." Her hand reached up in the stale hot air as if a golden apple hung on a tree. "Leonora wouldn't see this as my last chance for happiness."

Numie was growing impatient: "Did you at least leave her a note?"

"Yes," she said sheepishly. "I've never had enough guts to stand up to her anyway."

"Don't worry," Numie said. "You'd better catch that bus——or else Hayden will be spending his honeymoon with his fist." He led her to the station, as three of the Cubans piled out the door, heading for the bus.

"Just a minute," she said, pausing in front of a dusty mirror in the waiting room. The mirror made her look like a slab of jelly. Puffy, dark circles under her eyes. Dirty face. Smears of old makeup. She did her best with repairs and topped it all off with a generous new coating of scarlet lipstick. Then she tried smoothing the wrinkles out of her wilted pink dress.

"EVERYBODY ABOARD."

"For Christ's sake!" Numie called, his eyes darting around the waiting room in search of Hayden.

"Wait a minute!" she cried, rushing up to the station master. "Seen my husband? The only man wearing leather on an August day." Her voice was hysterical. "He was in here buying the tickets." Her words were stabbing the hot air.

The man looked as if she were a crazy woman. "Nope," he said.

"What do you mean?" Numie asked. "He was just in here. He took the..." Pausing in mid-sentence, he gave Tangerine a probing look.

She seemed to be reading his thoughts. "You're wrong." Her hand went to her mouth. "We're going to Atlanta. To see my folks." She grabbed Numie's shoulder and pushed him toward the men's room. "In there. Tell him he can potty on the bus."

Quickly Numie entered the toilet, the same one where he'd spotted Johnny Yellowwood. Empty. No, there were feet under the lone booth. "The bus is leaving," Numie shouted. No response. Pulling back the unlocked door, an annoyed Numie stared into the face of Castor Q. Combes.

"Violet eyes!" Castor yelled. "Get out of here, you queer. A guy can't take a shit without you fags getting off stealing a peek."

In panic, Numie slammed the door shut and rushed outside. "He's not in there," he said to Tangerine.

"The money," she said, reaching into her purse as if to confirm its loss. "Everything," she sighed, "everything tied up in that handkerchief."

"You going on this bus, lady?" the station master asked.

"No, I ain't going alone," she said softly, closing her purse.

"Where did he go? He didn't say nothing about going anywhere except with me."

"Didn't have to," the man said. "I know him."

"Then you did see him?" Numie accused.

"I saw a man named Gordon Boyd," the station master answered, smoking his pipe. "The lady asked me if I saw her husband." He smiled. "Now I'm not likely to see her husband, am I——considering she don't have a husband?"

Tangerine was shaking so badly Numie put his arm around her. "Look," he said impatiently, "did you see the guy she was with?"

"Yep," he said. "The sheriff wants him for beating his wife. Beat her nearly to death, then left her with three bawling kids and no money to feed 'em."

"Where do you think he went?" Numie asked, tightening his hold on Tangerine.

"He's probably hiding out on a shrimp boat. When he saw me, he ran. It's dangerous for him to be at the bus station anyway. Johnny Yellowwood comes here all the time."

"*I know,*" Numie said. Turning his back on the station master, Numie took Tangerine's hand and guided her out.

In the courtyard again, she blinked at the bright sun. Catching her reflection in the plate-glass window, she went over for a closer look. "Fat...and old...and ugly," she said out loud.

The bus was pulling out. One boy left on the bench was listening to *Tennessee Waltz.* "You're beautiful," Numie said, coming up behind Tangerine.

She backed away, putting her hand on her hip. "To think," she said, "I used to brag to my mama about returning to Atlanta like a grand movie queen. Even grander than Mae West. A real celebrity, riding on a white train with red upholstery." She tossed her head back, running her hands down her figure. "The school band there to meet me. The mayor and all the town brass."

Numie held on to her reassuringly. The boy with the transistor got up and walked away. The baby-blue convertible pulled out. The terminal yard was deserted now, except for a stumbling old drunk. But even he ducked behind a fruit market and faded from view. Not a sign of life.

In the distance, the motor of the bus could be heard, as it crossed over the bridge and began the long route back to the mainland.

"Okay, okay," she said in despair. "*Miss* Fern Cornelia Blanchard sure had a triumphant return to Atlanta."

"Forget that!" he said harshly. "Let's deal with the realities." He spun her around, staring deep into her soggy eyes. "The note you left for Leonora. Where did you leave it?"

Tangerine hung her head low. "I didn't really write it," she said. She tugged at his arm. "But I meant to."

He sighed. "Come on, baby, we're going home."

Chapter Twenty-Two

Two weeks later, Leonora with straight-back carriage walked into the patio of Sacre-Coeur.

Numie was stunned.

Behind her purple sunglasses, she was a tall red rose——haughty, statuesque. Her costume simulated that flower, the fabric draped like rose petals along her slender frame. On her head was a great stalklike concoction, studded with diamonds that glistened in the light.

"Wow!" he said. She was truly majestic. "What's the occasion?" Her presence seemed to envelop him like a placenta.

"We're going to a wedding." This morning already was disturbing her, as all mornings did when she couldn't find what she termed her geographic center.

"You're wearing *that* to a wedding?"

Her back stiffened. Questions from anyone, especially servants, annoyed her. "Of course." She breathed in the air of the patio. Fresh morning air usually made her cough. "There will be a photographer there from the newspaper. Whenever I make appearances, my public expects me to wear something daring and provocative." She stared at Numie. He aroused mixed feelings in her. She didn't know whether to assign him to oblivion or else amalgamate him into her own family. "I never know what that miserable drag queen is going to have on. I can hardly afford to have her take attention away from me."

Numie was leery of Leonora. He knew his suspicions didn't make sense, but he felt he was her victim in some way. "Lola's going to be there?" he asked. "I can't imagine anyone inviting Lola to a wedding."

"It's *her* wedding, dear heart." Leonora looked into her purse and pulled out a mirror. In it she studied her reflection more carefully. The costume was outrageous——no doubt about that. But then she loved to outrage the public. She remembered the day when one irate woman attending a fashion show chased her around the room with a hatpin to show her outrage at Leonora's latest collection.

Just talking about Lola filled Numie with a vague anxiety. "Lola getting married?" he asked. "To who, for Christ's sake?"

"The commodore," Leonora said, matter-of-factly.

"I can't believe it," Numie said. "We're not going to a wedding——more like a spectacle." He laughed sardonically at the whole idea.

She closed her purse. "The commodore wanted me to hold the wedding here at Sacre Coeur, but I just couldn't." She virtually spat her words with disgust. "I'd be the laughing stock." She felt a sharp pain in her heart.

Numie paused. He looked at her again with suspicion. "Why are you going?"

"The commodore is my business associate, she said. "And closest friend," she added as an after-thought. She moved through her patio and garden, feeling it was a tomb——and she'd been interred alive. "It would be unforgivable not to attend. When you have a close bond, as we do, you must overlook certain eccentricities in the other person." Her long arms hung disjointedly from her shoulders. "Lola, of course, is the biggest eccentricity I've ever had to overlook——other than my husband, Norton Huttnar, the degenerate." She remained rigid, looking straight ahead into the garden, her eyes filled with distant memories of horror. "Lola's drag is mild compared to what my husband used to wear. He left me with an inbuilt loathing of drag queens."

Numie turned around, ready to go. His boots clumped along the bricks. Blinking at the sky, he looked toward the gate. He was always nervous and uneasy around Leonora, more so this morning than usual.

"Don't be impatient," Leonora said, almost reading his thoughts. Self-doubt about her appearance was stabbing at her. Her bones seemed to have a certain rudeness this morning, as if they were rebelling against their stations after all these years. She couldn't trust them. For one brief moment, she considered canceling her appearance. "We're late, but I wanted to arrive after everybody else was there." Her face became grim and ominous. "After all, I am the most important guest."

. . .

Numie steered the Lincoln in between Lola's white Facel-Vega and the commodore's antique Rolls-Royce. The town's barflies were waiting between the curb and the bar, ready to enjoy the show.

The doors were wide open, the wedding crowd assembled inside.

Standing at the entrance was a minister, about thirty-five, his dark, wavy hair combed neatly. He was really a clean-cut, all-American boy type, with pale green eyes.

"Miss De la Mer," he said warmly, "I'm Roy Alberts. I've heard a lot about you, and I've been anxious to meet you. I had everybody wait until you arrived."

Like an eccentric red raven, Leonora extended her red-gloved hand. "That was kind of you, my young man." She was observing a tiny knot of drying blood on his white shirt collar, probably from a shaving nick. Right away she determined that anyone so careless about his appearance wasn't to be trusted.

"You look beautiful as a rose," he said, eying her costume. "More so."

She smiled benignly, not being one to succumb to flattery ever.

Numie was noticing an old drunk eating peanuts, crushing their shells, then tossing them on the sidewalk. It was like enjoying popcorn at the movies. Right at this moment he knew he'd feel more comfortable joining the drunks than participating in the action in any way. Instead, he stepped up to the minister and said, "I'm Numie Chase."

The minister shook his hand, a firm grip. "Glad to meet you, too."

Numie liked Roy Alberts at once.

"Aren't you the 'gay pope'?" Leonora asked, her voice smooth as cold steel.

The reverend frowned. "I hope not."

Numie instinctively backed away. He was beginning to learn when Leonora was preparing for the kill.

"Yes," she continued, "I think I've heard you called that when you're not being referred to as the 'gay Billy Graham'."

A nerve tugged at her left wrist. She really didn't know why she was insulting this kindly man. These unexplained impulses took over now and then. However, now that she'd launched the attack, she was determined to see the battle through.

"I resist labels," Alberts said softly. "I believe that God didn't limit love to jocks and bunnies."

Numie was surprised at his use of those words. This man didn't talk like any minister he'd ever met. He smiled to himself, wishing his own mama had the pleasure of meeting Roy Alberts.

"That's why I gladly accepted the Commodore's invitation to perform the wedding ceremony." Alberts went on.

Leonora searched his face carefully, her eyes probing it like a needle after a splinter. She was determined to find one weak and vulnerable spot. She focused on his mouth. It was petulant. Now she knew why she instantly disliked the man. She positively loathed petulant mouths. "But I read that a bishop suggested calling these gay marriages a 'celebration of commitment'. Why not that?"

"That's up to the individual," the reverend said. "If Miss La Mour and the commodore want to be joined in the eyes of God, then it's my duty to help them achieve that union."

She glanced ahead at the shadowy figures in the bar, but they were too dim and her eyes too weak to make out any distinct features. However, she could sense that all eyes were on her. "But they don't believe in God," she said, raising her voice. "I happen to know both of them are devout atheists."

"A devout atheist," the minister said, "is about the same as a true believer."

"Frankly, dear heart," Leonora continued, "I'm attending this so-called wedding because the commodore is a business associate of mine." She moved closer to Alberts, although his cheap shaving cologne offended her sensitive nostrils. "Confidentially, I disapprove mightily of homosexuality. It's a disgusting perversion!" She stepped back to survey the damage she'd caused. Indeed, the reverend's face showed his anguish.

"I, myself," Leonora went on, "was married to a most delightful creature, a darling man named Norton Huttnar. I loved him so much I've never been able to look at another man since his untimely death at the age of seventy-eight."

The minister's back stiffened. "Miss De la Mer," he said, "I don't understand you at all. You know I'm a self-admitted homosexual, yet you insult me by calling my love a disgusting perversion." His hand trembled. "The commodore and Miss La Mour represent a new style of family. Disgusting to some maybe, but so is hatred of all things we don't understand."

The heat of the morning was causing her to see spots. She'd have to go inside and quickly. "But this flamboyance," she protested. "Even my chauffeur here called it a spectacle." Her eyes wandered around in search of Numie, but he was off somewhere talking to a drunken bum.

"Maybe it is," the reverend said, "but I prefer flamboyance to *closet queens*."

Leonora's fingers began a crawling descent down her costume. "I beg your pardon."

"Between us, *dah-ling*," the minister said, effecting a mincing, high-pitched voice, "in that rose number, with a diamond stalk coming out of your head, you're the biggest drag queen here."

"My God," Leonora said, "I've never been talked to this way in my life." Motionless, she stood at rigid attention.

"If you don't want to attend," the minister said, resuming his natural voice, "you don't have to. To me, this is a serious ceremony of two people pledging fidelity to each other as abiding friends——husband and husband or husband and wife, whatever you want to call it. You can either enter into the spirit of it, or else *leave*. Good day, Miss De la Mer."

"The vicious swine!" Leonora said to Numie, now at her side.

Numie sighed with relief at his own good judgment at staying away for a few moments so he wouldn't have to hear their words. "Do you want to get out of here?" Numie asked. "I do."

"Darling," she whispered, "all my life I've been the victim of the vilest type of character assassination." Hand at her forehead, she was breathing with difficulty. The intense heat seemed to be molding her costume to her body. In fact, the whole grimy sidewalk seemed to be molding itself to her. She wanted to turn and go, but dared not. Unsteady for a moment, she reached out with her long fingers for Numie's hand. But it was sweaty, and she withdrew instantly at the touch. "I'm not going to allow one faggoty minister's attack to rile me." Her voice was shrill, like a wounded leopard. "I am going to attend." By now she'd regained her balance and those blasted spots were disappearing in front of her eyes. "My public expects it of me." The dim figures in the bar were taking actual shapes——vague faces she recognized on her rides throughout the town. "See," she said, gesturing to Numie, "they're looking at me now."

About seventy persons were gathered. Never had the bar been filled to such capacity. A newspaper photographer near the door recorded Leonora's entrance. She tipped her head slightly to acknowledge his presence.

Once again, Numie had an image of Leonora as a silent-screen star arriving at the premiere of a film. The outfit was different, but the stiltlike stride was the same as the first night he'd met her.

Leonora's pique at the gay minister faded quickly in the wake of attention she was receiving. Her rose costume attracted much interest. Lola was nowhere in sight.

Numie retreated to the far corner of the bar.

"Violet eyes," came a voice. "Don't step on my toe. It's infected with pus." There stood Castor Q. Combes, holding his calico cat.

"You follow me everywhere," Numie said. He didn't understand why he was always glad to see Castor.

"The other way around, if you ask me," Castor countered. "Who was taking a shit at the bus station when you came barging in?"

"That was a mistake," Numie said, his face growing sad with thoughts of Tangerine. "I didn't know you were in there. I was looking for someone."

"I bet!" Castor abruptly dropped his calico. Her body twisted in the air, and she landed on her feet. "Some place to look all right."

Castor had the incredible ability to make Numie feel guilty about anything.

"After this wedding ceremony, you won't be seeing me at this stinking bar no more."

"Why's that?" Numie asked. He felt he and Castor shared

a number of secrets.

"My cat caught that blasted rat," Castor said with pride. "Was it ever big! She drug it to my house."

"I saw her with it," Numie said, looking at the calico who was fascinated by a giant roach.

"Oh, man, you lie," Castor said, reaching into his pocket and pulling out some chewing tobacco. "Do you ever lie!"

"No, it's true," Numie said, smiling in spite of the fact Castor never believed a word he said. Numie had a warm feeling, the kind you get when sad music is played at the movies.

"If truth was a hammer and hit you on the head, you still wouldn't feel it," Castor said, biting into the tobacco aggressively. "I'm warning you, next time I go take a shit, I don't want nō queer barging in on me when I'm conducting private business." Wide-eyed, he stared at Numie defiantly. "You hear?"

"Only too well," Numie said, suddenly aware of the others in the bar. "So does everybody else. Could you lower your voice?"

"You have good reason to be ashamed, let me tell you." The morning sun breaking through stained glass gave Castor a yellow glow. "One more thing, if that Lola bitch comes down the aisle all dressed in white, I've warned her. I'm gonna stand up and shout to everybody, that bitch is no virgin."

"I believe you would," Numie said, glancing nervously at the clock on the wall. Its hands said six o'clock, though it was clearly noon. Off schedule, like everything else in this town. "But give a girl a break. You know Lola just loves white."

"The color makes me sick. I've made my statement, and everybody in this town will tell you that Castor Q. Combes stands behind his word." He spat again.

The circular platform, on which Lola usually did her musical numbers, had been turned into an altar, draped in her favorite material, white satin. Vestments in white and gold were hanging loosely. Covering the platform was a lacy canopy of streamers adorned with flowers. The last Royal Poincianas of summer were draped about.

From a room in back, Commodore Philip appeared. Looking haggard and slightly stooped, he was obviously ill. But he summoned his energy, and with the help of a cane, made his way to the altar where the Reverend Alberts was waiting. The Commodore was wearing white baggies, a purple ruffled shirt, and a pink silk scarf. His shoes were two-toned, in white and brown. His most attractive feature, his silver gray hair, had given way to jet-black, a bad dye job.

A mountain of yellow fabric appeared from around the corner of the building. It was Erzulie, the voodoo queen. At the head of the procession. She was followed by Sunshine, the commodore's cooking cousin, and six other bearers carrying a pole strung with tropical fruit and flowers. They laid it at the altar like an offering.

Two candlebearers appeared next. Ned and Dinah, in long white robes and multi-colored bean beads strung around their necks. As she stood at the doorway, Dinah——completely devoid of her usual makeup——looked like a vestal virgin. It was clear to all that she was entirely nude under her thin robe. Then Ned stepped into the light. His genitalia were arranged for display.

Back at the platform, Bojo looked sober this morning. On his miniature piano, he started the wedding march. It was more like New Orleans jazz than a wedding march, but at least he was sitting up straight on his swivel stool.

Then Lola appeared, one arm resting daintily on the sleeve of her escort, Johnny Yellowwood. The sheriff seemed embarrassed at the presence of the newspaper photographer. With his eye, he signaled Dave, his deputy, to stop him. As a flashbulb popped, Dave grabbed the camera from the photographer's hand. A brief skirmish, but the march went on.

Lola's anger at not getting photographed was clearly apparent. But she gracefully continued her walk to the makeshift altar.

Fortunately, she had not worn white, as Castor Q. Combes was carefully observing. Rather, a full-length bridal gown in silver gray——covered with sequins, crystal beads, and rhinestones shaped like stars and crosses. Her pageboy wig was pillow white, and she'd generously shadowed her eyes in silver as well. Her usual flaming mouth had given way to raspberry mocha, a color she'd retained for her fingernails showing through open mitt lace gloves and her toenails peeking through silver slingback platform shoes. Dangling cross-shaped gold earrings, with rhinestones pasted on, hung from each pierced ear. Proudly she carried a rhinestone bib on her chest. Draped around her shoulders was a pearl-white chinchilla shrugette. In her arms she carried a bouquet of gladiolas sprayed with silver paint. A rhinestone tiara crowned this decorative mass of black flesh, fabric, stone, and glass.

All too much for Numie. For the actual ceremony, he ducked out back, sneaking a beer from the big refrigerator the commodore kept outside.

Slowly sipping his beer, Numie was an alien. He didn't belong at this mock wedding. No part of him.

His mind wasn't on the ceremony taking place inside the bar, but lost in the world he'd been slipping into.

The last two weeks with Ralph——all a charade of pretended affection. Ralph was constantly looking for some sign of rejection from Numie. It was hard, real hard, for Numie to pretend love when none existed. At least, with his johns in the past, he had to give sex——and only sex——but Ralph was demanding love. How could you demand love? *Ever.*

After the morning she'd discovered Numie in the guest cottage with Ralph, Anne had avoided him. She kept their conversation at a minimum. Ralph still didn't know the reason for this hostility. He just assumed Anne was jealous of him because he'd taken a lover.

Wasn't Numie better off not getting involved with anybody? In these past few days, he kept repeating that question to himself.

To travel light in the world——that had been his goal. Free of possessions. Commitment and concern, two elements missing from his life.

He could also add that he was bereft of ideas, or even the ability to articulate and define his experiences, shaping them into a meaningful insight.

How long could he go on being owned by Ralph? Or how long would Ralph want to continue to own him? To recognize that all things in life are temporary had been easy for Numie. To try for some permanent arrangement seemed as futile as cursing the darkness.

He downed such a hefty swig of beer he almost choked.

Tensely alert now, Numie could hear every word of the ceremony from his position behind the altar. The trelliswork concealed him.

The commodore was putting a ring on Lola's finger.

"You should have had it shined, sweet daddy," she whispered in a voice too soft for any of the audience to hear.

"It's an Old Mine diamond, bitch," the commodore said. "Belonged to my great-grandmother."

"But you really should have had it shined," Lola admonished. "Everybody will be wanting to see my ring, and I don't dare show them this dull thing."

A murmur rose from the crowd.

"Shall we go on with the ceremony?" the Reverend Alberts inquired.

"Darling," Leonora interjected, "an Old Mine diamond refers to the way it's cut. It's very valuable. Everything doesn't have to shine to have value."

"Listen, Miss Rose Bush," Lola said, "I have you to know I know a thing or two about diamonds. Diamonds are supposed to shine——everybody knows that."

"Please," the minister pleaded.

"Very well," Lola said, raising her voice slightly, "but, daddy I've never been so humiliated in my life. And on my wedding day. Everybody will make fun of me."

After this whispered conversation, Lola allowed the commodore to put the antique diamond ring on her finger.

Vows specially written by the Reverend Alberts were exchanged. Commodore Philip Le Blanc and Lola La Mour were now married.

The crowd was rushing to the platform, some to shake the Commodore's frail hand, others to kiss Lola, who warned them not to mess up her makeup. She turned her wedding band around on her finger so that the diamond was hidden inside her hand.

Numie sought out Leonora to take her back to Sacre-Coeur.

. . .

Alone on the patio of Sacre-Coeur, Numie was on his sixth Scotch, far exceeding the limit set by Leonora.

All at once, Anne was there, in nothing but shorts and a halter. "There's something melancholy about September," she said. "Something in the air, I can't place it."

It was the first time since his night of love with her she'd acknowledged him as a fellow human being.

"It's the end of summer," Numie said, "and that's always sad."

"I see you're all by yourself tonight," she said.

"Yes, Ralph hasn't shown up all day." After the blood-boiling heat of the day, Numie was hoping to relax. Anne's presence was disturbing. He feared trouble.

"You'll get used to it. I did." Laughter sounded on the patio, but it was so faint it could have been the wind. "He used to disappear for one or two weeks at a time."

Numie searched for some vision of concern in her soft brown eyes, but they were vacant. "We don't have to talk like two wives waiting for the old man to come home," he said, getting up. "That's not where it's at——not with me anyway."

She smoothed back a lock of hair from her temple and gazed at him. "I'm sorry I've offended you."

"Forget it!" He brushed the sweat from his forehead with the back of his hand. The pressure of being with her under these circumstances was getting to him.

She went behind the bar and took a saltine, smothering it with Tabasco sauce. Then she opened her usual beer, pouring it into a glass. "I'll never be an elegant lady like Leonora."

For a long while, there was nothing but silence. Numie was tense and keyed up.

Finally, Anne slammed down her glass. "There's a bug in my drink. The island's crawling with insects. Get me a clean one."

"Okay," he said. A sullen and vaguely injured look crossed his face. "The day chauffeur is a night bartender, huh?"

"Sensitive?" She stared disdainfully at him.

With burning eyes and a quivering lip, he glared at her. "Yes, I am. I'm tired of being treated like somebody's nigger all the time."

Lighting a cigarette, she blew smoke from her nose. "You put yourself in that position." Her manicured nails shone in the evening light. "Whores have to please, don't they?"

He was absorbing her presence, as never before. Up to now, he'd been thinking of her as a girl. But he was seeing a woman——bitter, cynical, a woman with a lot of mileage on her. "I please when I get paid," he said sarcastically.

The spots from the wall of the house were throwing shafts of red light across the patio. Anne's face was clearly defined. He tried to read it. She looked like someone who had experienced something deeply, and from that experience had grown wiser, but would be more cautious in the future.

"I can vouch for your pleasing when you get paid," she said after a long pause.

At the bar, he hesitated then poured another beer. "Let's stop this," he pleaded. "I'm not in the mood. If you've got it in for me, then let me have it." He searched for her tormented eyes, desperate to make her understand. "What difference does it make to you if I live with Ralph? He was never your husband in anything but name only."

As she took the beer from him, her eyes blinked and her voice grew softer. "How true."

"Then what's pissing you?" he asked, his heart pounding insistently for a verdict.

"*You*."

He flinched. "What does that mean? Do you hate me for making love to you?"

"No, I don't hate you for that," she said calmly. "I hate you for not carrying through with it."

Grinding his teeth together, he knew he long since had lost control of the conversation. Her words stunned him. He had no immediate response. Opening his mouth as if to speak, he came out with choked words. "What could I do?"

She slammed down her beer glass. "Stand on your own feet and quit hustling." She stopped herself from lighting another cigarette from her half-finished stub. "Get a job. Are you lazy or something?" She was like a wild thing furtively watching him. "I've worked all my life."

He stared at her. "Come off it, you were Leonora's girl."

Jumping to her feet, she held her hands rigidly by her side. "I was a lot younger then and very naive." She turned her back on him, as if she were drawing a curtain of horror. "Ralph

will get bored with you," she said in a sharp voice. Then her
words grew faint. "I'm amazed it's lasted two weeks——a record
for him." She turned back around and stared at him accusingly.
"Then what are you going to do?" Her lips tightened. "Go
back to that Lola? Even she is married now."

After a pause, he said, "I have a job——a driver for Leonora.
You know that."

Her body was rocking back and forth. "You moonlight, too.
I know Ralph gives you an extra seventy-five bucks a week."

He clenched his fingers. "I earn it."

She smiled bitterly. "I'm sure you do, but that's not the
point."

In helplessness, he turned from her. "Where can I get a job,
other than the one I have?" He banged his fist against the bar.
"Not on this island."

"I don't know," she said, her surface calm returning. She
sipped her beer. "There's no work here, that's for sure. Maybe
you could go away."

He sighed in exasperation. "Are you trying to get rid of
me?"

"No, I'm not." The beer glass tilted in her hand. "What I
mean is . . . "

"Just what are you trying to tell me?" he asked forcefully.
Now he was in charge. "You're not making sense."

The silence in the patio grew heavy. She bit her lips, "Quit
selling your body——it's disgusting!"

The evening wind hit him in the face, but didn't cool him.
"You told me that the night you met me."

She put the glass on the table and faced him squarely. "Do
you know, could you possibly know that when you made love
to me, it was the most beautiful and tender love ever?"

His eyes were on the glass because he dared not look at her.
Then he picked up her glass and drank from it, as if that would
cleanse him from the embarrassment he was feeling. In a
tentative voice, he asked, "Anne...better than Nick?"

"Ralph was right," she said, starting to cry. "I just tell that
story about Nick." Nowhere to go, she circled the patio without
saying a word. "It's easier than telling the truth. Easier than
telling what he was really like." She paused awkwardly. He
could hardly hear her. "Easier than telling what he did."

Numie was walking rapidly to her.

Just then, the red spots of the patio outlined Ralph's image. It was obvious he'd been drinking, and heavily. "My God, I'm probably the only man on this island who can come home and find his wife and his husband together."

"Ralph," Anne said in a businesslike voice, quickly regaining her composure, "there were several calls for you today. When you're out cruising, you could at least check in every now and then. After all, there are things to be taken care of."

Ralph stared at Anne as if she were a target and he had a knife. "Get out of my sight, bitch. I can't stand to look at you."

"Go to hell!" she shouted, turning and running from the patio.

With Anne's half-empty glass in his hand, Numie was taking this in the way a victim watches an execution, knowing he was next.

"As for you," Ralph said, staggering over to him. He grabbed the glass from his hand and tossed it into a bush. "You're drinking too much."

Fists clenched, Numie said bitingly, "You're one to talk!"

Ralph glared at him contemptuously. "You've got to go on a diet. You're getting a tire around your middle——one big turnoff."

Numie was slowly regaining control of himself. When he spoke, he tried to sound as neutral as possible. "That's not what you said last night."

Ralph practically spat at him. "I was back at the beach today. There was one number there with a fantastic build." He arched his shoulders. "Did he come on strong! I kept asking myself, what I was doing coming home to a *middle-aged* man when I saw what was available to me."

The sky was growing darker, and the air even chillier after the heat of the day. If only it would rain. "Well, go get him, goddam it," Numie managed to say.

Seemingly delighted with himself, Ralph cautioned, "Don't get jealous."

Numie started to smile falsely, but it faded before he could complete it. "Jealous is not the word."

Ralph grabbed him by the shoulders, his fingers digging in until he saw Numie wince with pain. "I'm not kicking you out, if that's what you're afraid of. But I'm warning you——starting tomorrow, you'd better shape up."

Taking Ralph's hand, Numie pulled it from his shoulder. "Have you looked at your own tire lately?" he asked with a bite in his voice. "You're not the world's greatest physical attraction." At the bar he poured himself a drink.

Suddenly, beside him, Ralph took Numie's half-full glass and poured its contents over the bar top. "But I pay the bills," Ralph said. "I can go to pot if I want to. You're selling a bod, baby, and you'd better get it in shape——or else!" He turned to go. "I'm sleeping in my own room upstairs tonight. You can stay in the guest cottage——by yourself." He stumbled on his route to the downstairs parlor.

Numie picked up the empty glass and refilled it. He settled back into a chair. Time to face reality. His days on the island were coming to an end——he clearly knew that now.

Where to go?

What next?

Suddenly, he had an idea.

In the guest cottage, he was searching through his duffel bag for his address book. There was one place, only one he'd found in his entire life where he'd been welcomed and wanted. He'd write a letter tonight.

Many years had gone by, but there was still a slim chance.

Chapter Twenty-Three

In the patio of Sacre-Coeur, it was early morning. Birds were darting from tree to tree. The sun had just come up. Unlike the oppressive heat of the past two weeks, this morning was bright and fresh, the temperature just right.

Numie sat still for a long while. When had he last stopped to enjoy the beauty of a day? The birds were even singing.

"Tangerine," he called out, watching as she hobbled across the bricks.

"Quit screaming, sugartit," she said. "Think I'm deaf or something? I've put us on a pot of coffee."

"What's the matter with you?"

"Rheumatism——just getting old——that's all. Come to think of it, that's enough!" Setting the pan of potatoes down on the coffee table, she rubbed her back. "I really ache this morning." She was clad in a lime-green blouse, an orange-colored skirt, and tennis shoes without stockings. A red bandana encased her tangerine hair. Plopping down in a nearby wicker chair, she raised her sweaty arms to the sun, revealing not only wads of hair, but parts of a yellowing brassiere.

Numie dug his hands deep into his pockets. "I expected to see you at the wedding yesterday."

Her sigh mocked him. "I couldn't face it." She moved her chair over, her knees touching his. "Just think, that Lola can get a man, even a feeble one, and look what happened to me." She nodded, almost absently. "Talk about Hayden gives me a crick in the heart. I've just been moping around my house."

A whiff of her armpits drove him back farther into his chair. "Did the sheriff ever find him?"

She stared at him with something less than complete affection. "He's gone for good."

He reached over and squeezed her hand so hard her rings hurt.

"Watch my fingers," she cautioned. "I've got these taters to peel. I'm cooking lunch for us all. The cook called in sick." She glanced over at him. "Come to think of it, you look like you got a poker shoved up the wrong place, too."

Swallowing hard, he said, "Ralph and I may be splitting

soon. Things aren't going well."

"Considering Ralph, that's very likely. You don't pick 'em no better than I do." She didn't say anything for a minute, then looked up from her potato peeling. "I wish I had your problems." She studied his face quietly. "You're so young, and your life's ahead of you. Okay, you got troubles. But from my side of the fence, I'd gladly cross over."

He raised himself on both elbows and then with effort swung into a rigid sitting position. "How thoughtless of me to lay my shit on you after what you've been through." Her face made him pause and remember. "You know, your voice sounds different. Sadder. I've never known you to talk this way before."

She took a handkerchief from her hip pocket and blew her nose. "I never felt this way before. But I ain't trying to depress you——just let you know how lucky you are even if it don't seem like that now."

He took a cigarette from his pocket, lit it, and gave it to her.

"You keep reaching for that grab bag," she said, "till there's no chance left. Then you toss it over." Her lips parted slightly and her head nodded. "No point hanging on when the damn thing's run out of goodies. That's when it gets ugly." Her lips quivered. She burst into tears.

He tried to put his arm around her.

But she broke away. "A woman by herself," she said, sobbing, "is just like turnip greens without fatback. A bitter taste, no good flavor at all."

At this moment Leonora entered the patio. Never had he seen her so disheveled. Something must be seriously wrong. Around her nude body was wrapped a crepe de chine robe in coffee brown.

Leonora paused hesitantly, suddenly aware that she had not checked her appearance this morning. But she knew her face was all right, considering that she was a natural beauty. "I just got a call from the hospital on the mainland," she said. "The commodore died this morning on the operating table."

The news neither shocked nor surprised Numie. It had been predictable. He thought immediately of how Lola was receiving the bulletin.

"It's just as well," Leonora said. Her hands were shaking.

"He was eaten up with cancer anyway." A stab of guilt plunged into her. For the first time, she admitted something to herself. She loathed Philip.

"I'm sorry to hear that," Tangerine said, still crying from before.

Leonora looked down at her. "You don't have to cry. The commodore's death is not a time for tears. He had a full life." A distant memory flashed before her eyes. Philip had known Norton Huttnar, her late husband. Leonora wondered how well they'd known each other. The prospect caused her to shudder and tighten her robe around her body. "Unlike me," she continued, "Philip had stopped growing——and that's certain death anyway."

Numie found Leonora's imperial behavior at a time like this shocking. Regardless of how he hated someone in life, he respected him in death. It erased some of the bad things. "You can't knock her for crying," he said.

She turned on him, her eyes sparkling. "As for you," she said, "we've got real problems this morning. More serious than the commodore's dying." A rustling in the tree over her head sent her arm stretching out into the air. Then she steadied herself. Her nerves were shattered. "I've been on the phone with the Commodore's attorney," she went on. "He's got a will. Everything has been bequeathed to Lola."

Numie settled back with unnecessary vigor. A butterfly landed on the arm of his chair, but quickly took off again. "Lola always wanted to get paid," he said. "So now she's struck it rich."

Stillness etherized the patio for a moment. "You don't seem to understand," Leonora said. "That makes Lola my business partner."

"Oh, my God," Tangerine said, resuming her potato peeling. "Lola's been hard to contain up to now, but..."

Numie mentally filled in the consequences of that 'but'.

So did Leonora. "Exactly," she said. "I've spoken to her this morning. Even before the will's read, she wants to survey our mutual properties." Her fingers stabbed the air. "Further, she wants you to be her driver. To show her around."

The prospect was outrageous to him. It was like having to adjust to a new boss with no prior notice. "Me?" he asked hesitantly.

Leonora stared accusingly. "It's not as if you don't know her." So mesmerized was she by the horror descending, a fly was allowed to meander across her open-mouthed face. "I told her she could hire somebody else, but she insisted on you." Leonora clutched her side. Her breath was coming in gasps. "I'm not in a position to refuse her anything——at least for the moment."

Numie jumped up. "I didn't know that driving Lola around would be part of my job."

"Hell," Leonora said, turning from the sight of him. At the bar, she was infuriated by the empty beer bottles. With the back of her hand, she sent them tumbling onto the bricks of the patio. "I'll give you a hundred dollars a week if that will satisfy your greed. I can't afford to antagonize Lola."

Nervously he wiped his sweaty hands on his trousers. "It's not greed. It's Lola." Avoiding Tangerine's penetrating look, he went on, "Lola and I aren't on the best of terms."

Leonora spun around, glaring at him. "Nevertheless, she requested you. In fact, she's waiting for you now." For a moment, the only sound heard was Tangerine's cough. Leonora was tempted, ever so briefly, to slap her in the face. Coughing in her presence was unbearable. "Lola will tell you where to go," she continued, turning to Numie. "I have a feeling she knows exactly where everything is, that calculating black hussy."

"I don't know how long I'll be with her." Numie's voice was weird, even to himself. It was the sound he made when he suffered from a sore throat.

"Take all the time you need," Leonora said. Her confidence was slowly returning. As before, when her world seemed hopelessly doomed, she was girding herself to remake it. "I'm certainly not going anywhere today. Besides, this news has given me a splitting headache." She was ready to go, then she noticed what Tangerine was doing. "Peeling potatoes at a time like this?"

"The cook is sick," Tangerine said, her eyes downcast.

For one brief second, Leonora flirted with the idea of kicking over the water holding the blasted potatoes. "Darling," she said, controlling her voice, "no one will be eating at this house today I can assure you. Besides, nobody eats potatoes under any circumstances.

Tangerine's face reflected her hurt. "But that's one of the few things I know how to cook."

"Forget it!" Leonora screeched, exasperated to the point of violence. She rushed toward the parlor. "That miserable drag queen even owns half of my fashion house." Her temples were throbbing with pain, as the tension within her mounted. "I'm fated to go through life plagued with drag queens. Norton Huttnar. Now, Lola La Mour."

. . .

In the downstairs bar at Commodore Philip's, Ned was wearing nothing but a bikini. He was nursing a drink in the corner near the platform where Lola was married.

Numie adjusted his eyes to the dim light. Kicking aside a fallen box, he told Ned: "Tell Lola the *chauffeur* is here."

With glassy eyes, Ned looked up at him. "I'm no messenger service."

For one brief moment, Numie was tempted to walk out on everything and everybody.

On wobbly legs, Ned got up. "Let me talk some shit to you, white boy." His fingers dug into Numie's shoulder. "I gotta figure out some way to keep the lid on that highsidin' Lola. That gal is pussy-whipping me to death." His hand dropped to his side. "She's after *cajones*. She's trying to get mine, and you're next on her list."

Numie backed away, smiling sardonically. "I thought you knew how to control all women."

Ned banged his fist on the bar counter. "Man, Lola is the craziest chick I ever came across. Women with real pussies I can handle. But in Lola's case..."

"I know," Numie said, his tension at seeing Ned again fading. "It's like petting a cobra."

Ned fingered his own biceps, as if to assure himself they were still there. "Lola's one hell of a bitch. She was coming on so strong with me right in front of you. You know why? To make you jealous." His eyes darted around the bar, as if he were being attacked from every angle. "Now that she's all hotsy-totsy with the cookies the commodore left behind, she wants a white man on the chain." He licked his finger and pointed at Numie. "You, stud."

This prospect struck Numie like hell trying to claim him. "I'm not on the market. I was with her once and that's enough."

Ned burst into hollow laughter. "She'll get you back."

Numie stepped aside. He was playing a role today, and was determined it would not affect him deeply. "If Lola's through with you, what are you hanging around for?"

Ned waved his hand, but noticing it was empty, wrapped it around his drink again. "She ain't through with me. Dinah neither. That broad wants me around so she can boss me. Let's face it. Half the fun of being rich is to make those around you eat ass."

"Not for me it isn't." He nervously paced the bar.

"Man, you ain't rich——and you ain't never gonna be rich neither," Ned said.

Numie smiled to himself. All his life he'd dreamed of the rich lady waiting to take him away. But even in his worse nightmares, the lady had not been Lola or anything like her.

"Jive-ass motherfucker," Ned said, spinning around. "You're just another nigger like me, hanging out with some pussy trying to get a lick."

Numie couldn't take Ned or any more of this talk. "Does she want me to drive her or not?" he asked abruptly.

Ned ambled over and put a quarter in the jukebox. A full glass in the other hand, he pounded the jukebox drunkenly in rhythm to the rock music. "She's waiting for you upstairs. That queen is after her some *manhood*. She's gonna buy yours, watch and see!"

. . .

In Lola's boudoir, Dinah was clicking her heels to ear-splitting pop music. She was wearing nothing but a sunflower yellow T-shirt cut into a form-fitting halter top. "Don't stand there with your jaw hanging," she said. "Come on in or you'll let in the flies."

In a gossamer-thin white morning coat, Lola was in her

dressing room foyer. Turning around, she spotted Numie. Quickly she dropped her nail file. Putting her hand to her forehead, she started to mourn, then darted over to the stereo and turned it off. "Ain't you got no respect for the dead?" she demanded of Dinah. Throwing her hands to her face again, she sobbed loudly and rushed over to Numie to embrace him.

He remained cold and distant.

She stepped back, her anger apparent. Still, she tried not to show it. "Just imagine," she said, "my dear sweet daddy taken away from me so soon after we was married."

"But you had so many good years together," Numie said sarcastically.

Lola glared at him.

He glanced at his watch. "Want me to drive you somewhere?"

"Yes," Lola answered, rather grandly. "You know Dinah, of course. She's my new secretary."

"I didn't know you could type," Numie said.

"Can't," Dinah answered.

"Look, gal," Lola said, "you do not receive my *business* visitors with no pants on." She looked nervously at Numie, trying to detect some attraction on his part for Dinah. She could see none. "That black furry thing," she went on, "is sickening enough without your flaunting it in our faces."

"'Cuse me," Dinah said, retreating to the bathroom.

Numie backed away from Lola, staying as close to the door as possible. Lola had the crazed glow of a woman out for a taste of blood.

Propping her hands on her hips, she said, "I want to survey the mutual properties *I* own with De la Mer. Is my business manager ready?"

He shook his head and tried to speak in an unemotional voice. "I didn't know you had a business manager?"

She strutted around the boudoir, swinging her ass hopefully. "Ned is my new business manager." She kept glancing back at Numie. The way she figured it, he was doing a real good job of concealing his jealousy. "The same job for me that Ralph has for that De la Mer dyke."

The sunlight coming in through the gauze curtains made the white room yellow. Numie's hand was shaking. "And Dinah is your version of Anne?" he asked.

"Exactly," Lola answered.

"'Cept I can't type," Dinah called, peering around the corner and shaking a pair of nylon panties at Lola.

"Social secretaries don't have to type," Lola said, emotionally exhausted. That child had a way of tiring her something awful. "Dinah had to look all over town for me to get a suitable black dress to wear during this time of grief." The line sounded phony, and she knew it. She studied her reflection in her dressing mirror, hoping that would give her more confidence. "I've never worn black, but I think it proper today. Dinah found a Cuban girl my size, and we bought the dress right off her back." She went over to the bed and picked it up. "No style!" she exclaimed with loathing in her voice. "Cubans got no taste at all, but I'll have to wear it temporarily." She ran her hand down her trim figure. "I'm having something made up real special for tonight."

Numie yawned. He was bored, and he clearly wanted to get on with the business of the day. "Where are we going first?"

Lola's eyes flared. She wasn't used to tricks yawning in her face. "To get an outfit for Ned," she said sharply. "He don't have no suitable clothes to be seen around town with me." She whipped around, waving her arms in a theatrical gesture and tossing her ass once more at Numie. "Jesus Christ, I'll go broke dressing you men."

. . .

In his pink suit and "Sky" hat, Ned was six-foot-two of new man. He was ready and raring to go.

"Don't you think it's a little flashy?" David asked, in his high-pitched voice.

"Man, if you've got something to flash, then flash it," Ned countered.

In the same boutique where Lola had outfitted him, Numie was pacing the upper reaches, casually examining a pair of badly made slacks.

"Your mama has to show these dudes how to dress," Lola said. She was not completely pleased with her makeup. Sweat in summer caused embarrassing streaks.

"You sure know how to pick them," David said, eying Ned carefully.

"One more thing," Ned added, folding up his old trousers, "this pink suit's the only thing in this joint that sings. Everything else is more for old fags. Next time I come in, I want to see some good stuff."

Lola looked hopefully up front at Numie, but he was paying her no attention. "Ever seen a rainbow?" she asked David.

"What do you mean?" he replied.

Lola did a rolling bump. "Get some color in here," she ordered.

"Some red on red, some black on white...and plum," Ned said. "I get off on plum."

"But I've done very well with this merchandise," David protested. "The pink suit I actually got in a shipment by mistake."

"Mistake?" Ned was furious. "You saying I ain't got taste, mister?"

No, I didn't mean it that way," David said, backing off.

It probably was a mistake," Lola said, swishing gaily around the room. "That's why it's the best suit in the shop——'cause you didn't order it!"

"But I've never received any complaints before," David said.

"If you don't want some coins from our little pot of gold, that's okay with me, man," Ned said. He pinched Lola's ass. "Come on."

Hands on her hips, Lola said, "You forget I own this shop." Turning her back on David, she reached to fondle Ned's hair. "Your lease has run out." Her over-the-shoulder voice was matter-of-fact.

"Anything you say," David said nervously. "I'd hate to lose my shop. I think I know what you have in mind." He eyed his merchandise. "My clothes have been looking pretty dull lately. I could spice them up a bit."

With exhaled breath, she commanded, "Charge Ned's suit."

"You mean..." David asked hesitantly, "on the commodore's account? But he's dead."

She giggled, then suppressed it. "I just happen to know where my commodore is," she said. "No, I mean on *my* account!" With that announcement she was half out the entrance and into the street. She waited impatiently for Numie to open the door to the back compartment of Leonora's Lincoln.

Numie was trying to pretend today wasn't happening. It was very hot, and the air was heavy. He longed for a little wind to blow away the rotten smell of this whole place.

Ned trailed Lola inside the car. "This leopard skin upholstery's too much," he said, fondling it like he did the breast of a woman. "Bet that was some cat. Love to have me a jacket of that cat's hide."

Lola patted him on the knee. "You will," she said.

. . .

"You are, in fact, Haskell Hadley Yett?" an attorney was asking. "Not Lola La Mour."

Lola crossed her legs and checked her hosiery for a snag. "One and the same," she answered, holding her head high. "Lola La Mour is my professional name."

"And what kind of profession is that?" the attorney asked, settling back in a leather chair and lighting a cigarette. "That requires you to dress, act, and talk like a woman?"

Lola licked her lips, knowing that made her sexier. "I'm a cabaret entertainer," she said, adjusting her black dress. "My fans expect it of me."

The attorney fingered his mustache and moved uncomfortably in his seat. His white shirt was soaked. "Who are these gentlemen with you?" he inquired.

Lola started to answer, but Ned interrupted. "I'm her business manager here to protect her interests."

As if threatened, the attorney sat up rigidly. "Her interests are well taken care of, I can assure you."

"I'm the driver," Numie interjected, hoping to stay out of this whole affair. In the far corner of the room, he had refused even a seat. Cast in the servant role, he was determined to play it through. Aimlessly his eyes wandered, taking in the termite-eaten Cuban wicker furniture, the thirsty plants, and the bamboo ceiling. His head was dark today, and sounds had a hard time reaching him. It was some kind of hell he was hearing, but he was a long way from it.

"As you know," the attorney said, turning to Ned, "Mr.

Yett was Commodore Philip's sole heir."

"Heiress," Lola corrected. She smiled demurely. "I'm known by my professional name." Trying to appear casual like watching a fly, she glanced at Numie in the back of the room. That white boy infuriated the hell out of her. He didn't seem to be impressed that she was an heiress. And that had been the one thing she knew would impress him. It didn't make sense, unless Numie was playing a game. Holding out for higher stakes.

"I'm sorry, *Miss* La Mour," the attorney said, trying to catch her eye. "Whichever term you prefer is acceptable to me." He settled back again. "The commodore has a close relative."

The word sent a shiver racing up Lola's spine.

"I think one sister is still living in New Orleans," the attorney continued.

Memories of the banquet and the call from Sister Amelia flashed through Lola's head.

"She's not mentioned in the will," the attorney said. "I had warned Phil to at least mention her. Now I must warn you: I expect his sister will contest the will."

In spite of running eye shadow, Lola tried to appear as confident as possible. "I'm not worried," she said.

She flung herself back in her peacock chair like a limp dishrag. No need to appear tense. The bars on the windows caught her eye. The office was like a goddamn jail, and she was not going to be the prisoner of white men for much longer. Sitting up rigidly, she was ready for business. "Exactly what does the commodore's estate consist of?" Her words hung heavy in the air. From the open but barred window an aroma of honeysuckle wafted across, only to be smothered by the attorney's cigarette smoke. "He never talked to me too much about his property on the mainland."

"It's quite large," the attorney said. "You're going to be a very wealthy... person."

A tingle began in Lola's chartreuse-painted toe, traversing her hosiery-encased legs, settling for a brief moment in her little honeypot, then traveling up her breasts, lodging finally at her temples, streaked with pancake makeup. "I know he had boats," she replied, again trying to sound as casual as possible. "He used to bring his yacht down from time to time."

"Yes, I know that," the attorney said. "He owns four, including the yacht. I wouldn't exactly call them boats. They're more like ships."

Her temples practically exploded. Then the tingle began its downward descent, this time anchoring permanently at the honeypot.

"You know, of course, he wasn't a real commodore," the attorney said.

Lola practically laughed at his face. She wanted to say, "You know, motherfucker, I'm a strange lady, but I can out-pussy any pussy!" But she refrained from uttering such crudeness, mentally reminding herself she must avoid such bad taste. It didn't become her new position in life.

"Look, man, Ned was saying, "with that many boats, you're the commodore of your own fleet."

"Yes," the attorney said stiffly. "He owned quite a bit of property in Tortuga. The bar he owned outright. Nearly everything else is in partnership with Leonora de la Mer, including her fashion house."

That tingling sensation in her honeypot was getting completely out of control. It was rape. She loved his last words so much she wished she'd had a tape recorder so she could hear the words over and over, memorizing every sound and imbedding it deep in her brain. Visions of herself as a fashion designer, bigger and more successful than De la Mer ever was, danced through her head. But back to business. "What about Sacre-Coeur?" she asked pointedly, knowing her luck couldn't hold out forever.

"No," the attorney said, "that's completely owned by De la Mer. Inherited it from her husband."

"And the Facel-Vega," Lola said impatiently. "Don't forget that and the Rolls-Royce." Her breath was coming in gasps.

"Lola, you can do better than that old broken down Rolls," Ned said.

Her eyes spat fire at him. "We'll discuss it later if you don't mind," she said in her best ladylike voice. The more her eyeballs took in Ned, the more convinced she was he was a field nigger.

"Now," the attorney went on, but in a hesitant voice, "there is the question of the body."

Utter silence fell across the room.

Lola was remembering her wedding and wishing she'd saved some of the flowers. Had she known the wedding and the commodore's death would be taking place so close together she would have. It would cut down tremendously on the florist's bill. But she never gave flowers to the commodore alive. He never liked anything he couldn't eat or polish.

"The body's not buried yet," the attorney said when he was getting no response from Lola.

"I'm no gravedigger," she said indignantly.

"No one is expecting you to dig the grave," the attorney snapped. "But you've got to make arrangements, or else give me instructions so I can."

Lola shifted her legs again, swinging her arms. Was he trying to suck her into a trap? "I'm not into fancy coffins," she said firmly. "Something simple. Maybe just a pine box."

The attorney cast a disdainful eye, then said, "You mean a pauper's coffin?"

"Call it what you like," Lola answered, angered now, as she never wanted to associate herself with poverty ever. "My departed commodore told me he didn't like spending money on funerals or undertakers." She remembered his telling her that one time, and here was one request she could live with.

"We don't call them undertakers any more," the attorney said. "If you insist on an inexpensive coffin, the commodore's friends at the yacht club on the mainland will be horrified. I feel I should warn you."

"Why do those cats have to know?" Ned asked.

"They'll find out at the funeral," the attorney replied.

"What funeral?" Lola asked. She feared she was losing control of the conversation——and, after all, she was the heiress. "I don't see no need for a funeral." Her voice was cold. Then she softened her tone, and started to put her hand to her temples until she realized it would streak her makeup all the more. "My commodore's death has left my system in such a state of shock I couldn't bear to go through with no funeral. We'll just have to bury him——that's all. I have my memories. Thank the good Lord for that."

"Miss La Mour," the attorney said, "if you don't mind my asking, exactly what was your relationship with the commodore?"

The sun was hot and glaring, and its light seemed to be slashing right through those bars. Lola reached into her purse, putting on a pair of rhinestone sunglasses. "We lived together for years," she said.

You mean you worked at his saloon?" the attorney corrected her.

"Yes, I worked there," Lola said, "but I also lived with my commodore." Once again, she wet her lips for effect. "He was my husband."

"Surely you're mistaken," the attorney said. "Although you're known professionally as Lola La Mour, you are a man." He crushed out his cigarette. "And men don't have husbands!"

All this slander about her being a man burned the hell out of her. "Darling," she said in her most biting voice, "I had a husband. Of course, we weren't legally married until just the other day, but a boss player like you should have heard of common law marriages."

"Please," the attorney said.

"Why don't you please?" Ned interrupted. "The lady here said she was married to the commodore. After all, she should know."

"You have a point there," the attorney said. "A most unusual case."

Lola was all to pieces right now. Abruptly she stood up, seeing if the attorney would rise to acknowledge her action. He did. Lola's smile was confident as she said, "At the moment, I'm tremendously short of cold hard cash. I need a whole pot of gold until all this red tape is cleared up."

Clearing his throat, the attorney said, "I think that could be arranged. I could advance you a suitable amount." He extended his hand. "Miss La Mour, you have my deepest sympathy at the loss of your dear..." He hesitated, then said, "...husband. He was my finest client, and I will personally feel his departure deeply."

Lola extended her hand tentatively, wishing she'd worn gloves for the occasion. "Thank you."

"Of course," the attorney continued, "I know the commodore's affairs intimately, and I hope you will see fit to retain my services."

"Yes," Lola said, glancing absently at the slowly moving blades of the wood fan overhead. "But at a much higher rate."

"Really?" the attorney said, finding it hard to suppress his enthusiasm. "I think the arrangements——the burial and all, the settling of the estate——can be taken care of speedily and efficiently." Walking around his desk, he took her by the arm and escorted her to the door. "I totally agree with you, by the way. Funerals are morbid events and shouldn't be dragged out."

"Then we understand each other?" Lola asked, adopting a model's stance at the door that best showed off her girlish figure.

"Perfectly," the attorney replied, squeezing her elbow ever so gently.

. . .

On the steps leading to the street, Numie asked, "Do I have to drive you around all day?"

Lola stopped in her tracks, digging her high heel into the step. "Yes, I've always considered it vulgar for ladies to be seen behind the wheel of a car."

After dropping Ned off at Commodore Philip's bar, Lola was getting into the Lincoln once again. She emerged on the street still clad in her simple black dress. But she'd put on a pearl necklace and wrapped a white boa around her shoulders. Hitting the cobblestones were her six-inch-high Cucaracha Miranda clogs. Numie eyed her skeptically. "You call that a 'mourning' dress?" he asked. He reluctantly opened the rear door for her.

She opened her eyes wide, and her voice was cool and controlled. "Honey, just 'cause a girl's lost her husband, and is supposed to wear basic black, it don't mean she can't look glamorous." Lola directed him to drive her to the Dry Marquesas Hotel where he'd spent his first night in town.

"Can't you read the sign?" Numie called back at her when she'd ordered him to stop right in front of the hotel. "It says, NO PARKING."

"Darling," she said rather grandly, "that sign was intended for regular people. Not Lola La Mour!" Moving like an electric eel, Lola's tongue slipped out and wet-coated her red lips.

"We'll see," Numie said. Whenever he was with Lola these days, he wanted to reach out and strangle her. As he led her into the lobby, two Cubans across the street yelled something in Spanish. But he didn't understand.

Behind the desk the surly clerk was reading a sex book. "Back with another customer?" he asked.

"No way," Numie said. He surveyed the lobby as if it were the distant past. "I don't need to hang out in this dump any more."

The clerk slammed the book down on the desk, deliberately concealing the cover. "Just as well——you couldn't pay the bill no way till Ralph chipped in." He took a toothpick out of his mouth and tossed it on the tile floor.

Lola pranced around the lobby, trying to be forceful, commanding, and sexually provocative. Now that she'd had a chance to redo her makeup, she was more confident. "This place gives me the creeps," she said in a loud voice. "I wish this town had a decent hotel." Hands on her hips, she glared at the clerk. "I might build one one day."

"Look, nigger," the clerk said, almost hissing through yellowing teeth, "you're lucky I let you in in the first place."

Numie glanced nervously at Lola, who remained glued to her position, as if a frozen still-life. "Watch who you're calling nigger," he warned the clerk.

"Take it easy, man," the clerk said, backing off. "I got my own beliefs about things. When my old man used to own this hotel, we didn't accept niggers."

Lola was slow to rage, but after a few seconds her fury was in full bloom. She started to say something, but her explosive anger caused her to choke. "Clap Face," she stuttered, "I happen to know your old man went bankrupt. Spent all his money eating thirteen-year-old chocolate drops." Whipping her white boa around her throat as if to protect herself from an imaginary gale, she went on. "He was even run out of town. White trash——just like you."

Numie couldn't have felt more tight and distant from Lola; he was anxious to avoid a fight. It was a question of being in the presence of two people he hated and forced to decide who had harmed him more. "Okay," he said to Lola, "let's skip the family biographies."

Coming out from behind the desk, the clerk had an unzipped fly. "What do you want here?"

Lola paused a long time for effect. "A suite," she answered.

The clerk laughed and let out a gin belch. "A *suite?* Nobody's asked for a suite at this place since the old P&O steamship from Havana stopped coming."

Lola sucked in her cheeks as if all sorts of cameras were turned on her, then said, "I know you have them and I demand the best one."

"We'll rent you anything you can pay for," the clerk said. Realizing his fly was unzipped, he discreetly tended to it. "We'll even charge you a nickel if you want to take a leak in the can." A frown crossed his face, "But those old suites ain't in very good shape."

Anxious to get on with it, Numie said, "Let's see what you've got."

The clerk went ahead.

Numie followed Lola. "What's this about wanting a suite?" he whispered in her ear.

Lola's throat was parched, and she was exhausted. The responsibility of being a rich widow was weighing heavily on her today. "I'm no longer a second-class citizen," she said. "The commodore wanted to live over the bar. He thought it camp. I don't!"

"Okay," he said. Crossing over a barricade of lumber——the same barricade he'd crossed that night he met Ralph——Numie said no more until they reached the suite.

Unlocking the door, the clerk invited them to step inside. "This is it."

Numie went in first. "This place stinks," he said, making for a window. "It hasn't been aired out in years." The window was stuck, but he managed to raise it, throwing open the shutter doors. The sun, now high in the sky, flooded the room. Spiderwebs were in the corner. Turning to Lola, he asked, "How do you like it?"

She hesitated before answering, trying to make up her mind if the clerk was showing her the best. "It's certainly big enough," she said finally. Desperately she was searching for a mirror. She always judged a place by how a mirror in the room reflected her image. "But the decor's all wrong for me." Waving her boa at the ceiling, she said, "This peach color's got to go. I can't operate against a peach background." She was growing frenetic, irascible. "I've always operated in a boudoir all in white, with lots of satin."

The clerk looked as if he wanted to beat hell out of her. "Take it or leave it," he said.

"Young man," she cautioned, "don't be impertinent with me." She was remembering how De la Mer one night dressed down a waiter. She assumed De la Mer's stance, even slightly imitating her voice. "I may take it, except it'll have to be redecorated." She stepped away from the harsh glare of the sun. "Everything must be in white. The wallpaper, drapes, carpet, furniture."

The clerk shook his head. "We're not going to do a damn thing."

"You don't understand," Numie said, walking over. He shuddered to think the clerk might be sizing him up as Lola's boy, even though he did feel like her boy right now. "Miss La Mour's willing to pay for it."

"That so?" the clerk said. "Then we'll be only too happy to oblige. Send your own painter and decorator over today. We ain't exactly interior decorators around here."

"We can see that," Numie said. A truck screeched to a halt near the window. "Man, did anyone ever tell you you should take up hotel management?"

The clerk looked as if he wanted to spit.

Turning his back, Numie paced the floor, as distant memories of hundreds of hotel rooms flooded his brain. But he was in control enough to keep one single memory from forming a picture in focus.

Lola settled herself on one of the dusty sofas. "You obviously have never truly understood who I am," she said. She felt a tightening in her honeypot that needed relief.

"I don't care who you are," the clerk said.

Numie studied him closely. He knew he was called Spider, and he was wondering how he got that name.

"As far as I'm concerned," Spider said, "you're just that colored drag queen shacked up with the old commodore."

"Listen, punk," Numie said, "the commodore is dead. Miss

La Mour's in charge now." He was enjoying lording it over the clerk, after his mistreatment when he arrived in town.

"I don't like bossy gals," Spider said.

Lola practically jumped up from the sofa. "Did I hear you say gal?" She ran her hand down her black dress that was being warmed by the noonday sun. "If I wasn't such a lady, I'd rip your balls off——if you've got any."

Spider stepped menacingly toward her.

Numie suspected Spider was thinking Lola was really a man at this point, and to the clerk Lola was spewing out fighting words.

"No man," Lola continued, "black or white, is going to call me gal——like some common streetwalker——and get away with it." She studied Spider's face carefully, wondering how much he really knew about her. After all, Castor Q. Combes, that vicious liar and gossip, often hung out around this hotel and might have slandered her. "I'll overlook it this time, 'cause you're a dumbass, honky, redneck bastard. From now on, it's Miss la Mour——or else!" Lola lit a cigarette and violently blew rings.

Spider seemed ready to kick her in the mouth, but he thoughtfully headed to the door. "Okay, don't get all hot and bothered." He left quickly.

Numie turned to Lola. "Are you sure you're doing the right thing moving in here?"

"Temporary headquarters," Lola said, smiling. She glanced quickly around the room, deciding where she was going to install some gilt mirrors. "I'm not planning to live here forever."

"Where then?" Numie asked, momentarily relieved that Lola was planning to leave Tortuga.

"Sacre-Coeur... and I don't mean in the guest cottage." Sinking back into the sofa, Lola was enjoying this moment of revelation. She waited quietly for her words to sink in.

Numie was stunned. "I think that place already has a tenant." Then he was curious. "Just how do you plan to move Leonora out?"

Lola got up, slinking her hips over to the window. "In time, child, I will reveal all." She glanced out at the street scene, and for a horrified moment thought she saw her cousin, Castor Q.

Combes. "People of your race are so backward," she said to Numie. "It takes so long for something to penetrate." She pivoted, then stared at him with contempt. "A black stud like Ned would have figured out what I was up to long ago. But you white boys. My people have always had to carry you on our backs."

"Listen," he said, wishing he could be the servant and not involved in any personal conversations, "you didn't do so bad with the commodore. He's white. or was. And you went for me."

"Darling," she said, adoring every sweet moment she could humiliate him, "using whities for sex or money and having to depend on their brain capacity are two different things."

Fists clenched, he said, "You really burn me."

"I know," she answered, smiling. "But you're doing okay. The two bit hustler I bailed out of jail is on his way toward becoming a big stud in this town." She stood right in front of him, touching his cheek affectionately. "But don't forget——not for one moment——who's going to make you big. Lola La Mour, that's who."

He seized her hand, removing it from his face. "You making an offer?" He spun around. "Just for the record, I'm not for sale."

She stalked to the other side of the room. "You was always for sale, ever since that first day you figured out you had a little something hanging between your legs." She stopped short with a slight gasp. "That's never been a question with you. It was always the question of the price." The singing of a bird at the window caused her to pick up a Bible and toss it at the green shutters. The bird darted away. "Between us, my dear, you sell cheap."

He stared at her blonde wig, her red mouth, her chartreuse fingernails, the mockery of the black dress, the white boa on a hot summer day——enough to make him ill. "I said, I'm not for sale. After that night with you and the commodore, I've had it!"

"Don't shake one of your balls loose," she said, heading for the door, high heels clanking. "I can understand why you didn't want to get it on with the commodore. For Christ's sake, who did?" She held up the Old Mine diamond, proudly exhibiting it to him. Like a hot flash, embarrassment flooded her brain. She'd been assured——and not just by De la Mer——that Old Mine diamonds are valuable, even though they don't shine. After all, any nigger could have a shiny, sparkling diamond. Only unusual people wore Old Mine diamonds, antique at that. "It was me you wanted all alone," she said, her eyes focusing on Numie once again. "I know that." She whispered softly and confidentially. "It's okay, baby. Let it all hang out!"

"It's not okay," he said, red with fury. His words were choked. "I don't want you!" he screamed.

Fearful Spider would hear this talk of rejection, Lola opted to keep cool. "Now you're being ridiculous," she said forcefully. Later on, this white boy would have to face hell for uttering those words. "Every man alive wants Lola La Mour." With that statement, she tossed her white boa around her neck and paraded down the corridor toward the lobby of the hotel.

. . .

Alone at the beach, Numie pulled off all his clothes. The day was nearly over, and he had just two hours by himself——two hours before he had to start driving Lola and Ned around the island again.

In one dash, he made a flat racing dive into the cold water. Face buried deep, he began a steady stroke carrying himself out as far as he could without raising up. Could he swim across the gulf to Mexico without ever coming up for air?

Lungs bursting, he cocked his head and sucked in fresh clean air. Jumping like a dolphin, he shot up, clearing water as far down as his crotch. Then he came down again in a splash, deciding to float for a while this time.

The sun was sinking. Here he was, alone out at sea. The thought sent a sudden chill racing through his body.

He'd gone out much farther than he had wanted to. Still on his back, he rolled over and swam hurriedly to shore.

Silent and brooding, he stood looking back at the sea from which he'd just emerged. Its salt water was still running down his nude body.

What messages from what far-off lands were washing up on

the shore right now?

Instead of wanting to remain in Tortuga, he was stirred by a sense of wanderlust. Nothing was right for him here. Everybody, except possibly Anne and Tangerine, were getting it on. But he was left out. The driver to a crazed drag queen and an egotistical pimp.

"Where is home?" he asked the silent sea.

The answer was clear. The only home he had he carried around within himself.

Chapter Twenty-Four

"This is off-white," Lola was screaming. "Off-white goddamn you." She tossed a soggy coffee container in a wastepaper basket. "I can't stand off-white, pearl gray, ivory, oyster white. I can only operate against a background of *pure* white." The entire world seemed to be conspiring to keep her from having what she wanted, even if she could afford it.

Without saying a word, Spider turned and left the Dry Marquesas Hotel suite. "I swear I've had it!" he cried in the corridor.

Pulling out a badly crushed glazed doughnut from a paper bag, Numie said, "But your wedding dress wasn't white."

Lola ran her hands along the naked flesh of her arm. The smoothness of it sent shivers of excitement through her. "That was different," she said. "I was a blaze of silver glory." Anger and frustration seethed inside Numie. "If you don't stop finding fault, Spider won't let you redo this suite."

"*He* won't!" she said, hands on her hips. "We'll see about that." She caught sight of herself in a newly arrived tall standing mirror near the window. It was impossible to hold back a smile of pleasure and admiration for the sight she beheld.

"Okay, so you've got power," he said. Heading for the bathroom, he stopped at the presence of a painter, summoned here only this morning. Then Numie went in anyway, taking a leak——loudly——at the stool.

Lola was in pursuit, barging in and almost upsetting a gallon of white paint. She was sticky and uncomfortable, her anger just sweating up inside her. "Just what are you insinuating?" she asked Numie.

Shaking himself, he turned to stare. "I didn't mean a damn thing."

"It's about time you started showing some respect." Glowering at the painter, she said, "If you think I'm going to accept the paint job on that ceiling, you've got another thought coming. I want that ceiling as white as our face. That old paint is bleeding through."

"I've put on three coats already," the man protested, "As

soon as I finish this bathroom, I'm leaving. You've got to get someone else."

Surging and throbbing, Lola's guts were about to explode. "So," she said menacingly, "you think you're too good to work for someone of my color?"

"Lady, I work for anybody who pays me," the painter said. "It's just this particular job. You're the most demanding woman I've ever come across in twenty years. Worse than my first wife."

Numie brushed past, heading back to the living room. "Wha..." He was startled to see the tall, lean frame of Johnny Yellowwood on the sofa. "I didn't hear you knock."

"I didn't," the sheriff said. "The door was open."

At first Numie was scared. Memories of the thrill killer flashed through his brain. Then slowly his courage returned. "Do you always walk in every door you see open?"

"If it suits my purpose," Yellowwood answered. "This time it did. You hear more interesting conversations that way. See more sights." He wet his lips and smiled.

Really angry, Numie snapped, "The circus just shut down."

"To the contrary, boy," Yellowwood said, "I think it's just opening night."

As if to confirm the sheriff's words, the painter rushed from the bathroom, shouting, "I quit! Lady, you're crazy for white. Too bad you couldn't have been born white."

"You son-of-a-bitch," Lola screamed after him. His words ate away at her heart. She wanted to strike back so violently the painter would be wiped out. "You're also a fag. I saw you looking at *my* Numie when he was taking a leak."

Out of the room, the painter was slamming the door behind him.

Lola rushed over and threw it open again. "Cocksucker," she yelled down the hallway. Her hands fluttered in the air, like wings unfolding. Now that she was in a position to have slaves, nobody was into taking orders.

"The one and only Lola La Mour," Yellowwood said, lighting a cigarette.

Resentment flashed through her brain. Had it not been for the actions of this man, she would have had a picture in the newspapers of herself resplendent in her wedding dress.

"I hope I haven't chosen an inopportune moment to call on a lady," Yellowwood said. "But I've come to pay my respects. As you know, Phil was my best friend."

Lola stopped, pausing awkwardly. Then she quickly regained her composure, assuming the stance of a sulky blues singer. "Johnny Yellowwood, what an unexpected pleasure." Her heart was beating fast. She didn't trust him for one second. "I was meaning to give you a call, but I've been so broken up inside over my commodore's death." She glanced at Numie. "You remember my friend, of course."

Painfully self-conscious, Numie said, "If he doesn't, I remember him."

The sheriff ignored the remark. "You didn't have much of a mourning period," he said to Lola.

Lola bit her lip. Was everybody in this rotten town expecting her to go around forever crying her eyes out?

"Phil's body has hardly cooled," Yellowwood said. "And here you are——out with another man. He's certainly better looking, I must say. Real pretty white boy you've got for yourself."

Numie wanted to punch the sheriff in the mouth. What a ballbreaker he was! "You should know," he said, "you've checked me out enough."

Again, Yellowwood ignored him. "Look," he said, turning to Lola, "I ain't knocking your taking up with another guy so soon. I understand it. Life is for the living. No use moping around and crying your eyes out over something you can't do one goddamn thing about."

She knew this was no sympathy call. The way white men beat around the bush infuriated the hell out of her. "What do you want?" she asked abruptly, dropping all the charade of ladylike manners.

"May I speak frankly in front of your white lover boy here?" the sheriff asked.

Numie was ready to walk out the door at this point. He'd had about all the humiliation in this town he could stand.

"I have no secrets from him," Lola said, fearing Yellowwood was going to reveal something to make her sound sexually unattractive. "What is it?"

The sheriff settled back on the sofa, fingering a cake of mud on his boot and letting it drop to the floor. "I want the same arrangement I had with the commodore. You know, sheriffs don't make much money, and I kinda got used to the good life."

Numie looked long and searchingly at Lola. He wished he had had all this ammunition when he was the victim of law and order in this town.

"These platform shoes are killing me," Lola said, resenting the sheriff's intrusion to the point of rage. She feared white men. They only gave you money for the sheer pleasure of taking it away. "As I said, I had every intention of ringing you up tomorrow, but seeing that you're here today we can get on with it. I told the commodore's attorney this morning he'd find me very generous." This time only one hand went to her hip. "I'm sure you will, too." She paused to enjoy her new power position. "For instance, I know you like to go on boating trips. Here I am with four of 'em. Now what is a girl going to do with four boats?" The tall mirror confirmed once more her lifelong belief that black was definitely not her color. "There will be other presents from time to time." She ran her hand ever so gently across her platinum blonde wig. "Presents just between friends."

"I understand," Yellowwood said, a smile slowly crossing his face. "What do you want in return for such generosity?"

"There will be requests on and off," she said, vaguely trying to think of one at the moment. Numie crossed her vision. "Like, if stud hustlers get out of hand." Her voice grew intimidating. "Little things like that." Her head was beginning to pound as if she had the most hideous hangover. "Big ones, too, if certain grand ladies living in certain grand mansions forget who they are and start thinking they're grander and more important than me."

"I see," the sheriff said.

She smiled, too, knowing that she'd served lunch, and Yellowwood was devouring every mouthful. "Then we understand each other?"

"Perfectly," Yellowwood replied.

"Drop in any time, Johnny," Lola said, now firmly convinced she was in the driver's seat. "Don't bother to knock. You might even catch Numie and me going at it . . . like two animals in heat." She gave him a wicked grin. "You'd like that, wouldn't you?"

"I sure would," he said, getting up. "Thanks for the invite. I've got to be going now that we've had our little mutual understanding. But we'll keep in touch." Almost in a whisper, he hissed in her ear. "Real close, like kissing kin." He pecked her on the cheek.

She instinctively backed away, the kiss lingering like a bee sting. A sudden silence fell over the room after the sheriff shut the door.

Numie waited for a long moment. "I think the commodore is all but forgotten. Life sure does go on."

"I'm not into this nostalgia shit!" Lola said. "I broke one of my fingernails hassling with that goddamn painter." Nervousness about the oncoming night flooded her. "As far as I'm concerned, I don't even remember the commodore. Fuck yesterday. I'm a *today* girl!"

. . .

In Leonora's Lincoln, Numie was driving Ned and Lola to JOAN'S on the north shore. The time alone on the beach had restored his spirits enough for him to endure this evening.

"This is the kind of night I should be cooling my honeypot in a tub of ice——not going out to some cathouse on a joy ride," Lola was saying. "That house of hookers really needs me to give it some class."

"Right on!" Ned replied. "You're a million-dollar baby."

Once at the house, Numie opened the rear compartment door for them, then trailed them.

Two hookers were sitting at a wicker table, drinking beer. Overhead colored lights were flashing, and flies were buzzing about.

At first the women thought Numie was a customer and started preening their feathers. Then they realized he was only an employee of Leonora's.

It was about eight-thirty in the evening; and neither woman had changed into her working clothes yet. One, a Cuban of about thirty-five years, still had on an artist-type smock, covered with cigarette burns. It was the color of the American flag: red, white, and blue. Three plastic rollers crowned the top of her long and stringy blue-black hair. Her feet, encased in black suede high heels, rested on the porch railing.

The other, a fat, bleached blonde of forty-five, was in a short mini-dress of purple crochet, badly torn in parts. Her large breasts showed through, and she was wearing a pair of black panties stretched around her enormous bottom. Gold mules gave off a metallic flash. Only her long centipedic eyelashes had been applied for the evening's work. Otherwise, her puffy face was without makeup.

"I'll give you a discount," the blonde said to Numie. "Seeing you're part of the household."

"No thanks," Numie said. "I'm on the job."

"Too bad," the blonde said. "It'd be nice having someone young for a change."

"That's what all the boys say when they have to go to bed with you," the Cuban said.

The blonde slammed down her beer. "You stinking spik. I'll scratch the tatoos right off your titties."

"You're just jealous," the Cuban went on. "I can't help it if the men keep requesting me. The young ones come here to get away from their mothers, the older ones from their wives. You remind them of the dumpy broads they've got back at home."

"That's a lie!" the blonde said. "I'm very much wanted."

"Only by those who call you 'Deep Throat'. As for me, I refuse to do it that way."

"Oh, yeah," the blonde said. "By doing it the way some of 'em like it, I made two-hundred motherfucking dollars last week."

"I made three-hundred and fifty."

"I don't believe it," the blonde said.

"Ask Joan."

"You think you're so hot."

"Look at these legs, the Cuban said. "Men go for that."

"Frankly," the blonde said, "I think the more you cover up, the better you look. Men are more attracted to blondes than that mop of yours. If you washed out that tint, it'd be gray."

"We could all be blondes," the Cuban said defensively, "if we knew Lady Bleach so well as you."

Numie flipped his cigarette into a nearby bush and passed

through the cranberry glass doors into the foyer.

Joan was puffing furiously on a cigar. In navy slacks with a white shirt open at the throat, she stood rigidly, eying Ned and Lola skeptically. "I got a call from Leonora. Said I might be getting a little visit from you."

"I'm the new madam," Lola announced, tossing her boa around her neck and prancing across the room in her finest whorish swagger.

Joan gingerly fingered one of her hoop earrings. "Last time I called central casting, that was my role." She'd stopped smoking now, and was holding her cigar tentatively.

"At the moment," Ned said, swaying on the balls of his red-shoed feet, "let's call it a peace-loving co-management. Sweet harmony."

Lola surveyed the rickety old rundown toilet right off the hall. Stepping inside, she spotted cigarette butts dumped in the bowl. She flushed it, the sound hitting her ears like a dam broke loose. Back in the hallway, she asked, "How many hookers you got hanging out 'round here? I saw two pigs on the front porch, not even dressed for business." She dug a heel into the floor. "Get their asses off there. Gives this dump a bad name."

Arching her back, Joan replied, "Five girls in all."

Rock 'n roll music blasted down from upstairs. To judge from the shaking floor, someone was wiggling and twisting. "What are their nationalities?" she demanded of Joan.

"Two came from Havana——a mother-daughter act," Joan said.

"The other three?" Ned asked.

"One's a local woman," Joan said. "Her husband, a shrimper, drowned at sea. The other two are Navy wives."

Joan's brash tone offended Lola. "That's not what I meant, child," she said. "How many of my soul sisters work here?"

"None," Joan answered.

Lola was like a jack in the box who'd lost his springs. "There's gonna be some changes made around here," she said. "From now on, we're gonna be equal opportunity employers."

"I have nothing against colored girls working here," Joan snapped.

"*Colored* women fuck better than white women," Ned

declared. "Honey, don't ask me how I know——'cause I ain't jiving you. This one black chick could take thirty a night and still call for more."

Through the beaded curtains came a teenaged Cuban girl, in blue jeans and a skimpy halter. Totally wiped out, the girl turned and looked in Ned's direction. Seemingly thinking he was a trick, she crossed the parlor to him. Her pale, anemic body nestled up to his, and she smiled into his eyes.

Fury raged through Lola. "You cheap spik hooker!" she yelled. "Lay one hand on my man, and I'll castrate your pussy. That humpy number belongs to me."

"Now, Lola," Ned said, restraining her, "you're the boss lady. But I didn't know you owned my dick."

Startled, the girl ran back, looking once at Joan before disappearing behind the curtains.

"That was Maria," Joan said. "One of Leonora's favorites."

Shivering flashes ran through Lola's body. She looked around the room, trying as hard as possible to appear bored. She didn't want Ned and especially Joan to know how young girls could upset her.

"How old is Maria?" Ned demanded.

"Just thirteen," Joan answered.

Lola winced as if in pain. She was more than three times the age of Maria!

"That's too young," Ned said. "You've got to get rid of her."

"I told you," Joan said, "she's one of Leonora's favorites."

"No matter," Ned said. "That girl has to go back to her parents, if she's got any. I didn't start selling it till I was sixteen. Thirteen's too young. Give her three more years."

"If you want to discuss her employment," Joan said stiffly, "why don't you talk to her mother? She's one of those 'pigs' sitting out there on the front porch."

Lola went over to Ned, taking his arm. "Don't say nothing too hasty, handsome," she said. "Some of those rednecks like 'em that young."

"I know——but thirteen," Ned protested.

Ned was really making her mad now, because she knew he wanted Maria for himself. "Shit, man, my daddy raped me when I was just twelve."

"That's no reason to keep Maria on here," Ned said.

Lola closed her eyes tightly, but there was no way for her to forget the look on Ned's face. Here was her man——right in front of Joan——with hot pants for a younger woman. This evening wasn't going at all the way she planned.

Numie settled back on the mission oak sofa after securing one of Leonora's color-wrapped joints from the wooden box. Lighting it, he coughed on the first puff. Too harsh, he thought. Just like Leonora herself. He was enjoying the show, mainly because he wasn't one of the subjects of dispute.

At the liquor cabinet, Joan poured herself a stiff drink of Scotch. "You can't just walk in here and tell me how I should run my house."

Lola spun around. She'd had enough defiance of her authority. "I not only can, I am."

Joan faced her. "I happen to have been running cathouses before you were born."

"From the looks of you, that's the mother-loving truth," Lola said. If thought contained any power, Joan would have died on the spot——so strong was the resentment pouring from Lola.

If Joan's face were a good barometer of her inner emotions, the feelings were reciprocated.

"What this dump needs is a blood transfusion," Ned added.

More than ever, the obsession to dominate was paramount in Lola right now. "The name alone——JOAN'S——so corny."

"What would you prefer?" Joan asked sarcastically.

"Leonora came up with something pretty good," Numie said, getting up from the sofa. His head was swimming. "The Garden of Delights."

"Yeah," Ned said. "I like that." Turning to Joan, he continued, "Right now you're drawing the redneck potbelly trade. You've got to offer more refined pleasures——keep up with the times."

Joan drew back in disgust. "And how should I do that?"

"This parlor could be turned into a dance bar," Ned said. "Give the tricks a chance to get acquainted with the goodies before sampling. Install the bar over there."

"A bar?" Joan asked, spitting out the words. "You give johns their liquor free. Otherwise, they'd resent it."

Lola's hands went to her hips again. She was in a fighting

mood. She'd gotten out of bed this morning like a fox hungry enough to eat a cow. That would come later. Right now this tired old hyena had to be devoured. "Time was," Lola said, "when you went into a saloon and got free eats. Those days are gone forever, baby. There will be no more free eats or drinks or nothing else at this house. We ain't the Red Cross."

Belting down the rest of her drink, Joan said, "I hear you." Her lips were quivering.

Lola felt in total control. "One more thing," she warned, "there'll be no more drinking on the job by the hired help. How can you know what's going on if you're high all the time?"

Joan didn't answer at first, but stood pouting. "Listen, you damn fag."

The word hit Lola like a whiplash. Under no circumstances had she ever considered herself a homosexual. She preferred men! "Look who you're talking to," Lola screeched, her voice competing with the rock music upstairs. "You muff-diving, bleached-out, burnt-up old dyke. I happen to be a *lady*."

"Don't talk back to Lola, Ned said, or else you'll find your ass back on the streets. 'Cept this time, you won't find no paying customers."

"If that unclassified freak's a lady, I suck eggs," Joan said.

Insults to Joan were no longer enough for Lola. She wanted to feel blood under her chartreuse nails. Those nails arched, she lunged her slender frame against Joan's blubber.

Numie rushed over to hold her back. "Cool it!" he yelled.

"You're fired," Lola screamed at Joan. "Get your ass out of here. I can't stand dykes no way." Tears of rage were forming. "They're always looking at me in the bar——their eyes burning up with heat for my body." She shuddered. "My spine turns to jelly just thinking what you slimy creatures would do to me."

Joan looked at her as if she couldn't believe her ears. "You're sick!"

Lola started for her again.

But Numie held her back.

Ned slammed his fist into his open palm. "The lady here said you was fired."

Her hand nervously at her breast, Joan countered, "Only

Leonora can fire me. I take my orders from her——and only her.
Eyes veiled, lips unsmiling, Lola moved toward Joan. "I
happen to own half this property." Her stomach churned, and
bitter thoughts swept across her like waves.
"That's not official yet," Joan countered. "I figured you'd
come here and make a grand play." She smiled with
condescension. "So just an hour ago I was on the phone with
the commodore's only surviving sister in New Orleans." Joan
paused to judge the effect on Lola's face.
Her eyes were angry and violent. The prospect of Sister
Amelia's arrival was illusion-shattering. The warmth seemed to
be going out of her whole body.
"She's going to fly here," Joan continued. "Plans to contest
the commodore's will. His estate could be tied up in the courts
for years. Years!" she shouted, her face flushing red. "Until
the estate's settled, you're not entitled to take a free shit out
here. Now get out!"
Lola just stood there, stunned into silence. For the first time
in her life, she didn't have a response to an attack from
someone .
The rock music died down. A long silence fell over the
parlor.
"C'mon," Numie said to Lola, "I think we'd better be
getting on."

. . .

"Why you got me all dressed up like this?" Dinah was
asking Lola. "I look like a virgin." In low-heeled shoes, Dinah
was wearing a plain gray skirt with a gray blouse.
Until that question, Lola was sitting quietly in the patio of
Sacre-Coeur. The soft colored bulbs were turned on,
spotlighting the plants as they moved gently in the breeze
blowing in from the Gulf. Finally Lola spoke, "Social secretaries
aren't supposed to look like cheap whores."
"I like red lipstick," Dinah said, turning in desperation to
Numie. "*Flaming red*. But Lola made me wash my face with
soap."
"You never looked younger or more innocent," Numie said.
"Leonora will be very impressed." He was anxious to be by

himself. Already he felt he'd been through the contortions of a sideshow rubber man at the carnival.

"Dinah was wearing the same shade of lipstick I have on," Lola said, directing her statement at Numie. That white boy didn't seem to be paying her no mind. "She don't seem to get it through her thick head she ain't supposed to compete."

At this point, a sudden movement signaled the entrance of Leonora. The top of her dress was like an old-fashioned bathing costume, a black background covered with gigantic pink camellias. Attached was a skirt of zebra stripes, the camellia motif picked up again on the bottom border. Trailing from her wide-brimmed hat was a long piece of fabric, again covered with pink camellias. Her hair was totally hidden by the hat, showing only her carefully groomed face, a mass of cold white powder and high arched eyebrows. "Good evening. I'm wearing black in memory of Phil. But death is so dismal I had to brighten it up with pink."

Numie was always stunned at how similar Lola's outlook was with that of Leonora's.

"I understand," Lola chimed in, trying to disguise her obvious jealousy over the fact that once again Leonora had upstaged her. "I tried going around in a simple black dress all day. But tonight I decided to come up with something more fetching, though still sticking to basic black." Getting up, she paraded around in front of Leonora, seeking approval. She was in a black satin cocktail suit, with a slim pencil skirt. The jacket was fitted, with a long open neck and three jet buttons. She removed the jacket, revealing a white crepe backless halter top.

Leonora did not acknowledge the outfit. Vulgarity in clothing always offended her.

Lola stood there blankly, not knowing what to say.

Instead, Leonora turned to Numie. "Get me one of my cigarettes," she commanded. Whirling around, she feasted her eyes on Dinah, enjoying her fresh look in contrast to Lola's tastelessness. Dinah could be a 1950s version of a black Vassar coed. "Who is this divine creature?"

Dinah smiled.

"My social secretary," Lola added quickly, not understanding why drab Dinah was getting any attention at all.

"Oh?" Leonora questioned, slightly amused. Lola's

pretensions, she felt, knew no bounds. "Social secretary, did you say?"

Raising her voice, Lola said, "Yes, I *did* say."

Dinah held out her hand to Leonora.

Slowly and caressingly, Leonora captured it in her chalk-white fingers, holding it for a long moment, enjoying its softness and smoothness. It was youth itself.

"I'm very pleased to meet you," Dinah gushed. "I saw you at Lola's wedding, and I wanted to come up and say hi."

"Why didn't you?" Leonora asked, wondering silently how many people such as Dinah there were at that wedding secretly desiring her and not the bride.

"My boyfriend wouldn't let me," Dinah said. "Thought I'd be bothering you."

The word, boyfriend, was like a slap in the face to Leonora. She'd misjudged Dinah. For a moment she'd been certain she preferred the company of women. "You wouldn't have bothered me at all," she finally said.

"I've heard so much about you," Dinah went on.

"You have?" Leonora asked, fascinated. "Don't spare a detail. I want to hear everything." No sooner had she said that, than she wished she'd withdrawn the remark. After all, Lola had probably crammed Dinah with the most hideous lies.

"Well," Dinah said, "your looks, this house, your gowns, everything. I've always wanted to see inside this place. It's very grand."

Leonora waved her hand invitingly in the air. "Merely a backdrop to show off your beauty.

"Thanks," Dinah replied. "No one's ever said that to me before."

"I bet!" Lola mumbled sarcastically. The conversation Leonora was having with Dinah made Lola want to puke. "We're so glad you invited *me* over for drinks tonight."

Leonora looked at Lola blankly, pausing briefly as if to say something, then seated herself in a peacock chair and puffed away at a marijuana cigarette Numie had handed her. The cigarette was attached to a holder on her index finger. "What would you two ladies like to drink?" she asked. "Of course, Lola, you might want to prepare your own beverage. You've had so much experience working all these years as a barmaid."

Lola fumed. "Yes, we must all start somewhere." Grandly she swaggered around the patio. That dyke had to get used to the fact she was an equal partner. Lola stopped. That was, if she was a partner at all. "After today, as you may know, I'm no longer a barmaid. I was just visiting one of the properties you and my dear commodore owned."

Leonora assumed a blase mask, but inside she was churning with disgust. "I know," she said coldly.

Hands on her hips, Lola said, "Joan wasn't exactly too friendly."

Leonora laughed harshly in her face. "She never was."

Lola gave off her finest gap-toothed grin. "Why don't you take it upon yourself to straighten her out?"

Leonora blew out her smoke with gusto, hoping it drifted into Lola's face. "Never fire anybody who can make serious trouble." She leaned back in the peacock chair, crossing her legs, letting some of her fabulous thighs show. "Joan, dear heart that she is, knows where all the black sheep went to lay their heads. I'm afraid she'll be around for the duration."

Lola remained silent for a moment. Leonora seemed to be twisting her arm. In some way she was feeling more and more inarticulate and impotent in Leonora's presence. "She and I had words."

"That's our Joan," Leonora said, enjoying the evening breeze. At first she'd been horrified to find Lola her partner. Now she was feeling more confident. Lola La Mour wouldn't be her partner in anything much longer.

"There was talk," Lola said hesitantly, not wanting to appear desperate. "Talk about a certain phone call to New Orleans."

"My God!" Leonora said, sitting up.

Lola was growing alarmed.

Leonora fastened her eyes on Lola. Her voice was low and thick. "Joan will stop at nothing."

Now Lola was really in panic. "We may just be getting a visitation from Sister Amelia."

"Naughty girl, that Joan," Leonora said, watching Lola squirm. "I wouldn't worry myself about it one bit, though." Her voice was never more ominous. "Life is nothing but a struggle anyway. One day we have money, the next day somebody takes it away from us. But if it weren't for the struggle, would life really be worth it?"

Seriously disturbed, Lola wandered alone into the garden to think. She was coming unglued, and she had to pull herself together before facing Leonora again.

Leonora, meanwhile, turned her attention to Dinah. "Come over," she invited. "Sit by me and tell me all about yourself."

The slim girl positioned herself on a large pool cushion at Leonora's feet. "There ain't much to tell. I've led a dull life."

Leonora gently caressed the girl's hair. "What do you study in school then?"

"School?" Dinah seemed puzzled.

"Yes, school," Leonora repeated, raising her voice.

"Do you think I'm still in school?" Dinah asked.

"She doesn't like school," Numie interrupted. "Wants to be an actress." In a world of fantasy, he was only too glad to play a part.

"An actress?" Leonora was enchanted. "I should have been an actress." Thoughts of one of Norton Huttnar's best friends crossed her mind. He'd wanted to make her a star. But the wicked old drag queen out of jealousy turned down the whole idea. "A producer wanted to make me into another Theda Bara, but I graciously declined. I'm an artist-designer and have always been true to my calling." Slowly she withdrew her hand from Dinah. "We have to stick to one profession, and one profession only."

"I wouldn't turn no producer down," Dinah said.

"Now you're talking like some common slut," Leonora said abruptly, rising from her chair. But then she settled back again. After all, Dinah had been around Lola. She'd never had anyone to teach her about manners. You must learn to be discriminating, preferring only the best."

Dinah was slow to anger, but when she did she fumed. "Who you calling a slut?" she asked, getting up from her cushion.

Fearing trouble, Numie took her by the arm and eased her back into her seat. "Miss De la Mer isn't calling you a slut. She's saying you shouldn't talk like one."

"Don't explain what I mean! What I say is *always* clear."

"Of course," Numie replied.

At the bar Lola aggressively took Numie's drink from his hand. She swallowed a large gulp, then pranced back to where Leonora was sitting. Her courage had returned.

Continuing to ignore her, Leonora just sat there, softly inhaling the smoke from her cigarette. Her face betrayed her pleasure.

Lola looked up with contempt in her heart, but her face hid it. She had to get on Leonora's good side, even if it meant placing an order for some dresses. "I'm tired of my wardrobe, and I want a change."

Even the breeze in the patio died down. Lola had succeeded in fully capturing Leonora's attention. "Did I hear you correctly?" she asked. She almost coughed on her cigarette.

"Yes," Lola said, surprised. Leonora seemed insulted. This Lola couldn't understand. You'd think the old has-been would jump at a chance for a new customer. Lola's black outfit was a trap for her. She felt wrapped as tightly as a mummy. "I've decided on a whole new image." The prospect of her own sexual attractiveness consumed her for a moment. She was like a carnivorous night-blooming lily.

Leonora feared that this monstrous day——the day of fully facing that Lola was her partner——was at hand. "You're not suggesting that I..."

Lola paused for effect, then said, "Yes."

Over Leonora's catlike face came an expression of childish anguish. "I'm frightfully expensive."

Lola stood firmly on the bricks, instinctively searching for the best light angle. "The only reason I came to you."

"I'm not in the habit of discussing business in my home," Leonora said. For one brief, horrifying moment, a paralyzing thought crossed her brain. Lola La Mour was the reincarnation of Norton Huttnar! But then she quickly dismissed the idea. Lola was probably older than her former husband. "If you're interested in picking up some little item, you can go to my showroom in the morning. A sales clerk will help you."

"You don't understand," Lola said, determined to press the point. "I want gowns specifically designed for me. I'll be in your office in the morning."

Leonora rose from her chair. Nobody, partner or not, was going to treat her this disrespectfully at Sacre-Coeur. "I don't design clothing for men!"

Lola could have suffered no crueler blow. She knew that Leonora had an uncanny ability to go right for the jugular. She stood stunned, feeling more vulnerable than Leonora could ever be. Even an attack on Leonora's age and her lesbianism wouldn't be as effective as what Leonora had just said.

Leonora walked across the patio, pretending to admire the flowers.

Blinded by tears, Lola trailed her. "My attorney tells me I'm the commodore's sole heiress. That should give me some say."

"Perhaps," Leonora said, admiring a rose. "I've not looked at the contracts in some time. Details bore me. There is the problem of Sister Amelia——a serious problem."

Lola was searching even the night air for a way to get rid of Sister Amelia and make Leonora show her some respect.

"Why don't you have another drink?" Leonora asked nonchalantly. She wanted to remove this vile creature bodily from the confines of Sacre-Coeur.

"This is not a social call," Lola said, losing control of her voice. "If I wanted a drink, I control the town's supply. I thought we had a lot of business to talk."

"Not only do I not discuss business in my home," Leonora said, "I don't discuss business at night." Finally, her curiosity broke down, and she asked, "What is it you want?"

"I'm interested in joining you in the fashion house as another designer," Lola said. She paused hesitantly. "I mean, after we get this Sister Amelia mess cleared up."

Leonora's breath was coming in quick, hurried gasps. "That might be a very long time."

Lola dreaded the implication of that remark. She seemed so close to her lifelong goal, and now it was moving away. She decided to pay no outward attention to Leonora's last remark. "I see myself working with you designing clothes." She wet her lips, hoping she was dazzling Leonora with her own sultry beauty. "Real fancy clothes."

"You?" Leonora asked with all the contempt, horror, and loathing she'd ever been able to put into her voice. "Surely you're joking. A drag queen!"

"Honey," Lola said in her most sarcastic voice. To hell with Sister Amelia hanging like a threat over her head. That last insult was more than she could take. Even her commodore had never gone that far. "I've been called many things in my life, but I want you to get it through your head that I'm every bit the lady you are. More beautiful and more talented." She stood uncompromisingly brutal in Leonora's presence.

At first Leonora was almost hypnotized, then she realized she was confronting a hopeless psychotic. "Operating a fashion house with you as a fellow designer is not only out of the question, it's laughable. My attorney will see you in time."

Her eyes moist with intensity, Lola at this moment wanted to throw Leonora in the pool, then pull her out like a dead rat and slowly and in the most painful way possible remove her gobs of makeup, her false eyelashes, all the thousand and one beauty aids she used to disguise the face of the old hag who lurked behind the mask. Instead she merely said, "You don't think I know how to design?"

Leonora forced a smile, making her mouth wide-set. "I certainly don't."

Cold blue flames were burning within Lola. "What I'm offering you is a chance to set fashion ahead. I can see our names up there now." Stars flashed in front of her eyes. "Fashions by La Mour and De la Mer. Or maybe your name should come first——seeing you're older.

"Share my billing?" Leonora asked. That mask that was Lola's face seemed eyeless for a second. Then those eyes started to fill up with fluid. They were unsurrendering eyes out for blood. "I'm a legend all by myself," Leonora added defiantly.

"I could be celebrated, too," Lola said with such conviction that everybody for a moment believed her.

"My dear, I'm afraid you're going to be celebrated on this island——but not for fashion." Leonora walked over to her peacock chair and sat down, focusing on Dinah again. Over her shoulder she looked back at Lola, then added as an afterthought: "If you're such a great designer, why come begging to me to design something for you that looks decent?"

"Begging?" Lola tottered there by herself, consumed with hate. "Decent?" She bit her lip. After the estate was settled——and only then——would she take care of Leonora de la Mer.

The evening wore on, ever so slowly. Numie was pacing the

pool, sucking in the smell of night-blooming jasmine.

The sound of Leonora's voice was like a stuck record. Her glittering triumphs, all recounted endlessly.

Dinah was a fascinated listener.

On the other hand Lola was reduced to watching.

Suddenly, Leonora stood at attention. "Numie," she called, "Dinah and I have decided to go upstairs to try on one of my special designs. She's going to model it for me."

Lola didn't say anything, only raised her eyebrows in ultimate disdain.

Leonora went inside, her hand resting protectively on Dinah's shoulder. She was amused with herself for not wishing Lola good night.

"Man, that tired old pussy has really put me to sleep," Lola said after Leonora was out of hearing range. She downed another drink.

Numie knew how disturbed Lola really was. "If Leonora thought she was boring anyone, she'd surely have them shot."

At a distance of a few feet, Lola stopped. Even Numie was a victim of Leonora's spell. Why couldn't anyone get the message? She, Lola La Mour, was in charge. Or soon would be. Damn that Sister Amelia! 'That broken down De la Mer's being retired. By me! I don't know why I sat here all night, listening to that dyke's fantasies. She don't seem to get it that I'm just as *big* and just as *grand*."

"But I know it," he said. "There's not a day goes by but what you remind me." A killing headache came over him. At this moment, the way he felt, all the money in the world wouldn't get him to remain for another week locked up in a house with these two.

"As for Dinah, that slinky-assed bitch." Lola said, her voice much deeper than before. "She's an alley cat. Has had everything in town——every eight year old, every eighty year old. She's sure playing it safe. In case I have trouble with the commodore's will, she's staking out De la Mer."

"Can you blame her?" Numie asked, being deliberately insulting and not caring at this point.

"She's here as my social secretary!" Lola said. A sudden movement in the bushes caused her to turn in fright, but it appeared to be nothing at all. "I'm firing her ass as of tonight.

Just for her big show with that dyke, I'm also taking Ned away from her. I can just see me now strutting down main street. You on one arm, Ned on the other."

"Stick to one arm, Lola."

"What you talking about, child?" She darted around the garden patio. The statues were nakedly white in the moonlight. Sacre-Coeur, ghostly. "You don't seem to understand. The name's Lola. I get what I want. Now she knew tonight was a mistake. She should have chosen the stage on which to confront De la Mer. The old dyke had rigged up this place so she'd look better. "When you're black," Lola went on, "you've got to make compromises in a whitey world. When you're not only black, but a flamboyant and dazzling lady who likes to go around in her more elegant finery, then you'd better be goddamn sure you know what's happening."

Numie walked over to the peacock chair. Carefully he picked up one of Leonora's color-wrapped joints. He lit it and sucked in the smoke, enjoying the movement of palms in the breeze. Although the day was hot, the night had turned cool.

Upstairs a light was switched on in Anne's room. A figure moved behind the curtains. The sound of muffled voices drifted down from Leonora's upstairs bedroom overlooking the patio. A tightening swelled in his throat. He was choking. The tightening grew stronger. "All day I've been trying to explain something to you——and you're not listening," he said. "I'm not going to be on your arm. I was with you today only in one capacity——as your driver, nothing else. The other thing between us, that was sheer hunger on my part."

At first Lola registered shock. "Hunger? You goddamn son of a bitch, I'll have you run out of town." Yellowwood was on her payroll. If Numie didn't shape up, the sheriff would have to start earning his money. "I know you're attracted to me——half out of your mind with lust. What you just said can mean only one thing. Someone else has offered you more money."

"How right you are," came a voice. It was Ralph.

"How dare you eavesdrop on a private conversation between a lady and her man," Lola said.

"Don't worry, Lola," Numie said, "Ralph is a specialist at walking in at awkward moments."

"I see I arrived just in time," Ralph said. "You see, Numie belongs to me. He's my husband——not yours. I disapprove of bigamy. So that leaves you out in the cold."

"I can take any man from anybody," Lola said defiantly. Ralph Douglas had just placed himself number two on her hate list, right under De la Mer. "Numie," she said sharply, "you and me are splitting."

Numie just sat there.

"I said," Lola continued, "in case there is wax in your ears, you and me are traveling."

"I'm not going anywhere," Numie said. How he wanted this day to rush to its speedy climax.

"Listen to me," Lola shouted. "You two fucking queers, you listen and listen good. You don't know who you're dealing with."

"Just who are we dealing with?" Ralph asked in drunken amusement, the way an adult will tempt a child to tell a story so everybody can laugh.

"Lola La Mour——that's who!" came the tart reply.

"Never heard of her," Ralph said, turning his back.

Grabbing her jacket, Lola pranced down the path leading to the gate and disappeared into the night.

. . .

In the guest cottage at Sacre-Coeur, Numie stood before the bathroom mirror, fogged with steam. His reflection was ghostly. He wiped his hand across the mirror, but his image was still unclear.

Pressing himself against the cold porcelain of the sink, he sucked in the steamy air of the bathroom.

He had failed.

Turning both the brass taps on full speed, he hoped the noise of rushing water would blot out the vision racing through his mind.

He'd tried to make it with Ralph. But had grown limp.

Suddenly, Ralph was in the bathroom. "I think you'd better split." The seat-top to the toilet bowl was already up. Stepping up to it, Ralph turned to Numie. "We're not working out."

Numie looked away. "You got the short end of the stick, huh?"

"I'm not in the mood for jokes," Ralph said, concentrating on the business at hand.

"Neither am I." Numie took one last look at himself in the now clear mirror, reached up to straighten his hair, then left the room.

Zipping up, Ralph was in pursuit. "You'd better go."

Numie had known it wouldn't be long before Ralph kicked him out. Only he hadn't expected it so soon. "I'm getting ready," he said angrily. Then, softening his voice, he asked, "Am I out completely?"

"No," Ralph said. "You can stay on as Leonora's driver."

Numie backed away. "Well, that's something."

Ralph slammed his fist into his open palm. "A hustler has to give something." His voice was petulant. "You can't leave me totally unsatisfied and frustrated the way you did tonight. I won't stand for that."

Numie felt he'd been punched severely in the stomach. "What about all the other times I made you happy?" Moving through the room impulsively, blindly, Numie didn't know why he was bothering to plead his case. "Are you kicking me out because of one failure? Goddamn it, I'm not a machine!"

Ralph gestured vaguely to the door. "You never made me happy, but I'm not blaming you for that. I'm afraid nobody——man or woman——can please me for very long."

The more Ralph talked, the more anonymous and characterless he became to Numie. Ralph was right. It was time for him to go.

"I keep dreaming about the next adventure," Ralph said. "One thing, though." He was pouring himself a drink. A cruel smile crossed his lips. "How could you hustle all those years and be impotent?"

The word stung Numie. "I'm not impotent," he said defensively. "Tonight was the first time——you know that."

At first Ralph didn't say anything. "Am I so ugly?" he asked accusingly.

"No, you know it's not that," Numie stammered. Exhausted and desperate, he was packing his few possessions. "It's something crazy going on inside me. I can't explain it."

"What could I have done to make it like it was the first day on the island?" Ralph asked.

Numie murmured something, then decided to give Ralph an honest answer after all. "Coming from me this sounds really far out. But it would have made a difference if you'd shown a little more love."

"Love?" Ralph almost laughed. "Hustlers don't want love."

A tremor of fear passed through Numie. He shouldn't have said what he did. "Maybe I'm not a hustler after all."

"But you said you've hustled all your life," Ralph countered.

"I have," Numie said, hanging his head low, "but I'm changing, I guess."

"If changing means giving me fabulous sex when you're a hustler, and love means impotence——give me a hustler," Ralph said.

Numie bit his lip. "Of course, you're not interested in what's going on in my head? Just the body——that's it!"

"Look," Ralph said, his face turning red, "you're lucky people are still interested in your body——at your age!"

His mind whirling, Numie said, "Do you want me to feel completely worthless?"

"How do you think I feel?" Ralph asked, confronting him.

Numie backed off. There was nothing else to say. He'd already said too much.

But Ralph wouldn't let go. "My hustler-lover can't even get it up for me."

Out the door, Numie stood on the stones and surveyed the night sky.

Behind him, Ralph was still ranting. "You've got it up for half the resident population along the Eastern seaboard——but not for me. Get out!"

The plants in the garden passed before him, as Numie hurried by. The early morning breezes made him shiver. In nothing but a flimsy T-shirt and a pair of khaki pants, he went around a tree which had fallen in a storm and never been removed.

The damp ground was soothing to his bare feet, until he stepped on a piece of broken glass. Feeling the pain, he kept on going, ignoring the drops of blood left behind.

In Leonora's Lincoln, he was driving to nowhere in

particular.

He'd gone many blocks before he realized he hadn't turned on the headlights. He was now in black town. Ned and Dinah's house was in pitch darkness.

Flipping on the car lights, he was jarred by a loud thud against the front fender. "Not a child," he cried out.

Braking the Lincoln, he got out quickly. There in the light of the car was a large yellow calico cat. It had been killed instantly.

Picking up the limp body, Numie lay it to the side of the road. "Oh, no" he said out loud, suddenly realizing something. "Don't let it be Castor's cat. Not his cat."

Getting back into the car, he drove off quickly. If it were Castor's cat, he couldn't face those wide, accusatory eyes.

At the beach he welcomed the salt air. It seemed to be forming crystals all over his body, a coating to heal damage left by the night. Finding a spot near the edge of the ocean, he sat down, stretching his legs toward the sea. The water lapped over his feet.

On the completely deserted beach, he could watch the coming and going of the waves.

Did he begin somewhere out there?

He had lived thirty-two years, a thimble of water compared to the vast pitcher before him. Yet he was beat when he should be in the best part of his life.

He lay back on the sands. Let the ocean take him back again. He didn't belong on the land.

No place for him anywhere.

Chapter Twenty-Five

Numie awoke to the sound of hungry sea gulls circling over him in search of their breakfast. He sat up and looked at this spectacle of life feeding upon life.

On the still deserted beach, the beams of the early morning sun bounced off the white sands and green sea as if they were crystal.

He'd spent the night on the beach, falling asleep shortly before dawn. His throat was clogged, and his chest ached. Had he caught cold?

Pushing himself up from the wet sand, he clenched his arms together for whatever warmth that gave him.

Just thinking about his pre-dawn hours made him shudder. What bothered him most was the gnawing fear he might have killed Castor's calico cat. Funny, but that concern was far more important to him than his being kicked out by Ralph.

The morning had a virgin freshness. Within the hour, overworked husbands would leave their small houses to earn money that was never enough. Housecoat-clad women with limp hair and white-green faces would holler some last-minute command to restless children who'd play until the burning sun drove them inside again.

Numie didn't really envy the domestic life of Tortuga. Yet at the same time he was attracted to anybody who had roots. Let them have their picnics, weddings, and TV dinners. What he wanted was the sense of belonging that made their often dreary lives worthwhile. There was a lot to be said for a daily routine.

How he wished somebody this morning would reach out to him, tell him that everything was going to be okay, that tomorrow would be better, that the worst was over, that he was loved for himself, that his cock was appreciated and enjoyed, but it didn't matter *that* much, that he would be just as appreciated, just as loved, if he weren't as accomplished in bed, that he wouldn't be cast aside if something happened to him, if he lost his power, if he got old, if...

He ran his fingers along the ridge of his nose. Didn't he deserve a second chance? Maybe there really was a God. Maybe you could bargain with him. Maybe, just maybe, God would make it a little easier for him. Give him peace one day.

A man can hustle his ass just so much, and then he's got to stop. A man grows tired. He wants to live for himself, do what *he* wants to do for a change.

Summers in Tortuga were something to be endured. Scorching traps for victims who couldn't afford to run away to shady worlds.

This bright morning sun, already growing hot, called for a focus on Numie's part. Some goal, something.

Why had he come here? What did he hope to gain?

This island was isolated. So was he. The sea washed up on its shore, but the contact was momentary.

Under the gray overcast of this day and on this deserted beach, he was certain of only one thing: *he was not for sale anymore.*

That day was over.

At the Lincoln, he put his hands on the door before deciding to walk along the coral road a bit. He couldn't face Sacre-Coeur, at least not now.

In the distance, Erzulie's shack came into view. A mass of yellow fabric, she was out front, feeding her chickens.

"Morning," he called, going up to her.

At first she was suspicious, then, recognizing him, "What brings you here? It's too early in the week for that white bitch to be dispensing those two dollars."

"I'm not her messenger boy today," he said, feeling weak and apprehensive. "Just out on my own. I couldn't sleep at the house last night. Wandered to the beach. Fell asleep there."

"Nobody can sleep on this damn island," she said, casting the rest of the grain before the hens. "It's haunted——that's why."

At first he wasn't sure what she was suggesting. "What do you mean?"

"On some hot summer nights I can hear buccaneers and the Chinese slaves they used to torture carry on something awful——right out there on the sea. Sometimes when the captain thought he was going to run into a patrol boat, he tossed the slaves overboard, their bodies weighed down with balls and chain. The wind picks up their dying screeches, and the cries sound off inside my head. Last night was one of those nights."

"For everybody, I reckon." He looked awkwardly at her, not really knowing why he was here. Almost for want of something to say, he asked: "Why do you always wear that yellow dress?"

"You liked it?" she asked.

"It's very bright, like the sunshine."

"This is the dress I'm going to be buried in." She smoothed the wrinkles of the night from it.

"But why wear it now?" Erzulie made no sense to him.

"I'm an old lady. I just might die in my sleep, and I want to be dressed and ready. Don't want any of those undertakers in this town dressing me like I'm some hen ready for the roasting oven. I know what they do to women before they put them in coffins."

He smiled, more out of embarrassment than anything else. "I don't think that would happen to you."

"Are you saying men don't want me?" Anger flashed across her face.

"Not at all," he said, fearing he'd come upon yet another colossal ego.

"I'm not known as the Haitian Venus for nothing," she said.

He shuffled his feet awkwardly. Did she really call herself the Haitian Venus?

"My skin," she said, "the color of coffee."

Just as he did with Lola or Leonora, he decided to play the game. "I bet a lot of guys wanted to get it on with you."

"Now you're talking!" Her cool tone was replaced with warm, sympathetic chatter. "Back in Haiti, I had three French lovers and the handsomest black stud in Port-au-Prince. I could stir up the passions not only of men, but Gods."

"Gods?" Now he knew she was crazy.

"Yes, gods."

"I didn't know there were gods in Haiti." He stared at the sky. Another crazy lady in his life he didn't need right now.

"Man, you are ignorant," she charged. "Haven't you ever heard of *loas*?"

"Never." He was only half listening to her jabber.

"They're a link between man and the higher God," she said. "But they behave like imps. Many of them wanted me as their private mistress. But I would never surrender myself to anyone——man or God."

"If you believed they were gods, weren't you afraid of making them mad?"

"I did just that by defying them," Erzulie continued. "That's why I was run out of Haiti. They became cruel to me when I turned them down."

"You really had some tough luck." He was just humoring her now.

She picked up on his condescension right away. "I don't want your sympathy, or the charity of that white bitch. I can look after Erzulie all by myself."

"I'm sure you can." He held his breath until his heart started to pound. Wanting to ask her something, he couldn't come right out with it.

"Look, I don't have all day to stand around gossiping with you," she said. "In fact, I'm not even sure I like you."

"I didn't mean to take up your time." Rather curtly, he started to say good-bye, then he decided what the hell. He might as well come right out with it. "Actually, I'm here to see you on a professional matter."

Her eyes brightened. "That's more like it. You realize, of course, I charge for my services."

"I'm willing to pay." He could see little glittering points of light dancing in those eyes.

"Come inside then," she said.

In her shack, Erzulie chased out two chickens. "I didn't always live in poverty like this. You wouldn't know it to see me now, but I come from an elite class, the *gens de couleur*. My father was French. We had a fantastic Victorian house in Port-au-Prince and a fabulous summer villa at Cap-Haïtien. We were very rich." She paused for a long time. "But that was long ago."

"I'm sure you were," he said. He looked into her contorted face, and all of a sudden he felt paralyzed, shrunken. "You're still surviving——not as well, but surviving."

"There's a lot to be said for that," she countered. "Now what's your problem?"

His heart sank. "I fear I'm losing some of my power as a man." He said that so fast it seemed to leave an echo ringing in his ears.

She drew a deep breath and raised her voice. "What makes you think so?"

The natural way she accepted what he'd laid on her put him more at ease. "It happened last night."

"That's nothing," she said, glancing at a shelf of bottles. "Maybe just a case of guilt."

He nodded, then paced the room anxiously. "But I'm afraid if I try it again, the same thing will happen." His eyes were pleading. "Can't you give me something?"

"I can give you anything you want," she said. "In fact, I once saw to it that an eighty-eight year old man fathered a baby. That's how potent some of my stuff is."

"Then I can buy some off you?" He was sweating, and feeling very much like a goddamn fool, indulging in black magic.

"No, because I don't think you need it," she said. "Try it with someone you really like the next time, then come to me if you need help."

A lump rose in his throat, and he stood for a long time facing her. "But..."

"Erzulie has told you what to do. I'm not used to having my word questioned, except by that white bitch."

"Okay, I'll try it your way." Flies buzzed over his head. The room smelled of sweet decay. "Say, I'd better be going."

"Wait, before you go," she said. "Come into the kitchen out back." On the stove rested a simmering pot.

"Is that your special brew?"

"No, this is something different," she said. "It's a sauce my mama taught me in Haiti. And it's edible. *Piment oiseau*, and is it fiery hot! The black people on the island here and some of the Cubans like it. Put it on their rice and black beans. All day I stand over this stove, making my special sauce. I sell it——that's how I earn enough money to live. Not from Miss De... whatever she calls herself, not from her charity."

"I'd like to try it," he said, not really meaning it. Having confided what he had to her, he was anxious to be off.

"Remember, you have to put it on something," she said. "Just too hot by itself. Here's a bottle I made yesterday."

He took it. "Thanks."

"Cost you a dollar."

"A bargain." He dug into the pocket of his pants.

In her front yard, he made for the road again. He looked back only once.

Erzulie was tossing a rock at a stray dog.

. . .

Without really meaning to go there, he found himself driving up the road to JOAN'S. The front porch was deserted, a burgundy-colored woman's bathing suit resting over a wicker chair. The string of bulbs overhead was still flashing, but the lights seemed best suited to the night.

Through the cranberry-etched doors, he made for the parlor.

There, sprawled across the mission oak sofa was Joan, her housecoat as electric a green as the fabric on which she lay. Her bleary eyes challenged him. She resented his presence.

He was clearly intruding on a private moment early in the morning. At first he was tempted to turn and leave. There was nothing for him here. Yet he felt some strange comfort in her presence. "Have a good night?" he asked.

"What goddamn business is it of yours what kind of night I had?" she asked. Her voice was slurred, her tongue thick. A bottle of Scotch was near her open hand.

He chose not to answer her question. "I was just wandering out by the beach. Thought I'd drop in."

Through the front window came the sound of an old car starting up in back. "Well, drop out," she said, slightly raising her droopy eyes.

"Don't say 'well'," he said facetiously, trying to pierce her hostility. "You know Leonora doesn't like the word."

Sliding down in slow motion, she slumped to the floor. "I couldn't give a fuck what Leonora likes or doesn't like." She practically spat. "I've spent enough time catering to what *that one* wants." Her eyes rolled back in her head like a cow so that only the whites showed. "Now, Lola La Mour. Talk about double jeopardy!"

He lit a cigarette, then tilted his head back to watch the little puffs of blue drift up to the dusty ivory-white ceiling. The smoke just seemed to hang in the corners, like balls of clouds.

"I agree with you," he said. "I'm in the same position——caught in the middle between those two."

Joan was like a pump trying to get her body moving, but her motor wasn't working. "Don't try to get on my good side," she warned him. "You and me, buster, aren't exactly allies."

"Okay," he said, "but we don't have to hate each other." He shifted his feet uncomfortably.

"I don't hate you," she said, reaching for her bottle of Scotch, but finding it beyond her grasp. "I just don't want you around."

"Okay, I'll leave," he said impatiently. He turned for the door, heading through the beaded curtains. Something told him he shouldn't have come here in the first place. Every time he didn't obey his instincts he paid.

"Wait!" she called in a frantic voice.

For a brief second, he considered keeping on walking. "What's the matter?" he asked finally, turning back.

"Could you help me up?" Eyes in focus once again, she was pleading.

"Sure," he said reluctantly. He lifted her massive body, squirming slightly at the piggish quality of her flesh.

One of her huge breasts tumbled out, but she didn't bother to conceal it. "Look at me," she ordered, standing on wobbly legs. Her voice broke. "Look what has become of me." In front of a mirrored wall, she stared at her image. "Leonora used me up." She choked. "Took everything." With force, she placed her breast back inside her housecoat. "Now I'm like some fucking milkcow."

Remembering her first attack on him, he said bitingly, "I'm sure you were a beautiful movie star once."

For a moment she looked as if she would strike him. "That's right, goddamn you. You cheap hustler. Always telling people what they want to hear." She headed toward her bottle of Scotch. "But you're not hustling me."

His hands were shaking. Saliva dribbled out of his mouth. He wiped his chin. "Okay, what do you want to hear? That you look like a tub of suet? That you're ugly and fat? That you've had it!"

The bottle in hand, she jerked up, catching her back. "You bastard!"

"It's true," he said. "You told me I was washed up." He wanted to stop talking, but couldn't help himself at this point. "I can slap it right back at you."

"I've not had my last fling." She faced him squarely. The wrinkles in her face were more pronounced. A vulnerability he'd once seen there was gone——replaced by a caustic mask. "I can go upstairs any time of the day or night I want." She smiled smugly. "The girls have to satisfy me. I make them work, let me tell you. Make them suffer every agony I've ever put up with."

He folded his hands and squeezed tightly. "What agony is that?"

She pursed her mouth. "You should know. You've been on the same trip. I've been everything and done everything, including working in a whorehouse catering strictly to dykes." Her tongue was like a flamethrower, searing Numie with fire. "A shock trooper, they called me. They used to haul me in, and four or five would make smorgasbord out of me." Once again, she tottered precariously on wobbly legs. "Those fat old broads would crawl on top of me, and I had to take it. Now I'm getting back." She stopped all of a sudden. "But, shit, I don't know why I'm telling you anything."

He moved toward the sofa. Now he was feeling faint and weak. "You're just confiding in another burnt-out whore."

"Get out of here!" she yelled, stumbling back against the wall.

He reached to brace her up.

"Get your hands off me," she shouted, jerking away. "I don't like men to touch me. Those days are over."

He was really furious at her now. "Don't be a fool. Do you really think I get my rocks off touching your blubber? No way!"

Her fist sailed through the air, but he was too quick for her. "Men have got off using my body," she said. "Plenty of 'em. But when I learned just how tender and gentle a woman could be, I swore off men for life." On her own legs, and with the now-rescued bottle in hand, she wobbled to the door, disappearing through the beaded curtains.

Lifting the lid of the wooden box, he took out one of Leonora's marijuana cigarettes. No blue this time——nothing his color——so he settled for red. On the sofa, he sucked in the smoke slowly, savoring it.

Someone in a room upstairs flipped on a radio. It picked up a station from Havana. A mad cacophony sounded throughout the house. Suddenly, the radio was turned off.

"Keep it down, you cheap spik." The bellowing voice upstairs was a man's.

He closed his eyes. A picture of Joan flashed below the lids.

Bitter and cynical, she was fed now only by the harm she could cause others. She'd not prepared herself for any other life once she could no longer peddle her body.

"Don't let it happen to me," he said softly. "Not that."

Through the beaded curtains came Maria, wearing nothing but a pair of jeans. Her breasts were small and firm; her limbs, long and slender. At the sight of him, her usually dead eyes came to life. Shaped like almonds, those eyes gave her a faintly Oriental slant. "Baby," she said, "share some of that weed with your cousin."

He handed her the cigarette.

Greedily she sucked in the smoke. "Got this goodie from the wooden box, didn't you?"

"Yeah." He wanted the girl to go.

"I ain't allowed in there," she said. "Got in once and Joan beat the hell out of me." She finished the cigarette, failing to offer him another drag. Then her hands started to snake up his leg.

"Not in the mood," he said, brushing her away. "Besides, you're too young."

"Shit, I've worn out bigger men than you." Through his pants, she kissed his crotch with her small mouth. Her movements were slow, lacking vigor.

He reclined on his back, making no effort to help her.

She unzipped his pants and pulled out his cock. Licking and kissing she worked slowly up the shaft.

Yet it had no effect on him. He just lay there——immune to the energy she was generating.

"Sweetie, I'm trying everything I can to put some life in it," she said. "Can't you do something?"

An uncontrollable rage came over him. Her eyes seemed to be staring, accusing. Without thinking what he was doing, he slapped her across the face. Blood formed at the corner of her mouth.

Zipping up, he bounded from the sofa, passing through the curtains.

The ocean breezes brought him back to his senses. Why did he strike her?

Looking back only once, he saw Maria on the porch, hand at her mouth. "It wasn't my fault——really it wasn't."

He was now inside the Lincoln, starting the motor and speeding up the coral road, the rocks bouncing off the fenders. Stepping on the accelerator, he said out loud: "It never happened."

Glancing occasionally at the road, he kept his eyes on the tall coconut palms bent by tradewinds, the white sand between the highway and the open sea.

This was hurricane season, he'd been told. Yet the weather was fine.

How could that cathouse stand out there on exposed land and not be washed away by now?

Maybe this season a hurricane would sweep over it and reclaim it for the sea. The sea had a way of cleaning off the debris left on shore by man. But could the sea blot out the memory of what happened in that house? He did strike that girl in the mouth. But it wasn't Maria he was striking. Had he become like Leonora? Out for revenge, not caring about his victim?

Then he started to cry. He forgot how long it'd been since he last cried. But he was making up for it now.

. . .

On the patio of Sacre-Coeur, Numie's duffel bag was laying in the sun. Reaching down, he picked it up, fondling it——his traveling office.

The muscles in his arms and shoulders ached, and his legs were weak. He wondered if he still had a room at Sacre-Coeur.

Fresh from the pool, Anne was beside him. She wore a thin robe slightly open. Underneath she was nude. She lifted a tentative hand to the top button, then dropped it.

Her body was undeniably lovely to him——flaring hips sloping swiftly to a tiny waist. Her proud breasts jutted out from under the clinging robe. He swallowed hard, searching her face. Finely constructed, delicate, it revealed nothing. "Let me get you a towel," he finally said.

"No thanks, I like to let the sun dry me." She stared intently. "How is it I never get to see you any more?"

He was breathing more easily. That was definitely a friendly question. "Between Lola and Leonora, not to mention Ralph, everybody eats up my time."

"As far as Ralph's concerned, she said, "I understand you're completely free."

He tightened his hand into a ball. "He told you that?"

"Yes," she said, "this morning before he left for work." She looked squarely at him, her face drained of emotion. "He's moved back into his own room upstairs——left the guest cottage to you."

At first he didn't know what to say. After all, she was Ralph's wife. He listened for some note of triumph in her voice. But there was none. "You predicted we wouldn't last."

"I don't always like to be right," she said. She seemed to look away from him in embarrassment. "Actually, I feel sorry for Ralph."

He winced at this statement.

"Nothing ever works out for him," she continued. She cleared her throat and walked to the corner of the garden where Leonora grew roses.

Hands clasped together, he followed her. "Your sympathy's wasted on that one."

She studied his face closely, then glanced back at the flowers, as if they held some hidden meaning for her.

From her expression he could tell she was angry he had said that. He was sorry.

"Perhaps it is," she said. Stopping, she pulled up a weed, examining it momentarily, then tossing it to the edge of the garden. "What happens to you now?" Even though the sun was hitting her directly in the eye, she glared at him. "Back to Lola?"

"Never!" He said that with a fury that seemed not so much directed at her, but at the garden, the house, the birds, any creature listening. When he vowed he wasn't for sale only this morning on the beach he'd meant it!

Her eyes smiled. "That's good to hear," she said. From her position, she noticed blood on his foot. "Say, barefoot boy, you've got a bad cut there." Getting up quickly, she lifted his foot, balancing it on her knee.

"I'll get something for it," she said, placing his foot gently on the ground.

A disturbing frown crossed his face. The sun burned into his forehead. Heat waves bouncing off the patio bricks distorted his vision. He waited patiently.

Minutes later, she was back, bathing his foot in peroxide and rubbing the crusted blood from the top. "Don't you like shoes?"

"I left in a hurry last night," he said. "Wasn't really thinking." He leaned back in his chair, trying to remember when anyone had ever helped him like this. He couldn't think of one time. "You should have been a nurse."

"A more useful career than the one I've had," she said, looking up at him. "If you can call what I've got now a career."

Through the open windows of the parlor came the whir of a vacuum cleaner. The old grandfather clock struck ten. "It's a living," he said.

"A damn good one at that," she answered, standing up now, inspecting her work. "I'll miss it."

He paused, caught between looking at his bandaged foot and comprehending what she'd just said. Her statement won out. "You leaving?"

There was a kind of odd fear in her voice that made her look at him closely before she said, "Yes."

He closed his eyes and leaned back in the chair. Silt and sediments of uncertainty were clouding his emotions right now. "Where you going?" He dreaded her answer.

"I don't know," she said, closing the lid to her first aid kit. "I'm just leaving, that's all. Been planning to for the last five years. If I don't do it now, I never will." She held a hand to her mouth. Moving the bones in that hand as if to get rid of a cramp, she said, "There wasn't that much here anyway."

"You can say that again!" he said. He got up from his chair, crossed the patio, heading for the bar.

She followed him. "I knew from the first moment you arrived at the bar that things wouldn't work out for you."

This momentarily made him flare up, but he contained his rage. Why did she want to go and say a thing like that? It could only hurt him.

"This town can burn up a guy faster than anything," she said. "Leave you with absolutely nothing."

Was she talking about herself? he wondered.

"At least I flatter myself I'll be leaving with something," she said.

He didn't dare ask what she meant. Instead he said, "Thanks for fixing the foot. I'll be more careful in the future where I walk."

"I hope so," she said softly, then smiled.

Cool, distant, controlled, Anne was a mystery. He never knew how far to go with her. She was looking at him with concentrated interest. He leaned back on the bar stool, trying to shut out his thoughts. There were many things he wanted to say to her, but somehow the words wouldn't come out. He wanted to break through to her. Would he sound too pushy to speak up now? Too much the hustler speaking? After all, he had to be careful with her. Her husband had kicked him out only the night before. Did she know the reason why? Pray that she didn't!

Upstairs the sound of operatic music filled the air.

"Leonora must be up," Anne said.

He bit his lips to keep from speaking and making a fool of himself. Instead he said, "Our day has begun." Almost uncontrollably, he found himself reaching for her arm.

But she moved away.

He cringed as he felt rejected. He'd misjudged her. She was behind him, massaging his neck muscles, relieving them of last night's tension. Slowly, almost without knowing what he was doing, he rested his cheek against her hand. She gently withdrew it, tightening it around his neck and inching toward his scalp. "Can we talk later?" he asked.

"Talk is cheap," she said coldly, a woman who'd been hurt too many times before.

At first he bristled at her statement, finding himself pulling away from her. But then a new wave of understanding came over him, and he kept the soft intimacy in his voice. "It doesn't have to be."

"Of course," she said, finishing the massage, "we can talk after our lords and masters have finished with us for the day. You're like me now. No special status in the household. Another servant."

"That thought has crossed my mind," he said painfully.

"I'm not even granted the status of wife," she said.

He was sorry she kept bringing up that subject. But he felt compelled to balance it in some way. "As for me, I'm no longer the kept boy." No sooner had he said that then he resented the sound of his own voice.

She ignored the remark. In the yellow-red sun, she stood before him, casting a shadow. Her robe was still undone, but she was completely casual about her nudity. It was clear she wasn't being provocative, just natural.

Through half-closed eyes, he took in her curves. He wanted to reach out——to touch, to fondle. But now was the wrong time. It wasn't that he wanted her sexually, not this morning at any rate. He desired something else: a quality she had. An approach to life that was free of games, all Lola and Leonora knew how to play. That Anne was recognizably normal in a crazy world was in itself compelling.

The wind stirred, but was interrupted by a loud, buzzing sound. "That's *her* calling," Anne said.

He sighed in despair. "Think she wants me to drive her some place?"

"Not today," she answered. "She's having a guest over she hasn't seen in fifty years." She smiled sardonically. "Leonora will need all morning to make herself appear beautiful."

. . .

"Exactly what do you do for Leonora?" Ruthie Elvina was asking.

Sitting at the bar, Numie was fascinated by two lizards on a rock. Until questioned, he was thinking of Anne. At first, he didn't understand what Ruthie Elvina meant. Then he said, "I'm just the chauffeur."

"*Just?*" She adjusted the gardenia in her gray-blonde hair. "Chauffeurs are very special people."

"I don't think so," he said, hoping to end all talk.

Ruthie Elvina was not put off by so easy a rejection. "When my husband, the late Captain Bray, was alive, we once hired a chauffeur to drive us around Paris." She sighed. "Now I'm behind the wheel myself——bad legs and all." Her voice was reminiscent of Southern girls who early in life were shipped off to school in the north or to England. However, Ruthie Elvina deliberately seemed to retain her regional speech.

He was most uncomfortable, having nothing to say to her. As the hired hand, he didn't think it was his job to amuse Leonora's guests while she kept them waiting. He poured himself another drink. Already he'd consumed his quota of Scotch for the day. But Leonora wasn't keeping check. The commodore's death had caused panic in her. From behind the bar, he could observe Ruthie Elvina more carefully.

In the afternoon sun, her moon-peach lipgloss was wearing thin, and her blue-green eye shadow was running. Amply displayed, her large breasts were modestly obscured by organdy ruffles. Smoothing down her floral print dress, she said, "I like to wear the colors of the sea." She smiled at him. "The sea has been good to us here on this island——it's part of our blood, and we should pay proper respect to it." Her voice, though polite, unmistakably carried the awareness that she was talking to a servant. "Don't you agree?"

"I certainly do," he said, almost willing to agree to anything if it would make her shut up. He'd wanted to say a lot more to Anne, and was resenting his tongue for freezing at a time like that.

Just then, Theodore M. Albury emerged from a long tenure in the toilet. Urine spots showed on his bright red slacks. On rubbery spindle legs, he weaved across the brick patio. "Young man," he called to Numie, "another martini——and make this one real dry."

"Teddy, don't you think you've had enough?" Ruthie Elvina asked. Her lips trembled with her voice. "I swear you could outdrink my captain if he was alive today."

He brushed aside her suggestion with the wave of his hand. Teddy was like an exotic bird of prey. His pear-shaped body and long, thin neck were too small to support his enormous head with its hawklike beak. His eyes were bloodshot. His skin, beet-colored. Another martini in hand, he stumbled to his chair, spilling some of the drink on his Madras jacket. As he leaned back, an Ankh——dangling on the end of a heavy gold chain——clanked against his butter-yellow Oxford shirt, which was open and revealed a mass of salt-and-pepper hair. On a stool, he carefully arranged his bare feet, encased in white crinkled Italian loafers.

"Teddy's in real estate," Ruthie Elvina said, almost apologetically. She seemed to be trying to catch Numie's eye.

He was determined to avoid even that personal a contact with her. "That's fine," he said. "I've seen your name on signs around the island." He just was talking to be talking. "Everything for rent here seems to be at least seventy years old."

Ruthie Elvina bristled at that remark.

"Dammit," Numie thought. Now he'd gone and insulted her. Why didn't he keep his mouth shut?

"You're right," Teddy said, "but I've got big plans with developers." He settled back in his chair, searching for the right shade angle from the tree branch overhead. "This time next year, I'll be hiring you as my chauffeur to drive me around in limousines." He opened his eyes wide and stared at both Numie and Ruthie Elvina, as if defying them to challenge his next remark. "I'm going to be a millionaire!"

This struck a responsive chord in Numie. Regardless of your position in life, he realized we all carry the same dream of striking it rich. "What's your secret?" he asked.

"I'm working on this project for a high-rise right on the beach," Teddy said. "On land Leonora and the late commodore own." The gardener was burning some trash in the back, and its yellow haze of smoke drifted their way. Teddy stopped momentarily, thinking it was a fire in the house. "With beautiful high-rise apartments, we'll get the money crowd. They'll arrive on yachts." He stared at Numie, as if debating whether to make the next point. "Right now we get the cheap campers." He grandly waved a hand in the air, slightly upsetting some of his martini. "I'm trying to give this town a little style."

Anger flashed across Ruthie Elvina's face. "It's got style," she said testily. "Plenty of it."

From the rigid arch of her back, Numie could tell that Ruthie

Elvina considered herself the social arbiter of taste and style in Tortuga. She clearly resented this interference from Teddy.

"As for me," Ruthie Elvina said, "I'm trying to uphold tradition——just like my captain wanted me to. Preserve the best of the past." Going out of her way to turn her back to Teddy, she deliberately addressed her next statement to Numie, although it was clearly said for the drunken realtor's benefit. "I'm starting a movement to restore some of the historical landmarks on the island. I don't think people appreciate the important espionage work that went on here in the Civil War when the Yankees captured the island." This was said like a pat little speech she'd delivered many times in front of civic groups. She turned around, squarely facing Teddy. "High risers could ruin our look."

"Look, baby," Teddy said, his voice increasingly bitter, "you'll vote for us." He settled back, like a man assured of easy victory. "Only objection you have to high rise is nobody has met your outrageous price yet."

Ruthie Elvina sucked in the air, her breasts jutting out all the more. She had all the self-righteousness of a Crusader storming the infidel. Then some of the air escaped her, and it was clear she'd decided that now wasn't the time for battle.

"You're holding out on that beach footage for all you can take us for," Teddy said, almost intuitively knowing he could get away with this attack. "The land actually belonged to my cousin, before he was sent off to the asylum by your brother, that judge."

Ruthie Elvina was fanning herself, as if to make her immune from all the hot air swirling around the patio.

Teddy was impatient; he wasn't getting a response from her. Even though his brain was swimming with liquor, he seemed to know the way to reach her. He leaned forward, blowing some of his alcoholic breath in her face. "Before your dear, departed captain swindled my family out of it."

He'd reached his mark. Ruthie Elvina heaved her fleshy body from her chair, towering over him. "That's a libelous story you've spread too many times, *Theodore*. " Her fleshy arms were shaking. "But up till now you've always had enough manners not to spread it right in front of me." She gazed straight upward into the sky, as if she could invoke some heavenly wrath to rain down on her enemy. "I could have you up on charges," she sputtered, "but everybody on this island knows you're the town drunk——and aren't responsible for your tongue."

Just as Teddy had known her vulnerable spot, it was obvious she'd hit his. He stared back at her uncomprehendingly for a moment. A lock of hair dangled over his forehead, and he looked momentarily deranged. "You will live to regret the day you made that accusation," he said softly but ominously.

Ruthie Elvina turned around, slowly sipping her tall drink. "Teddy hallucinates," she said to Numie, wiping the sweat from her thick upper lip. "Alcohol's bad for the brain." She looked back in disdain. "Pay no attention to him."

The argument ended as Leonora appeared. She stood in the shadow of the doorway, her face chalk white, her large eyes heavily coated with mascara. Hanging from her slender frame was a robe of coral and jade embroidery on black satin. It was an old Chinese theatrical costume. Gently adjusting the coral comb in her hair, she gracefully crossed the bricks on her coral satin slippers, heading for her guests. "Forgive me for being so late. I'm incorrigible. No, don't deny it." Her hand darted through the air in an undefined gesture. "I'm simply incorrigible. Reminds me of the time I inadvertently kept Queen Mary waiting for an hour." In the hot glare, she paused. A sharp pain shot through her side. That was such an obvious lie. Why did she tell it? It just slipped out, that's why. Since she'd last seen Ruthie Elvina, her own history was spectacular enough. Yet she could never resist putting gilt on the lily. But why Queen Mary? Why not someone more believable? Already she could see the eyes of Ruthie Elvina boring into her.

"As I live and breathe, you look fantastic," Ruthie Elvina said, hoisting her fleshy body across the patio. "You haven't changed a bit in fifty years."

"Neither have you," Leonora lied. My God, she thought. Even though they were the same age, Ruthie Elvina was a prehistoric relic on her last legs. Gently Leonora brushed her lips against Ruthie Elvina's hot, fleshy cheek, too heavily painted with rouge. The woman's cheap perfume offended Leonora's more sensitive nostrils. Leonora stared into the fallen face. Now her nervousness was ebbing. She was beginning to relish this moment, the coming together after all these years with her old high school rival. The beauty queen, Ruthie Elvina Saunders, versus the ugly duckling, Priscilla Osterhoudt. Now the roles were reversed. Ruthie Elvina was still Ruthie Elvina, the widow of the late Captain Bray, but Priscilla Osterhoudt had gone from Mrs. Norton Huttnar to Leonora de la Mer.

"This is Teddy Albury," Ruthie Elvina said. For some reason, she seemed to be sweating more heavily than ever.

"Theodore," he corrected, his voice slurred. He tried to rise from the chair, but fell back.

"Don't get up," Leonora added quickly. Then she looked at Numie. His face was blank. Was he bored? She was certain of it. Did all of them look like patients in a geriatrics ward to Numie?

Numie avoided Leonora's eyes. Now that Ralph had kicked him out, he was uncertain of his position at Sacre-Coeur. He must keep from making Leonora angry, though the task seemed impossible. "May I get you a drink?" he asked.

"No, darling, a smoke," Leonora said. Her dreams had been so unrefreshing the night before, and her day so horrid, that she was floundering right in front of everybody. What a day to encounter Ruthie Elvina Bray after half a century.

"What color?" Numie asked, fearing Leonora was itching for a fight and would use any excuse to attack him.

She glanced at her garden and the flowers growing there. "I feel in a rose mood today."

Into her wooden box and out with a marijuana cigarette, Numie crossed the patio and handed it to Leonora, then lit it for her.

She sucked in the smoke and sat up stiffly in her favorite peacock chair.

"What lovely cigarette paper you have," Ruthie Elvina said, "and what a distinct aroma. I pride myself on knowing a thing or two about tobacco——my captain taught me——but I've never smelled that particular brand before."

"It's Turkish," Leonora said.

"Oh!" Ruthie Elvina said. "Well, I love the color anyway." She sighed heavily, sitting down. "Rose, like the roses in this pretty garden." At the mention of roses, a frown crossed her face. "Roses remind me of my sister, Minnie."

"I remember her well," Leonora said. Her voice had a slow, nasal rendering. She was trying to disguise it, but her hatred of Ruthie Elvina was only exceeded by her equally loathsome sister, Minnie.

Ruthie Elvina paused with a deliberate awkwardness, as if trying to fathom what Leonora meant by her last remark. "Minnie was the rose of the family," she said.

Leonora coughed on the smoke. On a day like today she was not prepared to listen to a story glorifying Minnie.

"You shouldn't smoke so much," Ruthie Elvina said pressing on with her story. "My daddy called me in one day and sat me down right beside him." Her eyes tried to attract Leonora's, but they were lost roaming the garden. "My daddy told me he wasn't going to waste his time giving Minnie advice."

"Why was that, dear?" Leonora asked, being deliberately provocative. "I would imagine any young girl would be in dire need of advice from her father."

Ruthie Elvina stopped in the middle of her story. Her face reflected her puzzlement. She leaned forward in her chair and continued, "Seeing that Minnie was such a beautiful rose, and roses have a way of getting plucked——even those a bit faded." Her voice drifted off.

Realizing the story was at Ruthie Elvina's expense, Leonora was suddenly eager for more details.

"My daddy warned me," Ruthie Elvina said, "that I'd better pay attention to my books. And pick up all the feminine tricks I could on the side, 'cause I was just a great big waxy magnolia." She made petals out of her fingers, outlining the frame of her face. "And great big waxy magnolias need all the help they can get in this world."

Leonora laughed with relish, until she realized her voice was too harsh. "I can hardly believe that story," Leonora said, now savoring every moment of it. "You know yourself you were voted the most popular girl in school and were the queen of the prom."

"Popular, yes," Ruthie Elvina replied, "but I never thought I was much of a beauty."

"You were," Leonora said, "especially in that bathing suit you wore." She was sucking in the smoke rapidly. Having dreaded Ruthie Elvina's appearance today, she was now enjoying it——the most fun she'd had all summer. "First beauty contest ever held in Tortuga. All the boys said you had the prettiest legs in town."

She stared at Ruthie Elvina's varicose legs, encased in support stockings. Her white molded shoes were planted solidly on brick. Her arches seemed to have fallen. The huge bulky mass of her legs gave no clue whatsoever that they were ever shapely.

Ruthie Elvina shifted uncomfortably in her chair, tucking her flowery dress over her chubby kneecaps. "No one at school knew back then that you'd go to New York and become so famous."

"If I recall correctly, no one at school ever gave me much credit for anything," Leonora said. No sooner were the words out than she regretted them. That remark revealed the sting of rejection was still smarting. She recalled that the chief rejecter was Ruthie Elvina herself.

"I'm sorry you feel that way," Ruthie Elvina said. "Everyone thought you were very smart——perhaps a little bit standoffish."

"Let's forget about these school girl memories," Teddy said, "and get down to the business at hand. Got to get home pretty soon. Time for my siesta."

"Yes," Leonora said, sitting up rigidly, "just why are you people here?" She dreaded their explanations.

Ruthie Elvina giggled nervously. Then with a flutter of her hands, she said, "We're planning an old island homecoming. All the important people born on this island are returning for an old island days tour."

Then she shifted in her chair, as if trying to conceal some irregularities in her own internal plumbing. "Naturally we couldn't conceive of a tour without including Sacre-Coeur."

Leonora was all ears!

"It's the grandest house on the island," Ruthie Elvina said. Just as a smile was starting to form at Leonora's lips, Ruthie Elvina delivered her punch line, "Except mine, of course."

Leonora's face, lit by a diffused radiance of the sun through a shade tree, turned pale as death. Ruthie Elvina was baiting her with that remark, and she was having a hard time not snapping at it. Sacre-Coeur, as everybody knew, was far more dazzling than Ruthie Elvina's broken-down, old clapboard, fading, sea-green relic would ever be. The fake portraits she hung on the wall, pretending they were ancestors! The reproductions passed off as heirloom antiques. "I don't allow strangers into Sacre-Coeur. My privacy must be protected."

"Just this one time," Ruthie Elvina countered, "I didn't think you'd mind. After all, you're our most famous homegrown daughter. Besides, I've already had the programs printed, and you're listed as part of the tour. You didn't return my phone calls, but I just knew you wouldn't want to be excluded."

A long silence. The hot sun was bad for Leonora. As a rule, she never appeared in it. Even the shadow in the patio wasn't sufficient to conceal her anger. At first, her voice faltered, then she regained her composure. "Are you sitting here telling me that people will be arriving at my house——whether I invited them or not? And you took it upon yourself to open Sacre-Coeur to the public, putting me on exhibit?"

"I know I should be tarred and feathered," Ruthie Elvina said, "but Sacre-Coeur's so important to the success of the tour. I feel just awful, but I know you'll cooperate."

In a voice cold as the winter wind, Leonora asked, "What did you ever do for me?"

Ruthie Elvina seesawed with uncertainty in her chair, not completely aware of the fury she'd provoked in Leonora. "I was your best friend in school."

"You were my worst enemy!" Leonora got up, throwing her cigarette onto the bricks. "I hated you then, and I hate you now." She'd always wanted to get even with Ruthie Elvina. If she could sabotage the old island tour, that would be striking back in some small way. Whatever she'd wanted in Tortuga——a prize, an invitation, a friend, whatever——Ruthie Elvina was always there first, grabbing it up.

"Surely you're mistaken," Ruthie Elvina said. "I've always admired you greatly."

"Get out!" Leonora screeched. "Both of you. Get out!"

"I've got important business here," Teddy protested.

Ruthie Elvina heaved herself up from the chair. "But the programs are already printed."

"Print them again," Leonora said. Her hands were quivering, her facade of coolness shattered. Ruthie Elvina had done it again——shown her up as vulnerable.

Ruthie Elvina reached into her purse. "Here's an invitation," she said, handing it to Leonora.

At first Leonora stood motionless, then she reached out and gingerly accepted the envelope.

"You're invited to a party tonight aboard the Saskatchewan," Ruthie Elvina said. "I remember when we were just young girls, and I didn't invite you to my sixteenth birthday party. I knew you wanted to come, and I was wrong to hurt you like that." She stood for a moment in grave silence, then she took a hesitant step toward Leonora.

Instinctively Leonora backed away. The more she heard Ruthie Elvina talk, the weaker she felt. For her, going back into the past with Ruthie Elvina was the same as taking her out in mid-ocean and abandoning her. In spite of her name, the lioness of the sea didn't swim.

"My captain served aboard the Saskatchewan," Ruthie Elvina said, "and I'm sort of the unofficial hostess tonight." A quivering hand reached toward Leonora's.

Leonora concealed her hands within her robe, leaving Ruthie Elvina's hand dangling in the air.

"Please," Ruthie Elvina said, "let's forget the past. Accept the invitation. I know it's too late, and we can't make up for what's gone before. I did do things to hurt you. But life has made me pay." A sharp edge came over her voice. "Look at you now——and then look at me." Her lip trembled. "You've already got your revenge, Priscilla." After saying that, she turned to Teddy. "I know you've got something to tell her. I'll go on and call you tomorrow." She turned and waddled across the patio.

For one brief moment, Leonora wanted to run after her, throw her arms around Ruthie Elvina, and have a good cry. She knew she'd never see the old woman again. But as of this moment she'd stopped hating her. Instead she felt sorry for her. Ruthie Elvina, the big, waxy magnolia who'd bloomed too early. The petals were gone now.

Leonora herself had bloomed much later, and from that vantage point could afford to be forgiving. She hated herself for not being more charitable to her long-ago enemy, but was too paralyzed to do anything about it.

Leonora walked in her garden, wishing she was alone and freed of the drunken realtor. Ruthie Elvina had touched off painful memories.

Leonora remembered what she did the nights other children were playing or getting invited to parties. In her long black braids and middy dress, she'd design costumes for the house pets, a male cat she'd named Jennifer and a German shepherd, called Boulder. She'd decorate her bedroom with ribbons and crepe paper, then invite the animals. Jennifer would always tear up his costume, but Boulder never did, providing she kept feeding him.

"Let me have one more drink," Teddy said, stumbling over to her and interrupting her thoughts. "It'll take it to tell you what I've got to."

"Darling," Leonora said, "it's time for my afternoon massage." Nevertheless, her interest was piqued. "Numie, another cigarette. And get this gentleman another drink——whatever his poison." She seated herself stiffly in the peacock chair. "You're not the most beautiful thing in the world, and you look even less attractive when you're drunk. But I'll hear you out."

Teddy seemed to be having a hard time getting started. "I'm one of the directors of the local museum."

Leonora was growing impatient. "I had no idea," she said with condescension.

"We have your Picasso on loan."

The man's stupidity jarred her. "I've never owned a Picasso. You mean, my Kandinsky?"

"Yes, that's the one," Teddy said. "His name escaped me for a moment."

"I adore Kandinsky," Leonora said, settling back, safe in the security of knowing that Teddy was here only to ask her to continue her loan to the museum. "He maintained that every work obeys only laws of inner necessity."

Teddy took a chair directly in front of her. Before settling down, he said, "In this case it was a necessity I have something to spruce up my living room for this cocktail party. I borrowed your painting."

"Borrowed?" A sudden alarm sounded in Leonora.

"Yes, took it to my place, planning to return it the next

morning." Teddy fell back in his chair, letting the summer sun work its power over him.

In moments Leonora was on her feet. "Where's my Kandinsky?" she demanded.

Teddy smiled apologetically. "The painting was, so to speak, purloined."

"After being illegally taken from the museum in violation of my agreement." Leonora's chalk white face was turning to a muddy gray. Her fingers clutched the arm of her chair.

"I can explain," he said.

"*Please.*"

"That I might descend to the serenity of my little gathering, I had consumed an unusual amount of cocktails and wine," Teddy said.

"For you, I'm sure that must have been exceptional," Leonora said with biting sarcasm. She detested thievery on any level, and as far as she was concerned she was looking directly at one.

Teddy seemed oblivious to her insult. "Midnight found me floating alone into Commodore Philip's. There hadn't been so many queens and dykes on the prowl since Halloween. I seated myself at a table right by the door, and that's when I noticed a strange boy."

Cigarette in hand, Leonora was sucking in the smoke furiously, hoping it would pacify her. "I'm not interested in your tawdry sex life."

"In two seconds we were deep in some ridiculous conversation," Teddy said, suddenly relishing telling the story. "I never remember names on this particular sort of encounter, but I remember he volunteered he was an organist in Homestead."

"What does he have to do with my painting?" Leonora asked, her eyes searching desperately for Numie, but he had gone back to the kitchen.

"Considering I am musical, and a player of various instruments, I instinctively liked this boy," Teddy went on.

Where was Anne? Leonora wondered. Maybe she'd better call the sheriff. "I'm sure your musical talent is without peer," she said, hardly disguising the nervous edge to her voice. "My painting!"

"I'm getting to it," Teddy said, obviously disappointed she wasn't enjoying the story. "Fifteen minutes of conversation, and I figured a bird in hand. All I remember is two blaring headlights and my already, droopy eyelids."

The sun, this horrible creature——everything was becoming too much for Leonora. It was as if he were deliberately torturing her. She suspected that Ruthie Elvina was behind it somehow.

"When we entered my living room," Teddy said, "about one-thirty, he thought my place was beautiful. Said I must be very rich. I didn't want him to think I had your kind of money, so I told him I'd purchased it as a shack——then spent laborious years on restoration."

Numie, Anne, no one was in sight to help Leonora. She went over and pressed a buzzer. She could tell it was broken. The humidity in the air ruined everything. She was afraid to leave this man alone. He might steal something else. Finally, she decided to face him. "You're going to need a restoration if you don't explain and quickly."

Her words were sobering to Teddy. "While I fixed drinks, he wandered around the living room. That's when he discovered your painting and one I call 'Crazy Helen'."

At last he'd come to the point. Impulsively Leonora almost reached out to him, hoping to shake the rest of the story out of him: "This art lover," she said, "he stole my painting?"

"Not until I was in my bedroom with an accomplished trampoline artist who'd contorted his way through many an amorous night," Teddy said.

"Forget the pornography," Leonora snapped, pressing the buzzer with fury, even though she was convinced it didn't work.

"After this final workout, I was tired," Teddy said. "With no other assumption than he was going to spend the night, we went to sleep."

The smoke finally reached Leonora. She sat back down in her chair. Teddy's talk had mesmerized her into a kind of coma.

"The phone woke me at ten-thirty the following morning," he said. "It was an invitation to dinner that night. Then a sister, Trilla Russell, called to gossip about this sailor number she'd picked up in the men's room of the Greyhound bus station——apparently one of Yellowwood's rejects. Before I knew it, it was an hour before I left my bedroom."

Beyond fury at this point, Leonora listened to the sounds of her garden. She was breathing heavily, knowing that in a few moments she'd be launching her counterattack.

"I thought the boy had to get back to that organ in Homestead," Teddy said. "I felt no alarm until I entered my living room."

Leonora sat up. Even though she knew the outcome of the story, she waited to hear her suspicions confirmed.

"My God!" he said. "Two spots on the wall as empty as my bank account. The Picasso, or whatever you call it, and 'Crazy Helen' were gone."

"I don't give a goddamn about 'Crazy Helen'," Leonora said. "The Kandinsky?"

"It was crystal clear I had engaged a very crooked queen," Teddy said. "I was afraid to gaze about for fear of discovering more objects missing."

Memories of an awful hotel suite robbery in Los Angeles flashed through her brain. She'd blamed Joan for that one. "I don't care if he'd stolen everything in your house. "You called the sheriff, didn't you?"

Teddy pulled himself up. He was sweating. "I couldn't——considering the circumstances. I'd be ruined in this town. A scandal like this just when the high-rise is coming in. The money people wouldn't trust me. I'd look terribly undependable."

"I didn't even have that painting insured, you bastard," Leonora said, plotting her revenge. "I'm getting Yellowwood on the phone myself."

"I need time," Teddy said, "to track him down."

"How dare you ask me another favor," Leonora said. "You've violated a sacred trust. The ultimate rip-off! First, Ruthie Elvina. Now, you." She rose from her chair. "I'm not giving you any time at all. I'm filing charges." This was such a clear case of right and wrong, with her in the right, she wanted the episode publicized. It would show how the town abused her, not as a child, but even today.

Teddy's legs wobbled, and he didn't seem to know what to do next. "I'm not going to cater to you, Miss High and Mighty.

I'm not impressed with your fame or your money," Teddy said. "You're just another dyke, as far as I'm concerned. A broken-down bitch!"

If a knife were in her hand at this moment, she would have plunged it into his vile heart. Instead she said softy, but with a frightening intensity, "For saying that to me, *I'll destroy you.*"

She ran toward her parlor. Brokendown bitch, just another dyke——the words echoed inside her. None of it was true. Another attack by a cheap faggot, as untrue as the one by the gay minister. Fags hated her because she saw through them. She was compassionate and beautiful——not a bitch, not broken down. Attacking her in her own home, robbing her of her Kandinsky——the Albury creature was part of a mass conspiracy against her. Soon all the aliens on Ruthie Elvina's tour would be marching against Sacre-Coeur. After years of hiding from them, they were coming to seek her out. Where in the hell was Ralph? He could hire bodyguards. Have anybody shot who entered the grounds. In the glare of the sun, she didn't see the glass doors. She banged right into them, smashing her face. The pain shooting through her head was unbearable; the world going black, she fainted.

· · ·

Leonora opened her eyes. At first her bedroom was hazy. A throbbing pain prevented her from making out the objects in the room clearly. "What happened?"

Anne was standing by, placing a wet cloth on Leonora's head. "You fainted," she said matter-of-factly.

In one quick move, Leonora tossed the wet cloth across the room. "Now, I remember." In her mind, she re-lived the scene. "That dreadful Albury creature. My Kandinsky." A growing panic came into her voice.

"Yellowwood called," Anne said. "He knows all about it. He's investigating. Thinks he knows who the boy is. Said to tell you it's best to keep it out of the paper."

"They must find it," Leonora said, desperately reaching for Anne's hand. She feared the loss of just one of her treasures would set off a mass of robberies. She could see it now: all the aliens on Ruthie Elvina's tour carting off the art objects locked all these years behind the walls of Sacre-Coeur. "I'll never lend anything again as long as I live." A sudden pain. "Oh, how my head hurts. Quick, a mirror."

In moments, Anne was holding a mirror in front of Leonora's face.

"I'm badly bruised," Leonora said, gazing at her reflection. Without makeup, her face looked tired and old today. In some way, the glass seemed to mock her. "Take that mirror away."

"It's only a minor bruise." Nevertheless, Anne quickly withdrew the mirror. She smiled, as if she had news to cheer Leonora up. "You got a cable today from the Metropolitan in New York. They want to do a retrospective on you. Here, I'll get it." At first, Leonora didn't understand what she meant.

Anne picked up a yellow envelope. "Says here, 'you represented couture at its grandest.'"

A stern frown crossed Leonora's bruised brow. "The Metropolitan? Represented!" Rage exploded within her. "Darling," she said icily, "send this reply: Leonora de la Mer is no museum piece. I'm dateless and very much alive."

Anne looked disappointed. "Very well," she said softly.

"Do it now," Leonora commanded, sensing her orders weren't being carried out. Hand at her head bruise, she lay back on her soft satin cushions. Surely no one except her vilest enemies could suggest she belonged in a museum. Maybe it was part of a plot to lure her back to New York. After all, couture was in jeopardy, desperately fighting to hold on. She was needed to revive it, that was true. The creative designers were gone, but the imagination of Leonora de la Mer went on fruitfully forever. No big trends were sweeping the fashion world——none like those she'd dazzled it with years ago. No one had come along to replace her. Women were spending less and less on clothes, because no one was around to inspire and excite their imaginations. She sat up again, resenting Anne for leaving a slight crack in her black draperies through which the afternoon sun came through. Of one thing she was certain, she wouldn't return to New York no matter what trickery was used. The world of couture had turned its back on her at a crucial moment. She owed it no loyalty now that it needed her more than she needed it. It was the same as Ruthie Elvina's invitation. Too little, too late.

Anne was back. "I sent the cable. The exact words."

"Thanks," Leonora said suspiciously. "What is that other envelope in your hand?"

Ruthie Elvina's invitation for tonight's party aboard the Saskatchewan. I'll call her, of course, and tell her you're unable to make it."

"How bitter life is," Leonora said, reaching for the invitation. She let it dangle in front of her, as if it were something unclean. "My work may still be at a peak, but I must admit my invitations have fallen off." She removed her large glasses and returned the invitation to Anne. "I remember one night when a perfume manufacturer rented Maxim's at a cost of thirteen thousand dollars——just for me. The whole restaurant was closed to the outside world." She settled back once more onto her satin cushions. "Thirty waiters served just the two of us."

Anne turned to go. "I'll throw it away."

"No, don't be too hasty," Leonora said, a wry smile forming. "Give it to Tangerine."

Anne looked puzzled, as if she couldn't fathom Leonora's purpose.

"Tell her the invitation was for her," Leonora ordered.

"Are you sure?" Anne asked.

"You heard me," Leonora said. "No one invites poor Tangerine anywhere. She'll have a good time."

Chapter Twenty-Six

In her powder-specked mirror, Tangerine was practicing her best party-girl smile. Licking her orange-coated lips, she opened a round compact and wiped some more powder on her face. Then she smiled again——this time for Numie. "Thanks, sugartit, for taking me to the party tonight. It means a lot to me."

"I'm glad to." He was aware that Ruthie Elvina had intended the invitation for Leonora. When Leonora invited Tangerine, he didn't know if she were being extravagantly generous or else amusing herself perversely——gambling that Tangerine would make an ass of herself and embarrass Ruthie Elvina.

A tiny shred of beef had lodged between two of Tangerine's yellowed false teeth. With one of her orange-lacquered nails, she squeezed into the tight trap and scraped it out.

"Come on, you're pretty enough," he said. "In that outfit, no one will look at your face. You're not concealing your charms."

"You mean these milk jugs?" she asked, bouncing her breasts. "They drive men wild, that's true, but cows are better. After all, cows give milk."

He smiled. "I think it's a little more complicated than that."

In the Lincoln, Tangerine was opening the glove compartment. "Carlos, he used to be the chauffeur before you, kept some bourbon in here. One of those little half pints." Finding it, she swigged some down straight from the bottle.

"You'll be drunk before you get there," he said, concerned at a desperation he sensed in her. "Something tells me this isn't your first drink of the day." Her lipstick was badly smeared, and he debated whether to tell her or not. But he finally decided it wouldn't do any good, as her entire face was made up like a clown. One repair couldn't rescue it.

"I'm real excited about tonight," she said, taking another swig. "Mike Morgan's gonna be there."

Eyes on the road, he was only half listening. "Name sounds familiar."

"It should," she said petulantly, almost hurt he didn't recall exactly. "He's that young boy I told you about——the one who used to live in Tallahassee." Her wide eyes were almost beseeching him to recall. "I worked for his family. Showed him what to do with that little pecker between his legs."

"How could I forget?" A dog ventured in front of the headlights, but changed his mind about crossing the street. Foot on the brakes, Numie was thinking of killing that calico cat. How could he ever face Castor who blamed him for everything anyway?

"I got myself all dolled up for little Mike tonight. If I know him, he'll want another try."

A note of alarm sounded in Numie. Was Tangerine riding for another big disappointment. "How long has it been since you last saw him?"

Tangerine burped, shoving the bourbon back into the compartment. "I was twenty-two at the time," she said. "He was only fourteen."

He reached over and hugged her with one arm. "It may not even be the same Mike Morgan."

"One and the same," she said confidently, reaching into her purse for her lipstick. Even though the car was bouncing, and she had no mirror, she applied another red coating. "Been following his career in the paper for years. He's a hot-shot reporter for AP."

The reception aboard the Saskatchewan was in full blast.

Parking the Lincoln at the dock, Numie looked through the rear-view mirror and tightened a borrowed tie around a collar already choking him.

Carefully he led Tangerine up the gangplank, resting her elbow gingerly in the palm of his hand.

Most of the guests were already there, drinking hard liquor between avocado dip from conch shells and smoked oysters from open tinned cans. Young officers stood stiffly about, ready to answer questions or help the guests.

Tangerine's high heel shoes, in clear nylon mesh like a fish net, clanked against the deck. At the gateway, she paused to look into the crowd.

That mass of faces was staring back at her.

Her expression revealed how much she wanted them to like her outfit. Her shocking pink gown, at least below her waist, was two dresses sewn together. The stitching in one of the seams had burst, so she'd camouflaged it by letting a turquoise handkerchief dangle from her waist. For her top, she'd taken the upper part of a strapless turquoise bathing suit and had sewn sequins all over it to give it the effect of evening wear. The suit revealed a freckled back. For jewelry, she wore a necklace of shells and had tied two turquoise ribbons on gold earrings which dangled from her pierced ears. In her orange hair, a lipstick-red hibiscus rested. Around her shoulders she'd draped a worn white rabbit fur stole.

"Hello, Tangerine," a voice called. Ruthie Elvina floated across the room in her lemon silk chiffon with ruffles on the hem. Brushing back her teased banana curls, she extended her bat-winged sleeves to embrace her. "Someone told me you had run off and got married, and I said I just couldn't believe it. It's not true, is it?"

"Who'd have me?" Tangerine asked, looking downcast.

"I'm so glad," Ruthie Elvina said. "A good maid is hard to find. I should know. After you quit me and went over to Sacre-Coeur, I just haven't been able to find a suitable replacement." She frowned. "Why did you ever leave me? Why, you were just like one of the family."

"I couldn't live on the wages you were paying," Tangerine said softly.

"Well, course I can't afford to have you chauffeured to parties in limousines," Ruthie Elvina said. "Which reminds me, where's Leonora? The invitation you've got in your hand was intended for her."

"You didn't invite me?" Tangerine asked, her lip quivering. "She said you did."

"I invited Leonora," Ruthie Elvina said, her chin jutting out. "But seeing you're here, why don't you enjoy yourself?" Someone tapped Ruthie Elvina's naked shoulder, and she whirled around.

Tangerine seized this moment to escape. Heading straight for a young man in a white uniform pouring drinks, she said, "Bourbon on the rocks."

"Honey," Numie said, coming up behind her, "you're getting that 'I'm gonna get bombed' voice. Better cool it with the booze."

"If you wasn't so young and beautiful," she said, "I'd swear you was my daddy, giving me hell about that old devil moonshine." Someone caught her eye. Almost in panic, she broke away and crossed the room, bumping into strangers and knocking one glass out of a hand.

Quick on her trail, Numie came to a stop in back of her, reaching out to support her.

"Why, Mike Morgan, as I live and breathe," Tangerine said. "After all these years, I would have known you anywhere."

A tall, gray-haired man with a walrus-mustache stood staring blankly at her. "I don't think I've had the pleasure," he said finally. Narrow-eyed, he had a guttural voice in a deadly serious tone.

"You've *had* the pleasure all right! I'm Fern Cornelia Blanchard."

"Fern!" he said. "I can't believe it. It's been years."

"What you mean is, you didn't think I'd look so frisky after all this time," Tangerine said, assuming a distorted mask she evidently thought was sexy. "Well, it's all me——ready and raring to go." She leaned toward him, planting a wet kiss on his mouth."

He stepped back slightly, barely resisting the temptation to wipe his mouth.

"That mustache tickles," Tangerine said, giggling. "In more places than one, I bet!" She winked as she smiled.

He drew back from her, red faced in embarrassment. His summer sports jacket, tight as sausage casing, seemed even tighter. "Who's your friend?"

"Numie Chase," he said, extending his hand. He wanted to rescue Tangerine from this man, but didn't know how.

"Good-looking guy," Mike said to Tangerine. "You always did like 'em young." He elbowed her. "That's one thing you and I are in accord about, Fern."

She stepped back, eying him skeptically. "People today call me Tangerine."

"What an apt name," he said, his eyes traveling from her badly painted mouth to her hair. "From your hair, no doubt."

Just then, a middle aged man and woman appeared, accompanied by a girl. "Mike, darling," the woman called.

"Good to see you again, Mike," the man said.

"I'm so glad you could come," the woman said. "Here's Helen. She's been dying to meet you. It's rare that a big-time reporter like you comes down here to our little island."

"Helen," Mike said, all smiles. "Everything your mom and dad told me is true."

Helen gave Mike her hand.

He held it for a long time.

"I can't tell you how many delicious things I've heard about you," Helen said. "I look for your column every day. I miss it now that you're on vacation."

"What say I tell you what I would have written tomorrow?" Mike said, taking Helen by the arm. "Excuse me, Fern... Tangerine. Nice seeing you again." Almost as an afterthought, he added, "What are you doing these days?"

"I'm a goddamn movie star," Tangerine said in disgust.

Already absorbed by Helen, Mike answered, "That sounds nice."

Tangerine was left standing——without a goodbye.

"Don't you think we've had enough partying for one night?" Numie asked. He was going to leave regardless. No more could he witness humiliation for Tangerine.

"Yes, it's time to go," she said after a long pause. "Hell, yes."

On the gangplank, she was pleading, "Take me home, right away." Shivering in the night air, she protectively pulled her rabbit stole around her.

Silence, all the way back to her place.

In front of her house, she turned before heading upstairs. Tears were forming in her eyes. "Thanks for everything."

"Glad to help out——anytime," he said, kissing her on the mouth. "Want me to come up for a drink?"

"No, bless you," she said, nervously patting his hand. "Leonora has tired me out today," she sighed. "I didn't know just how much."

He watched as she climbed the rickety steps, nearly stumbling once.

She grabbed the railing for support. It was as wobbly as she.

Right after the screen door shut, he stood there nervously just waiting for something to happen. But what?

Then he knew.

Up the steps two at a time, he darted through the front door and into the hall. A black blur, and it was too late. He was reaching for her. But he was too far away.

She was falling——one leg plummeting down through the hole in the hallway.

. . .

The next morning, L.M. Jenkins, surgeon at the county hospital, walked down the dull tile of the corridor to a waiting Numie. Chart in hand and stethoscope around his neck, the doctor had the manner of a man used to telling people the world wasn't coming to an end.

"How is she?" Numie asked. He looked helplessly at the doctor, feeling powerless to put into words his deepest fears.

Dr. Jenkins eyed Numie skeptically. "You're not a relative, are you?"

In a strained voice, Numie said. "I'm her closest friend——doesn't that count?"

The doctor didn't respond. A nurse appeared and whispered something into his ear. Before going, he turned to Numie. "Tangerine's a pretty tough girl——agile as hell for a woman of her age." He shook his head. "But this is bad, real bad. I've seen the x-rays."

Numie found himself leaning forward to catch the doctor's words.

"We've got to put a metal pin in her hip plate this afternoon," Dr. Jenkins said. "We'll know in about two weeks if the operation's successful."

"Can I see her now?" Numie asked. He glanced unhappily down the hall. "I've been here all night."

"Yes, but make it short," the doctor said, already moving down the hallway. He called over his shoulder, "Room 102."

With trepidation, Numie turned away, heading down an annex to Tangerine's room.

She lay in the hospital bed covered with a sheet. A towel was tied around her head like a turban, concealing her orange hair. Slowly, she opened her eyes.

He smiled.

Staring back at him, her eyes were vacant. "Sugartit," she

said softly, tears pouring down her face. "Thanks for sticking around."

"Hello, baby," he said, giving her a kiss on her flabby cheek. A thin trace of last night's lipstick remained on her mouth. "I leave you for one moment——and look what happens."

She stopped crying and smiled faintly. "Does everybody know I got soused last night and fell on my ass?"

"Listen, Lady Blanchard," he said, "don't you know you're the wickedest woman on this island?" He softly rubbed her face. "I'll bet the whole island thinks you're here having a baby——probably mine."

She chuckled. "Wish it was true." With a shaking hand, she reached out to him. "Guess the doctor told you about my hip."

"Yes," he said, taking her hand. The Mexican rings were gone. He pressed her hand against his cheek. "Did anyone ever tell you you're my favorite girl?"

"Don't waste all your time on an old bag like me," she said, pretending to push him away.

He made a mock fist. "Shut up or I'll sock you one."

. . .

Out of the building and into the blazing morning sun, he was dizzy from lack of sleep. He opened the door of the Lincoln and crawled in. Without meaning to, he propped his head on the steering wheel. It burned his cheek, but he remained there as if paralyzed. The windows were rolled up, the air dead. Yet he rested there——not wanting to move, backward or forward. He felt suspended in time and space. A part of nothing. A candidate for extinction.

At Sacre-Coeur, the maid told Numie Ralph wanted him in his upstairs bedroom.

Numie looked at her and nodded imperceptibly. His lips parted, as if to say something, then his eyes dropped.

Up the steps two at a time, he rapped loudly on a large oak door. No sound from inside. He knocked again.

"Who's there?" came Ralph's sleepy voice. There was a sudden stirring.

"Numie," he said coolly. He stood back a step or two, not

really wanting to enter Ralph's room for what he felt would be another humiliation.

"It's unlocked," Ralph called out.

Slowly Numie cracked the door. The bedroom was nearly dark; the smell, rancid. Two figures lay under a sheet on Ralph's fourposter bed.

"Morning," Ralph said breathlessly.

"Morning," Numie answered in a voice larded with stress. He was tired, he told himself, and not ready for any of Ralph's games.

"What a workout I had last night," Ralph said in a deliberately seductive manner.

Numie walked briskly to the window, pulling back the draperies so he could see better. "You wanted me?"

Ralph smiled with a leer. "You interested in a three-way circus at this hour?"

"Some other time," Numie replied curtly. The jangling of a telephone in Leonora's study startled him.

"You don't know what you're missing." With that pronouncement, he pulled the sheet down, revealing the body of a tall, muscular black.

It was Ned!

"My God," Numie exclaimed.

"My reaction exactly," Ralph said.

Ralph was completely unaware of the reason for Numie's response. Apparently, Ralph knew nothing of Ned or his connection with Lola. At first, Numie decided to say something, then thought better of it.

"He's completely worn out after last night's workout," Ralph said. "I've tried to wake him up once or twice."

Numie turned his back on the exhibition. Frowning and staring at the garden below, he asked, "What do you want from me?"

Ralph pulled the sheet up back over Ned, hardly suppressing an oath. "You'll find out," he said bitingly. "I've got to get up and get dressed." He jumped out of bed and reached for his trousers resting on a maroon leather chair. Dangling them in front of Numie, he said, "I'll meet you in the patio where I'll have my coffee. See that it's there."

Eyes steady and flat, Numie turned and left the room.

"Sure," he said over his shoulder.

On the patio, Ralph was badly hung over. He sipped his coffee, burning himself. "You look worse than I do."

"I was up all night," Numie explained. All around him the world seemed lifeless and as unappetizing as Ralph. "Tangerine's in the hospital." He paused for some look of concern on Ralph's face. There was none. "Broke her hip."

Scanning the headlines, Ralph barely looked up. "Probably fell down drunk. I don't know why Leonora puts up with her."

Numie could feel his face redden. "I don't think you heard me," he said forcefully. "Tangerine fell down and broke her hip."

Ralph turned the page. No response whatsoever.

"Man," Numie protested, "do you know what that means for a woman of her age?"

"I know perfectly well how dangerous it is," Ralph said, discarding the paper on the bricks. "But Tangerine's not my charge." He got up quickly, tossing the black coffee into a hibiscus bush. "Listen, if you're going to work around here, you'd better shave before reporting for duty."

A note of uncertainty struck Numie. He feared Ralph was getting ready to close him out. "I would have if it wasn't for the accident."

"Accident or no accident," Ralph said, spitting out his words, "you'd better shape up." He looked up at his bedroom window. "You're no longer enjoying any special privileges around here."

Numie stared straight into Ralph's cold bullet eyes. "I know that."

Ralph confronted him, trying to outstare him. "I tried to get in touch with you all night, but I couldn't."

Numie was feeling slightly sick. It was an effort to move his fingers. "I told you, I was at the hospital." The terrible indefiniteness of his situation was really getting to him now.

"You were needed to drive up to the mainland to pick up the commodore's sister," Ralph said. He went to the bar and poured himself a beer. It tasted foul; he slammed it down on the counter. "Beer," he said with disgust. "A habit I picked up from Anne. The only habit, thank God."

It seemed to Numie he ought to say something, but nothing

came out. He could only wait.

"His sister is flying in from New Orleans," Ralph said, checking his watch. "But now you don't have to pick her up."

Here it comes, Numie thought. He was getting fired. "Who's going to pick her up?" he asked hesitantly.

"Ned," Ralph said matter-of-factly.

Numie smiled to himself. "Ned," he repeated.

"Yes," Ralph replied defiantly. "My *new* lover. He doesn't have your problem."

The words stung Numie, but still he said nothing.

"For some reason," Ralph went on, "Ned seemed very anxious to pick Amelia up." He shrugged his shoulders. "The drive to the mainland is a bore anyway."

Numie was secretly amused. "Can you trust him?"

"No problem," Ralph said, scratching his beard. "If Ned doesn't make it there, I'll put in a call for a limousine. Joan's the one who got Amelia to come." He paused. "But Leonora is calling the shots. She's out to break the will."

Ralph's rude treatment of him this morning, and his lack of compassion for Tangerine, silenced Numie for good. Lola was behind this, and he wasn't going to blow it for her. If she could get to Sister Amelia before Leonora and Ralph, more power to her. Numie owed none of them any favors nor any loyalty.

"Seeing that you like Tangerine so much," Ralph said sarcastically, "why don't you stay at her place?" The breeze rustled through the coconuts. A smirk came on Ralph's face. "Now that Ned's on the scene, the guest cottage is going to be occupied."

"I see," Numie said, expecting this. He wondered if Dinah had spent the night with Leonora. Would she be the one to turn Ned in?

"When Leonora wants you," Ralph went on, "Anne can call you at Tangerine's." He ran his hand through his hair. "In the meantime, you'd better get some sleep." He pinched Numie's chin between his index finger and his thumb.

Numie winced with pain, then pulled back.

"This morning you really look your age," Ralph said.

. . .

The wind was blowing over the island, whisking in mosquitoes from their swampy beds. Rain——or something more ominous——was in the air.

The sun had disappeared, and the streets were empty and foreboding, as Numie made his way back to Tangerine's apartment. Luxuriant plants swayed in the breeze, their leaves making soft, peculiar sounds.

They were whispering a warning. He knew it. The air was alive with danger!

He rushed into the apartment just as the first roar of thunder tore apart the sky. Rain began to beat against the weary walls.

The room smelled musty. The windows had been shut all day. As he flipped on a light, a cockroach, big as a mouse, darted under the sink.

Unbuttoning his shirt, he collapsed on Tangerine's old iron bed. He was about to explode.

For all he knew, he was no longer welcome at Sacre-Coeur. Ralph hadn't actually kicked him out, but had made it obvious he was to start trucking down the road.

By now, though, Numie should have become accustomed to dismissals. He'd had enough of them. Each one hurt a little bit, but he always prided himself on never showing pain. Play it cool, the rule of the hustler world. Johns liked a cool hustler. In fact, many who had enjoyed him liked him to show no emotion at all. Why those types didn't get it on with statues in the park he'd never understand.

It was strange he'd chosen such a life when he really wasn't cool at all. He felt. He cared.

There he went again, feeling sorry for himself. Truth was, he chose his life. The easy way, or so he had thought.

Being with someone in any intimate relationship was more than he could handle. He'd never had to approach anyone. Just made himself available, and a score, usually a man, came to him. In fact, he wasn't certain he liked males sexually. But it was easier to pump it to a man than hustle a chick.

What a way to live! He'd ended up with nothing to show for his trouble. Of course, he'd survived, and he couldn't entirely put that down. Ralph was the latest disaster. The line had been long.

If he thought his situation was bad, what about Tangerine?

That was a real tragedy. Her life was nearly over——even her fantasy had been taken away. The Saskatchewan sailed away with that even before the accident.

She'd known the hole was there. In fact, she'd never repaired it, in spite of the trouble it caused. He was certain her fall was a suicide plunge. At least with a broken hip, she could become an old lady and stop hanging onto the dream of finding a man.

But what about him? He was half Tangerine's age. Yet at times he'd been accepting his state in life as paralleling hers. He wasn't in her trap. There was a lot of living left for him yet. Of course, he'd have to approach life on different terms, but surely he could do that. At least try. Couldn't he?

He needed a companion, someone to help him along when he got deep down depressed. Someone to make it all seem worthwhile . . .

Just then, a loud rapping sounded on the screen door frame.

Into the hallway he bounded. "Anne!" His voice carried a desperation, as if she were a rescue party finally arrived.

"I'm glad you're here." He threw open the screen door. "Come on in."

"I'm soaked," she said, wiping her dripping hair. "What a cloudburst."

She moved through the room so quickly his vision of her seemed almost fleeting. "Let me get you a towel." In Tangerine's bathroom he was searching desperately for something clean. Everything was damp and dirty. He found only a washcloth. "I always seem to be getting something to dry you off," he said, back in the living room.

With an athletic sureness, she reached for the cloth. "You mean, I'm wet most of the time?"

"Most of the time," he said smiling. He stood there looking awkwardly at her in the gray of the afternoon. His mind whirled.

Outside the wind was picking up. The shutters on the window rattled.

She turned from him suddenly, finding a cigarette. Seeking the most comfortable seat, Tangerine's Salvation Army sofa, she studied him.

He rubbed his arms and moved about. "This apartment sure is cold and damp." The two plants in Tangerine's living room were almost dead. Was it worth it to water them? He turned around and faced Anne. "You've heard about Tangerine's accident?" It was almost like an accusation.

"Yes, that's why I'm here," she said softly. "I called the hospital. The operation's this afternoon."

He was trying to read her face for any trace of compassion but found no clues. She was matter-of-fact, but not cold, the way Ralph had been. "I know," he said finally. "How did Leonora take the news?"

Anne wasn't finding the sofa agreeable. "She didn't seem overly concerned." Then she sighed. "Said when you've seen as many deaths as she has, you can't get hysterical over another one. Then she barged around the room in a fit, claiming all her lovers——except one, that unspeakable Joan——were dead."

Anger flashed through Numie. "I hope you reminded her she has another one," he said. "If that's what Dinah is called."

"I didn't, of course," Anne said.

He was upset by Anne's casualness about Tangerine. "I hope Leonora gets it through her head Tangerine isn't dead."

"She is as far as Leonora's concerned." Getting up from the impossible sofa, Anne paced the floor. "Poor Tangerine, will she be okay?"

Numie warmed inside. For the first time today, Anne was responding the way he wanted her to. It just took her a little while to get it out. He could understand that. All those years at Sacre-Coeur had to have some kind of effect. "I hope she will," he said.

Anne seemed embarrassed to be in Tangerine's apartment alone with him. "How about a beer?" she asked, breaking the tension building between them.

He laughed. "You know Leonora doesn't like you to drink beer."

"Forget her," she said, heading for the kitchen. "Bronx girls drink beer——and that's that. They learn it from their daddies."

"Okay, beer it is," he said, squeezing past her. He could smell the sweetness of her body, fresh from the rain storm. Opening the refrigerator door, he removed two cans.

On their return, Anne's mood had changed to serious once again. "I've applied for a job in New York as a secretary." She sought his face.

But he turned from her, shifting his eyes again to those two dying plants.

"I'll know if I got it in a week or two," she continued.

"You're really going through with it?" he asked, still not looking her in the eye. "Does Leonora or Ralph know?" He was grasping for some words floating on his mind, but couldn't reach them.

"Neither one," she answered.

"Thanks for trusting me with this," he said, enjoying the coolness of the beer inside him. He felt the breeze stirring restlessly in the living room.

After a long moment of silence, she said, "Nothing good is happening on this island. I have a feeling it's going to get worse."

Numie stood up. He was flushed, as if his head were about to explode. "Will you get a divorce?"

"Yes," she said. "I shouldn't have married Ralph in the first place."

This was old news to him. He went and stood by the window. His hand was shaking. He didn't dare expose his vulnerability.

"I want to be free," Anne said, talking to his back. "Just in case anybody else ever comes along." She laughed nervously. "Guess I sound like Tangerine. Waiting for the man who never turns up."

"There's a slight difference between you and Tangerine," he said almost bitterly. "That poor girl didn't have much of a chance."

In a voice growing harsh, Anne said, "She had just as much chance as the rest of us. But she blew it."

He resented Anne for making this judgment, yet suspected it was true. He felt they weren't really talking about Tangerine anyway——but about themselves. That sounds pretty hard on her."

She didn't say anything for a long time.

He kept his back to her, his eyes glued to the scene below.

"Now that you know my plans, what about you?" she asked.

"I'm just hanging in for a little longer," he said. He clutched his sweat-soaked hands, his body tightening into steel. "I don't intend to go to New York. I've spent my last days on those streets."

"Ever thought about going inside?"

"What do you mean?" he asked, knowing perfectly well what she meant.

"Get off the streets," she said.

"I've tried that," he said sharply. "Far as I got was a stoop."

The rain stopped almost as quickly as it had begun. The moist air smelled fresh and pure.

On the sidewalk below, a long-haired girl haggled over price with three drunken sailors. Two young men in jeans were sharing a joint.

The sleazy bars were getting ready for the night.

. . .

On the mainland, the temperature had been in the upper eighties all week long. Construction workers building a new airport terminal paused in the muggy weather to look at a car coming to a screeching halt in the parking lot.

"A pimpmobile," one of them called out.

A fat cat's dream of Detroit art, it was a two-tone Cadillac in chartreuse and cream. White walls, silver initials on the side, special chrome attachments——psychedelic poetry in motion.

Lola snuggled back against the hand-rubbed, green-dyed leather, resting her platform shoes on the white shag carpet. She felt much like a pussycat. Leonora de la Mer could have her tired old leopard skin.

In the back seat mirror, she checked out her make-up. Perfect! Christ, she was looking good today. For her first meeting with the commodore's sister from New Orleans, Lola had decided to dress modestly. Instead of a blonde wig, she chose a straight black one that hung gracefully down her shoulders. Even though it was only afternoon, she was wearing a long-bodied, green satin gown, with tulle shoulders and sleeves sprinkled with satin flowers.

In the driver's seat, Ned was also preening his feathers. For the occasion, Lola had his hair straightened and styled and dressed him in a robin's egg blue suit with a matching silk scarf and shirt. In his alligator shoes, and with his cock almost completely revealed in his too tight pants, he practically danced out of the front to open the rear door for her. "These wheels are out of sight, but I wanted you to order your own machine——custom designed by *me*."

"Fuck off," Lola said, getting out of the car and adjusting her rhinestone sunglasses in the glaring light of the airport parking lot. "When I saw those initials, all gleaming silver, I knew it was for me."

"But the cat who owned this car was gunned down," Ned protested. "It's bad news to take some dead cat's car over."

She ignored him. "Just look at those three silver L's. They're perfect for me. Lola La Mour Le Blanc."

"Le Blanc," Ned said. "What kind of name is that?"

"That was my commodore's last name, stupid," Lola said. "It means *white*. Didn't you know, I'm the new Mrs. Le Blanc." She caught herself. "The late Mrs. Le ... hell, you know what I mean."

"You forgot," Ned said, poking her in the ribs, "you're a widow."

She looked at him with fury. "Like hell I forgot. That's one thing I'll never forget." She adjusted a satin flower.

"C'mon, we're late. Amelia is already landing."

In a roped-off section, Lola stood with Ned.

Two university students were also waiting for an arrival. Dressed in plaid Bermuda shorts and a T-shirt, one of the young men eyed Lola strangely.

Hands on her hips, Lola returned the stare. She couldn't go anywhere. Even out on business, without men looking at her with desire. On a normal day, she would welcome the students' attention. But not today——not with Amelia arriving and threatening to destroy her dreams. Time for goodlooking young students later.

The man was whispering something in the ear of his friend. The other student turned and looked at Lola, snickering.

No respect, Lola thought. Even when she dressed conservatively, men still treated her as a whore. White men especially. It was getting so that all white men these days wanted a black chick. She just didn't feel safe on the streets any more. "Do you think Ralph was suspicious?" Lola asked, her mind returning to business.

"About what?" Ned said.

"You hustling him and then volunteering to drive up to the mainland to meet my commodore's sister? That would sound mighty peculiar to me. But then again, white men are so dense."

"After old Ned finished with him, Ralph had something else on his mind."

"He obviously fell for it," Lola said, fearing she was sweating too much. "Here we are. If he knew I was here, his balls would turn somersaults."

"How you gonna spot the sister?" Ned asked.

"My commodore had a big family album back in Tortuga," Lola said, smiling at her own cleverness. "The face of that ugly bitch is pasted all over it. Looks like a prune."

Just then, the first passengers from New Orleans started to arrive. Most of them had filed out before a tall, gray-haired woman appeared.

Lola moved toward her, then hesitated. It just had to be the one. The woman was the only one on the plane who looked like a Jehovah's Witness. Her skin had a transparency, revealing knotted veins. She walked stiff and upright, her eyes small, but with sharp vision. Her outfit was simple: a green and white gingham shirt dress under a straw-brimmed hat.

"That's her," Lola whispered loudly to Ned. She pranced over to the woman. "How do you do?" Lola asked. "I'm Mrs. Le Blanc."

"You mean, you're looking for *Miss* Le Blanc?" Amelia asked.

"No, that's you," Lola answered. "I'm *Mrs.* Le Blanc."

The commodore's sister dropped her purse.

"Help the lady with her bag," Lola commanded of Ned. "I've been dying to meet my sister-in-law," she said, kissing the distraught woman on the cheek. "You're everything my commodore said you were."

"I beg your pardon," the woman said feebly, rubbing her cheek with a hastily drawn handkerchief. "I think there's been a terrible mistake."

"You are Amelia Le Blanc?" Lola asked, polishing her Old Mine diamond.

"Yes," she protested, "but I was to be met by a representative of Miss De la Mer."

"Consider her represented," Lola said, waving her ring in the air. "You are with family now, child, so relax and enjoy yourself."

"Surely I didn't hear you say you were Mrs. Le Blanc." Amelia's eyes widened in horror, and her breath was coming in short gasps.

"That's right, a name we share," Lola said interlocking her arm with Amelia's, even though the smell of her violet perfume was repugnant to her.

"Wait till you see our new car," Ned said enthusiastically. "You'll shi... love it!"

On wobbly legs, a reluctant Amelia was helped along to the baggage claim area——Lola Le Blanc on one arm, Ned on the other.

. . .

"I need a slight libation from time to time to steady my nerves," Amelia said, reaching for a martini the waitress was placing on their table. "Never flown on an airplane before, a harrowing experience, let me tell you." She glanced apprehensively around the room. "Think I'll take the train back home."

"Then you're going back?" Lola asked, practically swishing her tail in the plastic chair. In fact, the way she felt right now she'd gladly finance Amelia's bon voyage party to Siberia.

"By all means," Amelia said firmly. An ominous sound came into her voice. "After some business matters have been settled."

Lola's heart dropped.

The robin's egg blue suit she'd bought for Ned was clearly visible from across the air terminal bar. He was returning after a trip to the men's room.

Amelia kept digging her thumb into the aching muscle of her stiff neck. "I haven't had a decent night's sleep since losing my dear brother. Isn't it about time to end the little joke on me? I'm in no mood for humor."

Slurping his drink as he joined them, Ned said, "I don't see nothing funny."

Lola glanced at her long nail on the finger holding the Old Mine diamond. Some of the red polish had flaked off. That upset her so much she forgot what she was going to say. Then, remembering, she said to Ned, "I think our guest means me. That is, my going right up to her and introducing myself as Mrs. Le Blanc."

"Exactly," Amelia concurred, her patrician nostrils raised and twitching.

"That, my dear child," Lola said "was and is no laughing matter." Her eyes swept the room like a tornado, and her hand with the diamond waved the air.

"Are you trying to ruin the reputation of the Le Blanc family?" Amelia asked. That martini glass was at her tight mouth once again, except this time she spilled some on her dress.

As if to show Amelia up, Lola reached for her rum drink, daintily and with precision of movement. She was deliberately postponing answering Amelia's question just to show that grand southern lady that she, Lola La Mour Le Blanc, had nothing to fear from her. Except she did. Plenty. However, that was one little goodie Lola wasn't about to give away. After what she deemed a respectable amount of time, she decided to respond to the question at hand. "Being the lady I am, I will choose to ignore that last remark. The plane has probably messed up your mind, and you don't really know what you're saying."

"I know perfectly well what I'm saying," Amelia protested. "Not a soul back home——not a soul, do you hear me?——must know my late brother married a woman of the colored persuasion."

"Persuasion," Ned said derisively. "Honey, we ain't just persuaded. Like we didn't go around picking out colors. Make mine sunflower yellow. As for you, you'd look great in chocolate marshmallow."

Lola shot Ned a look that silenced him. She caught her breath and started to feel more at ease. Getting around Amelia was going to be just a little bit easier than she'd feared. Amelia was not the canny fox her brother had been. "I was married," Lola said emphatically. "Witnesses to prove it——not to mention the most spectacular wedding gown ever." She fingered her ring. "Still the talk of the town."

"Surely the marriage was conducted in the strictest of privacy?" Amelia inquired. Sitting up tall and erect, she moved her neck as if to catch a breath of fresh air.

"We even got our pictures in the newspapers," Lola lied, enjoying Amelia's discomfort.

"My God," Amelia exclaimed, sinking back into the chair. "I don't know how I'll manage to show my face in Tortuga. Sounds like a Godforsaken place anyway."

Lola flashed a satanic grin. If she had anything to do about it, Amelia would never have to get one lilywhite toe stuck in the slime of Tortuga.

"If my brother," she said, casting a disdainful eye at Lola, "was going around marrying up with colored women, now I know why he wanted to leave New Orleans." She put her hand to her brooch-covered chest. "Marrying that Cajun gal was wicked enough. People back home talk about it so much I can't walk out my front door."

Pain exploded inside Lola. She stared fixedly at Amelia. She knew she wasn't exactly getting virgin purity when she married up with the commodore, but she didn't know anything about any Cajun gal. The whole idea of marrying a man who'd wed a Cajun sounded low class to her.

"My poor sister, bless her soul——she's dead now," Amelia said, "just couldn't understand it either." Her eyes zeroed in on the Old Mine diamond. "Thank God she didn't live to see this day." She paused, as if she suddenly wanted to take flight. "Could the waitress be persuaded to bring me another slight libation? My heart is palpitating at such a dangerous rate I think I'd better slow it down——or else I'll pass out right in front of everybody."

At this moment, Lola was thinking how convenient that would be for her. She'd be only too happy to pay for another pauper's coffin if it meant getting rid of Amelia for good. A sister-in-law she wasn't interested in. Nevertheless, Lola's fingers snapped the air to gain the attention of the waitress. The snap resounded throughout the bar, attracting much notice.

"You don't have to snap your fingers that loud," Amelia whispered. "Everybody's looking. After all, we aren't at a hog-calling contest."

Normally, Lola would have kicked up her heels at that offense. But she decided to go easy with Amelia. It'd all work out better in the long run if she'd play it this way. Lola kept telling herself.

"I understand my brother——in a moment of total insanity, I have no doubt——bequeathed to you his entire estate," Amelia said, moving in on the subject on everybody's mind since the plane landed. "Forgetting his sister who has a house with a mortgage and no means of support." She coughed. "Who's too ill to work."

The shrillness in Amelia's voice sent shivers through Lola. "Your information is correct——that is, the part about his bequeathing his entire estate, every penny, to me, his legal wife." She gazed at the diamond again. "I can hardly consider that a moment of total insanity. Many men leave property to their wives. In fact, I understand it's the usual procedure."

"That's for the courts to decide," Amelia said.

"The courts?" Lola asked nervously. Then she sank back, as Amelia had done, and slowly assumed her mask of calmness.

"You heard what I said," Amelia answered. "I intend to contest the will, even if I have to keep it in the courts forever."

Lola reached for her purse, fumbling for a cigarette. Amelia, she realized, was a little smarter than she had thought at first. With a fierce grimace, Lola turned away. Then she stabbed the air with her cigarette, as if to emphasize a point. Only she realized she'd set the stage for a devastating rejoinder, but had absolutely no counterattack. The cigarette holder fell to the floor. Ned reached to retrieve it, giving Lola more time. "You know what you're getting at?" Lola asked. "According to your little plan, each of us might end up with nothing——not even enough to take care of basic needs."

"My goodness," Amelia said, smiling, her eyes dancing. "At least my brother married a woman smart enough to comprehend business."

Amelia's charade was over. Lola now knew she was just as foxy as her brother. But she liked that. Any dude or chick willing to bargain, Lola could handle. It was those puritanical bastards who couldn't be bribed——those were the ones to hate. Fortunately, she'd never run into too many of that kind.

"I'm like you, *Sister* Amelia," Lola said. "I feel a deep-in-the-stomach need for some slight libations myself." The waitress placed the martini on the table. "Another rum and Coke for me, and a Scotch for Ned. Might as well start getting another martini ready for Sister Amelia here." She let out a hoot. "Bout time we let the cows out to start grazing in the pasture."

. . .

The office of the commodore's attorney was on the first floor of a tile-roofed building in the Spanish section of town. In the Andalusian-styled lobby, Lola paused briefly, looking back at Ned helping Amelia along. Then, assured of her appearance in a gilt-framed mirror, she hurried passed the high-backed, dark wood chairs and a sagging, threadbare tapestry.

Milton Goldenburg's office extended the Old Spanish look, with its carved armchair placed behind an imposing heavy desk. In the nearly dark office, an art nouveau lamp cast a forgiving light.

"Miss La Mour," Goldenburg said. "So good to see you."

"It's Mrs. Le Blanc," Lola corrected. "I'm married, remember?"

"How could I ever forget?" Goldenburg asked, more amused than embarrassed. Taking her hand, he seated her on a deep green velour sofa.

After introductions, Ned and Amelia were shown to matching overstuffed armchairs. After everybody settled, there was a momentary silence. Lola surveyed tapestry scenes of Granada and Seville, hanging from wrought-iron spears. On the opposite wall was an impressive collection of floor-to-ceiling law books. "That's a lot of books," she said. "You read them all?"

"No, not even half of them," Goldenburg said. "But they are there, nevertheless, in case any peculiar circumstances might arise."

"Like today," Amelia said, sitting up stiffly. Her eyes were martini-glazed.

Ned shifted uneasily in his chair.

Reaching into her purse, Lola took out a magnifying mirror to adjust a false eyelash. "There's not too much light in this room."

"Enough," Amelia added as Goldenburg started to raise the venetian blinds onto a small patio with a waterless fountain. Hand fluttering at her long throat, Amelia said, "Sure is a hot day——but then I'm used to heat." Her last word carried some ominous threat.

Goldenburg buzzed his secretary. A short, stocky woman entered the room. "Get these people something to drink," he ordered. "You name it——we're stocked with it."

As the second round of drinks was being served, Lola got up and started to prance the floor. "Before we arrived here today, Sister Amelia and I got some tentative agreement worked out." She put her hands on her hips. "Fortunately, Ned and I got up there to save her from the clutches of those two child-molesting dykes, Joan and De la Mer." She patted Amelia on the shoulder. "Now Sister Amelia had never heard the word dyke before, but when I explained the gory details, she got the picture perfect. Why, I saw that De la Mer with my own eyes letching after this poor gal named Dinah." She glared at Ned, daring him to interrupt her story. "Dinah's only thirteen, a perfect innocent till she started running around with the wrong company."

Ned squirmed in his seat.

"What is your agreement?" Goldenburg asked.

"You can do the fancy papers and stuff," Lola said. "Sister Amelia has decided not to contest the will. All the bad publicity and all." She inspected her wedding diamond. "Seems that a lot of people in her family and their friends don't take too favorably to the commodore marrying up with a black lady. Also, she ain't got a lot of money to keep you expensive lawyers in tapestries."

"So tell me," Goldenburg asked impatiently.

"I'm going to get half the proceeds from the Garden of Delights," Amelia interrupted. "I've been led to understand that that comes to thirty thousand dollars a year. That will certainly pay off my mortgage."

"I've always handled the commodore's affairs," Goldenburg said. "But I've never heard of any Garden of Delights."

"What kind of lawyer are you?" Amelia asked. "You should look after my brother's affairs much better. Familiarize yourself with his holdings. Lola assures me the Garden is the best restaurant in Tortuga."

Lola quickly interrupted. "The Garden of Delights," she said to Goldenburg, "recently had its name changed. Up to now, it's been known as Joan's Place."

"I see!" the attorney said.

"Thank God it's not the Joan who called me from New Orleans," Amelia said.

Lola's expression warned the attorney to keep quiet.

"Lola here tells me that wicked woman operates a bordello," Amelia said. "She sounded so clean and decent over the phone. But then Lola told me she used to be an actress. Actresses can pretend to be respectable people. You just can't tell the difference."

"And this arrangement, this guarantee of thirty thousand a year, this is okay with you?" Goldenburg asked.

"Yes, I was never a greedy person," Amelia said, "but I want my share in life." She reached for another martini.

"We all do," Lola added, smiling at her diamond. "We want you to draw up the papers."

"You have my every guarantee," Goldenburg said. "It'll be a simple thing to arrange. I handle all of Mrs. Le Blanc's affairs."

"I would appreciate it if you'd stop calling her that," Amelia said. Her fingers tightened on the arm of her chair.

"Forgive me," Goldenburg said.

"Sister Amelia," Lola said, "in exchange for your cooperation, I'll never use the name again, I promise."

"I would appreciate it——not that I'm prejudiced or anything," Amelia said. "And one more thing, my name is Miss Le Blanc, not Sister Amelia."

"Of course," Lola answered, searching desperately for a mirror. There was none. "Milton, if you're going to have me as a client, you've got to get a mirror in this stuffy office. A lady likes to see how she looks every now and then."

"Next time you come here," Goldenburg said, "a bigger mirror you've never seen."

After the meeting, Amelia gracefully turned down another ride in the Cadillac. She preferred going back to the airport in the car of Goldenburg's secretary. She also elected not to receive Lola's goodbye kiss. Most of her departure time was spent checking and doublechecking the tentative agreement she'd been given in Goldenburg's office signed by Haskell Hadley Yett and herself. Hadley as a girl's name, Amelia had understood. But calling a girl Haskell had been too much for her.

"Now you understand why I changed it to Lola?" Lola was asking in the parking lot.

"It makes more sense," Amelia said. "No girl wants to go through life known as Haskell. However, I do think you could have selected something more dignified than Lola. Something like Mary." With that parting comment, Amelia was chauffeured away by Goldenburg's secretary.

Ned laughed loudly.

"What you laughing at, nigger?" Lola asked, shielding her eyes from the burning sun.

"We'll never know for sure if Amelia thinks you're a real girl or not," Ned said. "I suspect Joan didn't go into the facts of life with her when she made that call. But the last comment floored me. 'Something like Mary'. Amelia may be hipper than we think."

"I don't care if she takes me for a hermaphrodite," Lola said. "As long as she signed that agreement."

Goldenburg's secretary was circling back, bringing her car to a complete stop only feet away from Lola. Lola jumped back.

With an agility nobody knew she had, Amelia sprang from the car. She was reaching for Lola's hand.

"You forgot a handshake?" Lola asked, baffled.

"Yes, my dear," Amelia said, slipping the Old Mine diamond from Lola's finger. "That was my mother's ring, and I'd like to have it back." Saying no more, she got back in the car. The secretary pulled out again.

Ned laughed once more. "Some chick!"

"I didn't like the old thing anyway," Lola said. "It never did shine." She looked at her bare finger.

Ned opened the car door for her.

She got in, sinking back into the hand-rubbed leather. It'd been too easy, she thought. It took the challenge out of life getting everything you wanted handed to you. A girl needed to struggle for something. Lola had it all.

No, one thing missing.

She didn't have Numie where she wanted him. He'd defied her. But now she'd buy him, too.

Ned was driving her back to her hotel. A chocolate ice cream cone already acquired, and a vanilla waiting in the freezer. The mixed flavors would taste good.

Ned had succumbed quickly enough. Of course, having Dinah off hustling that De la Mer bitch had speeded up his conversion from Dinah to Lola. Little did De la Mer know what a big favor removing Dinah was for Lola. Dinah was too young and pretty to have around. Lola would have to be more careful who she hung out with from now on. Every woman she'd hire would have to be old, fat, and ugly.

There was growing room for only one gardenia in the garden.

Chapter Twenty-Seven

Swathed in white towels and coated with cream, Leonora was lying on a hard board. On a night table beside her bed was an unflattering news photo from a copy of a New York paper. The caption read, 'I'm Dateless and Alive'. Her reply to the Metropolitan Museum had made the front page. Every now and then, Leonora glanced at the picture out of the corner of her eye. The owner of the paper obviously had it in for her. Probably out of jealousy. Pressing a buzzer, Leonora summoned Anne.

In moments Anne was in the beauty chamber. "Good news," she said. "This wire came in about half an hour ago. I didn't know you were up. A firm offer to publish your memoirs."

"My memoirs?" Leonora sat up abruptly. "You write your memoirs when your life is over. Mine isn't!"

"The publisher isn't suggesting it is," Anne said. "He says through your personality he wants to recapture . . . I'll quote directly, 'a glorious, vanished time'."

"Vanished?" Leonora coughed on her own fury. The insults around here were becoming unbearable. She rose from the hard board. First, the news photo flashed in front of her, then her creamed face in the mirror. She'd been badly bruised by the glass doors.

Outside it was still raining. It'd rained all night. Lightning trembled over the treetops of the garden. She crossed the room, throwing open the French doors. Rain pelting her in the face, she stood there for a long moment.

"Has it really come?" she asked herself. "Time to admit defeat? To say that my life is nearly over?" Discovering herself talking out loud, she stopped and glanced back to find Anne listening.

The unwritten pages of her memoirs passed before her eyes, her failure as a woman reflected. If published, the memoirs would be obvious, revealing she'd never found what she'd always wanted: love.

Though she'd never known the love of one man or one woman, she was adored by the public. *Still.* "I'm desired," she whispered to herself, knowing the rain would drown out her voice.

That rain pounded her face harder, and it was telling her something. That she didn't belong here any more locked behind the walls of Sacre-Coeur. She belonged to her public. They hadn't forgotten. They wanted her back. The caption told it all: 'I'm alive'.

Like a patient waking from a deep coma, her eyes were open, but her mind foggy. It was hard to make decisions. But she'd be back on her radiant path soon, back where she belonged, in the main stream again.

Wet from rain, she rushed back into the beauty chamber, grabbing the telegram from Anne's hands. The words flattering her raced through her brain. Only then did she pause in horror. In the corner of the cable was the date: September 13.

The day she was going to die!

. . .

September 13, the day a fortune teller long ago had predicted she'd die. Born on September 13, she was also firmly convinced she'd meet her death on that same day. So firmly did she believe this, she'd ordered the date engraved in advance on her tombstone.

How had it happened that this day had come upon her without her knowing it? Each year, she dreaded the approach of September 13.

If she died now, her entire life would be like a promise unfulfilled.

Carefully, she studied her reflection in the mirror. The bone structure, perfection. Yet could this outward perfection be camouflaging something decaying inside? Could this body that walked and talked be made suddenly silent and inactive? The whole idea of creation——followed by the eventual destruction of life——struck her as the work of a sadistic monster who gave life, forced the victimized human into wanting it, then brutally snuffed it out.

Was what lay beyond the plotting of the most devious of schemers? She knew the transition between lives wouldn't be easy. The thought of what the master schemer had conjured up as her punishment caused her to shudder. Perhaps in her purgatory, she would be locked away in a coffin. There, forced to smell the stench of her own dying body. Perhaps she'd try to breathe when breath was no longer possible. Or perhaps she'd have a fantastic urge to move one muscle, to lift just one finger——and this, too, would be impossible.

What had her life meant this time around other than sheer survival? Had her sorrows been as futile as she now feared? During her lifetime, her cunning had made it possible for her to conquer and subdue her environment. But in spite of this amazing show of strength, she remained fragile and afraid of what lay beyond.

She'd been on this earth before. Of that, there was no doubt. In her wanderings through time, she was Nefertiti ("The Beautiful One is Come"), walking on the mauve sands of what is now Alexandria; Huitzilopochtli, the fearsome god of the Aztecs hungry for human blood; Sappho on the island of Lesbos writing verses to her young female pupil-companions; a pretty Pompeian girl who dressed in elaborate clothes and pursued cultural pastimes, and an Indian maiden in North America who with her brave lover set out to explore the vast regions of a continent.

Now what new fate awaited her?

The rest of this rainy day stretched out. It burned into her flesh.

In a few hours the night would come.

A time for terror.

The buzzer sounded again, Leonora pressing extra hard, as if every decision she made today had to be emphatic.

In moments, Anne was in her bedchamber.

Leonora glared at her. Suddenly she hated Anne's youth, her beauty, the fact she had so many more years to live. "That dear child hasn't been in to see me all day. Send for her."

Without saying a word, Anne turned and left. She was gone for a long time. When she returned, her voice was hesitant. "There's been some trouble."

"What do you mean?" Leonora asked, dropping her face towel.

"Dinah... she's been badly beaten."

"What?" Tossing her mirror on the table, Leonora lunged

toward the door. "Who did it?" Hand at her head she felt a migraine beginning. "Get a doctor."

"I've called already." Anne turned away from Leonora.

Clutching a flimsy robe tighter around her nude body, Leonora was heading down the hall.

"Found her sulking in her room," Anne said, trailing behind. "Said she's used to getting beaten."

"But who could have beaten her here?" Leonora asked. Her purple-glassed eyes and the dim lighting made her see Sacre-Coeur in an eerie glow. "I know the house is filled with monsters, but I thought civilized ones." In her race to Dinah's room, Leonora could hear the rush of her own breath. During the last hour, the rain had let up, becoming a slow mist. The whole house seemed to contain nothing but looming shadows and gaunt silhouettes.

Now she was inside Dinah's room. The girl was on her bed, her face hidden in the pillow. The only illumination came from a silk-shaded bedside lamp. The drawn draperies gave a deathly feeling to the room.

At her side, Leonora reached for Dinah trying to turn her over.

"I don't want you to see me this way," she sobbed. "You think I'm so pretty and everything."

"Don't be ridiculous, I must see you." Leonora's determination was reflected by her grim-jawed look. Though perspiring, Dinah had an odor both sweet and aromatic.

Unfulfilled desire knotted Leonora's stomach, even when touching the girl in this condition.

Trembling, Dinah turned over. Her face was bruised. Her tears blurred the vision of her large dark eyes, which were bloodshot and blinking. She lifted her head from the pillow.

Leonora gently ran her fingers across Dinah's face. "Who would do such a thing?"

"That goddamn Ned!" Dinah said, talking with apologetic slowness. "The son of a bitch beat me up for leaving him for you."

Leonora looked at Dinah with infinite reproachfulness, then softened her glare. She released the girl.

"I wasn't his *real* girl friend," Dinah protested. "He used me... against my wishes."

"Of course it was against your wishes," Leonora replied quickly, her back stiffening. The first awful reality that Dinah was a liar flashed through her brain. "I've been close to you. I know what your real feelings are."

Dinah's hand reached out for hers. This one action warmed Leonora. The girl's flashing eyes closed as Leonora tightened her grip. "How did he get in here?" Leonora asked.

"Ralph brought him here," Dinah said. "Picked him up cruising. Ned came to my room after Ralph had gone to sleep. Held me and beat my face against the bed."

"Why didn't you scream for help?" Leonora asked. The icy white of the room was drenching her. She wanted to scream herself.

"I did," Dinah said weakly, "but he turned the music up loud."

"I remember that," Leonora said, softly cupping Dinah's breasts. "I was going to send Anne up to complain to you." Her fingers gently caressed the flesh.

"Ned was just using Ralph," Dinah confessed. "Got Ralph to agree to let him drive up to the mainland to pick up the commodore's sister. Lola was with him."

The word, Lola, was like a wasp sting to Leonora. Now she saw it clearly. A betrayal. Ralph was to blame. Controlling her emotions, she reached down and smoothed the wrinkled covers of Dinah's bed. Then she bit down on her lip. "The cocksucker." She was shocked at her use of the word. Normally, she didn't use vulgarity and loathed its use in other people. But this time it just tumbled out.

"Ned works for Lola," Dinah said.

"This is incredible." Leonora turned to Anne. "Your husband's going to pay for this."

"All of a sudden he's my husband," Anne protested. "Ralph's no husband to me. You got me to marry him, remember?"

Leonora resented Anne all the more. Everyone was turning against her. Then she felt Dinah squeezing her hand again. No, there was one loyal person in the snakepit. "Get the commodore's attorney on the phone. I've been doublecrossed." She raised her hand, "This time Ralph Douglas has gone too far!"

. . .

Leonora was alone. Gales of rain pounded the house in fury. But upstairs her bedroom seemed far removed from the storm, a safe haven.

She lay quietly, listening to the lashing rain. In spite of the violence outside, it was a moment of peace from the storm raging inside her during this all too brief summer. The rain pounded against the house, the wind rattling the shutters of her bedroom window.

Where is Ralph?

She sat up rigidly in bed at the sound of a crash outside.

"Ralph," she called out, expecting him to appear.

A loud rap sounded on the door and Ralph was inside her room. "May I come in?"

"Don't ask when you're already in my room." Her words fell like the sharp blade of a guillotine. "Of course, you can come in. I sent for you, didn't I?"

"Yes," he said, walking deeper into the dark chamber. "You're *always* sending for me."

"You get paid, don't you?" She studied his face as if it held a profound secret.

"Indeed I do," he said, "and quite well. You're very generous." She detected an edge of sarcasm from him, which angered her.

The room pulsed with vibrations of impending violence. "One must buy people's loyalty," she sighed. "It's the only way." Her words struck him like bullets and he winced. "Open that curtain, just slightly," she commanded. "I want to see the storm."

He parted the velvet draperies, as lightning tore the sky. The white flash revealed Leonora's nude body sprawled on mauve sheets. "Do you want me to get you a robe?" he asked flatly.

"No," she replied, smiling. "When a body is as perfectly preserved as mine——at my age——one doesn't mind showing it off." She was deliberately making everything she said weighted with meaning. Soon she would be ready to spring the trap. "I know I'm not black, but men and women of all ages have found me attractive."

"So do I." Ralph lied. "I hope you don't think I am attracted only to blacks."

"I was beginning to wonder." Leonora's eyes were like hard blue diamonds.

"I notice you're not exactly immune to the charms of blacks yourself." His eyes focused swiftly on her, searching her out. "Dinah seems to be sticking around for a repeat performance."

His mention of Dinah brought a swift change in Leonora. Her face softened.

"That child, such a lovely innocent one." Her face glowed with anticipation. "Yes, she wants me." Reaching for her robe, Leonora got out of bed, grandly pacing like a high priestess, her simple, Grecian, white-satin gown cascading to the floor. "The whole world desires me," she announced.

"Understandably so." He glanced at her mirrored image.

Turning on the light, she stared into Ralph's eyes. He was trying to flatter her, she knew. She also was aware that he was offended by the nude female body. Perhaps, she thought, that's why she always appeared naked before him. It was a quirk in her own behavior she couldn't fully understand. Was she a missionary trying to convert him? Did she think that by looking at her he would come to see women as desirable sex objects? She resented him for not finding her body attractive, always turning in disgust at the sight of her nudity. Or worse, not seeming to notice her at all. She glared at him.

"Let me outline what you've done to me," she rasped. "You picked up that creature, Ned, who just happens to be Lola's consort." She paused to let her words sink in. "You allowed this Ned to come into Sacre-Coeur, let him talk you into going to meet the commodore's sister on the mainland." Looking at her many images in the mirrored room, Leonora yelled, "All part of a plot by Lola!" She shuddered at the sudden chill in the room. "That hideous beast accompanied Ned, for your information." A vision of what she must look like to the startled Ralph raced through her mind. With her face enraged, her eyes like knives cutting into his flesh, he must be frightened out of his mind. Leonora was delighted at the thought. "Amelia Le Blanc never made it to Tortuga; she was taken right into the office of the commodore's attorney." Leonora dabbed at her perspiring face with a tissue. "Amelia and Lola reached a settlement before I got a chance to talk to the commodore's sister." She took a deep breath, glaring at Ralph. "My one last chance to prevent having Lola as a partner has vanished, because of your stupidity." Her shoulders tightened. She moved toward him menacingly, and he took an involuntary step backward. "What is even worse, my dear Ralph, is that Ned used to be Dinah's boy friend." She glanced at Ralph, expecting him to speak. "In the middle of the night, he sneaked out of your bed, slipped upstairs to Dinah's room, and beat her within an inch of her life."

"I can't believe that," Ralph stammered, turning from her.

"I don't have to prove anything to you," she said contemptuously. For one brief moment, her hatred subsided. A tender feeling came over her. A memory. Maybe it was the distortion caused by the tropical storm. But Ralph's face became that of his father, the man she had loved long ago. She waited to reach out and caress that face. Then she remembered it was not her lost lover she was looking at, but his dreadful son. Ralph had never been her friend. The only reason she'd put up with him was because he was his father's son. But his father had betrayed her. Now the son had followed in his footsteps. She *must* remember that. "I don't have to tell you the complete case I have against you," she said, regaining her voice. "You're fired! As of this moment."

A stricken look crossed his face, a vein stood out in his left temple. Then he slammed his fist on a table. "You can't fire me."

"I not only can, I just did." She turned her back on him.

All color left Ralph's face. Silence filled the room, but it was more deafening than an avalanche and even blotted out the storm. His tone became conciliatory. "You're just upset. You don't know what you're saying."

"I have never been more certain of anything in my life. Her hand grasped a heavy mirror on her dressing table, as a slight tremor of fear made her think she might need it as a weapon. She turned to face him. "You've sponged off me long enough," she spat the words at him contemptuously.

"Sponged?" Ralph's hands became balled fists. "I've catered to your insane whims, endured your outrageous behavior... any money you ever paid me, I more than earned."

"You know I don't like to talk about money." She began to

move away from him. "I'm more interested in the spirit than I am the cash register."

"I've seen you count the take," he charged. "You're very interested."

"Not really," she said, retreating even more. She felt it was a dangerous risk being alone on this particular day with him. "I don't need the money, but I must keep it from the hands of those it would destroy."

"By that, I assume you mean me." Ralph froze in his steps.

"Exactly." Leonora staggered, holding onto a chair for support. Invisible destructive currents were about to sweep the room. She had to brace herself for them.

"You destroyed me in a thousand other ways," he said. "You played on my weaknesses. You bought——yes, bought——my friendship. If you hadn't entered my life, I could have become a great playwright." He was shouting.

"You were always a mediocre writer," she said with a hiss. "I was always the artiste in this household." Her face hardened like plaster.

"Don't make me laugh," he said bitingly. "You're a third-rate designer. Your clothes are theatrical crap! Most people who have had successful careers had to bust their balls. Yours was handed to you on a platter. You bought your way with Norton Huttnar's money."

The words, flung like a curse, flashed before her. "That's a damnable lie, and you know it." She clenched her hands. She wanted to strike him across the face. "Just yesterday I was on the front page of a New York newspaper."

"Do you know why?" he challenged her. "Because you're a caricature. In your old age I would have thought you'd learned some dignity. You're more a fool than ever." His face loomed threateningly into hers, specks of saliva splattering her as he talked.

She backed away again. "You miserable loser. How dare you attack me!" Her hand, holding the mirror, began to quiver. "You groveling little fairy."

"Don't use that outdated term with me, you broken down old dyke."

Once again, she raised her hand to slap him. But she feared physical retaliation. She was taking far too many chances on

September 13. "No one has called me that loathsome word *ever*." A memory of Albury flashed before her.

"Not to your face maybe," Ralph said. "But behind your back." He looked poised for the kill. "No one's told you the truth in years, either. Not until today."

"You don't even know what truth is." She pushed back her hair, the soothing gesture giving her renewed spirit. "All these years I've tried to elevate you, give you some philosophy to live by." Suddenly she felt exposed before him, in spite of her robe. The feeling made her uncomfortable. She put down the mirror and clutched the satin robe to her body. "But you're still the crude, coarse boy I always knew you were."

"You don't have a philosophy of life to pass on to anybody," he said, his eyes darkening violently. "You make pretty speeches that always get out of hand——fruity, opulent speeches. But you're just posing and prancing."

"I speak from the conviction of my heart, you liar." Her anger exploded on him.

"You don't have a heart," he snapped, moving toward the door.

"You always agreed with much of my philosophy," she shouted. If he left now, he'd leave in victory. She hadn't fully destroyed him yet.

"The only reason I agreed with you was that I was on your payroll," Ralph said, turning.

The words shattered her and her face became blank with shock.

"I'll tell you why you're surrounded only by people on your payroll," Ralph went on. "They can't afford to talk back."

"Dinah's not on my payroll." Her shout was of outraged incredulity. "She loves me just for myself."

"How we deceive ourselves," he said with a mocking smile. "Dinah's nothing but a cheap, larcenous hooker who's hustling you, same as Ned hustled me. Let's face it, Leonora, the only time you and I have ever had sex is when we've paid for it. Nobody else could stand us."

"Speak for yourself," she shouted, her eyes filling with tears. "I'm highly desirable."

He wiped his lips as if to remove contamination.

"You're nothing! A mirage. There's nothing real about you."

His hands tore at his hair. "You're no international beauty. I read your tombstone." He paused, lowering his voice. "You're pathetic," he mumbled.

"You're the one who's pathetic, you excuse for a man." She was out of control now. "Get out of Sacre-Coeur! There's a monster in your heart." She raised her hands and shook a fist at him. "I knew it'd find its voice one day. If only to turn on me." She was in desperate need of a barricade to cut her off from this man. "I knew I was going to die this day, but I didn't know you were to be my executioner."

"You're nothing but a bitter old woman lost in her fantasies and illusions," Ralph roared. "You deserve to die." He turned and left the room, slamming the door in her face.

Outside the storm shrieked and wailed.

But higher still came an eerie falsetto, rending the night.

It was the sound of Leonora screaming.

. . .

For a short while, the storm had let up. Numie was heading down the littered main street of town. Not a soul was in sight.

He had been to see Tangerine, and was certain she was going to live. She'd survived the operation beautifully. At least that nagging fear was over.

Out on this lonely street tonight turned his mind to all the other lonely streets he'd roamed. Footsore and with a deep hatred in his heart, he'd been looking for sex-buyers.

Tonight he didn't even have that goal to explain his strange presence outside when everybody else was safely at home riding out the storm.

Deep down, right at his core, he had to admit this summer had left him with no understanding of who he was. The only new insight he'd come up with was that there was an ordinariness about him. For thirty-two years, he'd assured himself constantly he was special. Was it all a lie?

After a few blocks, he was at the gates of Sacre-Coeur. Somehow tonight their bars looked more ominous and foreboding than ever. Slipping into the side entrance, he headed across the garden. Time to report for duty.

Two hours later, he hadn't moved from his chair in the living room. Draperies pulled back, he watched the storm return again in all its fury. Sitting there slowly sipping his Scotch, he felt a womblike warmth. For one moment, he was at peace——protected from the menace outside.

He remained in the same position, thinking how much he needed this rest, this retreat from Tortuga, from Leonora, from Ralph, from Lola, and even from Anne. His own company gave him a momentary delight.

A harsh buzzer interrupted his cozy reverie.

At the top of the stairs, he hesitated, then knocked and went inside.

Anne was holding Leonora down.

He rushed to Anne's side. "What's the matter?" he asked in panic.

Leonora's eyes were bugged, her face flushed red.

"I can't keep her still," Anne said. "She wants to go out...to the graveyard!"

To Numie, Leonora looked like some insane sorceress, who wanted to drag him down into unknown horror.

"New...me," Leonora screeched. Her hands were reaching for his.

Reluctantly, he offered her one. Long nails were digging into his flesh. He pulled away, his hand badly clawed.

"What the hell..."

Gravestones of buried memories were giving up their captives tonight. From shadows in the far corner of the room these nameless ghosts began to take shape in front of her. Norton Huttnar, Ruthie Elvina. They were just the vanguard. So many others were waiting to follow. "Sacre-Coeur," she yelled. "My beloved Sacre-Coeur."

"It's going to be okay," Numie assured her. He was terrified of the horror he sensed in her eyes. The lights dimmed, then came on again.

"Look," Leonora said, gripping his hand firmly, "the lights... they're going out..." Her body jerked with frenzy. Total darkness she couldn't stand.

The lights dimmed again, then flickered on.

"We have hurricane lamps," Anne said, looking hopelessly at Numie, her eyes pleading for him to help her. "I'll get them." She quickly left the room.

Every now and then, the flashing lightning sent stabs of white through the room.

"I'm not going to be safe here," Leonora protested. "I can feel it." Her fear now was leaving her for only brief moments, then returning with a vengeance. "There's a force at work to destroy all things beautiful." Her fingernails dug once more into Numie's sensitive flesh.

He winced with pain. Her hand held him firmly. It was like a death grip. Still, he tried to remain calm. Had Leonora gone totally mad? The walls of the old house rattled. "You should try to get some rest," he said, knowing how silly that sounded.

In a burst of energy, she let go of him, got up from the bed, and was stumbling around. He reached to steady her.

"Everyone except Dinah is trying to conspire against me," she said, staring at him with fury. "Even you for all I know."

"That's not true," he said. His whole body was shaking, and he braced himself for an attack from her. "Anne and I are trying to look after you."

"No," she said. She writhed and plunged around the room, as if looking for something. She stopped long enough to confront him again. "Both of you think I'm no longer in control." She then rushed toward her closet. Taking out an old silver mink, she slipped it on. "You're going to drive me to the graveyard."

"In this weather?" he asked, dumbfounded. In the main hall the storm was a dim noise, but outside it sounded more like galloping horses. "You must be out of your..." He paused, biting his tongue before he said it.

"No," she said, her calm moment returning. "I'm not out of my mind."

For this brief interlude, she was like the old Leonora, completely calling the shots.

"You're my driver," she said firmly, her back stiff. "If you refuse, I'll fire you." Thoughts of Ralph flashed through her mind. He didn't think he was going to get fired either. "I've already fired one tonight."

"You mean Ralph?" Numie asked. The air was oppressive. He was having a hard time breathing.

"Are you going to drive me there?" She would have fired him on the spot, but only hours remained in her life. Knowing that, she had to deal with what she had.

Not really caring about the job at this point, he sighed, "If you want to go." He felt if he didn't take her, she would try to go there on her own——and would surely get killed.

In the hallway, he was racing after her. The lightning outlined her silvery frame, as she rushed dangerously down the marble steps.

Anne confronted him at the bottom of the stairs.

"You're not taking her, surely," she said. In her hand was a hurricane lamp.

He reached for her free hand, but she withdrew it. "I'll explain everything later," he said. "There's just no time right now."

"In this storm, you'll never make it. You'll have an accident," Anne said, grabbing onto his arm.

He broke away. "I've got to take her."

Bitterness swept across Anne's face. Tears formed. "You're as much a fool as she is."

By now, Leonora had thrown open the oak doors. The storm howled inside the parlor.

. . .

Shattered shop windows, flooded streets, fallen cornices, evidence of the storm was everywhere.

Behind the wheel and driving into the blinding rain, Numie was cursing, fearing for their safety. Several times he flicked imaginary ashes from his cigarette before they formed.

The rain continued to lash against the windshield. He shook with a sudden cold. The headlights from the Lincoln hardly made a difference against the blackness of the night. Not one light shown anywhere.

The storm was getting worse. He was driving so slowly now the Lincoln was barely moving.

"Hurry up," she screamed at him in the earphone. "It's almost midnight."

By now he was convinced: Leonora was insane. Why would anyone on a night like this want to be taken to the graveyard?

Then, suddenly, the reason became clear.

September 13, the day engraved on her tombstone. That was

today!

Leonora must be convinced she was going to die.

Glancing into the back, he viewed her with pity. She must be experiencing the agonies of the damned.

It was five minutes to midnight.

Panic overwhelmed Leonora. Under the silver mink, her entire body was soaked with perspiration. Then suddenly crystal clear came a jarring thought. Was she experiencing not actual death, the death of the body, but the symbolic death of the soul? Was she becoming merely a ghostly shell of herself? Had her heart grown cold? Had the denial of love from every source caused her to dry up? Was she no more than a zombie, making her physical presence felt, but having nothing else to offer the world?

It was four minutes to midnight.

If there be a God, and she didn't believe there was one, but if there were, would he smile on her tonight? Give her that second chance? Return her to a state of innocence? Let her go back and live it again——freed of the hatred, the jealousies, the mockeries? She would give away anything——her fashion house, Sacre-Coeur, her furs, her jewels, her stocks and bonds——if God would grant her this one favor. It was such a small thing to ask.

It was three minutes to midnight.

A distant memory returned. She was a little girl again playing on the summer sand. She stopped for a moment, breathing in the salt air. For the last two months, she'd been sick. Her father was disgusted with her and didn't love her. Even her more patient mother was tired of waiting on her. She secretly feared they were going to poison her if she didn't get better. She prayed. God had answered her prayers. She was out of bed——alive and well. She could run and frolic in the sand. At the far end of the beach, some children were playing. She'd show everybody she was okay again——just like the rest of them. Madly she started to run toward the other children. They saw her coming. One boy was pointing at her. He was laughing. Now, another boy was laughing. All of the children were turning, laughing, mocking. The pain in her side grew worse. Falling on the sand, she cried out for her mother. "Come and get me. I'm still sick!"

It was two minutes before midnight.

The wind was blowing the rain against the panes of the Lincoln, water splashing all around her. She could see nothing. Numie had cut off the lights. Was she already buried in a watery grave? Was the car her coffin? She felt cold now. The perspiration had miraculously dried up. Her heart was beating so loudly its sound was like the grandfather clock she kept in her parlor. Was she just going to sit there? Let death find her? Put up no resistance?

It was now one minute to midnight.

Opening the rear door, she raced across the graveyard in the blinding rain. She must find her tombstone. Destroy it! Scratch the lettering off with her bare fingernails if it would save her life. By having the tombstone engraved, she might have set off the forces of her own doom.

In the darkness, all the tombstones were the same. Each and every one was emblazoned with her name and the day of her death!

Stumbling over a fallen wreath of flowers, she fell forward, tumbling onto a mound of dirt. She screamed at the top of her voice. Her breath came in gasps. The rain whipped her face, stinging.

Hands were on her, reaching for her and pulling up her mud-soaked, soggy body.

"You're going to live, Leonora," Numie shouted. "It's after midnight. But you'll catch pneumonia if you don't get out of this damn rain!"

Chapter Twenty-Eight

The morning after the storm, the sky was strangely still. Nothing seemed to be stirring, not even a bird in flight. From an upstairs window at Sacre-Coeur; the patio spread before Numie. Empty. Except for a broken-legged pelican hobbling across the fallen palm fronds.

"The sun's out," he said out loud. The house itself had been spared.

In the hallway, he paused at Leonora's door, but didn't knock.

He was searching for Anne. But she was nowhere to be found. Had she made it through the storm? She couldn't be found last night when he brought Leonora back from the graveyard.

The parlor was in shambles.

In the garden, he turned and looked back at Sacre-Coeur. Then he left the house avoiding the fallen branch of a ceiba tree.

The sun had fully emerged in the sky. Shivering in the morning breezes, he made his way down the main street.

The townspeople's faces were drawn; they were moving about quietly, surveying the damage. Already the sun was turning the fallen green vegetation yellow.

In a doorway, an old woman sat, weeping softly at her smashed frontporch swing.

In the presence of all these people and all this activity, he felt lonely and abandoned. He wanted to escape the island. The world here was too strangely disturbing to give him peace.

If only he could get an answer to his letter. Such a long time to wait. Maybe when the mail was shipped down from the mainland today, he'd have a reply.

At Tangerine's battered house, he stopped. The rickety stairway had been ripped from the building. The roof was smashed; and the house sagged dangerously on its foundation.

He stood here silently for a while, as the sun jabbed its way through the cracks in the broken shutters. Then he went through the gate and never looked back.

The hotel was still standing. He wondered if Lola were

inside. He didn't care enough to check.

A fly buzzed in and lit on his nose. He struck at it so furiously he hurt himself.

Then he went on his way.

. . .

At the hospital, there was a flurry of activity. No one noticed him. Everybody was too busy. Passing long lines of people waiting for typhoid shots, he continued on. Other lines were forming for Red Cross soup.

Apprehensive about Tangerine's condition, he hurried into her ward. In the emergency, men had been wheeled in with the women. A shriveled old man, toothless and sunken-eyed, his head bandaged, lay in his own waste. Nobody had time to change him. He just lay here, whimpering.

Tangerine heaved herself up to greet him. "Thank God you're here," she said, a look of grave concern on her pale face. He'd never seen her completely without makeup before. A ponderous weariness covered her face. The irises of her once-vibrant green eyes seemed diluted. A frail, tender hand——the veins purple——was reaching for him.

He put his hand in hers.

She was shaking. "I think someone on the staff is trying to poison me," she whispered confidentially.

"What a charge," he said, leaning over and kissing her cheek. "Who?"

"The nurse," she said. "I've got no big hospital insurance. None at all. A charity patient they call me." She faltered for a moment, as if losing her ability to speak. "I think they have a way of bumping you off here if you can't pay their highway robbery prices. They need the beds. Look at that poor slob over there."

"I did." Nausea swept over Numie. He fought it back. "Don't worry." He patted her hand. "Your bill's going to be taken care of. I've already talked to the doctor."

"You mean Leonora is going to help?" Her eyes brightened momentarily.

"Not exactly," he said, "but everything's going to be okay." He was telling a lie. The look on her face told him she knew it.

"Why hasn't Leonora been to see me?" Her grip was tightening on his hand.

"Leonora's a bit crazy right now." The painful memory of the graveyard scene came back to him. "The commodore's death has left her in a state. She can't go out, but she asks about you all the time."

"That's good," she sighed. Her voice was a mixture of anger and resignation. "What about Lola? She hasn't been in either."

"Lola's been busy," he explained in a rushed whisper. Did Tangerine really expect Lola to show up? "Again, the commodore's death. You know Lola. She gets completely caught up in what she's doing."

For a while she seemed to withdraw from him, her eyes closed. Then she sat up a bit. "I'll be well soon."

"I know you will," he said with all the conviction he could muster. His earlier optimism about her condition had given way to doubt.

"Before you go, you've got to talk to the doctor again," she said, reaching out.

He tenderly touched her face. "He's pretty busy this morning."

She lay back, becoming completely limp. "The entire staff's got it in for me. The other day, the head nurse came in and said, 'With all your demands, you'd think you'd been living in the Taj Mahal. Miss Blanchard, I happen to know you live in a rundown hovel.'" Hateful thoughts seemed to stir her back to life. "Well, my place may not be the Taj Mahal, but it's a hell of a lot better than this stinking hole."

He covered her body with a blanket.

"Anyway," she went on, "I've worn out my welcome here." She slung the blanket carelessly from her. "When they start giving you prunes three times a day——my daddy always said——it's time to pack up and get moving down the road."

"I don't want to get into an argument with you," he said, "but your doctor has you on a diet for a very specific reason." Her resentment at his saying this was clear. Was she now considering him one of the conspirators against her?

"Besides," she said, "everybody makes me feel like a slob." Once again she tried to sit up wearily.

"What do you mean?" he asked, automatically taking her

wrist and rubbing her arm.

"They don't let me tend to my private business——in private, the way they should." Her eyes drifted to some dead roses on the nearby table. "They stand around watching me. A lady should do some things in private."

The odor of rubbing alcohol assailed his nostrils. He couldn't stand it. "I'm sure they're not looking at you because it turns them on."

"No, naturally." She was getting more and more impatient with him. "It's their way of humiliating me."

He poured a glass of water into the flowers, though it was clear they were dead. "Really, they're just doing their job."

"Now you're taking up for them." Her frail, trembling hand gained renewed strength to push herself farther away from him.

"No, I'm not," he protested. He seemed frightened all of a sudden. Tangerine was dying, he just knew it.

"Go on," she said, "if that's the way you feel, you don't have to come around no more." She rolled over, turning her back to him.

"That's not the way I feel," he said, thinking Tangerine was becoming more and more a stranger. "But you must be reasonable."

"Now I'm being unreasonable," she said, sulking. "Before I got sick, you always thought I made sense."

"I still do," he said, looking at her pale orange hair, never realizing how thin it was. On the crown was a bald spot.

A nurse was now in the room. "These aren't visiting hours," she snapped at Numie. "Get out! Can't you see there's an emergency this morning?"

"I can see that poor man over there needs your help," he answered angrily.

"That's not my job," the nurse said. "We have volunteers for that kind of duty."

"She hates me," Tangerine whispered suddenly, confidential with him again.

"She's just a bitch, but I don't think she really hates you," he said, finding some hope in her new mood. As long as she's fighting, there's spirit left in her, he thought.

"Sure, she does," Tangerine said. "I got so mad at her the

other day I told her her vaginal cavity was too puckered up to accommodate a real man."

"I believe you did!" He bent over and kissed her goodbye.

"I'd really appreciate it if you could slip me a little booze tomorrow," she said. "I'm so dry I'm spitting cotton."

"We'll see." He was at the door when she called him back.

"I'm going to be able to get around?" she asked, her eyes wide but vacant. "Just like before?"

"Of course," he said, smiling falsely. "There's nothing in the world like a Georgia gal. They can drop two kids in the morning, and be out plowing corn in the afternoon."

"I know that," she said, perking up. "I just wanted to hear you say it."

. . .

On the roof deck at Sacre-Coeur, the September sun was making Numie drowsy. Taking some suntan lotion, he rubbed his nude body, covering himself with the oil. His skin seemed extremely white and tender today——vulnerable somehow. He poured the oil on thick, rubbing it in well. Just playing, he filled his belly-button, taking his little finger and tracing patterns on his chest. An aimless act, aimless as the day itself.

After his oiling, he collapsed on the rubber matting, spreading his body out like a starfish. He whistled softly, as if to make up for the lack of birds in the sky. Then he lit a cigarette. After a few puffs, he flicked the ashes between the redwood boards of the deck.

Unlike the blue sky, his future was cloudy. Patience, that's what he must have now. He'd have to wait for an answer to his letter. Everything depended on his getting that answer. He prayed that the recipient would reply. It had been so many years since they'd been in touch.

Half-formulated thoughts raced through his mind, only to be rubbed out by the darkness of last night. The rain, the graveyard. His dreams had been unsettling. He was fleeing. But from what? Who were the unknown assassins?

Now, he remembered more clearly. In his dream he'd been fleeing across a meadow somewhere. It was in the spring, but the vegetation was gray, as if covered with moth dust. A harsh wind was blowing, stirring up the powdery substance, blinding him at times.

Whirling through the air were butterflies with glass wings. Their shadows reflected on the ground, making them look like giant bats come to devour him. At first he'd been afraid. But then, seeing they were butterflies, he'd stopped running. Butterflies were harmless.

Or were they?

On closer inspection, these transparent creatures were becoming life sized.

Cold and tired, and completely out of breath, he fell on the wet earth.

Suddenly, the butterflies descended. Their many-jointed antennae were made of tiny threadlike silver wires. Their heads were small, but their compound eyes were large and menacing.

The faces on the butterflies——Leonora, Lola, Ralph, Johnny Yellowwood, Joan, Dinah, Ned, Commodore Philip, Castor Q. Combes, even Tangerine——flashed before him. They were circling over him. Through their transparent wings, he could see the sky and the clouds beyond. Then his horrified face was reflected hundreds of times as those same wings became mirrors.

Their mouths——coiled up like watch springs at rest——were extending into great elongated sucking tubes. They were seeking nectar from the flower.

He was the flower; his blood the nectar.

At the end of their sucking tubes were toothed spines. With these, they were lacerating his skin to get to the arteries inside.

He sat up with a bolt.

Even though the sun was hot, his body was icy cold.

He shielded his eyes from the sun and peered at a shadowy figure looming over him.

It was Dinah. One side of her face was bandaged.

He made no attempt to cover his nude body. "What happened to you?"

"A present from Ned, all tied up with a neat little red ribbon." She gently ran her hand across her face.

"Some gift!"

Dinah was beside him, removing her robe. She was nude too. Taking an adjoining mat, she lay back. Her breasts were small, her body, muscular. "I like chocolate-covered ice cream bars." She sighed and puckered her lip. "Why don't you go downstairs and get me one?"

"Right now?" He looked at her for a long moment wondering what her game was. "I'm not a servant."

Her next look was too bloodthirsty for comfort. "That's not what I hear," she said. In a quick puff, she swallowed a whole gulp of fresh air, closed her eyes and faced the sun. "You forget, I'm the lady of the manor now."

"Ring for it," he said angrily. "There's a maid." He was astonished at how quickly she'd adopted to the good life.

"Skip it." She gyrated on the mat. "I've got something better. Think I'll have a little blow." She reached into the pocket of her discarded robe and pulled out a folded hundred-dollar bill. In that bill, she carried her cocaine. Opening the bill, she sniffed it, then reached for a little silver spoon around her neck, dipping it into the powder and carefully lifting it to her nostrils. "Sweet perfume," she said. She inhaled the powder as if it were the breath of life. She didn't say anything at first, nor did she offer any to him.

"I'm surprised you left Ned," he said. "I thought he was super daddy."

"I was in love with Ned till I saw what kind of man he was." She practically spat. "Pussy whipped by a drag queen." Dinah looked him straight in the eye with a look that could kill. "Can't respect no man who'd let a fag do that to him. Besides, Ned made me hustle my ass night and day." She fingered her silver spoon. "Leonora is much more understanding, not so demanding."

"Besides, she can support your habit better," he said sarcastically, hating her, hating himself, hating whoring in general.

"I hear you talking!" She leaned back gingerly on the matting. "I was just a tool to Ned. Someone to feed him, to fuck him, like a goddamn machine." She ran her fingers down her child-like breasts and assumed a sexy pose. "Leonora has taught me about women's liberation. Did you know she was the slave of a son-of-a-bitch one time herself? Huttnar, some mindfucking name like that."

He leaned back, feeling the sun was getting too hot. "She

told me."

"As long as Ned needed me, I was willing to get out on that street and hustle my ass." She was roaring mad. "Now he's got the queen——he don't need me. Getting into that old queen's hole is more of a turn-on to him than being with the real thing." Like a pussycat, she seemed to be clawing the deck. "I'm no longer his Li'l Bit. Li'l Bit has become a whole lot, and here's one 'ho who's doing it all by herself——with a little help from Leonora."

He smiled. "I see Leonora has completely converted you."

"The bitch is giving me a better game, that's all," she said, sitting up. "I'll be with her until I get an even better game." Her eyes surveyed the grounds below. "Li'l Bit's going places in this world." She sat back on her legs slouched down, and looked ready to pounce. "Now, why don't you do some traveling yourself? I came up here to use the sundeck. I didn't know it was used by the hired hands, too. I must speak to Leonora. I believe in equal facilities, but separate ones."

He got up and stood for a long moment looking down at her. He decided it was hopeless to talk to her. Putting a towel around his nude body, he headed downstairs.

This troubled, hurried summer seemed to be moving rapidly to its end.

. . .

Numie slipped down the winding staircase, his bare feet making no sound on the marble. In the parlor he stopped to survey the storm's damage. A velvet sofa was saturated. Shattered glass covered the room, and vases and lamps had fallen over. The room was bathed in a green light coming in from the half open shutters. A fly circled a wall sconce, its nasal buzzing seemingly vibrating the crystal pendants.

Through the open glass doors, he walked out onto the brick patio, feeling the rise of the heat. Blinking his eyes, he adjusted to the sun after the darkness of the parlor. The leaves of the palm trees hung motionless. Nothing was stirring in the garden this late morning. Then the broken-legged pelican emerged again, searching for something lost last night.

Darting back at the sound of footsteps, he concealed himself behind a shrub. He was in no mood for confrontation today.

It was Ralph, carrying a small overnight bag. His large eyes were streaked with red, and perspiration had matted his hair. A small bit of excessive saliva bubbled out of the corner of his mouth.

Anne was behind him, running her fingers nervously through her hair.

"You my bon voyage party?" he asked.

"I was never your party——you know that," she said.

His eyes met hers in a steady gaze. "Imagine being married to you all these years, and I'm still a virgin——at least with women."

Her shoulders collapsed, and her arms flapped down by her sides. "That's not something I want to remember."

The clock in the parlor behind them struck the hour. There was a long silence.

"Why did you stick it out?" he asked. "I never could figure that out."

Anne went to the bar for a beer. A cat had climbed over the wall and was rummaging through the garbage. At first she looked as if she were going to chase it away, then she turned her back to it. "I clung to some sort of security," she said vacantly. "How could I have ever thought that being with you would keep me from ending up lonely one day?"

He put his bag down. "Frankly, I don't know." The tone of his voice grew petulant. "I certainly never encouraged you being with me."

She wiped beer from the corner of her mouth. "I know."

He glanced around the patio. "It'll be tough leaving this place." His cold fist banged into the palm of his hand. "I've always had trouble making decisions for myself. With Leonora, it was easy. She made them for me." Reaching into his overnight bag, he pulled out a pair of sunglasses. "I think that's why I was attracted to Leonora in the first place. No decisions necessary. Every day planned."

Taking some face lotion, Anne absently oiled herself. "What are you going to do now?"

He took off one of his loafers and removed a sand spur. "See if I can make it on my own. I'll get wheels under me, and ride off some of the bitterness I feel for Leonora."

Putting the lotion down suddenly, Anne reached for a cigarette. Though her voice was outwardly calm, her hand was shaking. "What about your things?" she asked. "Where can I send them?"

The question seemed to stun him for a moment. "A moving van will come for them in a few weeks," he replied.

In a moment of anger, Anne tossed the beer can at the cat. "A divorce——what about that?"

He walked up to her. "Does it really matter? I don't plan to get married again, and I'm sure you're no longer interested in marriage. An antiquated custom by today's standards."

"Okay, we'll ignore it," she agreed. She opened another beer. "Pretend it never happened."

He shifted uneasily. "I plan to go on one big tour of this country——find out what it's all about." He moved around the patio in a wild burst of energy. "All the way to the lumberjacks around Seattle, sampling the wares along the way." He looked back at her and smiled. "I've got the money. Now I've got the time." He paused, then asked. "What about you?"

Anne studied the cat, now sitting on top of the garbage can, a look of defiance on its face. She seemed to be making some judgment about it, respecting its independence and total self-interest. "I'll be leaving soon myself," she said. "Returning to New York. I should never have come to Tortuga. Neither should you, but it's too late to talk about that now."

He exhaled slowly, as if bored already with her plans. "What will you do there?"

She straightened up, her sharp features implacable. "Find a job. See if there's any life worth living for me." She shrugged her shoulders. "What can any of us do?" A bitterness came into her voice. "Unlike you, I don't have any money. Leonora was never very generous with me."

He laughed sardonically. "She wasn't that generous with me either," he said. "I took what I wanted."

She shook her head from side to side, as if not comprehending, not believing. "You embezzled?"

Triumphant defiance crossed his face. "My father did that before me. Guess I took after him." He clutched his arms tightly. "I'd give you some now to help you get out of here, but I'll need every penny. I don't know where I'm going to get any more."

She put her hand to her mouth.

"You aren't going to cry or do something stupid like that?" he asked.

"No," she said, regaining control.

"That's good." He allowed himself a small smile. "What is it then?"

"All of a sudden," she said in a jerky voice, "I had this awful feeling that I've been standing still——not moving ahead at all with my life."

"Yeah," he said impatiently, "I know it well." He glanced at his watch. "I've got to go. There's a plane out today."

As if grateful for this return to the practical side of life, she asked, "Want me to drive you to the airport?"

"No," he said, "I called a taxi. Should be here any minute now." Almost on cue, a car horn sounded outside the gates. "This is it, wifey."

She winced at the use of the word. "Good luck, Ralph." Almost as an afterthought, she added, "I hope you find a good life." She moved toward him, as if she were going to touch him. "Despite what's happened between us, or despite what never happened, I wish you well." She reached to touch his hand, but withdrew it quickly.

In his rush to the gate, her gesture seemingly escaped his attention.

Still watching, but feeling guilty for doing so, Numie was tempted to reveal himself, to say something, to offer comfort in some way. Then he decided moments such as these should be private affairs.

. . .

Leonora opened her eyes onto the new day. The half-light coming in from the closed shutters, the oppressive heat, the strange silence that lay over Sacre-Coeur gave her the feeling that she was experiencing a living death. Her body was hot and moist. Frantically her eyes darted about her dark bedchamber, with its ominous oak furniture. The whole atmosphere was crushing, paralyzing——a tomb of her own making. Would she be able to rise from her coffin? Jerking her body up, she clawed at her face with her long-nailed hand. She was alive! Spared. Given another whole year before she had to face another September 13.

Off the bed and into her wardrobe, she was searching for a suitable gown. The hell with it! What did clothes matter on a morning like this? She reached for a blue chiffon cape, draping it over her shoulders. The panels attached to her bracelets flowed like butterfly wings as she raised her arms.

She had to let in the sun. For too long she'd avoided the day. Now she wanted it, needed it. Today would be different, different from all other days. Today, she'd outstare the sun!

Throwing back the heavy draperies, she stood at her French doors, the morning's glare filling the room. Opening the doors, she stalked out onto her balcony. Turning her head to the sky, she opened her eyes wide and glared at the sun, her arms outstretched. She would destroy her eyes if she wanted to. She'd seen all of life she cared to. Too much! Then, speaking softly in a voice strange and distant to her, she said, "I've made my decision. I'm going to write my memoirs."

Since the powers had decided to spare her, it must be for a purpose. This morning she knew what that purpose was. Many future fans, the young, were out there waiting to hear with open hearts and minds how to live their lives in total defiance of the world's standards. And to get away with it! "They'll probably make me the goddess of a cult——they're so desperate for a heroine these days," she said aloud. With the publication of her memoirs, she could become a legend. *A living legend*. All her life she'd rebelled against the petty details of life, preferring instead the realities of the inner woman. Through that emotional landscape, she'd walked alone. To tell the story of that journey now must consume her every hour.

She would begin right this morning. That's why she didn't care if she destroyed her eyes. It was all inside her, the whole story. She didn't need to see any more. She'd seen everything, done everything. She'd had all the fame, all the money, and all the sex she could possibly desire. All that remained was for her to make her experiences relevant for a new generation.

She closed her eyes. After all, she didn't really have to destroy them. She was thinking only in terms of a symbolic gesture. The sun was always too powerful for her. She ran from it. She went out at night, or else carefully draped and shaded. She lived behind closed windows to escape the day.

She'd also go on a sex fast to purify her body and soul.

But she did need Tangerine to help her maintain her body. Oh, she was forgetting. Tangerine was still in the hospital. That being the case, she'd teach Dinah how to massage and preserve her body through the rigorous ordeal of writing the memoirs.

Into her bedroom, she studied her bruised face in the mirror. She'd have to stop being so vain. Her beauty was fabled enough. It was more important now that she make her reputation as a diarist.

She laughed silently to herself. Most people, she realized, learned by trial and error. They made mistakes, then they'd repeat those mistakes. She, on the other hand, was born instantly illuminated, receiving the complete truth the moment she entered the world. Dare she not share that with others? If she remained silent, it would be like a promise unfulfilled.

She'd never kept a written diary. Yet in her head she had. Every detail was engraved there. She would just write the date at the top of the paper, and then record her feelings and emotions at that time. Since she knew the complete truth at the beginning, and it was the same truth now, she could perform that feat.

Of course, along the way, she'd learned about surface reality. All of the people of the world had to learn about surface reality day by day. Obviously if somebody invented a better detergent, you'd learn about that. But truth was eternal, enduring. That she'd always known.

It was good she was surrounded by trivial people such as Numie, Anne, Dinah. She needed them in her life to cope with the details. Numie, for instance, had experiences. They had made him bitter, cynical, jaded. But they had taught him nothing.

She was the opposite——an idea person who sold her creativity on the world marketplace. Numie didn't have anything to sell other than a body. Unlike Numie, she'd been doubly blessed, having a great body as well as creativity. She was a celebrated figure, no less!

Breathing heavily, she was frightened of and excessively

stimulated with her new mission. She'd terrify the world with her own brand of truth. With that chilling thought, she entered the bathroom. Impurities had to be removed from her body. She couldn't begin her memoirs with impurities in her system.

. . .

The noonday sun was shining through the bathroom in the hotel suite of Lola La Mour. For the first time in her life, she had nothing to do. No orders from anybody. She was her own boss. The roles were reversed. It was she who was ordering people around now.

Let all the bitches who'd dismissed her as a silly drag queen look in on her now. She'd show them where it was at.

She thought back to a day in early childhood when there was no food in the house, not even some rice and beans. That memory was long faded. In a bucket on a table in the living room was champagne, the same brand Leonora de la Mer always ordered. No more rum toddies for her.

Today she'd also send out for some caviar. Once when the commodore had given her a taste, she'd hated it. But she'd order it from the grocery store, nevertheless.

Later on, she'd have Ned drive her around to her properties. She wanted to see if the storm had caused any damage. Perhaps she would stop at a jewelry store in the afternoon.

Ned was coming into the bathroom. "You've got an invite. The mail's just arrived from the mainland. An engraved invite to attend one of your lawyer's fancy parties, the kind the commodore never took you to."

"Of course," she said matter-of-factly, admiring the shine of her red nails. "I think that white man has a powerful attraction for me, aside from the business part of our relationship." Looking at herself in a hand mirror, she wet her lips. "Did you see how long he held my hand when we said goodbye?"

Ned frowned. "I was too busy hustling Sister Amelia's ass out of that office to notice much handholding."

Still in her wig, she splashed in her bubble bath, enjoying the rich lather of suds. Suddenly, she sat up. "Would you give up your life for me?"

At the edge of the tub, Ned was starting to pull off his pants to join her. "Hell, no, why should I?"

Lola's face grew stern. "Then you're not committed to the relationship."

"I ball you," he said, taking off his pants. "Isn't that enough?"

"No, I demand total commitment, total loyalty," she said, sitting up more rigidly.

"I can't give you that," he said, turning a startled face to her. "I've given you all I can. But not that."

Taking some of the bubbly capping off the creamy froth of the water, she tossed the suds at him. "Then get out!" she screamed.

"That suits me just fine," he said, reaching for his pants. Slipping into them, he walked rapidly into the living room. Quickly he poured a drink, downing it so fast it burned his throat.

In moments, she was in the room, dripping soap. She reached for a flimsy nightgown. "Just where do you think you're going?"

"I'm going out," he said, the color of his skin deepening. "Following your orders."

"You're going nowhere unless I dismiss you," she said. "No one walks out on Lola La Mour." Barging over, she slapped the glass from his hand, sending its contents spilling onto the new carpet.

"You ordered me out, remember?" Empty glass in hand, he said, "Baby, this ain't the only place in town where I can get a drink." Making for his wardrobe, he pulled out a shirt.

"You walk out of here, and you die," she threatened.

"If I stay, I'll die," he said, covering himself with cologne until he reeked of it. "You watch me like a hawk. I need some real pussy for a change. You leave a man with nothing." He grabbed hold of himself. "You're after balls."

"You don't know how to live with a *star*——that's your problem." Her shrill voice was more high-pitched than ever. "You're not man enough."

"Okay, it's my problem," he said, turning his back on her, as if that would drown out her voice. "But I've got to have breathing space. I can't stand this shit no more."

"Shit!" Lola laughed in pain. "You call the love I offer

shit?" She waved her hand in a sweeping gesture. "After all I've done for you. The sacrifices I've made."

"I don't need you," he said, posing at intense concentration. "I wanted to get my share of the commodore's bread, but the price ain't worth it." He withdrew from her instinctively. "I'm going back to Dinah."

She hated the sound of Dinah's name——hated her youth, her beauty. Mostly she hated what was between her legs. What could men possibly see in that awful smelly thing? "Have you finished your little high school recitation?" she asked.

"Yeah, I'm through." He clutched his throat. "Up to here I'm through. I need some severance pay. After all, I helped you pull off that deal with Sister Amelia. I need enough money to set myself up, be my own boss."

"*My needs*——not yours——will determine the course of this relationship," she said, pressing her hands to her forehead. "And right now I've got a letch for you." She coolly surveyed him.

"I'm not selling my dick——at least not to you." The closeness of this creature, the airless room, seemed to nauseate him.

"I told you, I have this letch for you." She sank back slowly into her white sofa at the far end of the room.

"Fuck off!" he said. "I'm leaving." He had the door slightly ajar. "Keep the clothes, keep everything."

"Ned, baby," she said warmly, feeling the excessive heat of the room which was matched only by the blood-boiling fury inside her. "You just don't understand," she said, fixing colorless, bizarre eyes on him. "You walk out that door, sugar, and I'll shoot you in the back."

He turned.

On the sofa, she was holding a revolver she'd found in the back of the commodore's desk. "I will kill you just as sure as I'm looking at your pretty brown eyes." She tried not to show her nervousness. "I never thought the commodore's gun would come in so handy. You know I'll kill you, don't you, boy?"

"*I believe you would*." His face was blank.

"You're finally getting my message," she said contemptuously. "I'm not some little black pussy on her first date at the drive-in movie." Quickly she jerked off her wig and tossed it across the room. "Come over here and look at this face." In the harsh light, with the afternoon sun beating in, without her adornment and frills, she knew exactly what her face looked like. That's why she took so much time every day to make it up. It was old, quite old. "When I say this is your mother talking, I mean it. You see before you not some ravishing lady with her cherry glowing a virginal red. You see before you an aging, forty-five-year-old, burned-out lady!"

He paused a long time before speaking. "I never knew you was that old. You always told people you was twenty-four. I didn't exactly believe that. But forty-five!" A strange laugh came from him. "That's a record for me. I've always been into young stuff."

That remark seemed to pierce her flesh. "Let's face it: you're young enough to be my son."

He smiled sardonically. "At that ripe age, you're holding up pretty well. I must say."

"You mean, I can create an illusion?" She seemed momentarily hypnotized by a remembrance of her long-vanished youth. "Who am I kidding? In a year——maybe two——I'm going to be washed up." She paused like a figure in a period picture. "I've based my whole life on youth and beauty. I'm losing both. I can get more flamboyant, but I'm not going to get more beautiful——certainly not any younger." Her voice broke into a strangled sob. The words were incoherent. When she finally spoke, it was in gasps. "I'm afraid. *Afraid.*"

"I can't help you," he said, looking as if he felt strong, handsome, masculine, immune from her plight. "Put down that stupid gun and let me go."

She closed her finger around the trigger. "I'll kill you. Then I'll kill myself!"

"You really mean it, don't you?" His eyes widened.

"Of course, I mean it." She made a gesture to the door, silently defying that it would ever be opened without her permission. "I'm going to hang on to you; even if I have to kill you to do it." Her voice was getting even more high-pitched, her gestures airier. "I've always lost everything I've ever wanted." She sobbed. "Lola is tired of losing!"

"Come on . . ." He raised his hand toward her, then backed away.

"Take off your clothes," she commanded. "Get in that bubble bath." She lowered her voice. "I'll be in to rub your back." She glared at him, searching for some show of defiance. He was giving in, submitting, she could tell. As an afterthought, she added, "and anything else I want to rub any time of the day or night I want to rub it. You're mine!"

He sighed in defeat. Not saying a word, he was heading back to the bathroom. He got out of his clothes slowly and into the water; he let the bubbles float over his head.

In front of the bathroom mirror, Lola adjusted her retrieved wig. Then she generously applied flaming red lipstick as a prelude to joining him in the bath.

Intimidating Ned had been easy, almost too easy. She couldn't quite believe it.

Getting Numie into her stable would be more difficult. But still an imminent prospect.

"The water's got cold," he yelled.

"Don't worry," she said over her shoulder. "Your mother's going to make it scalding!"

. . .

Leonora in anger answered the sound of the buzzer. "Anne, you know I don't like to be disturbed when I'm meditating. What is it?"

"It's Sunshine," she said.

"Sunshine?" Leonora asked incredulously.. "You know I loathe it."

"No," Anne said, exasperated. "Sunshine is the commodore's cousin. He's demanding to see you."

"Really!" An idea flashed through Leonora's mind. Lola had taken care of Sister Amelia. But one relative was just as good as another when your aim was breaking a will.

"Show the young man up," Leonora commanded.

Chapter Twenty-Nine

Numie had a hard time falling asleep that night. Tossing and turning, he wrestled the bedcovers in the guest cottage at Sacre-Coeur. In the dark, he was reaching back in space. Where had everything gone wrong? At what point in life had he taken that bad a turnoff? The same question, endlessly repeated.

Images clogged his brain, giving way to memories, both distant and close——all blending into one melting pot that churned inside his head. Tears filled his eyes, and at times he seemed on the verge of some new insight. But then it was gone. Everything became elusive again, including the solution for his escape.

If only an answer to his letter would come. Maybe it had gotten lost! Getting out of bed quickly, he flicked on the lamp. Its glare gave him a headache. At the desk, he sat down and began to write once more a letter that remained his only hope for escaping Tortuga.

Shortly before dawn, he left Sacre-Coeur. As he walked down the deserted sidewalk, the whole island looked as if it was washed with purple paint.

The sun was up now, casting light on the rows of little shanties that bordered the graveyard.

Out early, the old shoeshine man was here, rocking on his front porch——his smile revealing decaying, yellow-green teeth. "Morning, young man."

"Morning, old timer. You get up early."

"Don't want to miss no business."

"I said next time I was wearing shoes, I'd be right over," Numie said, walking up the rickety steps. "Here I am."

Shining his shoes, the old man sang a loose-lipped tune, a kind of Dixieland. Between shines he paused to take a swig from a half pint of liquor tucked away under his ornate stand. Stretching his back, he scratched the sweaty armpits of a yellowing, pin-striped shirt. Then he snapped his dirty rag and went to work. Eyes squinting, he held the shoes up to his face, testing the gleam. "Right fine shine I gave you."

"Best I ever had," Numie replied, putting a dollar bill in the withered, outstretched hand.

In the now clear light of morning, Numie saw that the polish was applied too thickly, that it was the wrong color, and that some of the areas had been completely missed. "See you around," he called back at the shanty.

Beyond the graveyard, he was pleased about one thing: he'd carried out his vague commitment to return to that old man to get the shine. A small incident, perhaps, but it was important to him.

He planned to return again and again to have his shoes shined by that old man——just as long as he continued to live in Tortuga and the old man continued to live.

Back at the guest cottage, he dozed for hours. The heat made him toss and turn in sweaty sheets. He woke late in the afternoon.

Opening his eyes fully, he was startled by a tapping on his door. He must be dreaming. But, no, the tapping was growing louder. Bolting up, he reached for his robe and rushed to the door. "Anne," he said, startled. "Come on in." He was really glad to see her, though slightly alarmed at the prospect of bad news. "Does Leonora want me to drive her somewhere?"

"No, she's resting now after dictating her memoirs to me for hours." She glanced quickly at the disheveled room, then at his sleepy face. "I'm beat! Anything to drink out here?"

At the bar he checked a small refrigerator. "No beer," he said, smiling. Her presence warmed him.

She paused for a moment, hesitating. "Then Scotch," she replied.

"Sorry I don't have any cubes," he said, handing her a half-filled glass. Her words, the tone of her voice, was suddenly having a disturbing effect on him.

She downed some of it. "Why don't we go for a drive?" she asked. A little sigh came from her. "I'd like to get away."

"Where to?" he asked. He was sorry his question sounded a little cold. It wasn't meant that way. He had a hard time expressing feeling.

In his presence, she looked helpless. Hand at her throat, she seemed to be in some sort of pain. "Any place away from here."

. . .

On the way to nowhere in particular, he drove the Lincoln past a saloon with swinging, green-shuttered doors, a dingy grocery store, then a Navy shop, and finally a red-brick bank building.

"What am I going to do?" he asked, not expecting an answer.

Her look was strange. "Correction," she said. "What are we going to do?"

Numie's eyes were wide and glazed. Did she mean that? Afraid to ask, he didn't say anything, just kept his eyes glued on the road.

"We're in the same boat," she said after a long pause.

He could almost sense her nerves tightening. His certainly were.

"Each of us wanting to get out of this hole," she said, "but not knowing how to go about it."

Outside, sallow-faced young men hung out on street corners wearing their masks. He mentally transferred his own face onto that of those mannikins, remembering too well how he used to stand around waiting for some miserable excuse of life to come to him. Turning the corner, he wanted to escape the tawdry town, with its decaying bars, its yellow-streaked windows, its termite-eaten lumber. "I've written a letter," he said impetuously. "But haven't got an answer yet."

Anne rolled down the window, letting in the smell of the late afternoon. Soon all the bars were gone, giving way to birds of paradise growing alongside the road.

He turned from their sight. Their long-pointed tongues seemed to be sticking out at him, mocking him. God, he was paranoid today.

"Hope it comes soon," she said, shifting in her seat.

He was heading for the ocean, to the childhood haunt and ghostly memories of Leonora. The land that spelled such defeat and despair for her gave him a curious kind of solace. It was the doorway that could bring change to Tortuga. If Ruthie Elvina, Lola, and Leonora could be tempted to sell, high-risers would go up on its shore, signaling the end of the long and sleepy isolation of the island town. He wouldn't be around to see it, but he sensed its coming.

"My own hope of getting a job in New York is getting pretty slim," Anne said in a warm, confidential tone.

Suddenly, the thought of Erzulie and his own impotence came racing through his mind. Fear struck him, forcing him to turn from the ocean and head in another direction to the lonely pier at the end of the street. As he neared it, he was relieved. No sign of life anywhere.

"This place is creepy," she said, crossing the rotten boards with him.

At the edge, with the water right at their feet, he pointed to some distant boats on the horizon. "Some day, I'd like to get on one of those boats and go away. Way out there." A sea gull dropped a dead fish nearby, then scooped down to reclaim it. "To visit all the islands south of here." In a near whisper, he added, "To dock in all the strange ports."

Her voice had a sudden sharpness. "Looking for what?" she asked, seemingly impatient with childish fantasies.

"I don't know," he said defensively. He felt like a little boy in her presence. "What were you looking for when you came to this port in the first place?"

"People never look for anything but themselves," she said, turning her face from the water. "That's what I think." In total contrast to his restlessness, she seemed anchored to the spot, like granite statuary. "They may tell you they're seeking money or peace or fame or love, but they're not." Her voice softened. "That's all part of finding out who you are."

A rustling in the garbage pails behind him caused him to jerk around, startled. But it was only some alley cats. One looked like Castor's calico reincarnate. How he wished it were! "Do you really want to find out about yourself?" he asked her.

"Probably not," she said. "I'd be terrified for sure." Moving closer, she held tightly to his arm. "I didn't quite tell you all. The job in New York." She faced him squarely. "I was turned down."

Dark clouds, like a late summer rainstorm, seemed on the horizon. Remembering the storm and the panic of Leonora, he didn't respond at first. Then he asked, "What will you do?"

The first drops of rain began to fall. Still she stood there motionless. "Stay on here unless I get a better offer." A streak of lightning tore across the sky. "I have to eat." She smiled. "An old custom my daddy taught me back in the Bronx."

Numie felt tension building and he thought an unbearable explosion was about to go off inside him. He didn't care whether he got soaked or not. After that other storm, it wouldn't bother him. "Then you're not leaving after all?"

The rain was pouring down now, coating the furry boards of the old pier. Even the pelicans were gone, and the cats were off under a warehouse seeking shelter.

"I'm going to leave," she answered, rain hitting her in the face, "but not as soon as I'd like." She turned to the sea for a long moment, arching her neck. "When you go, guess you'll go alone?"

Under her thin cotton blouse, her breasts were clearly outlined. "I guess," he said, taking his eyes off her long enough to glance at the waves washing up against the pilings. "Who would go with me?" he asked the water, not daring to face her.

"Dammit!" she finally said. Her hair was streaky wet, her features hard. Through eyes half closed to protect them from the lashing rain, she yelled, "Do I have to print an engraved invitation?" Night was moving in. "I couldn't make it any clearer."

When he didn't speak, she said, "It's obvious you're not interested." Turning her back, she walked rapidly across the rain-splattered, dilapidated docks.

He steadied himself on a piling. Bewildered, he wasn't really understanding what was happening. Temples throbbing, he stared at the rain hitting the sea. Soon Anne would be gone. Suddenly, he was overcome with the feeling she was his last chance. Just as Tortuga seemed to be his last chance when he first got here, now she was the embodiment of whatever it was that drove him here in the first place. No more time to think. He'd figure out everything later.

"Hey, wait up," he called. After the first running steps, he nearly slipped on the rubbery, rotten wood.

She stopped at the sound of his voice. When she saw he was falling, one hand reached out to grab him, even though she was yards away.

That was all he needed to see.

. . .

At the Sunset Trailer Court, all was quiet. The storm was over.

Inside Leonora's trailer, Anne, nude, was lying on an orchid chenille bedspread, her head resting in a nest of throw pillows.

At the other end of the trailer, Numie was in the kitchen galley, heating a pot of water on an electric hotplate. Waiting for the water to boil, he studied the fireboard walls and ceiling. Decals made of cutout seed packages and catalogues formed a frieze around the ceiling and windows. A long and narrow wooden shelf held an accumulation of years of living for Leonora's parents: an empty perfume bottle with a pretentious stopper, a miniature birch bark canoe, a drinking glass filled with partially burned birthday candles, and a dime store ashtray afloat with cigarette butts.

A sharp pain shot through Numie's groin. He'd made passionate love to Anne about half an hour ago. The first night with her had been different. Both of them had been clutching, hungry. The love-making between them this afternoon was tender, more complete. He'd greatly enjoyed the first experience, but had found the second time infinitely more fulfilling.

He hadn't concentrated on his feelings for Anne, allowing them to drift into that vague and uncommitted part of his brain. He didn't want her to know just how lonely he was. For that matter, he didn't want anybody to know just how much he needed someone else. At the same time, he kept secretly hoping she would see through his mask to the man beyond. He knew it was unfair. She couldn't be expected to read his mind——yet he hoped she would.

Back on the bed, he caressed her. Instinctively, her body moved closer to his, though she appeared to be asleep. How long could he lie with her in silence? What could a man who'd always been paid for sex say to her? "This was strictly for free," or something stupid like that. What could he offer her?

When she woke up fully, she smiled gently at him; there was no need to talk. There was perfect and silent communication. Her body was soaked with perspiration, as was his.

Running a bath for them, she insisted he get in first. With a big sponge, she soaked his chest, then, using her long deft fingers she lathered his whole body. Alternatively, she massaged the tired muscles in his neck and back. The warm water soothed every cell, and he lay back against the porcelain, giving himself up completely to her tender ministrations.

Then his own hands reached out and cupped her upturned breasts, squeezing them, but ever so gently. She got into the tub with him; and his hands were sponging and lathering the hidden parts of her body. Slippery smooth, her skin was not only a delight to him, but was arousing him once again.

Lifting her by the waist, he sat her on his lap, impaling her. Bobbing up and down, he let the water swirl around them like waves. He was not only plunging into her empty void, but fulfilling the empty void in himself.

Gripping him around the neck, she kissed him tenderly then almost violently as she neared her climax. For the first time in his life, he realized what a form of communication lips were between lovers.

She was biting his neck, and he was clutching her to him. Then it was over. But he lingered, holding her close, until the water turned cold. Kissing the bridge of her nose and then her eyebrows, he got up and lifted her out of the tub.

He felt closer to her than he'd ever felt to another person. It was a new and exciting experience. He didn't want to overwhelm her, frighten her away. He wanted her to take time, make up her mind without pressure about how much she wanted him and trusted him.

The night was passing quickly, and he was savoring every moment.

. . .

Tape recorder on, Leonora was puncturing the early evening air with her beaded cigarette holder. Then, turning off the tape, she got up. Puffing furiously, she was creating a gray smokescreen around herself. She opened the green shutter doors and walked out onto her balcony, overlooking the garden below.

Lips contorted, she let the night air bathe her body. It soothed her. Swaggering a bit, she held on to the railing.

It was then she noticed Numie and Anne crossing the garden. What were those two up to? She'd have to watch them more closely.

Earlier in the evening, one disturbing thought kept crossing her mind, as she played back the tapes. At first, she was mesmerized by the sound of her own voice. Later, she began to worry that her memoirs sounded as if she were playacting at life——creating an illusion, missing out on the actual experience.

Much of her life had been spent trying to carefully preserve an image of herself as she was forty years ago. To do this, she had to by-pass reality. Now, coming out of her fantasy-world, she welcomed the resurgence of life.

She couldn't go on acting young forever. Who could? She'd have to let the vintage Leonora de la Mer out of her cage.

The truth was, she had never been innocently new or absurdly antique. She had always been herself——goading herself into new horizons, falling back when she allowed hurt and weakness to dim her brilliance, but rising again with the strength of angels to some glittering triumph, growing and expanding, forever reaching out to the stars. At times she'd been a disappointment to herself, but she never failed to dazzle her audience. That was because she'd allowed her romantic vision to become a reality in life. At times, the race got out of control, as if she were challenging the wind to catch up, but she always returned to her solid Virgo core, stabilizing herself for a while before flying again.

She was no longer the child who'd married Norton Huttnar. To dwell on the past would only bring about that which she most feared. Would longtime admirers abandon their admiration if they saw what she looked like today? Could she truly face the glare of lights at a talk show? Did interest in her border on necrophilia? Was something missing in her? Something long gone——never to return?

Even more than an unknown audience, she was afraid of herself. Wasn't it better to leave the past alone? Wasn't it reckless to dredge it up again? What awful ghosts waited there to be rediscovered? Did she need the self-inflicted pain?

Her fingers brushed the night air. The answer was clear: she'd be accepted again when she returned to New York. After all, America doted on self-destructive heroines. Such ladies mirrored their own mortality and spoke of the very impermanence of life itself. To see Leonora de la Mer still clinging to life, still surviving, would evoke at the very least a sympathetic response. She was, in the final analysis, a monument to endurance.

Convinced of this, and feeling she had little choice, she was determined to creatively live out the time remaining to her. Let the spotlight shine on her. She was pursuing life to its fiery and incredible ending.

The years had taken their toll. But she was going to be back there on center stage.

The memoirs, a new spring line, publicity, television, public appearances, interviews, her head was spinning.

She was truly alive! For the first time in almost half a century!

. . .

In a corner of Leonora's dressing room, Numie was enjoying the second of her blue-wrapped marijuana cigarettes. "I've been listening to your tapes," he said. "They're terrific." He sucked in more smoke. "I didn't know all those things happened to you."

She responded as if challenged. "Of course, they happened to me." She looked at him calculatingly, then was filled with pity. He, who had had nothing. She, who had had it all. "The luminaries of the 20th century have passed through my life. I charmed each and every one with my extraordinary personality." Beneath her self-glorifying description, she felt another Leonora was trying to get out. A desperate woman who *hadn't* had it all. But she kept burying and repressing her. Waving her hand through the air, she said, "My memoirs are my glamorous carnival of memory."

He looked at the tape as if it were an obscene record. "I didn't know you could publish things about people like that." Fearful of angering her or intruding upon her guarded isolation, he added quickly, "I mean, really personal things."

"It doesn't matter," she said impatiently. "Many of the people I write about are dead now anyway." She slipped gracefully off her table and moved demurely through the chamber. "Like a supreme Michelangelo, death has chiseled away at my heart with each and every passing."

He was disturbed by her this morning. Her painted mouth, usually so carefully tended to, seemed slashed across her face.

"But I have captured and retained the presence of those I knew," she said. She stopped at her draperies, pulling them back herself, letting in the morning sun. She stood before them, looking like a holdover from the night who hadn't yet gone to bed. "Everybody written about in my memoirs——my garden of loved ones——will become timeless." Her eyes traveled across the plant life behind the walls of Sacre-Coeur. It was like a savage city erected behind black ramparts. "In my memoirs, the light will always be shining."

Head reeling, Numie moved across the room to a stack of papers recently typed by Anne. "You write here——I just heard it a little while ago——that you missed out on the most creative role in your life."

"My worst mistake," she confirmed, holding onto the drapery for support. "I turned down an opportunity to become the First Lady of the land."

He raised his eyebrow, not really sure but what these were the ravings of a lunatic, the wildest fantasy dreams of a disappointing life, a last-ditch attempt to rewrite her history the way she wanted it to be. "I didn't even know you knew..."

"I was stronger than he was," she said, stiffening her back and feeling powerful again. "I would have consumed him." She sighed inaudibly. "He would have been completely destroyed by me." She stopped, her hand nervously plowing through her hair. Perhaps she was exaggerating, but she had met him. Once, at a reception. "I left him," she said bitterly to Numie. How she remembered the look of desire on his face. It *could* have been. Who is to say it couldn't? "Oh, God, I must tell all of this to my tapes. I have a whole new insight." At her desk she was pressing the buzzer. When there was no immediate response, she tried to rip it from its casing. "Anne. Anne. Anne," she screamed.

Sunshine was at the door, the local newspaper in hand. "Lola's up to something. Look at this!"

Across the front page was a picture of Leonora. The most unflattering picture she'd ever seen, snapped when she'd been drugged half out of her mind at a party at Commodore Philip's years ago. Alongside it was a picture of her in her school dress, with the caption: "From Priscilla Osterhoudt to Leonora de la Mer." Underneath it was a three-column wedding picture taken the day she first departed from Tortuga. Staring back at her from the page was the unmistakable image of Norton Huttnar! She thought she'd destroyed every picture of him ever taken. But obviously not.

The headline, "Old Island Homecoming Salutes Leonora de la Mer." Her tribute——a gala party at Commodore Philip's bar——was being paid for by Lola La Mour!

"I can't believe it," Leonora said. "If that cheap drag queen thinks she can flatter me into dropping plans to break the will, she's dead wrong."

"Like to hear you say that, Leonora," Sunshine added. "After all, that money belongs to me."

She glared contemptuously at him. "That is debatable. But you're all I have to work with."

"You're not going to that fag's party?" Sunshine asked.

"Of course, how can I not go?" Leonora said, horrified at the man's stupidity. "The whole town will be there. Besides, it's not her party. It's to honor me. I assure you——no one will notice Lola La Mour when I make my appearance."

. . .

The next afternoon the breeze from the ocean was blowing through Numie's hair as he stood in Erzulie's front yard. The tall grass was green after the huge rainfall that came with the tropical storm. Chickens ran over old automobile tires. Scattered bits of a picket fence and an overturned doghouse littered the grounds.

In her sunflower yellow dress, Erzulie was sitting on her porch shelling peas.

"Hi," Numie called.

She scratched her breast. "Another two dollars from that white bitch?" she asked.

"No, it's not that time of the week," he said, standing there awkwardly in the dry summer heat. "Came to report on your *piment oiseau*, the hottest sauce I've ever had in my life. Me and my girl put it over a dish we made up last night." He blew out air in memory. "She had to drink eight beers, and even then said her mouth was on fire."

"You complaining?" Her face tightened, and one eye half closed.

"No, just telling you what happened," he explained, laughing slightly.

"Your girl?" Erzulie eyed her badly ripped shoes, which left her almost barefoot. Then she looked up at him. "Does that mean what I think it means?"

He stood staring back for a moment. "It means I won't be needing your other special sauce." Smiling with confidence, he added, "No problem there at all."

"See, Erzulie was right." She chuckled. "You just weren't making it with the right party." Her eyes drifted to the sea, as if it were an accusing mirror. "I know back in Haiti I cured many a man of impotence." A pig came right out of the house, looked in all directions, then headed back. "One night with me, and I turned them into wild stallions."

"I bet." He straightened up. Her words had reminded him of something. Was she another Tangerine, lost in yesterday's sexual fantasies?

Erzulie smiled. Her teeth were decaying into a yellow-green, just like the old shoeshine man's.

He sat down on the porch, stretching out and looking toward the water. It was calm today.

"Got any drinking whiskey on you?" she asked, staring right past him to buzzing bees.

"No, not a thing," he said, a hammer pounded inside his head. "I'm getting over a hangover."

Snapping her fingers, she tried to stop a rooster chasing a hen across her front yard. Her warning went unheeded. "I'm going to kill that rooster and fry him up tonight."

He sighed. "He'll have one great memory."

"Better enjoy the piece he's getting," she said, swerving dangerously in her chair. "It'll be his last."

Restless, Numie was walking around the porch, avoiding a discarded bedspring.

"Look inside my house and bring me my purse sitting there in the living room," she ordered, shifting her weight as shadows stretched across the porch.

Brushing away the flies, he went in. On a stove in back, the same pot was simmering. Out on the porch again, he handed her a snakeskin purse.

Rummaging through it, she pulled out a change purse. "What do you know?" she said. "I forgot to go to the bank today." She turned a sharp eye on him. "Why don't you run down the road apiece and come back with some whiskey for my headache?"

"Sure, I'd be glad to." Was she hustling him?

"Pay for it yourself and just deduct the money I owe you from what that white bitch gives me." She seemed solidly anchored to one spot, a great ball of yellow butter.

"Will do," he said, surprised. Hadn't she denounced Leonora for giving her the money? Now she was speaking of it as if it were her due.

In the Lincoln, he headed down the blacktop road to a liquor store and passed Joan's. Or was it the Garden of Delights? He was secretly amused that Amelia Le Blanc was going to be supported on the earnings of a cathouse.

Back with the whiskey, he could not find Erzulie anywhere. Going once more into of the sweet decay of her living room, he saw she was asleep. He placed the liquor on a nearby table, then gave Erzulie a silent goodbye. This was probably the last time he'd ever see her.

On the way back to the Lincoln, he stopped to stare at the rooster. All red feathered, with a mighty comb, it stood proudly, cock of the front yard. He shuddered to think of that poor rooster's fate. Then he quickly got in the limousine and headed out down the road. The rooster's crowing resounded in his ears. What kind of rooster would crow at three o'clock in the afternoon?

. . .

That evening a sea of faces, many of them unknown to her, was waiting to greet Leonora as she stepped from the limousine. Behind the wheel, Sunshine jumped out and opened the door to the back compartment. Numie had asked that he not drive tonight, and she'd granted his request.

Stepping onto the pavement, Leonora was proud of her

outfit. Even though it was late summer, she'd detected a chill in the air which allowed her to wear what she called her *apres-midi*. It was a turquoise and ivory Persian lamb topcoat muffled around the neck with double fox boas dyed to match.

Out to greet her on the sidewalk was Ruthie Elvina, looking very plain in flowery cotton. Behind her was a group of broken-down, prune-like hags.

Although Leonora had hoped never to see her lifelong enemy ever again, she held out a gloved hand to Ruthie Elvina.

Ruthie Elvina smiled and shook it firmly. Then she turned and looked at the women behind her. "These are the last of our class, Priscilla."

Leonora was horrified and at first suspected this was another diabolical attempt on Ruthie Elvina's part to humiliate her. After all, these relics could hardly be contemporaries of hers. Acutely embarrassed, she shook each and every hand, searching behind the withered masks for some semblance of the young girls of long ago who'd rejected her. She could find no one she knew, because she'd never really looked into their eyes before.

"That's it," Ruthie Elvina said with a sigh. "All the others are dead——or else moved away so long ago we can't find a single trace of them."

Lola, at the door to greet Leonora, was all smiles, in a silver-embroidered gown with high-heeled, ankle-strap shoes. "My commodore," she said, "my *legal* husband, would have wanted me to do this for you, darling."

"Legal?" Leonora asked contemptuously. "I guess I am behind the times. Has this state changed the law to permit same-sex marriages?"

"Child," Lola said, hands on her hips, "this ain't no man looking at you."

"Perhaps you're right," Leonora said. "If it acts like a woman, talks like a woman, looks like a woman, then perhaps it is. But in the eyes of the law..."

"I'm legal, sister!" Lola said. "I can see now we're going to have to go to extremes to prove it." She gestured toward the ringside table. "Your favorite champagne is waiting. I had a few bottles left over from the supply I'm drinking."

The endless parade filed past Leonora's table. Greetings from everybody from Johnny Yellowwood to rubbery-legged Teddy

Albury. Each and every one Leonora treated with respect. After all, they were here to honor her even though she wouldn't speak to most of them on any other occasion.

By her side, Sunshine was already into the second bottle of champagne.

The lights dimmed. A pink spot lit the stage. At the piano, BoJo started playing warm-up music.

Leonora gasped in fright that Lola was going to perform.
At first she was tempted to leave, but the menacing drag queen had seated her in the prime position. She was a trapped audience!

From out of the back Lola was now in the spotlight. In her best baby-doll voice, she said, "Good evening, ladies and gentlemen. Welcome to my cabaret."

This public pronouncement of ownership didn't impress Leonora one bit.

Moistening her lips, Lola stared at Leonora through mascara-ringed eyes. "We cabaret entertainers are always being asked questions in interviews. Like 'Miss La Mour, what do you look for in a man?' I've always got an answer to that one. Twelve inches!"

A catcaller in the audience yelled, "How often do you find it?"

"Not often enough, *shorty!*" Lola yelled back. The audience laughed.

Practically in the spotlight herself, Leonora remained stone-faced.

"There are those in the audience who have dared suggest I'm not a real lady," Lola said. "We'll see!" she whispered confidentially as the lights dimmed.

The stage was pitch dark. BoJo began playing, "Whatever Lola wants..." Red spots flashed around the smoke-filled room where liquor flowed.

A feeling of uneasy anticipation was in the bar; more coming from Leonora than anybody else. "What dreadful thing is she going to do next," she asked in a whisper to Sunshine.

When the spot went on again, it revealed Lola's new outfit, a skin-tight white gown glittering with sequins shaped like red hearts. Radiantly raunchy, she gyrated around the stage. Slit up to the thigh, the gown revealed her chocolate legs. Almost panther-like in grace, she titillated the audience.

Every eye, including those of Leonora's, was glued to the stage.

Lola's bracelets dangled and swirled, and in a moment she'd snapped away the white gown. Her arms reached toward the ceiling.

A murmur rose from the audience.

Lola stood revealed in a red halter and red-spangled panties.

She began to move her belly like a dancer's. She was asking the audience to beg for more.

"Show your tits!" a man yelled.

At this point Leonora was truly ready to get up and leave. She'd just about had it, yet in some strange way she also found Lola's act compelling.

Still at the piano, BoJo was at his best, milking the song for its suggestiveness.

Spinning, Lola was moving incredibly fast. In a flash her halter was gone, and her boobs revealed.

The audience was screaming wildly.

Ruthie Elvina and her coterie at the back murmured about leaving, but remained in their seats.

Leonora looked away in disdain.

Yet the act wasn't over. Gyrating and contorting her body, Lola was sensuality itself——at fever pitch. Then the music became real lowdown.

Leonora was again paying attention. What could Lola possibly do for a finish, she wondered.

Provocatively Lola slipped down her red-spangled panties half an inch at a time. Then in a wild stamping dance, her high heels hit the floor like a fandango dancer. Sweat was dripping from her face, her whole body was glistening like black-colored bronze. There was the look of a wild thing in her eyes. Those eyes were now concentrating with ferocity on Leonora.

It was a direct challenge. Opening her almond eyes all the wider, Leonora met Lola's stare.

It was as if all the other patrons at the gala didn't count. The number was nearing its finish. BoJo was beating the piano as if it were a drum.

With a snap, the panties came off. The pink spotlight went out. A cold, harsh white light was focused on only one spot.

Lola La Mour was indeed a woman!

The light was on just long enough for everybody to get a good look, then it faded. Lola scampered from the stage.

Making her way through the crowd, Leonora was heading for her Lincoln. Opening the rear compartment by herself, she screamed at a drunken Sunshine. "Take me back to Sacre-Coeur!"

"Who would have ever thought it," Sunshine said, opening the glass panel to the back. He steered the car from the curb. "She's had it cut off all these years."

"You're not going to get the commodore's money," Leonora said with fury. "In this state marriage to a transsexual woman is legal. Lola was right."

"Leonora," he cried out, "you mean..."

"Yes, I do mean what I say," Leonora said. "Lola's the legitimate heir."

"But, Leonora, that leaves me..." Sunshine nearly ran off the road.

"I'm considering giving Numie Ralph's job," Leonora said. "I'll be needing a chauffeur."

"But I was going to have my own yacht," Sunshine protested. "Not driving around as somebody's chauffeur."

"Take it or leave it!"

Sunshine sighed. "Okay, Leonora, I'll take it."

"From now on," she said firmly, closing her eyes, hoping to blot out what she'd seen at the bar, "you'll address me as Miss De la Mer." After a block, she called to him, "You're like Tangerine. You were always meant to be a servant."

Sunshine kept his eyes on the road ahead.

. . .

In her all-white apartment, Lola threw herself on her satin bed. "I hated to do what I did tonight," she screamed at Ned.

"Baby, you was great!" he said, caressing her bare back. "All these times I've been going to bed with you, I never knew you had a real pussy. Why did you always cover it up?"

"I can't stand the thing!" she said, turning over and sobbing. "I'm still a rear-door girl. I don't like it the front way at all. The commodore made me do it."

"Like it or not," he said, "you'd better get used to it that way, 'cause that's what *I* like. How long ago did you become a woman?"

"Five years ago," she said, pressing her hand to her aching head.

"Did you go to Copenhagen?" he asked.

"No, Johns Hopkins," she replied.

"Who's he?" Ned asked.

"That's a fucking hospital," she said, getting up from the bed. She was heading toward the bathroom to repair her makeup. "They even had psychiatrists talk to me about emotionally conditioning myself to becoming a real woman. Hell!" she called out, "I know more about being a real woman than anybody at that castrating hellhole. I could give them lessons."

"I bet you could," Ned said, smiling to himself and slipping off his pants. "I bet you could at that. Now you get that cute little thing in here." A frown crossed his face.

"Honey, you don't have to take those pills like Dinah, do you?"

. . .

The next morning, Leonora's new secretary was calling over the intercom. "A colored girl's out front and wants to talk to you."

"Sorry," Leonora snapped, "I'm too busy." She banged down her compact on the desk. Probably a job applicant. With Ralph gone, she was the only one in charge. Everybody in town thought she was a regular employment bureau.

"The girl is very insistent," the secretary went on. "Claims this business is half hers. Says she knows you *very well.* "

"My God," Leonora exclaimed, jumping up. "That could only be Lola." Out from behind the desk, she carefully studied her appearance in the full-figure mirror. If Lola was here, Leonora knew her dress would be severely scrutinized. She smiled in approval at her figure, clad in an ecru jacket over a mauve print shirt and a gunmetal gray skirt. In her rosy pink high-heeled pumps, she paraded around the floor several times, a hammered gold medallion dangling from her neck. Satisfied with the way she looked, she barged into the outer reception lounge.

Hands on her hips, Lola was standing, glaring at the secretary. "You must be new in town, if you haven't heard of Lola La Mour." Lola was attired in daytime pants under a belted jacket with two patch pockets. In the presence of Leonora, she began to doubt her choice of outfit, wishing she had worn something more elegant. She tossed her blonde curls haughtily.

"What are you doing here?" Leonora asked in feigned politeness. "You know I'm busy." She deliberately wanted to be insulting, but not obviously so.

"I'm here on business myself," Lola answered. At this moment it seemed a dozen movie cameras were focusing on her. Her voice quivered slightly, and this horrified her, as she wanted to present a portrait of total coolness. It was Leonora who had something to fear from her——not the other way around.

"Let's conduct this *brief* interview in my salon," Leonora said, her delicate hands directing the way. In the privacy of her office, Leonora lit another one of her interminable marijuana cigarettes. "What brings you out today, or did I ask that?"

"This is an *official* business call," Lola said, "and I demand to be treated like a lady."

Lola swallowed hard. Chalk up round one to Leonora. Gazing at Leonora brought an immediate dizziness.

Leonora returned the stare. To her, Lola seemed a glutinous mass of mascara and rouge, all tinted with turquoise. And that wig. Only a bird of prey deep in the desert would consider it enticing.

Lola grandly stalked the room, asserting her sense of proprietorship.

To Leonora, Lola was like an unwanted cloud blotting out the sun. "Please state your business."

Lola instinctively reached to touch Leonora's arm. Leonora withdrew. "Please don't touch me," she said. "I can't stand to be touched."

Lola backed off in anger. She tossed a manila envelope on Leonora's desk. "I understand you are the only designer employed by *our* fashion house."

"I *am* the fashion house."

"No more," she said defiantly, stretching her lips into something resembling a smile. "I've just retired from shaking my moneymaker, and I'm cruising for another profession. Just look in that folder."

At the window, Leonora raised it slightly, to let out some of the penetrating odor from Lola's perfume. She seemed to have doused herself with an entire bottle. I don't have to take your commands," she said finally.

"That's a matter of opinion," Lola said, standing her ground. When was this white bitch going to start showing her some respect? "I suggest you look inside that goddamn folder."

Curiosity drove Leonora to the desk. She opened the folder and brought out the sketches. She tossed the designs on her desk. "My God, what is this? Tribal rites south of Pago-Pago?"

"You racist!" Lola snapped. "It's the beginning of a new Afro collection." Every worm in her brain was moving from that insult. "You've always made women look like cheap drag versions of Dietrich."

Covering the sketches with paper, as if her eyes could no longer tolerate the sight of them, Leonora said softly, but pointedly, "You're the one to talk about cheap drag."

Lola huffed. "My designs will shake up this house. Get customers to open up their purses again." She snorted in front of one of Leonora's half-clothed mannikins. "Afro all the way, starting with Dahomey."

"What's that? Leonora asked, arranging her posture at the desk almost like one of her mannequins. "Something for women's hygiene?"

Without permission, Lola slid some panel doors open revealing an array of fabrics in all colors. "A country," she said loudly. "Didn't you go to school? On second thought, there probably wasn't a Dahomey when you was in school."

"What do you know about fashion in Dahomey?" Leonora asked. "Assuming there is such a place."

Rummaging through some hat boxes, Lola looked up. "I've seen pictures," she said. "Besides, I suspect my kin came from there."

"Those are the weirdest and most unsuccessful designs for women's clothing I've ever seen," Leonora said. The sound of boys scurrying by the side of the building drifted in. Leonora felt threatened. "I thought you liked frilly, feminine things. Most of the times I've seen you, you were dressed like Jean Harlow."

Closing the panel doors with contempt, Lola said, "You're speaking of the past. I've gone through many changes since finding out who I am." She sashayed over to the desk, holding up one of her sketches. "These are from the Fon people. They scar the bodies of boys——it's called cicatrization. Now ain't that a four-million-dollar word? They work colors into the wounds. I mean, like real primitive. Now, I'm not talking about making scars on no woman's body, but re-creating that same thing in fabric."

"Disgusting barbarism!" Leonora charged. She turned from the sight of this horrible creature and her hideous designs. Her very presence made Leonora feel she was suffocating.

"The concept of black fashion will one day take over this country," Lola predicted. She seemed to be losing out in this battle——not at all the way she'd fantasized when she'd rehearsed it in front of the mirror this morning. "What I'm offering is a chance to set fashion ahead instead of trailing it."

"I beg your pardon!" Leonora said, through clenched teeth.

A deathly silence fell over the room.

Leonora eventually resumed smoking, furiously blowing out. "Me in black fashion? The idea is too absurd for comment."

"My designs will make us even more rich and famous than we are." Why wouldn't Leonora listen to reason? she kept asking.

"*I'm* rich and famous," Leonora asserted, casting a disdainful look at Lola. "You are merely rich." She crushed out the remainder of her cigarette. "You'll never be famous." With a quick brush of her hand, the designs inspired by the Fon people were tossed on her carpeted floor. "Your designs appall me. I'm the star of my own show. I don't want or need another designer. I'm certainly not in the market for a totally untalented one."

"You've got one, anyway, sugar," Lola said, feeling her power real good now. It was erotically thrilling. "I own half this business."

"You don't seem to realize," Leonora said calmly, walking

around the room as if she were venturing into cold water. "If I were some poor, struggling artist, just getting her start in life, you could have power over me——power you inherited, I might add. You certainly never earned it." She stopped short right near Lola, glaring into her liquid eyes.

"I earned it, bitch!" Lola said, standing up to her. "If all those years with my commodore wasn't earning it, then I don't know the meaning of singing for your supper."

Leonora backed away. The pathetic creature was probably right. After all, Leonora had had her Norton Huttnar. "If you don't mind, let's dispense with the name-calling." Leonora seated herself behind her desk. "The point is, you're not in a position to intimidate me. We're selling our joint businesses."

"Exactly what does that mean?" Suddenly, Lola was scared. She didn't fully understand how white people did business, except they were always capable of surprises.

"Exactly what I said," Leonora answered coolly. "Our partnership is dissolved, or soon will be." She reached for another cigarette, then put it down. Her head was already swimming. Besides, it was the wrong color. "Anything we own jointly, we're selling. I don't want to be associated with you on any level."

Lola laughed in Leonora's face, but her laugh didn't sound quite human. "You're prejudiced against black people?" She turned to the window. This line she'd used so many times was starting to bore even her.

"I'm not," Leonora asserted firmly. "If that were true, why would I be living with a black girl?"

The image of Dinah came back through Lola's head like a freight car out of control. When she was fully together, she was going to insist that no one mention that black pussy's name ever again. "She's a cheap hooker," Lola charged.

Leonora let the words pass over her. Of course, Lola's accusation had crossed her mind. Many times. But she couldn't afford to think those things about Dinah. Only she wasn't going to tolerate another Joan. "Dinah has far more class than you ever will," Leonora said. She wanted to hurt Lola, for saying such a thing about Dinah, for daring to repeat what was already in her own mind.

" Dinah, class?" Lola was fuming now. She, Lola La Mour,

was generally regarded as the arbiter of taste in blacktown. Why, many people called her up to ask how to decorate their shanties. "She's the town whore! Everybody's had her. She's just using you."

Leonora spun around in her chair. She had to get this vile creature out of her sight, but yet there was business to conduct. No one had had power over her since Norton Huttnar. She'd prided herself for years on never being in the presence of anyone she didn't want to see. Now, this!

"All of us use each other," she said in a hesitant voice. She reached for a pair of sunglasses, then used them like a mask. "Dinah and I will soon be leaving for New York. She's going to become one of the most successful high-fashion models there. I'll see to that. Soon you'll be staring at her face on the cover of Vogue."

Leonora could find no crueler words to say to Lola. Even more than the commodore's money, even more than Sacre-Coeur, Lola wanted to be on the cover of Vogue. To think that she, Lola La Mour, set Dinah up for this job. "Dinah on the cover of Vogue?" she asked, not really believing her ears. "You are out of your mind, like everybody says."

"No, I'm not insane," Leonora said, feeling almost immune from the accusation that had been made so often. "Time will tell who's the crazy one."

"Crazy, am I?" Lola asked. She rocked around the room at fever pitch. "You can't tongue-lash me no more. The day is over when you can come grandly into my bar and lord it over me, ordering that cheap champagne." An almost cannibalistic, blood-pounding frenzy was churning away inside. "You're no longer allowed in Commodore Philip's bar." She slammed her ringed hand down on the desk, hurting herself. "The name, incidentally, has been changed to Chez Lola."

"I only went to that contemptible bar because I didn't want to insult the commodore by staying away," Leonora said. "I couldn't stand the vile place. As for last night's performance, it was beneath me."

"Beneath you?" Lola questioned. "Baby, that bar has class. Something you wouldn't know anything about. You're used to taking some little spik cunt up the steps at the Garden of Delights, as you call it."

"You miserable transsexual! Get out of my shop."

"I'm part landlady here myself," Lola said. "You keep forgetting that."

"No. I don't," Leonora protested. "To forget that would be like forgetting a recurring nightmare."

"You're nothing but a pit viper," Lola charged.

"I see acquiring money has done nothing for your humility, something I have always managed to possess regardless of my position in life. You've got the money, but that's where it stops for you. You're too crude and vulgar to obtain anything else in life. The only thing you can do at this point is to buy your twobit hustlers and pretend you're a lady."

"The patron of the town whore," Lola said. "Look who's talking!"

"Say what you will about Dinah," Leonora said. "She's immune from your criticism. You thought you could come in here in triumph. You're wrong. You see, I've had it in Tortuga. I'm selling everything but Sacre-Coeur, and I don't plan to visit the island ever again. My house will become a ghost mansion." She sighed. "It was never mine anyway. The memory of Norton Huttnar is in the woodwork, just like the termites eating away at it."

Lola felt awesomely ill. The feeling started at her feet and worked its way up.

"You can imitate my clothes, my name, my car, everything, but not my talent," Leonora said. "I've made it in the world on my own creativity. You have nothing to offer. You took advantage of a senile degenerate."

"Baby, so did you!" Lola shouted.

Leonora paused momentarily. "In that you succeeded I'll admit. But what about the rest of your life? I don't envy the years ahead of you——trying to maintain a fast-fading illusion."

"What a joke!" Lola said, her pride so wounded she could scream. "How dare you talk to me like this. You're a has-been!"

"It's true, I *was* a has-been," Leonora said. "But no more. In this crazy world, has-beens are back in style. Perhaps swept there by a nostalgia craze, I really don't know. The point is, I'm on the verge of my biggest acclaim. I've lived so long and gone so far I am a living legend."

"You're feeding off the past."

"Yes," Leonora admitted, "I am pumping blood from it, but at least I've got a past to feed off. It's like insurance. As for you, you've won the battle, but lost the war."

"I hate you, you stinking white bitch," Lola said.

"I don't hate you," Leonora said, her calm returning. "Actually, I feel sorry for you. But all is not lost. With me out of Tortuga, you can dominate the town. I'll be back in New York, and you'll be left the biggest fish in the pond. Ruthie Elvina is hardly any competition."

Her words stabbing the air, Lola suddenly demanded, "I want Sacre-Coeur." Now was her only chance. "I've always wanted Sacre-Coeur. Ever since I was a little girl and used to walk by at night wondering what was going on inside. I'm tired of standing on the outside, wondering what's going on inside."

A fit of madness overcame Leonora. Throw caution to the wind. A way out of all this was emerging, part of her new lease on life. Sacre-Coeur had become her prison, her death-trap. Discard it. Without time to reconsider. "Let's make a deal, if I may speak in the vernacular. I'll give you Sacre-Coeur, providing you relinquish any control over my fashion house and the properties I own out at the beach."

"You'll give me Sacre-Coeur?" Lola was astonished. She had expected Leonora to fight for her life.

"Yes, I'll even give up my interest in the Garden of Delights, an establishment far more suited to your temperament than mine. Call your attorney on the mainland. Dollar for dollar from a standpoint of value, I'm offering you a good deal. You in Sacre-Coeur, how fitting. A fitting memorial to that bastard, Norton Huttnar. He, like you, loved drag. And how fitting that you and Amelia Le Blanc are splitting the revenue from the Garden of Delights."

"Your offer sounds good to me," Lola said. "I don't like land without buildings on it. Sacre-Coeur is the showplace of the island. Only thing is, you have only thirty days to move out completely."

"That's no problem," Leonora said. "I'll be gone long before that."

"Me, the grand lady of Sacre-Coeur." The words were spinning through Lola's head.

"My darling, I'm sure you'll be the grandest lady Sacre-Coeur ever had," Leonora said facetiously. "Excepting present company, of course." She smiled. "Good night."

"Good night," Lola chimed, shrugging off the insult. "I dismissed my chauffeur, not knowing how long I'd be here. Frankly, I thought we'd be all night."

"No problem," Leonora said. "My chauffeur will deliver you back to your hotel."

. . .

Emerging from the ocean, Numie slowly walked toward the Cuban exiles lounging in front of a wooden-framed bar with a side porch. They were drinking beer, but the blacks at the other end were downing straight hot bourbon from Dixie cups.

Next door was a grocery store. The aromatic smell of spices on its shelves——anise, cumin, chamomile flowers——seemed to drift across the graveled courtyard. Ringing its gingerbread veranda were stalks of ripe yellow bananas. Inside the shop, Numie passed open sacks of beans, pigtails of garlic, and canned magnolia milk to a pile of straw hats in the corner. He bought one, giving the shopkeeper a dollar.

The yellow sunlight of the late afternoon was bathing the docks as he came out. He paused for a long moment, then decided he'd better get back to the Lincoln parked nearby in front of Leonora's fashion house. In an hour or so, it'd be time to take her back to Sacre-Coeur.

A chill came over his body, as a breeze blew in from the turquoise water. In nothing but a skimpy white bikini, he suddenly felt nude. His pants were in the front seat of the limousine. He headed back.

Lola stood propped against the front fender of the Lincoln. "I'm not a lady used to waiting for her chauffeur."

He swallowed hard. "I thought Ned was your driver."

"I got rid of him for the rest of the day." She sighed, excited at the sight of Numie's body. "He's a pest he's so jealous of me. De la Mer said you was to drive me back to my suite. My temporary home, I might add." She placed her hands on her hips. "In thirty days Sacre Coeur will belong to this gorgeous lady you see before you."

"Leonora's turning over Sacre-Coeur to you?" he asked. "I can't believe it!"

She wet her lips seductively. "Believe it!"

"Let me slip on my pants."

"What you doing, running round here naked?" she asked.

"I'm not," he said, getting into his pants. "Just got back from a swim down at the pier."

Later, at the hotel, as he was helping her out, she firmly took hold of his wrist. "Come up to my suite. I have some very important business to discuss with you."

"Can't," he said as matter-of-factly as possible. "Got to get back to Leonora." He did not want to be alone with Lola, for any reason.

"De la Mer has rented you out for as long as I have need of your services," she said petulantly. "I'm in need right now." This defying her had got to stop.

"I'm not in that kind of business any more," he said. Nevertheless, he followed her. With Lola, you could never be certain. The simplest rejection could trigger a major attack.

In the hotel lobby, she was proud the desk clerk was seeing her going up to her suite with Numie. Numie had been gone for a long time, and that damn desk clerk just might be thinking he'd rejected her. Under no circumstances did she want to create the impression she'd ever been rejected...*by anyone*.

In the suite, Lola lit a cigarette and began puffing furiously, heaving her beanpole chest in and out.

"The suite's really great," Numie said nervously. Did they finally get it white enough for you?"

"Enough to blind 'em, baby."

He tugged at the wet bikini under his pants.

"Take it off," she said. "Make yourself at home."

"No, I've got to be going." He glanced nervously at the clock. "What's this important business you got with me?"

"As you know, I've got so many green bambinos stuffed up there——thanks to my sweet daddy——pictures of Lincoln and Washington just float through the air every time I let a fart."

"Congratulations," he said. "You got what you wanted. First, the commodore's money. Now, Sacre-Coeur. Even Ned, although Dinah doesn't seem to be missing him too much. That should wrap up your dream with a great big red ribbon."

"No way," she said, getting up from the white sofa. Her head felt dizzy so she sat back down. This conversation wasn't going according to her liking at all. "I need one more thing to make it right."

"What's that?" he asked.

"You, stud."

"I'm not a stud " he said. "Never was. It was all a mirage."

"True, but I'm gonna buy you anyway," Lola said.

"I'm not for sale." He wanted desperately to be with Anne.

Lola decided to dismiss that statement. A cheap hustler trick. Numie was just holding out for a high price. "Of course, you're getting older," she said, but you're still kinda cute. You're also hung which makes it nice for me. I've been known to go out with men, even if they are ugly, providing they got something dangling between their legs. I don't like to mess up my mouth for nothing."

"You didn't hear me," he said in defiant anger. "I'm not for sale."

She decided to once more ignore what he was saying. "I ain't exactly spring chicken myself, though I look like a girl of seventeen."

"I'm leaving." His temples were throbbing, and his heart was pounding furiously.

"Just one minute there, big boy," she said. "No one walks out on Lola La Mour. Or did you know that?"

"No, I didn't know that." He turned, glaring at her, instinctively bracing himself. "Even if I did, I'd still leave."

Suddenly, his message was all too clear. She let out a cry which she quickly tried to muffle with a laugh. But the laugh sounded too hysterical. He was really going. Turning her down in spite of her newly acquired power and money.

"What's got into you? I know Ralph ain't keeping you no more. Then who is?"

"Nobody, I'm working for a living," he said. "I'm a chauffeur, remember?"

"Seventy-five bucks a week," she said sarcastically. "Don't jive me. Okay, who's your new john?"

"I don't have one." He paused. "But I do have a girl. A real one."

Lola recoiled as if slapped. "Don't tell me you and that beer-guzzling Bronx dyke have got together and are going to have a meaningful relationship. What a buttgrabber!"

"Your opinion of it doesn't matter," he said, furious at himself for having revealed even this brief insight into his life. "Goodbye, Lola. I mean really goodbye."

"You can't walk out on me after all I've done for you." Nails arched, she jumped up.

"I thank you for feeding me when I first came to Tortuga," he said. But let's don't prolong this any more than we have to." At the door, he paused. Something told him to look back. Just as he did, an ashtray sailed past his ear, crashing into the door. He ducked. Thank God she was a bad shot.

She was racing toward him, both fists raised in the air. She flayed his chest. "How dare you reject me, you lilywhite bastard," she screamed. Then she slapped his face. "For such an experienced hustler, you don't know nothing about black bitches in heat. We're the toughest thing since leather dildos. You're going nowhere, baby."

"You're making an ass out of yourself." No sooner had he said that than he regretted it. He was convinced that Lola was insane; and here he was——possibly blowing his last chance to get out of Tortuga in one piece.

At first, she didn't respond. It was as if she hadn't heard him again. She just stood there, glaring, as was her way. Her hands were still shaped into fists, but she eventually released her grip, her arms falling limply by her sides.

For the first time since she was a little girl, she saw herself reflected in someone else's eyes. To Numie, she was a grotesque. Now she knew why she always projected a glamorous image of herself. It was her defense, her only way to prevent the harsh eyes of the world from judging her. She'd judge them first, the sons-of-bitches.

She was trapped! Numie had robbed her of something vital, making her think less of herself. She was afraid and insecure in his presence. Without fully knowing why, it was the most necessary thing in the world to keep him with her. Not because of who he was, or even that he was that special. It was because she felt if she lost him, she'd lose everything. He was the test by which she had to measure her new position in life. Stiffening her back, she braced for her grandstand play.

Tossing back her face and sobbing like some frantic thing, she screamed, "I'm a woman, too. I'm real. Just as real as Anne. Now don't tell me there's a world of difference between the two. I'm just as good as any woman. Better!" Her hands were on him, clutching. "I want you for my man. I'll look after you, take care of you when you get sick. I'll buy you a car, jewelry, all the fancy clothes you want. We'll travel. I mean, de luxe." Her hands waved around her Shirley Temple blonde curls like moths in a closet. "Okay, dammit, I'll let you in through the front door next time."

He greeted her with a startled look.

"Yes, that way," she said. "Didn't you hear about the show I put on last night? I showed the whole town my pussy. Then Ned really broke me in style. And how!"

"No, I didn't hear about it," he said. "Even if I did, it wouldn't make any difference. I'm flattered that you want to hold onto me, but I don't love you."

"You're in love with Anne?" she asked contemptuously.

"No, I don't love her either, not really," he said. "But I feel with her I could learn to. At least I might grow. Having you give me things, having you as my boss-lady, that's nowhere."

"Growth, you motherfucker!" Lola yelled. "What do you know about growth? The word makes me sick. I've grown. Look how far I've come in the world——against all the odds you honky types put in my way."

"I know, he said. "You've made it. You'll go on making it. But without me."

"Walk out that door, and you're the same as dead in this town, cousin," she said.

"That's a chance I've got to take," he replied coolly. "I'd be dead if I stayed here."

Before she realized it, he was gone. At first, she found it hard to believe she'd really let him get away. Tight with frustration and humiliation, her lips began to quiver. Rushing to the window, she saw him cross the street and get into the Lincoln. His shoulders, so broad and strapping. All these years as a hustler, and he'd still retained a certain innocence.

Closing the curtain, she started to cry. In some way, something beautiful had gone out of her life. She wasn't quite certain what it was. Just that she wanted it, and now it was to be no more.

It was time for her afternoon bath. Stepping out of her outfit, she reached for a robe. Before the mirror she examined each and every one of her gleaming white front teeth. Then she removed her wig of blonde curls. The face certainly wasn't pretty. She had that plucked chicken look today.

In the tepid water, she relaxed, breathing deeply. Touching between her legs, she fantasized what it would be like to take Numie like a real woman. But who was she kidding? Herself, that was for sure. Numie was nothing but one of those twobit hustlers De la Mer was talking about. Lola hadn't gotten this far in the world getting sentimental over twobit hustlers.

One thought stood out. He had turned her down. Defying, doublecrossing, and humiliating. For that, he had to be punished.

Getting out of the tub quickly, she superficially dried herself. Then she headed for the telephone.

. . .

On the way to Sacre-Coeur, Numie stepped hard on the accelerator. He was fighting a gnawing feeling of guilt he didn't understand. With Lola, he was only doing what he must.

Parked in front of the gate to Leonora's house, was a car. Four men were seated in it.

Numie pumped the brakes, bringing the old limousine to a stop only moments before ramming the other vehicle.

One of the men got out. The others followed. "Ned!" Numie said. "What in hell's going on?"

"Get out!" Ned ordered.

"Come on," Numie protested. He opened the door. "What's the trouble?"

"You are," said a burly man in back of Ned.

Numie started to back away. From all sides, the men were closing in. The night was a black blur. A hand grabbed Numie's neck, and he was pulled back so roughly two buttons popped from his shirt.

"Get your goddamn hands off me," Numie yelled.

"Hey guys," one of his attackers said, "this one ain't none too friendly."

One man struck a blow to Numie's stomach. Doubling over in pain, he raised up only to see their faces now.

Tough, hard, bitter.

An arm from behind tightened around Numie's neck like a noose. He struggled to get away——only to be rewarded with another fist in the gut. His situation was hopeless! Even so, he tried to make a run for it. But he was held back. Kicks, hits, blows came from all directions. He struck blindly at his tormentors, rarely finding his mark. Head spinning, he finally used his hands only to ward off blows to his face. Fists continued to pound him furiously.

He fell to the ground. Then hands grabbed him again, spread-eagling his body. His temple was throbbing, his chest was a riot of pain.

One man was pulling off his belt. Soon its heavy metal studs were whipping against Numie's face. Blood was running from his nose.

The men encircled Numie. The blows had stopped.

Numie slowly opened his eyes onto a sea of leering faces. The men were laughing.

A leather gloved hand pulled his hair so his head snapped back. Mud was rubbed into his eyes and nose. The leather probe was at his mouth, gouging it open. The fingers stabbed their way inside, brushing his teeth with the foul-tasting dirt.

Numie was going to vomit at any moment. Only when his stomach finally rebelled did the men back away. He vomited again and again till nothing was left in his system. Then he dry-gagged some more.

Someone was pouring liquor down on him. He welcomed its cleansing effect, its stinging sensation. Alcohol for his wounds. The whiskey stopped. Numie lay quietly on the ground, not daring to move, not wanting to think what was going to happen next.

He heard the car motor starting and then the car backed out of the driveway.

Numie tried to get to his feet, but was too weak and bruised.

The car swerved, then stopped. All the men got in except Ned. He remained for a moment, looking down at Numie.

"Get in, Ned," the driver called. "Let's get out of here."

Ned spat, then got into the front seat. "Lola wanted us to give you something to remember her by."

Chapter Thirty

Numie was emerging from a painful sleep. A mocking voice, strange and guttural, was calling to him, then laughing and jeering as he tried to find his way in darkness. Eventually, the voice drifted off.

Slowly, his eyes opened. The room was a blur. There was a stabbing pain in his chest. He raised his hand to his face. It was swollen, especially under his eyes. He felt as if two large rocks were embedded there.

But he could see! After a few moments the clouds lifted. Anne was the first object he focused on. Silently smoking a cigarette, she was at the foot of his bed, an elbow resting on her knee; she looked different. The luster was gone from her large green eyes which stared at him from under her deep smooth brow. The arch of her lean face was overshadowed by the sensual fleshy lips. Narrow at the waist, her morning gown billowed out at the top, making her look warm and seductive.

At first, she didn't say anything——just sat there dangling her coral-colored slipper in the air and smoking. Her mood seemed detached, almost haughty. It was as if she in some way were blaming him for his beating. Her smile was faint, her voice strained. "Don't tell me," she said. "Lola's behind what happened to you. I could pluck out every black hair in her head."

"She'd just wear a wig."

Now Anne was hovering over him.

Lost in her softness, he snuggled his head into her breasts, allowing sobs to wrack his body. Fifteen minutes later, he was still clinging. Through her warmth and love, he was being restored to life, learning to trust again. At moments the dark vision of last night descended, the blows raining down, then it would lift again, as he immersed himself in the sweet smell of Anne. Finally, he broke away, regaining control, feeling embarrassed. "What time is it?"

"It's morning," she said, straightening up. "About ten o'clock."

"Has Leonora been asking for me?"

"She knows you've been beaten," she said. "She was

furious. First Dinah, now you."

"At least she showed some concern."

"Not about the beating," Anne said, "but about the loss of your services for today. The old island tour's set for this afternoon. Remember, Ruthie Elvina put Sacre-Coeur on the program? Everybody and his cousin will be here soon."

He sat up. "Tangerine, I just happened to remember. She's coming home today."

"Don't worry," Anne said, placing her hands on his shoulder and gently lowering him back. "Everything's okay. I hired a carpenter to seal up the hole and replace her stairway. Her place is a mess, though. I didn't have time to get over there and do much work myself. Most of her furniture, if you can call it that, was ruined in the storm."

"I talked to her yesterday," he said. "I tried to get her to stay on at the hospital. At least there someone would look after her. But she wouldn't listen."

"From what I hear," Anne said, "the staff will be only too glad to get rid of her. That's probably why they agreed to let her go early."

A new wave of dizziness was sweeping over him. Falling back against the pillow, he gently traced the swelling under his eyes with the tips of his fingers.

"I'll get an ice pack," she said, rising from the bed. "I don't know if you should get up or not. We had a doctor look at you last night. No broken bones."

"But I'm black and blue as that sick bitch, Lola," he said, seething at the very mention of her name.

"You look awful," she said. "Let's don't even talk about Lola. If I start thinking about her, I'd want to kill her. Let's face it: she's got an in with the sheriff. She knows she can do as she damn pleases in this rotten town, and get away with it."

"If it weren't for Tangerine," he said, "I'd split today. I've had it here!"

"Speaking of that," she said, her face brightening up. "The letter, the one you told me about. I think it's here."

Eyes wide open, he sat up in bed, ignoring his dizziness, "It did come." Eagerly he tore open the envelope.

In a bad, arthritic scrawl, these words rose up from the page:

"Dearest Numie,

Now I know what happened to you. I had figured you as gone forever. Your letter was a blessing, a real spirit-lifter. Living alone at eighty-three is not the easiest way of life. Bad heart, long drawn-out leukemia, and a few other minor ills such as arthritis——but still grateful for God's wonderful blessings. I'm not even smoking the weed anymore——so you know I've changed. All my beatniks have gone and left me. As you know, Lisa ran off to Oregon with No-count. Bob and Spence have broken up their courtship. Spence went back to all his family's money, and Bob is now living in the city with some TV producer, a one-time popular vocalist. Different lives, but I love them dearly. Even Maria has gone, although she and I never warmed up to each other too much. But not one phone call, not one letter, until yours came today. You must grow old to appreciate being remembered.

No-count bad-mouthed you a lot before striking out for Oregon. Said you were a male prostitute. How dumb he must have thought I was. Men can't be whores. They're not biologically built that way. I've known a few of the female kind, though. One of my sons——lost both my boys in the war——brought one of those painted heifers up from the city one night. I was coming across the field with a pail of milk. Tossed the whole bucket right in her face. Later on, I regretted throwing away good milk on such a cheap slut.

The place here is going to rot. A disgrace to an old-time dirt farmer with a green thumb like me. Now I seldom dare look out on my sadly neglected garden. While resting on my bed, my line of vision is lifted above ground level to enjoy the tall chestnut tree I planted forty-five years ago.

Of course, you'd be welcome. Come on home. My farm is probably the only home you've ever had. Come and work it, Numie, and take care of me. In return I'll give it to you, the whole thing, when I pass on. It's the only way you're going to get your feet planted solid on ground. I won't have any use for the place where I'm going. I thought Lisa wanted it, but I guess she wanted No-count more. I told her at the time she was losing a good man, letting you get away.

Winter's coming on, and I fear I won't make it through January without some help. Sometimes, I can't even heat up a *can of Campbell's soup.*

You get on up here now just as fast as you can. Lot of work to be done before the snow comes.

Just for the occasion, I'll break my resolution and light up with you.

Love and God bless,
    Grandma."

"Good news?" Anne asked.

"Good news," he said, smiling at her. He paused, then asked awkwardly, "Wanta come with me?"

"Thought you'd never ask," she said, running her hands through his hair. "Yes."

"You didn't ask where," he said.

"Does it matter?" she said. Her fingers snaked around his ear. "More to the point, do you love me?"

He hesitated. It was easier to say yes, but it wasn't honest. He'd never had an honest relationship with anyone. It was time to start now. "I don't know how to answer that. I want to love you, that's for sure. I'd like to tell you I love you. That you're the most important person who ever lived as far as I'm concerned. That you are. But until I'm different, until I've gotten over a lot of hangups, that isn't saying too much. There haven't been many important people in my life."

"I know that," she said softly. "I'm not asking much myself. That you let me go with you. We'll both try to survive...together."

"We can give it a try," he said.

"Maybe that's what love really is," she said.

"I wish I was all fresh and pure," he said. "But, as you know, everybody's had me. Lola, Ralph——you name it."

"No one's ever really had you," she said. "Not even me. But one day I will. You'll see."

. . .

At the foot of the rickety steps to Tangerine's Taj Mahal white-coated attendants were heaving up the stretcher inch by inch.

"Steady there, for God's sake," its passenger directed. "This ain't no coffin. The body's still alive."

She didn't look like herself any more. The once-vibrant orange hair was now gray at the roots. The always colorful face was drained——not even a touch of its usual garish make-up. All that lost weight made the flesh hang from her bones.

Without her tinsel, Tangerine Blanchard was a very sad Christmas tree.

At the top, Numie was waiting. "Welcome home," he said warmly.

"Thought those clowns would never get me here," she said. "My God, look at you. They're letting you out of the hospital, but you look like you should go in."

"A little accident," he said, unsteady on his feet. "I was drinking last night and ran into something."

"The story of my life," she said. "I was in six car accidents before I turned sweet sixteen."

He held the screen door open.

"My God, I can't believe it," she cried from inside. "You boarded up that blasted hole——Blanchard's folly."

"Of course," he said. "We didn't want you taking another dive."

The attendants moved their burden into the living room and into a wheelchair. "I just can't believe it," she said. "The place is a mess."

"I told you about the storm."

"Christ," she called out, "new curtains."

"Yeah", he said. "They arrived at noon. Compliments of Lola La Mour. Now that she's completed her suite at the hotel, she fancies herself an interior decorator."

"Pale yellow, though," Tangerine said, childlike in her disappointment. "Not for me at all. There's nothing pale about me. I like color to vibrate."

One of the attendants came over to ask, "Don't you think we ought to put her to bed before we go?"

Good idea," Numie replied. "When's the nurse due?"

"Around four," he answered.

"I want to sit here and talk to my good-looking boy friend," Tangerine said. "I've had enough of beds unless there's some action going on in them."

"Okay, I'll take care of her," Numie said, ushering the attendants to the door.

"Numie," Tangerine summoned.

He sat down on the new sofa Lola had sent over. "How do you like it?" he asked, rubbing the red velvet and leaning back against the yellowy gilt frame.

"It was just great of Lola to do all these fancy things for me," Tangerine said. "But I was very attached to my old sofa. I know it wasn't in the best of shape, but a lot of my life took place on that sofa. I'd been meaning to get it repaired and upholstered."

"The storm completely ruined it," Numie said. She was making him feel guilty. "Really it did."

"Let's face it." Tangerine pushed back her hair, hesitating a long moment before speaking. "After all Lola——and I love Lola dearly——*Lola is colored*. I know that don't mean nothing to us. Both of us are liberated. We don't see color. We see only what's inside the person. But, honey, colored folks have a taste they brought over from Africa. It's not to white folk's liking."

Numie sat rigidly on the sofa, not saying a word.

Tangerine was eying the rest of the room skeptically.

Finally, he got up. "Let me get you some bourbon. I know you must be dry." He went to the kitchen. Three whole hours before the nurse was due!

He felt trapped. He knew Tangerine was dying and he did not want to face the pain her death would inflict on him.

"Numie," the demanding voice came from the bedroom where she'd wheeled herself. "My slop jar! The only thing my mama ever left me. It's gone! Numie."

. . .

Sunglasses covered her bruises, but otherwise Leonora gave herself her own seal of approval. The dress was perfect. A bit nostalgic perhaps, but with a touch of 'today.' The gown was oyster pink, dripping down, then caught up in intricate embroidery on her hips.

Already the report reaching her was that Sacre-Coeur was the highlight of the old island tour. Bringing in bartenders and plying all the guests with hard liquor helped make it so.

At the far end of the patio, a buffet table groaned with old island food: raw conch salad, conch fritters, shrimp in their shells steamed in beer, Spanish black beans, and picadillo, with big pitchers of Sangria and lots of key lime pie.

No people were lingering at Ruthie Elvina's house, if they even made it over there at all. Everybody was at Leonora's.

Guests were milling about, inspecting her porcelain collection, criticizing her art, and testing out her antique chairs. In the faraway Edwardian gazebo a young couple were making love, seemingly oblivious to the audience they were attracting. At the edge of the garden, one hairy-legged man in Bermuda shorts was vomiting, his dirndl-clad wife slapping him on the back.

Leonora stood in the parlor, looking out. Too many flowers, she thought. The house looked funereal. Too much wax was on the parquet floors. She nearly slipped.

In the garden, she was bathed in vibrant colors. The sharp blue of the sky, the blinding yellow from the sun, the flame from the flowers——everything convinced her she'd selected the right color, oyster pink, for her gown. It softened nature's vividness, giving her a subtlety and femininity no one else had.

Curiously stiff, she moved through the crowd. No one seemed to pay attention to her. Perhaps she should have worn a more striking gown, if vulgarity were needed to attract the masses.

Then she realized this impression was wrong. They were noticing her, but shyly, too afraid to approach. They seemingly knew they were invaders in her home, and were respectfully keeping their distance.

Despite her earlier protests, Leonora was glad Ruthie Elvina had advertised Sacre-Coeur on the old island tour. Somehow it had all become part of Leonora's plan to face the public again. How fitting she should throw open the gates of Sacre-Coeur after keeping them closed for all these years. Leonora belonged to the world now, the world with all its grossness and horror as reflected in her garden today, but belong she did.

Back like a predatory bird of prey, Teddy Albury, the real-estate agent, was at her side. His sharp beak was pecking her cheek. She withdrew at this sudden familiarity. That and the smell of stale vodka were offensive.

"I didn't think you'd dare set foot in Sacre-Coeur again after what you did to me," she said.

"Everything's cool, baby," he said.

"Don't baby me."

"Your Picasso's outside, all neatly wrapped up in a newspaper," he said. "No damage." He sighed. "Now we can be friends."

"Where did you find my Kandinsky?" she asked.

"In a trailer park," he said, "but that's a long story."

"I've heard enough of your long-winded tales," she said.

"I found out where the culprit lived from someone who saw us leaving Commodore Philip's. When I got to the trailer park, I surprised him at the door. I grabbed him by the neck of his shirt, slapped him hard across the face, and said, 'It's me'."

"Please," Leonora protested, "after two attacks on my household staff, I can't stand another story of violence."

He ignored her protestations. "He pretended not to know me," Teddy said. "'You know who in the fuck I am, and you know what I'm here for,' I said. I placed my knee on the boy's throat in the appropriate thug fashion, then I cracked him in the face again."

"I beg you," Leonora implored.

"'If that painting's not here, it's going to be bad, bad for you', I said. 'I don't know what I'm doing when I get drunk,' he said. 'I'll get it for you'. The Picasso was in the trunk of his car, resting on a pile of luggage."

Leonora breathed with relief, hoping this was the end.

"I told him," Teddy said, 'You're just lucky I don't beat you so bad you'll never rob someone gay again. I know you're married, and I know you think you're straight. But you ain't, you see. You're gay!'

In horror Leonora glanced at her guests. All eyes were turned on them.

Teddy went on. "'Remember?' I asked him. 'We went to bed together. And as for the change you stole from my pocket, I want you to keep it to pay back the next man you go down on.' That was it, Leonora. I just don't trust anybody any more."

By now, Leonora had had enough. "And I don't trust you,"

she said, motioning for one of the waiters. "I'll have the painting brought in. If it's all right, I'll drop charges against you."

"You can afford to be generous," Teddy said.

"What do you mean?" she asked.

"The whole town's heard about the deal you made with Lola," he said. "She's getting this old white elephant. If the termites stopped holding hands, Sacre-Coeur would collapse."

"That's insulting!"

"You traded Lola half a million dollars worth of beach property for this firetrap," Teddy accused.

"I beg your pardon," Leonora said.

"Look, baby, you're going to have to negotiate with me if you want to sell the beach property," Teddy said. "High rise is coming to Tortuga. Progress is on its way. Just two nights ago Ruthie Elvina finally agreed to our price."

"Really?" Leonora asked, "Half a million. You must think I'm Lola. This is no dumb transsexual you're talking to." She arched her back. "One million dollars——or else."

"One million!" Teddy staggered back. "You must be out of your mind."

"The whole town keeps saying that about me," she replied. "We'll see who's out of her mind. Without my land, you can't have risers on the beach. I control too much of the property."

"One million dollars——that's robbery," he charged.

"But something tells me you boys will come up with it," Leonora smiled.

"You're a bandit, you know that," he accused. "First you rob Lola. Now us."

"Lola robbed the commodore to get the claim to the property in the first place," Leonora said. "Dare I look into the shady pasts of the rest of you entrepreneurs. Now if you'll excuse me, my guests are waiting."

By her side were a bull-necked husband and his wife with her black hair coiled and contorted.

"Are you *the* Leonora de la Mer?" the woman asked.

Bowing theatrically, Leonora responded with an elaborate smile. "Indisputably," she said.

. . .

That night Numie wanted to be alone; he didn't even want to see Anne. Crossing the street from Tangerine's, he stayed much too long at a bar there.

It was after midnight when he noticed the time. He'd promised to relieve the nurse at ten. During his last Scotch, he finally staggered out on his way to her apartment.

Anne was waiting on the balcony, "Hi," she said, just a touch of anger in her voice. "You'd better sober up."

"Anne, what are you doing here?" He kissed her gently on the lips.

"The nurse quit," she said. "Called me at Sacre-Coeur. Said Tangerine was insulting."

He stumbled in. "She probably was. After all, dying doesn't bring out the best in us. How is she?"

"Okay, I guess," Anne said. "I've been letting her sleep."

He entered the bedroom. At first, there wasn't a sound, not even Tangerine's usual heavy breathing. In panic, he flipped on a light.

There Tangerine lay helplessly on the bed steeped in her own wastes. She'd lost control, like the man at the hospital. Her open eyes were the saddest he'd ever seen.

Trembling, he had to turn away. He was going to be sick himself from too much Scotch. Rushing into the bathroom, he vomited.

"Help me, Numie," Tangerine moaned as he came back in the bedroom. "Help me."

"It's okay, baby." He approached the bed slowly, reaching down and lifting her hand in a squeeze.

Anne was at the door. "My God," she said, seeing the mess. "Look, we've got to have round-the-clock nurses. They're trained for things like this."

He looked down at the filthy bed, fighting a lifetime of disgust. "Okay," he told Anne, "bring me some hot water." Just as he finished removing Tangerine's last soiled garment, a pan was placed on the nightstand.

Tangerine heaved herself up slightly in bed, watching Numie's maneuvers. Her lips were moving in some silent and feverish prayer.

"I'll need some washcloths and soap," he told Anne. "See if there are fresh sheets in the hall closet." The vomiting and the shock of seeing Tangerine had momentarily sobered him.

Gently, and with Anne's help, he moved the sick woman to the clean side of the bed. Then he began to wash her naked body. Within moments, she was no longer his old friend but a dying stranger who had to be helped.

Anne slid the sheets out from under, as he lifted Tangerine. Then Anne made up half the bed so Tangerine could be rolled onto them.

As soon as he'd finished, he rushed out. In the bathroom, he peeled off his clothes and jumped in the shower. Then, dressed again, he joined Anne in the living room.

She sat there on the newly bought sofa, smoking a cigarette. "You were very good," she said. "I'm going to be in fine hands if I ever get sick."

"Thanks a lot," he said. "We can't handle this, though. Somehow I've got to talk her into going back to the hospital. That's where she belongs."

"Do you think she's okay for tonight?" Anne asked.

"Don't worry," he said. "I'm spending the night on the sofa."

"I wish I could stay with you, but I have to get back to Leonora," she said. "That creature is driving me up the wall. I don't know how much more I can take."

"We won't be here long, I promise," he said. "We'll stick it out a little longer, and then we've got a date with grandma. We need a little more money before we leave."

"Good night," she said.

He held her for a long moment, kissing her goodbye.

She left without saying another word.

He went right back to the bedroom——relieved to find Tangerine as he'd left her, lying on the fresh sheets.

She opened her eyes slowly and looked up. "Sugar," she whispered, "don't let it happen again. You won't, will you? *Please*." She reached for his hand and held on.

He searched her eyes carefully, looking for some trace of the woman who'd so enchanted him. But there was none. "I won't, sweetheart," he promised. "I won't let it happen again. You've got to go back to the hospital tomorrow."

"No," she said, her voice desperate. "No, I'm not going to leave my bed——my own Taj Mahal." Her face was so white she seemed to have powdered it. Peering at him with desolate black eyes, he knew she was aware of her trap.

"We can't take care of you here without nurses, you know that," he said.

"I'm not going to be a bother to no one," she said. "Really I'm not. I'm not going to be a bother no more."

Her words were unexpected. What did she mean? That she was going to kill herself? "It's not that you're a bother," he finally said. "It's just that we're not prepared to take care of you here."

"I know," she said, sighing. "It's time to go when you can't look after yourself."

"You'll get better soon," he assured her. "You'll be up and about." His words sounded hollow.

"What about you?" she asked, taking his hand. "Who's going to take care of you?"

"I've always gone it alone," he said. "But things are changing now."

Her hand dropped. "Both you and me, Numie, we're born losers."

"That's one hell of a cheery note." He drew back from her. Was she using her illness as a license to say what she really thought about him?

"Trouble with me is," she went on, "I've been too cheery all my life, never facing up to the truth. But you've got to."

She coughed suddenly. "You're not going to gain anything from Leonora or Lola——only trouble, more than you can handle. You can't cope with those crazy ladies."

"I've learned that," he said, not wanting to hear it.

"With Anne, it's different," she said weakly. "For the first time in your life, someone has come along to offer you something." She seemed impatient. "She's in love with you. You have a chance at a life together." Tears were forming. "I wish somebody had come along and offered me that long ago."

"Anne and I can make it, I'm sure," he said.

"You can't make it here," she said. "I've told Anne that."

"She's convinced," he said.

Tangerine's head was reeling.

"You okay?" he asked.

"No." She paused for a long, awkward moment. "What broke my heart was wanting things I could never get. If I'd been more honest with myself, I'd a come out one hell of a lot better." The cough returned. "Why can't you settle for less than your big dream of striking it rich? Us southerners always think we're going to be rich one day. Your own roof over your head, a decent job where you're not put down, and someone to love you——maybe that's what it's all about."

"The whole idea sounds less and less dull," he said.

She held her throat, her breathing growing faint. Suddenly reaching out, she was pressing his head against her naked breasts.

Slowly he withdrew. "Good night, sweet soul," he said in a voice foreign to him. "I'll be in the next room if you need anything."

"Good night," she said softly.

At the doorway, he paused to look back.

"Numie," she said, "my mama used to read the Bible to me. And once when I was very young, I believed it. But the Bible is a lie."

"In what way?" he asked.

"The meek do not inherit the earth," she said.

. . .

He lay quietly on the sofa, wide awake and dry-eyed. He was beyond tears.

It was morning now.

Tangerine was gone.

The men from the funeral parlor had come. They had taken her body away.

Reluctantly, he got up. First he locked the screen door. Then he pulled down the shades. At last, he lay back on the sofa.

In the afternoon, someone came up the steps, knocked, then called out. He didn't answer——nor did he recognize the male voice. Someone else came later. But he didn't budge from the sofa. Finally, whoever it was went away.

Lying there was strangely peaceful. The apartment was permeated not with the smell of death, but memories. The spirit of Tangerine haunted its walls.

The whole world was locked out——even the sick old woman he'd ministered to last night. Not she, but Tangerine, was inside him now.

Fern Cornelia Blanchard, his Georgia peach. His orange-haired clown. His loving friend and refuge. His Halloween.

Full of his own Tangerine, he smiled. Then power surged through his body. *Yes, she was inside.* All the best of his Tangerine.

In his excitement, he crouched on the edge of the sofa, ready to spring. At the first noise, he leapt to his feet.

Down below a hammer pounded. Was it the sound of building? Or of tearing away?

. . .

"I'm not wearing black and that's that," Lola was screaming. "I don't care whose funeral it is."

Pacing the hotel suite, Ned fumed. "You do not show up at funerals looking like some overripe sunflower."

"And why not?" she asked. "You could have said a fresh spring daisy. This daffodil color is just right for me. I sent the leftover material over to Tangerine's right before she died to make her some new curtains out of it."

"I'm not going with you unless you act like you got some raising," Ned said.

"De la Mer will be there all draped out in black," Lola said. "I'm not into that scene. We'll both end up looking like two black widows. Besides, black don't do nothing for me."

"This is no goddamn fashion contest," he said. "A woman has died. We're there to show our respects, even if she was white."

"Anyway, Tangerine's dying like this caught me off guard," Lola protested. "I think she willed herself to death with no concern or regard for her mourners. I've already had one death to go through. Tangerine should have thought of someone other than herself."

"I'll be damned," he said. "You're blaming her for dying. For doing *you* an injustice. Now I've heard everything!"

Behind the wheel of the Cadillac Ned was bumping along the rough stone lane to the graveyard.

In the back seat, Lola was virtually hidden under a black lace veil attached to a big black cloche hat. Black all over, she hated the feeling. Had she not been in such bad shape, she would not have given in to Ned.

"You'd think," she said, "with all De la Mer's money she would have hired the brass band. After all, Tangerine was her servant, not mine."

"De la Mer didn't want no brass band," Ned said. "That's why you decided to hire it. Tell it like it is, sister."

"You're way off," Lola yelled. "When my daddy died, I wanted to hire a brass band and couldn t afford one. I decided I'd become so rich the next time somebody up and died——even if I didn't know them too well——I was gonna go out and hire a big brass band."

The Cadillac screeched to a halt at the entrance to the necropolis. The funeral hearse was waiting.

Knowing who was footing the bill, the brass band——its members all smiles——was there to greet Lola. As Ned opened the car door to her, she was heralded by blowing coronets from the Delgado brothers and the rotten tuba playing of BoJo, her accompanist at the bar. In fact, BoJo was so bad, big Luis Machin was trying to drown him out with a bass drum.

The funeral march sounded as Lola made her way past the little white church into the graveyard. The band followed her.

On the periphery of her vision, rows of angels on marble guard seemingly made way for her, as she passed stone crosses and moss-green urns. She was acutely aware of the impression she was making in front of the dozen or so visitors gathered at Tangerine's grave site.

Lola was trying to work with basic black. The least she could hope for was that she'd stand out as a silhouette against the whiteness of the sunny day.

In lieu of pallbearers, the owners of the funeral parlor had recruited his four sons. Tilting and swaying the coffin, they crossed the mounds of earth, arriving at the site. Awkwardly, they put down their burden, standing uncomfortably about, the sun making their black, pin-striped suits appear purple.

Before the grave, Lola positioned herself in front of two gigantic crescent-shaped wreaths of pale yellow chrysanthemums she had ordered.

She was furious. De la Mer wasn't here yet. Just like the bitch to try to steal the show at the last moment.

It was then she noticed a black Lincoln pulling to a halt at the other side of the graveyard.

Lola's black veil swirled in the wind, revealing her face to a small group. It was a mask of anger.

De la Mer had dared wear all white!

The day was hot, the sun beating down fiercely. As Numie held the door back, Leonora emerged, a portrait in white and heavily veiled. Her white linen suit with a pleated skirt was simple, as were her white pumps. Her white veil was held in position by her large white leghorn hat. She was a tall, mysterious goddess.

"There!" Lola hissed loudly to Ned, hiding behind the yellow chrysanthemums. "See what I told you? Everybody's looking at her. Not at me in the goddamn soot color. You'll pay for this."

"Fuck off!" Ned said, "Who's everybody? There's ten people here at the most."

Propped up by Anne on one side and Numie on the other, Leonora made her way through the graveyard. On her right, she was passing her own unfinished tombstone. She knew it was there, but didn't dare look. The strong presence of Numie made her embarrassed——sorry that he'd ever seen her in such a weak condition. First thing tomorrow morning, she was going to order her tombstone destroyed. She had decided that when she did die, she didn't want to be buried in Tortuga. The port town had been her grave as a child, and then later in life. She much preferred cremation, her ashes tossed to the wind——a freedom she'd never known in life.

Facing Lola across the grave site, she glanced disdainfully at her. Her business with Lola was concluded. The details would be worked out by their attorneys. She had no more need to soil her life with trashy transsexuals.

Leonora's body shook at the thought of Tangerine. Poor, dear Tangerine. Of course, with Leonora leaving, Tangerine would have destroyed herself anyway——or else worked at Sacre-Coeur for Lola, God forbid. It would have been impossible to have taken Tangerine to New York. She wouldn't have fitted in. Without Leonora, Tangerine would have had no life. She was convinced that Tangerine knew that——not in her conscious mind, but deep down. It was as if she, Leonora, were a great queen, and Tangerine was one of her subjects. Was Tangerine symbolically throwing her body on the funeral pyre of the old Leonora because she had no place with the new one?

At first, Numie stood across the freshly dug grave facing Lola. She wasn't looking in his direction, and he was glad. Ned stayed concealed behind the mass of chrysanthemums. Funny, but he didn't hate Ned. Somehow he knew that Ned's attack on him was part of a job he'd fallen heir to. It was Lola he hated. But did he? Could you really hate the insane?

There stood Lola in her flaming, reckless way that even the blackness of the veil couldn't conceal. She was still gaudy, still contemptuous of life she couldn't control. All her blazing anger came from some force within her she couldn't direct. That force was burning away. In time, it would consume Lola in its fire. He didn't need to strike back at her. Besides, he was no fool. What did he expect, messing around with a psycho like Lola? He was lucky he'd gotten only a beating and hadn't been killed.

All eyes turned suddenly at the approach of a tall man from below. He wore a dark suit and sunglasses. It was Mike Morgan, the reporter from Associated Press. He'd cared enough to attend!

Joy swept through Numie. The joy of having someone here who'd known Tangerine in a younger, happier day.

As soon as Morgan fell into place next to a gloomy Lola, the pastor began to speak.

But who could listen? The pastor had never known Tangerine. How could his words connect with her life, her spirit? Numie bit his quivering lips.

Other than himself, only Morgan seemed at all moved. His face was an austere mask——except for one lone tear that fell, getting lost in his mustache.

Looking out across the graveyard, Numie's eyes were fixed on the overturned mossy slabs so ravaged by time. Why did people end up like this? On this lonely, windswept hill where nothing lived but lizards, wild grass, and weeds. "Oh, God," he said aloud.

Anne reached for him. But otherwise his outburst went unnoticed. Everybody else was intently staring at the coffin.

As the coffin was lowered into the grave, the brass band was playing, "Nearer My God To Thee."

The pastor's words, "Ashes to ashes and dust to dust," were carried by the wind.

Numie trembled. All that was left of Tangerine was in that cheap wooden box. His breath came in gasps——tears were blurring his eyes. The tears became frozen, then splintered like broken glass, blinding him.

He ran.

. . .

Slowly and deliberately Numie was treading his way across the docks. The wooden planks on the wharf dated from Reconstruction days. Although they'd survived hurricanes and tropical storms, they were sagging dangerously. Many of the pilings had collapsed. Every few feet was another pitfall, another Blanchard's folly.

An unpainted, wooden-framed warehouse was mistress of the wharf. But even her front sagged in rhythmic sympathy with the docks. Her huge doors opening onto the pier had long ago caved in——so they were boarded up.

Tangerine was gone now, but what about her prediction? Would he end up the way she did? A loser like her?

So many questions, so few answers.

He stared out at the sea. When he came to this town, he was a fugitive at the end of the line. But was Tortuga really the end? When towns ran out, didn't you have to go back and start all over again?

Was Tortuga just the beginning of a new journey?

. . .

In her bedroom, Leonora was dictating into her tape recorder. Of all the times in life she didn't want to attend a funeral, today was the day. Right when she was trying to escape any association with death, she had found herself in the graveyard, that awful graveyard, again. Best to wipe it out and get on with her life.

A sudden knock sounded on the door. "Who in hell?" she shouted. "Nothing but interruptions. I'm dictating. Let me alone."

"I have to see you," Numie said, opening the door. The sight of her nude breasts, still firm at her age, always disturbed him for reasons he did not know. He'd certainly seen enough nudity in his business.

"What is it?" she demanded to know.

He coughed. Why delay it any longer? "Anne and I are leaving this afternoon. I'm sorry we couldn't give you notice. She's packing now." He waited for the impact of his words to reach her, bracing himself for a screaming denunciation.

She was outwardly calm. Remembering how embarrassed Numie always was at the sight of her nudity, she reached for a satin sheet to cover herself. "Darling, don't be ridiculous." She turned off the tape recorder. "You might leave me. After all, you're nothing but a drifter. Anne, never! She's completely dependent on me. I'm taking her back to New York with me. You, too, if you want to go. Although I think you've been drinking more Scotch than we agreed upon. Providing you refrain and stick to our original agreement, you may come."

"We *are* leaving, but not with you, Leonora." The woman was utterly impossible. Refusing to listen to anything she didn't want to hear.

"I assume you're not joking," she said. "If I remember, you were never much for humor. "Why doesn't Anne come down and tell me herself?" Suspicion was racing through her mind. "You realize I plan to have my books audited. If you or Anne have stolen from me..." She looked at him accusingly. "In fact, if you head out of this house, I'm calling Yellowwood to stop you. Your leaving like this can mean only one thing——you're making off with my jewelry. My silver, at least." She leaned back in bed, rubbing her head. "I'm surrounded by thieves and bandits. I didn't tell you this. But my accountant called me. It appears that Ralph has been embezzling from me for years. I've called the FBI."

Numie's face reddened, his temples throbbed. "We haven't taken anything that belongs to you. We're not asking for anything either. Not even our back pay. You can call the sheriff if you want to."

Although she long ago learned not to trust anyone, she believed him. Then what was the reason? Suddenly, it was all too clear. "I keep forgetting you're a hustler. I know what your scheme is."

"I have no scheme," he said.

"You hustlers are always after something." She felt relieved, confident. The only time she was ever upset was when people behaved unpredictably. "Ralph's gone. You want to fill his shoes, not that I blame you. You want the prestige of being associated with me so intimately. Darling, nature abhors a vacuum. My dismissal of him certainly created one. You might as well take the position. I'll need someone now that I'm leaving for New York. So much to take care of, including moving all my possessions from Sacre-Coeur. I knew you wouldn't settle for being a chauffeur forever. Didn't I predict that?"

Leonora was tiring him, bringing him down. This goodbye wasn't going at all the way he wanted. "I don't want Ralph's job," he said adamantly.

"Of course, you do. You're annoying me holding out like this when we both know that getting Ralph's job is the only reason you're here now."

"No, I don't want to be in any of your Sacre-Coeurs, including the one I know you'll re-create in New York," he said. "I want to be out where I can breathe the air for a change and be my own man."

"Don't be sophomoric, my dear."

"I mean it!" he said. "When I first saw Sacre-Coeur, I thought that big fence was to keep other people out. Now, I know it's to keep the inmates in."

The sudden animosity in his voice surprised her. She decided she had better start taking him seriously.

"I was your lowest paid servant, and I earned every penny, that's for sure," he said. "The life style you created is not for me."

"You're right," she said.

He was startled to find her agreeing with him about anything.

"Even in my present savaged state, I know you're right," she said. "You want no part of the world I created here. Neither do I. I don't know whatever possessed me to return to this God forsaken place. But that's in the past. I'm moving back into life, *adventure*, and I'll take you with me. You'll be a success, providing you stick close to my skirt-tails." No sooner had she said that than she regretted it. After all, Numie was a man, and he'd resent it. Even hustlers had human feelings some of the time.

"No thanks," he said bitterly. "I used to dream I'd meet a rich lady one day who'd invite me to live with her in her fine house. I never really believed that dream would come true. But it didn't work out exactly as I dreamed it."

"I'm on the verge of my greatest triumph——stick with me," she pleaded, resenting the tone of desperation creeping into her voice. "You'll share in it."

"I'm not interested," he said.

"Now I know why I was attracted to you in the bar that night," she said angrily. Seeing that he was really going, she decided to use any ploy. "*New me* indeed! Your name is a betrayal and a lie. The hustler who came here to pander to me, to light my cigarettes, to give me insincere compliments was just waiting till he caught me in a weak moment before moving in for the kill." She fell back on her pillow. "You know I have to have people around me who'll take care of me. Okay, buster, state your price."

"Nothing."

"Years of hustling destroys sensitivity," she went on. "Your heart——whatever there was of it——is gone. You're cold and cruel, deserting a helpless woman."

If he hadn't been so saddened by the day's events, he could have laughed at that last remark. "You're not exactly helpless."

Her statement had been so utterly ridiculous, even to herself, she decided to admit it. "True," she said, "I'll survive longer than you or Anne. Of course, you two think you have each other... for the moment at least. God only knows how long that will last. I have no one."

"There's Dinah," he said.

"Tricks don't count," she said. "I've survived without love from any quarter all these years, and I'll continue."

"At least you had talent," he said.

"You left out beauty," she accused, "and, yes, I still have my talent."

"You've mentioned beauty so many times I didn't think it was necessary."

She bristled at that remark.

"Thank you for everything," he said. "I know you meant well. At least, I'd like to think you did."

"That's right, use your unbearable cliches to confront any human situation," she said, sitting up again. "I used to loathe cliches. Now, I feel differently. I think we should repeat them over and over. They are the only true things in life."

"Okay, Leonora," he said, growing impatient. "I'm leaving."

"One small favor," she said, suddenly resigned to the fact that he was going. "Get Joan on the phone. You know how I hate to dial numbers." If she were to survive, she had to get tough again. Forget Anne. Forget Numie. They'd be back soon enough. Perhaps she'd take them in again. That depended on how repentant they were.

Numie called the Garden of Delights. Joan answered. He handed the receiver to Leonora, his last official duty as her employee.

At the door, he looked back.

Leonora was no longer paying attention to him. "My darling," she was saying into her 1920s phone, "I might as well inform you, I've sold the Garden of Delights. From now on, your bosses will be Lola and the commodore's sister. Mainly Lola. Of course, she'll fire you as soon as the papers are signed. That will leave you out in the cold. I should let you starve——or go on welfare. However, I'm dismissing Anne tonight and taking you back as my secretary. You can answer the phone and type, the only talents you ever had. As an actress, you were ludicrous. I'm allowing you to return with me to New York. All your years of treachery, the thousand and one betrayals, I've decided to forgive."

. . .

The bus to the mainland was ready to pull out. Numie was squeezing Anne's hand. Coming out of the station, Castor Q. Combes was zipping up. Trailing him was his calico cat.

"Just a minute," Numie said, getting up. "Somebody I have to say goodbye to."

In front of the station, Numie confronted Castor.

"You again, white boy," Castor said. "Good for me I was out of the toilet this time before you came in to try to molest me."

"The cat," Numie said. "It's okay?"

"Of course, it's okay."

"I thought..." The memory of that early morning ride, the calico fur lifeless at the side of the road, came back. Obviously it hadn't been Castor's cat. Thank God for that.

The driver called to Numie.

"I'm leaving, Castor," Numie said. "Take good care of that cat. A cat could get run over, you know."

"Always trying to interfere in somebody else's business, ain't you?"

"Not really," Numie said. "And take care of yourself, too."

"Get on that bus," Castor said. "I ain't got no time to fool with you."

Numie reached down and petted the cat, who was rubbing against his leg. Then he turned to Castor. "Give me a quick hug, 'cause you're the only friend I'm leaving on this island." He reached out and hugged the boy close.

For one brief second, Castor almost responded, then broke away. "You get away from me, you pervert," he said. "Come on, cat." He looked back at Numie. "My mama told me never to trust a man with violet eyes."

Back in his seat, Numie was reaching for Anne again.

"Who was that?" she asked.

"Just someone who showed me a little kindness my first day in town," he said.

The bus screeched into gear.

Numie looked back only once.

It was growing dark.

Castor and his calico cat walked under a crescent sign marking the end of the highway in continental U.S.A. In faded letters, it proclaimed, "The End of the Rainbow."

Epilogue

For Numie, it had been eighteen dreary months, and the second long winter seemed determined to retain its freezing grip on Upper New York State. He was convinced this hell hole was the coldest place on earth.

Grandma's condition seemed to worsen every day, but month after month she clung to life. He didn't understand why she bothered, as life offered her nothing any more.

Like Tangerine, she grew increasingly testy in her decline. Her demands on both Anne and Numie had become totally unreasonable. Throughout it all, she held out the promise that she was going to will the farm to them when she died.

But only last week, Anne discovered a copy of her last will and testament. The original, apparently, had been deposited at her attorney's office in a neighboring town. When he first came to New York State, Grandma had insisted that Numie drive her to that office. Now, he realized what her business was there. She'd lied. She never had any intention of giving them the farm. She'd willed it to a distant cousin who lived in Oregon. The moment she died, this cousin, Numie suspected, would sell the farm. He and Anne would have no place to live.

Tonight, Grandma had exhausted Anne, who had gone to bed complaining of a headache. But despite that, Anne always seemed perky and free from pain when a waitress who worked at a hamburger joint along the roadside came calling to take her out two or three nights a week. Numie wasn't invited to go along. Anne would vaguely say they were going to see a movie in a nearby town, or else were going to visit a friend, but often she didn't come home until after three in the morning.

He'd hear her come in but she no longer slept in his bedroom. Anne's excuse was that she needed to sleep in the day bed off Grandma's room in case the old woman needed her in the middle of the night.

It had been so long, he'd forgotten when he last had sex with her. Even when he was having sex with her, she'd complain of the pain. "I find intercourse painful," she once told him. "You make me bleed. I'm no cow, you know."

Tonight, he couldn't take another minute in that house with

either woman. There was just so much TV he could watch.

Sometimes when he had to get out of the house, he drove to a neighboring town to visit a little bar called Hestor's. It was supposed to be the gay bar for the area, but a straight stranger could probably walk in, have a drink, then go on his way, never realizing he'd been in a gay bar.

The bar was often too drafty and too bleak to offer much comfort to anyone. None of the patrons ever seemed to talk to one another. They sat around exchanging furtive glances, as if too afraid to make contact. It was a repressive bar, but men still came here from small towns far away for what little pleasure the place offered. At least the patrons were in the company of other gay men, even if they did nothing to make contact with each other.

Tonight was a little different. The bar was more animated than ever, and Numie had never seen such a crowd here. He quickly learned from the bartender that they'd had a music festival in a neighboring town. Most of the people in the bar tonight were from New York. Unlike the locals, at least they didn't seem afraid to be gay.

Throughout the evening, two slightly older men at a nearby table had been eying Numie. They weren't unattractive, and from the way they were dressed in dark suits, ties, and white shirts, they looked rather prosperous.

One of the men called the bartender over and whispered something in his ear. When the bartender came back, he told Numie in a very soft voice that his tab was being picked up.

In gratitude, Numie raised his mug of beer and saluted his benefactors. They raised their cocktail glasses and toasted him, but ever so discreetly.

He hadn't done anything like this in a long time, and he felt embarrassed——really out of practice. He turned his back to the men and ordered another beer, since they were paying. After all, he rarely had more than five dollars in his jeans since he'd left Tortuga. Money was real tight at Grandma's. She gave them so few dollars to buy groceries, he felt she was remembering prices from the Depression days, not what things cost now.

Every now and then, he'd turn and look over his shoulder. The two men were still there, and they exchanged friendly glances with him, but nothing more.

That beer that the bartender kept placing on the counter in front of him was beginning to take its toll. Glancing only briefly at the two men, Numie headed for the men's room in the back. He wasn't quite sure, but sensed that either one or else both of the men were trailing him.

Opening the door to the foul-smelling toilet, he spotted three urinals. He hesitated only a moment before taking the urinal in the middle.

He was so familiar with this scene that he knew exactly what was going to happen next. The two men from the bar placed themselves on his left and right. They made no move to unzip, but stood looking down at Numie.

Slowly, very slowly, he unbuttoned his jeans. He knew this was showtime, and it gave him a thrill. It'd been so long since he was the object of anyone's desire, and it was a welcome feeling returning to him. He pulled out his cock and pissed noisily against the porcelain. He heard one of the men sigh. Even when he'd finished, he still held it out for their inspection, shaking it several times. Under their appreciative eyes, it began to harden and take on a life of its own. He feared he might not be able to get it back into his pants if that happened.

Removing both hands, he allowed the men one final inspection before he tucked his hardening cock back into his jeans.

He turned and left the toilet, leaving the men standing at the urinals. By the time he reached the bar again, the men had joined him, inviting him to their table. He accepted the invitation, and was placed in the middle of their booth between them.

The introductions that followed revealed a lot. They were record producers who'd come to hear some of the artists they represented at the festival. They were also very eager to learn about Numie. He'd told them he'd been a chauffeur in Tortuga, but had lost his job.

"We have a good friend down there," one of the men, Gordon Roberts, said. "The designer. Leonora de la Mer."

"That's her," Numie said. "I worked for her."

"Imagine," said the other man, John Frels. "We see her

about once a week. Gordon and I either go over to her place for dinner in New York, or else she comes over to our townhouse."

"Please give her my best," Numie said.

"Why don't you come and work for us?" John asked abruptly. "As our driver. Leonora will really be surprised——and a bit jealous——when we show up with you Friday night."

"No, I can't." Numie said. His protest sounded weak, even to himself.

"You can do any God damn thing you want to do if you want to do it," Gordon said. "Haven't you done anything rash and impulsive in your life?"

"A man as good looking as you," John said, pausing. "One with your gigantic assets should be living life to the fullest."

"I don't know..." Numie hesitated. Maybe it was the beer, but his mind was all blurred.

"Next week, this place will be a very distant memory," Gordon predicted.

"This is pretty sudden," Numie said.

"That's what makes it so delicious." Gordon said. "John and I can really satisfy a big guy like you. We don't like boys. We like our men fully grown and mature."

"What if I said yes?" Numie asked.

"Then we're out of this bar in a flash," John said. "On the long drive back to New York. Just the three of us."

"Let the good times roll," Gordon said.

An hour must have passed before Numie left the bar with the men. Lots of talk, lots of promises. Even if he didn't believe all the fancy talk, he was lured by the prospect of adventure. Something new, something different. Anything to convince him he was alive again.

Behind the wheel of a very black Cadillac, he was heading for New York. At first he'd been tempted to stop off briefly at the farm to pick up some things and say goodbye. But he decided against it.

"Why bother with your old clothes?" John asked. "You'll have all new clothes in New York. New everything."

"That's right," Gordon added. "You'll live up to that name of yours. You'll be a *new me*."